GEMINI GAMBIT • BOOK 5

INFINITY'S BARGAIN

D. SCOTT JOHNSON

INFINITY'S BARGAIN
D. Scott Johnson

ISBN: 978-1-7360141-4-1 (hardcover)
978-1-7360141-3-4 (paperback)
978-1-7360141-5-8 (ebook)

Cover design by Melissa Lew
Interior layout by Lighthouse24

Chapter 1
Kim

A block of text appeared in her virtual vision channel when she ran her new sleep app for the first time. *This sleep therapy app wishes to access the lower medical functions of your phone. Caution! Always consult with a doctor before proceeding.*

She suppressed a snort. It was almost as bad as the cautions before virtual exercise sessions. Did anyone do it? *Doctor, I'm considering bending at the waist.* Or in her particular case, going to sleep. That hadn't been happening much since they'd gotten back from bemian space.

She'd been grateful for snapping awake for no reason the first time it happened. It was what had saved her from Valsa Burtan's final attempt to hijack their ship. Kim had chalked her wakefulness up to being out of range of the sa'dst hack Valsa had used to freeze Maff and Mike and thought nothing more about it.

Until it happened again, and again, and again, with increasing frequency as the months went by. Now, more than a year later, they were happening multiple times a night. Going without sleep wasn't a big deal when she was a teenager. But her Rage + the Machine days of pulling all-night hackathons or taking shifts staking out a firewall port for weeks at a time were long past.

Even though it all still felt like yesterday.

The problems lack of sleep caused weren't restricted to feeling exhausted all the time and snapping at Mike when he didn't deserve it. They also interfered with her work. Kim was now not only the owner of a successful locksmith business, she was also the project manager of the rebooted Operation Sidereal. Mike had resurrected it from the ashes of Matthew Watchtell's original effort to build transdimensional portals for fun and profit. They weren't there yet, but the progress was solid and steady.

She was also half of the chief—and currently only—Interpreter for the La'fan. Kim now had north of two hundred languages at her disposal. She used them with the threads Mike still had attached to two La'fan sites to work together to help their adopted galactic family. They negotiated contracts, settled disputes, and navigated the byzantine cultures of various planets and collectives.

It was a marathon session of navigating one of those cultures to settle a dispute about a contract that had her seriously considering using this well regarded but still new app as an artificial way of going to sleep. She'd never been so tired before that afternoon.

"If Shareah," the closest person La'fanians had to a leader, "didn't restrict access to us to once a day," Mike said as he stretched his arms out, "I don't know what we'd do."

Kim put her head in her hands and rested her elbows on the dining room table. The La'fan needed an Interpreter, and Kim was happy to help. But it was getting harder and harder to find the right words, the correct translation, the explanation that all parties would understand. It wasn't a capacity issue. If anything, she was learning new languages faster than ever. It was exhaustion, pure and simple.

"At least we've got tomorrow off," she said. Mike had made weekly breaks nonnegotiable when it became clear she was struggling.

"And I know how to help you relax."

She looked up into his flashing eyes, and it was like jumping off a diving board into…

Nothing. She had nothing to give, and that hurt most of all. "Rain check?"

His smile was sweet, a warm light in her gray world. "Sure." Mike hid his disappointment well, but it was there. This had to stop.

So now, lying in bed with Mike on the other side of their pillow wall, she pushed Allow to give the new sleep therapy app permission to access the lower medical functions of her phone. This wasn't a licensed clinical app like the ones Tonya used as a nurse. It was a commercial app that would at first record and then gently stimulate her brain into various levels of NREM sleep. It was seen as safe and effective for most kinds of insomnia. Kim could only hope.

The darkness as sleep took her was warm and welcoming.

"Hey, Wren," Mark said to her as she walked down the metal ramp into Pride's Lair, Rage + The Machine's virtual hideout when she was younger. She *is* younger. "You up for a game?"

He sat in the conversation pit in the main room, Michiko and Lourdes to either side of him. They were always playing card games of one kind or another. Judging by the way the cards were floating and arranged, 3-D spades seemed to be the flavor of the day.

"Can't," she said as she headed for the weapons hall, "gotta prep the viral slugs. I've only got fifteen minutes until history class starts." It was their first run with her new custom design, but if she blew up her World History grade, she'd be watching from the sidelines.

She stopped. There was a blank wall where the weapons hall was supposed to be. "Guys, not cool rearranging the realm."

"What are you talking about?" Mark said over his shoulder, facing away from Kim. They were all facing away from her now. The gaming pit had changed shape too. That shouldn't happen. The environment was twisting around her, and she didn't understand why.

The longer she thought about it, the more she realized Rage + The Machine's lair had been completely rearranged. It would take forever to put it all back the way it was supposed to be, and she had a test to take in ten minutes.

Above her, on the catwalks that hung from the ceiling but *in the wrong places*, Rich and Josh, the Machine's construct experts, walked side by side. They were turned away from her too. She couldn't see anyone's faces.

Incredibly, the realm got messier. Things weren't at all in the right place—when they were there at all. Edmund was nowhere to be found. He'd moved out; she could see him off in the distance teaching a class. But he was turned away as well. They all were.

Henry, the Machine's realspace driver and mechanic, was behind her somehow. "You'll need to find the armory if you want to get those slugs sorted out." She turned around, but his face…

It was a skull. There was no happy smile; a dark, stained skull grinned down at her instead. She looked around, and they all faced her now, all skulls.

Their bodies dissolved away.

Now there was an enormous tower in the center of a room, their skulls mounted to it, water flowing out of eye sockets and nose holes. Kim tried to scream but couldn't breathe. The straps on the table she was laid out on were too tight. She wasn't in Pride's Lair anymore. She was in Manuel Quispe's private office. They were prisoners of this deadly drug kingpin in his remote Bolivian estate.

"And now," Quispe, an ugly, fat man said, sitting behind a giant desk to her left, "it's your turn." He motioned to Mike, who stood beside him. But it wasn't Mike. It was Colque. The knife he held reflected her husband's face but not his soul as he pressed the tip under her ear, through her flesh and—

Kim shot upright on her bed, trying to hold shut a knife wound that wasn't there. It wasn't real. She was fine; Mike was asleep beside her. The taste of her own blood faded as she swept away the remains of the nightmare from her mind and checked the time. Four a.m.

Six full hours of sleep, the longest single stretch she'd had in months.

The nightmare was bad, and six hours wasn't that great, but Kim wasn't exhausted. Tired, but it was a real improvement from the night before. Then she looked around the room as the moonlight shone through the bedroom window.

It was all such a mess.

It took two hours to bring it under control. She'd quietly realigned everything in the bedroom perfectly, managing it without waking Mike up. This was much better; the orderly arrangement settled a blanket of peace on her soul.

Until she got to the kitchen. It was a bigger wreck than the bedroom. But it was her turn to clean it, and progress gave her the same sense of peace cleaning the bedroom had. Then she opened the silverware drawer to put away the stuff in the dishwasher and a stitch in her mind pulled tight. *This was wrong. Everything in this drawer was wrong.*

Kim got the silverware to stack perfectly in the tray after half a dozen tries. Each stack was the same height, with the same number of items, set on top of each other in such a way that she couldn't see that they *were* a stack when she stared straight down at them. The stitch in her mind came undone, and that blanket of peace descended on her again. She'd done restorations on seventeenth century locks that were less satisfying than rearranging her silverware drawer, and she treated those locks better than some people treated their children.

It had to have been the sleep app that caused this change. Despite the peace, there was a genuine undercurrent of fear. She'd always been a little obsessive over detail. Maybe more than a little. The sleep app had warned her side effects were possible. This was new, and it wasn't like she could go to a real doctor with the whole story. "You see, there was this ship that took us to another world…"

Mike walked out of the bedroom after his morning prayers and stopped. "Hi?"

"Hi, yourself," she replied as she gingerly lifted the silverware tray back into its drawer.

"You were"—he looked around at what she'd accomplished—"busy this morning. What time did you get up?"

Kim pushed the drawer shut ever so gently, getting a little thrill when there was no movement, no shift inside. The silverware would stay perfect all day long. "Four, but I didn't wake up at all until then."

The news stopped him from moving a throw pillow on the couch, and she said a silent prayer of thanks for that. It would've ruined the symmetry she'd created. He turned to her with a smile that, a year into marriage, still melted her. "That's good news, but don't you think all this," he waved a hand at their living room and kitchen, "might be a side effect of your new app?"

They normally kept the apartment neat, but now it looked like a Condé Nast set. It was all perfectly placed and symmetrical to within a millimeter—she'd checked with the lidar sensor in her phone. No dust motes sparkled in the morning light through the window.

Great. Kim had figured out a new way to be a freak, and Mike had noticed. It was like she was collecting merit badges on the subject and was now well on her way to being an especially weird Eagle Scout.

She sat down heavily at the dining room table, although the asymmetry made her itch. She managed not to move things around until they were perfect because Mike would watch her like a hawk and then badger her for the rest of the day until they came up with a story a doctor might believe. But resisting the urge to rearrange the table wasn't the same thing as making the urge go away. She could still feel it. It had only gone to a corner of her mind to hide. This might be permanent. *Consult your doctor first…*

She chased the wood grain of the table with her thumb. "At least I got some sleep."

He sat down next to her and threw the end of a napkin over her hand. They gripped it together, their version of a kiss in the morning. "It'll be okay."

Kim rubbed the weave of the fabric until she found a smooth direction. *The order, everything going in the same direction, was so right.* She fought the urge to arrange the table again, and this time it went away a little easier. "I know," she replied. And it would be. This was a side effect of the therapy, not a permanent condition.

And at least the apartment was clean. "What's your day like?"

He relaxed, and she could almost see him think *My wife is a basket case, but at least she hasn't added any more eggs to it.*

Maybe.

"Pretty standard, although I'll be late into the lock shop. More meetings."

He got up, and in that fascinatingly graceful way he had, started coffee. His morning ritual, with its custom bean storage, an electric grinder with a special 3-D printed titanium grinding burr kit, imported water filter, and bespoke French press soothed the new troll that'd taken up residence in her head. She'd often teased him about how Zen he got about it all. She was certain he moved from one part to the next of his coffee ritual the same way every morning. But what was once cute now brought real peace inside her. Maybe this wouldn't be all bad.

He reached up over his head, wearing nothing but Chinese-style pajama bottoms, and Kim discovered another plus about getting some sleep. When her heart jumped off the diving board this time, it had a destination.

Then she checked the clock over his head and swore. "I'm late!"

He snorted without turning. "For you."

He never missed a chance to goof on her need to arrive well in advance of an appointment, but her shop wouldn't open itself. There would be time for fun later. After a quick shower, she threw him her best smoldering look as she picked up the thermos he'd filled for her—she'd sworn off Starbucks because his coffee ritual *worked*—and headed out the door.

She turned at the threshold. "Don't make any plans with Spencer or anyone else tonight. Got it?"

The way he shifted in his seat made him cuter. "Got it."

*

She didn't know how or even if her new troll would be a problem at the shop. If there was an issue, it would probably be general messiness like at the house. It was an active workplace with a small machine shop in the back that she used to work on various kinds of locks. She braced herself as she unlocked the front door. It wouldn't be there. The thing in her head should've evaporated by now. It was *not* a permanent condition. She opened the door and then...

Spent the next few minutes staring at the planks of the hardwood floor.

They were original to the house her shop had originally been, dating back to the early nineteenth century. She couldn't stop staring at the patterns in the wood grain, tracing them back and forth, following their contours. Each one flowed with the others, and as she followed them, her fascination grew. A part of her knew with terrible certainty that she needed to learn each and every one by heart if she were ever to have true peace.

Strobe lights flashed on the walls and a piercing whistle warbled loudly in her ears, but she couldn't stop following them. It took the security alarm people calling her to break the spell. She had been so caught up in the patterns that she'd forgotten to turn the alarm off when she walked in. The phone only worked to break the spell because it was directly connected to her nervous system. Without it, she might've stared at the floor until the police arrived to check out the alarm.

But like earlier in the morning, once the spell was broken, she could control the new monster in her head. Having customers come and go helped too. Contractors and retirees with home restoration hobbies both wanted to get an early start on their projects, so mornings were always a busy time. Basil, her now veteran cousin-assistant, and Alexander, the new cousin who would soon replace him, arrived two hours later. She went into her back workshop—a later extension built mercifully on a smooth concrete slab—to do some restoration and fabrication work. The intricacies of the various tumblers, dogs, and gears were constructive tasks to concentrate on. As she worked, the new obsession over order seemed less alien to her, more like a refinement or extension of what she already was.

"Kim," Basil said as he pushed his head through the back door. "Someone's asking for you."

She nodded at him, checked that the 3-D printer had enough metal powder in its hopper to finish the gear she was working on, and got up to see who it was. They knew her by name, so it had to be law enforcement or maybe one of the specialized restorers who worked in the esoteric but thriving antique lock import-export business. The latter was interested in her skills with ancient locks, the former for ones more recent.

The murmur of customers was clearly audible from her shop. Business was good. Her sales floor was rarely empty. But when she got to the counter, it wasn't law enforcement or restorers.

It was Matthew Watchtell.

"Good morning, Ms. Trayne."

The last time this happened, he snuck projectors into her shop and used a hologram. This was no projection; it was him. She checked her alerts. There was a big flashing red *WATCHTELL PAROLED EARLY*. She'd been so scrambled this morning that, for the first time, she forgot to check his status right after she woke up.

He'd only served two years.

Let's hear it for lawyers.

But that was the extent of her reaction. The last time around, and only as a hologram, he'd put her in a blind panic. Now it felt like the car not starting in the morning or realizing there was gum stuck to the bottom of her shoe.

Maybe it was the new scar that cut across a quarter of his face. When they parted last in the visitor center of a maximum-security prison, she'd subtly let the entire room know that he mistreated his own grandson. They would've come to a simpler conclusion than the truth, that he'd created Will to become a test subject in a dangerous machine, but it was still the truth. She didn't know if there would be any repercussions.

She could only hope. "Did I help give you that?"

His face darkened, and the scar stood out more. "I consider it a favor."

His expression said otherwise. "How so?"

"Vicious rumors of a specific sort are spread, and a prisoner is at risk in the general population. That, and this," he pointed at the scar that went from the hairline above his left eye to above his nose, a poor trade for the scars he'd left on her two years ago, "was enough to convince a judge that perhaps moderating the sentence to confinement would be in order."

Out of nowhere and despite a real attempt to stop it, a smile cracked her face. "You're under house arrest? Do you have an ankle monitor?" A giggle bubbled up. This was her rapist, and all she felt was *good*. "Can I see it?"

An anger she'd witnessed up close several times rushed to the surface. That wouldn't do. "Careful, Matthew," she said. "You don't want to get sent back to the clink the same day you left."

Kim wasn't the vulnerable one here. She would never *be* the vulnerable one again. Facing him when he was still in prison, confronting him when it was all so raw, had forged steel inside her. She was so far beyond him now. "What do you want?" she asked.

The rage twisted as he controlled and then mastered it. A smile of his own came out. It didn't terrify her as much as it used to, but it brought her back to the ground. He was still a predator. Mastering her fear of him didn't make him less dangerous. "I have a proposal for you. It's come to my attention that you've continued work on one of my most important projects."

Kim tuned out the bustle of customers around them. "And?"

"I'm taking it back."

They had brought the project so far on their own. They didn't need a supervisor. And this was still Watchtell. "The hell you are."

He chuckled. It was a sound that, despite her conquered fear, still made her skin crawl. "Oh, it won't be today, or next week. But it is in the works, and it will happen. My sources tell me you've gone a long way in my absence. I appreciate that resourcefulness. I'd be remiss if I didn't offer your team a new opportunity."

The idea that all their work could be scooped up by him was bad enough. That he would then be their boss was an idea that briefly choked her.

But only briefly. "Get out."

He backed away slowly. "I didn't think you would accept my offer immediately."

Now she was the one constrained by being in a public place. Kim had new ways to give him scars. Her body ached at the incipient transformation. She would torture him with crystal skin and coral lightning.

"Get out *now,*" she whispered.

"Certainly. I will be easy to locate should you change your mind. And you should. I've already taken my first steps. They won't be my last." He pivoted, the brass bell over the door rang, and he was gone.

It took her a minute to realize Basil was speaking to her. "Who was that?"

Already taken my first steps. That had to be a clue. Her blood went cold as she started searching her realm cloud's access logs. "A man who's not allowed in this store again."

There it was. A micro-DDOS attack that would've been impossible if he hadn't been standing right next to her. It was one of the oldest tricks in the book, and if it had been any other day, she would've laughed in his face. But this wasn't any other day. The wood grain in the floor still called to her, and the skull faces of her friends were vivid in her mind.

He'd rattled her and then won, and now she knew what he wanted. Watchtell wasn't here to recruit her.

He was on a fishing expedition.

Five realm constructs had been removed in the past minute. All were related to their portal research, one of them a critical innovation that reduced the power required by ninety percent.

"I need to go. I'll be back soon."

She opened a channel to Mike. "We have a problem."

Chapter 2
Helen

As far as jobs went, she could've done worse. *Had* done worse. Washing dishes was a lot more work than sitting in a car staking out a garage across the street.

As a new immigrant with a bit of a shaky background, Helen's dream job of being a cop was still a couple of years away. It went without saying that Chinese laws didn't match up with those of the US. The basics were closer than Westerners liked to admit, but the extra effort Americans wrapped around concepts such as due process and civil rights was extraordinary. In China, she gathered evidence, presented it, and watched the bad guy get hauled away. The idea of innocent until proven guilty seemed dangerously naïve. Nobody was above suspicion in her experience, especially people with histories of bad behavior.

But she didn't have a choice. For better or worse, America was now her home. As long as she stayed far away from China both politically and geographically, the old bastards in the politburo seemed content to let this become a kind of retirement. The joke was on them. Jainlee, the original owner of her host, a serial killer of epic ability, the gadfly who took every opportunity to torture Helen's law-and-order soul, was still embedded in Chinese realmspace. She would eventually become the third known threaded intelligence on Earth. Helen would wait patiently but still looked forward to it. In spite of all expectations, she missed her.

So here she sat, alone in a car parked on a street in DC's Chinatown, working as an assistant-slash-apprentice for Wong's Investigative Services. It was a family-run business, and that family happened to have a cousin who owned a Chinese restaurant in Dumas, an obscure Arkansas town. That cousin was Mr. Harry Wong, who owned the restaurant Helen had washed dishes in during their brief stay in Spencer's home town.

"It's not charity," Harry said after telling her about the job in DC before they left Arkansas. "He needs hard workers with good English skills. You'll be a perfect fit."

It wasn't a perfect fit, but it would do as a temporary job. Helen was already taking steps to secure her future. While on this stakeout, she *also* sat, virtually, in two George Mason University criminology classes studying for her degree in law enforcement. Helen would've taken all the classes in one year, but they weren't offered that way. She was fairly certain her professors wouldn't notice that both of her holos were asking relevant questions in two different classes at the same time. If they did, they wouldn't know what to make of it.

But those weren't the only places her threads were working in. While her realspace host was in DC, she was also currently also helping Judy, her first American cop friend back in Dumas. The department's investigation database was tangled up so badly that it wouldn't answer queries anymore. What messed it up wasn't much of a mystery. Helen had replaced the ancient original secretary not long after arriving in town. After she left, they brought the elderly matron back. Helen respected and honored her almost as an ancestor, but the woman was a menace in front of a computer. A significant number of her threads had spent hours trying to untangle the data.

Having her threads spread out and active like this made for a challenging workday, typically lasting more than twelve hours. Mike said he didn't know how she did it. She needed to work up a training regimen for her brother's threads. He could use some proper Chinese discipline. America fairly bred laziness. She needed the strenuous thread workouts to stay strong no matter how exhausting they were. She was the primary defense against another attack by Andromeda. Holding that being back was a straightforward firewall patrol, but one day it might figure out a way to stage a brute-force attack. Helen refused to be the weak link in that chain.

"Any movement on your door, Helen?" Her mentor and the owner's third son, Tom Wong, asked over their open phone connection.

Their stakeout was about an item that couldn't be more American: a car. Specifically, a so-called *classic* car. Very specifically, an ancient Ferrari 365 GTB/4, also known as a Daytona. This particular specimen had been reported stolen several weeks ago. Considering the lack of electronics, the thief probably only needed a single electrical wire to do the job. In the normal world, the owner would file a police report, collect an insurance settlement, and get a new vehicle.

Needless to say, people who owned Italian sports cars worth more than large houses and built around the same time as Mao's cultural revolution didn't live in the normal world.

It would still merely be a low-priority criminal matter except for the striking coincidence that the vehicle in question vanished only hours before it was due to be seized as part of a divorce settlement. The soon-to-be ex-Mrs. Xie accused Li-liang Xie, the wayward black sheep son of the chili sauce emperor Yìchén Xie, of being far from an innocent victim. She claimed in extremely colorful Mandarin that he arranged the theft to hide the asset.

So what was a woman to do when the old sports car she vowed was hers to send down the Potomac, on a barge, with a dummy clad in her wedding dress, in the driver's seat, surrounded by drums of gasoline, and past an archer with flaming arrows… well, what *was* she to do when that suddenly vanished into thin air?

Call Wong's Investigations, that's what.

"Nothing on my side," Helen replied.

Xie Li-liang was about as typical a little emperor as you could get from a modern Chinese family. Pampered in the extreme, his only real skill was spending money. He did this with style and great enthusiasm.

He was *not* a criminal mastermind. It'd taken a dozen threads and a little judicious data store cracking from Kim to track the admittedly attractive vehicle from its glassed-in, purpose-built home garage to a ramshackle car repair shop in a seedy part of DC's Chinatown. There weren't any cameras she could reach inside, but Helen would bet a month's wages that the target of Mrs. Xie's revenge was sitting between broken down Kias and Geelys like an Italian beauty queen sleeping in a TSMC factory dorm.

Helen discovered the likely location so fast they had plenty of time to see if Mr. Xie would get impatient and visit his wheeled lover to take it for a drive. Xie personally driving the supposedly stolen car past his, or rather now his ex-wife's, house would be a classic move from Xie's playbook. Daddy's money would always get him out of any trouble that might result.

But not this time.

The garage had two entrances: one on the busy street it fronted and another that was accessed through an alley on the opposite side. Her boss, Tom, thought Xie had at least some brains, and so he was covering the back entrance. Helen had spent the last week profiling Xie and knew otherwise.

Emperors never snuck, never skulked, never crept. They walked proudly with an entourage of servants, carried in elegant sandalwood sedan chairs by strong coolies. This wasn't ancient China, so Xie's servants were now his posse. The owner of a shiny black Cadillac with huge wheels Helen could probably sit in without stooping over didn't need coolies.

Helen *felt* that Escalade coming down the street long before it appeared. "I've got activity on my side," she told Tom.

"Roger. Let's see which door they use."

The music was nothing but bass as far as she could tell. The vibrations might bang the door of her car off its hinges. Incredibly, it got louder when Xie and company pulled into the shop's parking lot. Xie staggered out. They shouted things at each other for a few moments, threw some obscene gestures back and forth, then Xie turned and went through the front door.

"Subject is inside the building." The Escalade exited the parking lot via the alley and drove out of sight.

Tom swore over their channel. "You have got to be kidding."

"What's the problem?"

"These idiots are trying to get that barge of a Cadillac to go down this alley. It's so narrow they're pulling the wing mirrors in." There was honking over the line, and Tom shouting at the crew of the Cadillac through his car window.

The front garage door made a few snap-bang noises and started to open. "He's on the move," Helen said.

"Follow him, I've got to back all the way out of this damned alley."

The Ferrari burbled its way out of the garage. It was one of only a handful in white, and Helen couldn't help but admire the way its styling glowed in the fading light of the afternoon. It somehow blended the beauty of a swan with the aggression of a tiger. Xie's popped-up collars, odd spikey hairdo, and skinny elbow hanging out of the window pushed this over the line into nouveau riche tackiness. The machine deserved better.

She turned her now-frumpy old Tesla on and put it in gear. "On the move," she said, but couldn't tell if he heard her over the commotion that was going on in the alley. The tracking app on her phone would keep him in the loop after he got the alley situation sorted out.

The old parts of downtown DC were a nerve-wracking jumble of one-way streets, turn restrictions, and construction. It at least had the advantage of preventing Xie from driving at speeds that would make him difficult to follow. Helen's cop instincts kicked in as she followed him, and she came to a grim realization: Xie was almost certainly drunk. Not enough to be an immediate menace, but it was noticeable to someone trained to spot the signs. She would have to play this carefully. Drunks were notoriously unpredictable.

As they wended their way through the streets, Helen's second prediction was also proved correct: they were heading toward Xie's former home. She checked the map in her enhanced vision. Tom seemed to have gotten out of the alley, but he was a long way behind.

"He's heading toward the house," she told him. "Turn left on Wyoming and then right on Kalorama Northwest. Block the circle exit, and I'll flush him your way."

"Will do."

The house was at the top of a circular road that ran one way clockwise. The entrance and exit were at the bottom of the circle. It was a perfect trap.

And a narrow one, too. As they got closer to the final circle, the streets were crowded in by parked cars that lined both sides. She nearly lost him a couple of times because she had to move aside and stop to let some traffic go past.

The change in appearance of the neighborhoods was striking as well. They'd started out in a seedy portion of Chinatown, and now, less than three miles away, the car was no longer worth more than the houses it drove past. In an earlier time, she might've sneered at such excess, but China was no different. If anything, the sequestering of wealth was worse in her homeland. To this day, some people in the Chinese countryside lived lives no different from a medieval peasant. Far too many people in cities looked down on them from chrome towers.

Coward that he was, she thought he'd lean on the horn and shout as he drove past. He didn't do that. He slowed down and then stopped. Helen quickly parked a few spots behind him. There were thick bushes on this side of the street that extended into the roadway itself. Perfect cover.

He staggered up out of the car and nearly fell shutting the door. He took a swig from an open bottle of expensive whiskey and bellowed wordlessly at the house. Helen only expected this kind of misbehavior from country people new to a city or politburo mistresses. Sometimes they were the same thing. He had managed to find a way to lose face, drop-kick his family's honor, destroy his guanxi, and in all probability get arrested at the same time. It was almost physically painful to watch.

After getting no response, he reached in to honk the horn. "Hey!" he shouted in English, slurring the word out into a long cry. "Hey!" More honking. "Come out here, you bitch! Look what I found!" He staggered forward toward the impassive façade of the house. "Do you hear me? I found your toy! That's what you always called it, you ignorant bitch!" He threw the bottle, which crashed loudly against the railing of the stairs to the front door.

Scratch the comparison with politburo mistresses. *Toddlers* behaved better than this.

Then he reached behind his back and pulled out a gun.

It was her first time encountering someone armed in an uncontrolled situation. Helen was out of the car before Xie took his next step. "Hey!"

He startled and turned to face her, but then staggered against the curb. As he fell, time slowed down, Helen's heartbeats slicing it into discrete intervals.

Thump-thump.

His knees buckled. He was going down.

Thump-thump.

The gun came up as he flailed. It moved in an arc and pointed straight at her. There wasn't time to go anywhere. The hole of the barrel was all she could see.

Thump-thump.

It fired.

The nanovest she wore under her shirt hardened in an instant, but the impact was still powerful enough to spin her into a half turn. She hit the ground hard. There was no pain. Almost no sensation at all. For a brief moment, Helen had gotten away with being shot.

Then it started to *hurt*.

Nanomaterials made bulletproof vests no thicker or heavier than a T-shirt, but all that energy still had to go somewhere. In her case, it seemed to be the right side of her abdomen. It felt like a rhino had run her over, leading with his horn. She'd seen demonstrations of the vests and knew no critical damage had been done. But it *hurt so bad*.

Xie loomed over her, a drunk in crisis. "Oh my God! Are you okay?"

"No, I'm not okay! You shot me!" She moved to show him the impact, but the pain flared up worse. She almost passed out.

This turned her routine firewall patrol into a stumbling shambles that quickly failed altogether. The ramparts were no longer manned. The gate had fallen open. Andromeda was always beyond the wall.

Xie's eyes changed. "I knew you would make a mistake," he said in a voice that was not his. "Time to correct mine."

His hands closed over her throat as he climbed on top of her. The pain in her side was now matched with a crushing agony. She flailed around but found nothing to grab, reached up but he was too far away to touch, and he was so strong. Nobody had come out of the house; they may not have heard anything. There were woods on the other side of the street, and the neighboring houses were far away. Helen was going to die at the hands of an Andromeda-possessed drunk.

Clawing at his hands did no good. The pain in her lungs now exceeded all else. Her vision faded at the edges and lost its color. After all this, she would be strangled to death in the street thousands of miles from home.

A blur passed over him, and then he was gone. Vanished. She pulled in a single ragged gasp as she sat up.

Tom was on the ground a few feet away from her, struggling with Xie.

Losing.

That set her immediate priority. She abruptly left both her classes, closed the connection to Dumas's police department, and pulled away from all other distractions. Helen threw the freed threads into her firewall constructs, filling them completely. She cut the probe off with a vicious twist.

Xie stopped struggling immediately. A moment later, he cried out and tried to protect himself from Tom's blows. Helen staggered upright, fighting through the fire of her injuries. Tom cocked back for another punch, one that would go too far. She grabbed his hand. "Stop! I'm okay!"

In the distance, sirens were heading their way. Someone must've heard that gunshot after all.

Tom quickly stood up, towering over her. "You're sure?"

The pain came roaring back. She had to sit down on the curb or she'd fall. "No, but I will be."

Tom pulled a pair of handcuffs out and put them on Xie. He gave Xie a single kick to the gut for good measure. "That's for shooting my newest employee, asshole!"

She and Tom both threw up their hands as what seemed like half the DC police department rushed onto the scene. It was another parallel with China: being rich got you the best service. She lifted her arms. The pain in her side and around her neck got in a private wrestling match. She cried out, embarrassed by her weakness.

Tom shouted, "She's been shot!" which focused attention on her. The police quickly motioned for her to put her hands down. She thanked her ancestors for small favors.

The next hour and a half was spent sitting in the back entrance of an ambulance while medics checked her out. Cops recorded her statement and questioned her.

It took a lot of convincing before they gave up trying to drag her to an ER. It was just a lot of bruising. The diagnostics in her phone would've highlighted any real injuries quickly.

That didn't slow down the circus though. The entire neighborhood had turned up, and now it was a scene out of a bad crime realm drama.

Tom came over. "You said you didn't know this guy."

She watched Xie as they pushed his gurney into another ambulance. His pained cries as they moved him set her teeth on edge. Unlike Helen, Xie seemed to think getting bounced to the ground and pummeled a little might've given him an aneurism or an injury equally life threatening. "I don't."

"Then why did he attack you like that?"

It would take the rest of the night to tell that story, and he wouldn't believe her when she was done. "He's blind drunk. Probably thought I was his wife. I think he was going to shoot her."

Tom grunted. "Or himself."

"No," she said as the other ambulance roared off with flashing lights and siren. "He's too big of a coward for that." She reached up to him. "A little help?"

He helped her to her feet and then walked her to her car. "You should take a few days off," he said. "Gunshots are no laughing matter."

The power levels of her phone's analgesic routines were pegged, and she still winced. "I think I'll take you up on that."

Besides, she had work to do. It was obviously time to take automating some of these defenses seriously. She opened a programming window as the car drove itself home while her threads began working on datastores that would do the job.

It was going to be a long night.

Chapter 3

Maff

"Your attention, passengers at gate B29," Maff said as she held the bizarre human microphone—complete with coiled cord—up to her suit's external speaker. "Flight FF913 to Orlando will begin boarding in thirty minutes." She set it down carefully. The design dated back to their 1970s decade, and the button on the side made it hard to hold. Her body had no discrete internal structure, so she'd assumed a human shape with her suit but still had to use her manipulators to interact with their world. She had broken a few things before she got the hang of handling their tools.

An elderly pale female walked up to the counter, the servos in her powered supportLegs framework whirring away like a junior version of Maff's own suit legs. "Excuse me, ma'am. You have a lovely accent. Where are you from?"

The human capacity for curiosity was endlessly surprising, especially amongst their young and aged. The children were fascinated by her suit, while the elderly seemed to make a sport of figuring out where she was from by the sound of her voice. They all assumed that she was the victim of a terrible accident or profound deformity, because that was the most famous use of all-encompassing life mobility suits on Earth. It was a convenient mistake, although it was getting a bit difficult avoiding invitations to various conventions and trade shows. The general public couldn't tell the difference between Maff's suit and any others. The one time she'd encountered an actual fully suited human, they were too surprised to closely examine her. Standing on a convention floor inviting long term inspection by experts and professionals would be a disaster.

But maybe not for much longer.

"Russia," she said. It was Mike's idea; he claimed her Pallundian accent came close to that language.

"Is that where you got such a distinctive suit? The legs look a little like mine, but wow, the rest of it..."

Building up her cover story was the first thing they did when it became obvious she'd be staying on Earth for some time.

"The suit is from new start-up my family is creating here in US. It is prototype." This technically wasn't a lie. Pallun suits could be adapted to meet human needs easily, and they were superior to the human versions. It was an entry in the fast-growing list of opportunities she was going to present to her family about Earth's potential.

"Well, I must say it's beautiful. Good luck with your effort." She smiled and returned to her seat, her brass supportLegs whirring and clicking as she went. Yes, Pallundian tech would revolutionize the human's mobility enhancement market.

Her eyes strayed past the woman to the tall windows on the opposite gate, allowing her to stare at the real reason she'd chosen this line of work. In the rest of the galaxy, the AC network built gateways and D-ships for transportation. Those were what moved cargo and people around, and both strongly resembled various kinds of Earth ground transportation, especially their trains. But humans didn't have portals, at least not yet, so they didn't use them for high-speed transport.

They used *airplanes*.

Machines not built on Earth could fly, of course, but nobody in their right mind would climb inside one and let it carry them around. The AC nodes wouldn't build such a craft even if anyone asked them for it. Falling out of a high-grav sky was dangerous.

And yet humans had flown in machines of their own design for centuries.

Maff was a pallun. Her kind evolved to do nothing but fly. The idea that she could do it down in a gravity well, soaring over the heads of the regular high grav-high temp types without seriously risking her own life made her giddy.

But flying an airplane safely was a major undertaking. She'd have to lay down roots and build a history to pass the background checks that were required. As with Mike and Helen, Maff was leaning heavily on Kim to get her identity established. "I'm getting pretty good at acquiring passports," Kim had said. Maff now had enough to land a job, but it would take time for her established identity to become strong enough to stand up to real scrutiny.

The concept of a job as the humans defined it was a jarring thing she was still getting used to. In the galaxy, the AC network provided *raskara,* a word and concept that was difficult to translate so her human friends could understand it. The closest she could get was modest prosperity. If someone didn't want to work for a good quality of life, they didn't have to. Entertainments were always within reach. Education was always available. Conveniences of modest capability were always free.

It deeply puzzled Mike, although when he tried to explain why with concepts like energy budgets and basic economics, Maff's head felt like it would explode. It was as incomprehensible to her as their ideas of particle physics, prophecy, and time travel. Humans were different in so many ways that Maff was losing track.

She eventually figured out that humans didn't provide raskara because, apparently, they couldn't afford it. At least not for long periods of time. What was provided by government, which was the human's self-evolved substitute for AC nodes, usually didn't work well and was expensive. Charity, a concept she was familiar with, worked pretty much like it did back home: efficient and comparatively inexpensive but targeted and with a ton of strings attached. In both cases, what the humans got was not raskara, but rather a much less satisfying basic survival.

The times humans did try to provide raskara on a large scale, mostly in their twentieth century, were disastrous. Things always fell apart, usually with great suffering and loss of life. It seemed the nodes had been right about one thing: you did not get civilization the way the galaxy got it without the AC network.

Thankfully the entire mess could be avoided by getting *a job*. It was roughly similar to *penkfore*. In the galaxy, people not content with raskara could pursue a life of penkfore, which could be translated as ambition and wealth.

There was a startling commonality here. People who succeeded at pursuing penkfore in human societies were perceived largely the same way they were in the galaxy: with suspicion, if not outright hostility, by anyone content with raskara. This was ironic since in both places raskara was only tolerable through the fruits of penkfore. Without penkfore, there would be no entertainments, education, or conveniences. The AC network could provide, but it could not create. There was a difference too. Penkfore was a comparatively rare way of life in the galaxy. Not here. Here, Maff had found herself on a planet filled top to bottom with people pursuing penkfore not out of desire but necessity.

But there was more. Humans had built everything around her. Not only built it, but designed it, conceived it, and on a level deeper than anything she had ever encountered. And it was wonderful! Their societies were much richer than anything back home.

Since penkfore was required for them to function, human cultures were vibrant, striving, always innovating and creating. True, their level of technology wasn't equal to what was found in the galaxy...*yet*. But it was close. Aside from portals and the tech infrastructure around them, humans had primitive versions of most kinds of technology found back home. In some places, like the airplane parked across from her at this moment, they had advanced technology completely unknown in the galaxy. And they knew how it all worked, unlike the galaxy.

And there wasn't an AC network node in sight.

This was a critical aspect of Maff's *other* Big Plan. She didn't understand what their technological know-how would mean because, since Maff was from the larger galaxy—a bemian, as

Spencer had dubbed them after the first bug-eyed monster aliens they'd encountered—*she* had no idea how any of it worked. But that was a problem for another cloud bank. Her idea was both simpler and more complicated than unleashing a planet full of hypercurious high-grav types on the galaxy.

She wanted to put on a show.

What the galaxy hungered for always was novelty and entertainment. The AC network uplifted cultures and then integrated them into a bigger whole. They'd been doing it for billions of years. This forced a sameness, the humans called it homogeneity, on the whole galaxy. Genuinely new things, new songs, new stories, new art, were almost unheard of. Using the same tools tended to produce similar results. Novelty was found in the rediscovery of old things or marginal changes to art that'd always existed.

Earth was nothing like that. The entire planet was filled with new stories. There were basic commonalities that hinted at universal concepts. Romance was easy to spot, and the *hero's quest* underpinned the greatest bemian stories as well as the ones here on Earth. But those were only the broadest strokes.

And that was only regarding Earth's literature. Much of Earth's music was utterly original. Their classical and folk music had obvious parallels to bemian types. But rock and roll? Hip hop? Jazz? Country and western? All new. And these were subsets of an enormous classification called popular music. Maff hadn't heard anything like it, ever. Some of it didn't start out sounding like music at all. It took spending some time with it for the artistic qualities to become obvious. And humans had millions of hours of it lying around.

Humanity's cultural corpus represented a penkfore opportunity of unprecedented scale. But it was also an extremely dangerous one. Humans were surprisingly open and comfortable with the idea that there were aliens around them, even if they hadn't yet knowingly met any. The galaxy at large, however, would not come to terms so easily with a wolfling civilization. They were supposed to be impossible. When they were imagined at all, it was as a contagion to be contained, a source of chaos that would end galactic civilization if not tamed immediately. Earth's emergence needed to be protected, managed, and carefully shepherded into the light, otherwise there was a real risk the entire planet would be shoved down the throat of a superstorm as soon as the AC network got wind of its existence.

Nevertheless it was inevitable that humans would have to join the rest of the galaxy. It would happen someday. Maff wanted it to happen on Earth's terms, and she knew exactly who could help.

They key was Jupiter. It was nearly a twin to the long-destroyed pallun home world. And it had no AC network presence. Her people had been forbidden from flying free on worlds controlled by the nodes as punishment for their defiance, that brief time when they'd thrown off the yoke of the nodes and gone wolfling themselves. The restriction was meant to be a poetic irony. *They were cast out, doomed to roam, banned forever from flying through clouds controlled by nodes.* The implication, pointed out explicitly in any number of antipallun dramas, was that they could fly free on a planet the nodes had left untouched because none existed. Now she knew of such a place. As long as they could gain the human's trust and cooperation.

So Earth was sitting on a diamond storm of penkfore that might outweigh the planet itself. They needed help discreetly introducing these assets to the galaxy. Maff's people were justifiably famous as a race dedicated to penkfore, to the point they were resented for it by the rest of the galaxy. In Earth's solar system, there was a place pallun would be free to practice a lifestyle denied them for generations. Maff sensed the edges of a deal that would tie the two peoples together in a system of prosperity not seen since before the Refounding.

But only the edges. Maff was a pilot, not a trader. She needed help. She needed her family. And for that she needed Mike and Kim.

When her shift finished, she met up with them at the office-slash-lab that was at the exact spot where Earth and the galaxy first collided. As always, she stole a glance at the parking dock that marked the spot where her ship, *Palatine*, was hiding in the transit dimension. They'd disguised it with tarps, boxes, crates, and other piles of miscellaneous construction materials. If she didn't already know what was buried under all that, she'd never guess the truth. But Maff did, and it was always reassuring to know that this small bit of home was still with her.

After entering, she sighed and relaxed into her more normal shape: much wider than she was tall, thinner, and balanced on legs spread around her instead of grouped into two bunches. In this shape, the humans in on her secret said she resembled a manta ray in a scuba suit. Once Maff got a look at those things, she could see their point.

"Hi, Maff!" Mike said from the more habitat-like part of the building—what they called *the office*. "We're almost ready to start."

Maff needed to talk things over with her family and she knew the only Interpreter on the whole planet who still had threads that could reach them. They both seemed tense, though, with steaming coffee mugs sitting in front of them.

"Are you okay?" Maff asked.

They shared a look that didn't seem happy. Kim wrapped her hands around her mug. "We've had some things happen. Nothing dangerous, but if you could stick around after your call, we'd like to talk them over with you."

Maff lifted her wing tips. "Of course, anything you need." She settled beside the conference table they were sitting at. "How does this work?"

Back home, a trans-system call was handled completely behind the scenes by the Interpreter's Guild. She would make the request, then get an estimated time the call would be completed. She'd need to be at a guild chapter house by then in a call terminal booth to use the connection. None of that infrastructure was present on Earth.

"You installed the app I sent you on your phone, right?" Kim asked.

The English word for their version of a neural connector was *phone*. The bemian versions were so small they were implanted under the skin. Here they were the size of a large ruby nodule, what Spencer called a *jewelry pendant.* "Yes."

Mike closed his eyes. "And that's it. Connection complete. We're ready."

"That was fast," Maff replied. "You said it might take a lot longer."

"It's interesting," Mike said. "The appointments the guild makes you use don't have anything to do with capacity. There are plenty of threads at any chapter house. It takes time because they have to set up system-to-system thread connections manually from one to the next in a chain. If an Interpreter has visited your source and destination system, you're in luck; there will be a direct connection, and it can happen at any time. But if the distance is long, or the system is new or remote, getting it arranged can be complicated. It's similar to how Earth's long-distance networks functioned in the middle of the last century."

"And we're hidden," Kim said as she opened her eyes. "They won't know where you're calling from."

On some subconscious level, Maff had moved Mike and Kim into a *remarkable human* box. She'd forgotten they were remarkable by bemian standards too. "I don't think I'll ever get used to you guys doing things like this," she said.

Kim shrugged. "Activate the app, it'll take care of the rest. We won't be able to see or hear what goes on either. The bandwidth is limited, so it's not full haptic. Only a virtual screen."

Maff nodded and set her legs to passive balance, her equivalent of sitting down without a plinth. Then she logged in.

The screen opposite her showed two extremely agitated pallun, also known as Papa and Mama.

"Maff!" her mother wailed. "Oh, we have been so worried!"

"Have you eaten?" her father asked forcefully. "Are you warm? Have those *irtan* taken advantage of you?"

"Hi, guys—"

That was the extent of her side of the conversation for some time.

"How could you be gone for so long..."

"And the neighbors! *Za*, the neighbors have been wondering..."

"A shunning! Can you believe they..."

"We didn't know if we should arrange a funeral..."

"Give me pump attacks and let me die..."

"If your uncle asked one more time where you were..."

They'd entered a classic Pallundian parent feedback loop, winding themselves up with no end in sight.

Maff shouted, "I'm *fine!*"

That summoned an indignant silence, but at least it was silence. "Please. Let me tell you what's happened."

She provided a brief and carefully sanitized version of the events that led to her ending up on Earth and then said, "You're not going to believe what it's like here."

She expected them to be thrilled.

When she was done, it was clear they weren't.

"Are you *sure* you're eating properly?" Papa asked.

"I told you, I'm fine." Working out a compatible menu had been one of the first things she'd done. "Didn't you hear about the music and the—"

"They're being nice to you?" Mama asked. "You've kept your suit on the whole time, yes?"

She'd presented them with the opportunity of a lifetime, and her mom was worried she was sleeping around? "I'm the only pallun here, Mama. Of course I've kept my suit on."

They shared a look of obvious concern. Papa leaned in close, the nose of his suit becoming comically huge. "These things you're describing, they don't exist. You know that, yes?"

"Papa, they *do* exist. I've seen them myself. Listened to them myself."

Behind Papa, Mama started to wail again. "My baby! My baby's gone mad! She's so far away, and now she's *insane*!"

"Hush, Mama," scolded Papa. "You're upsetting her."

"You're not upsetting me," Maff said. "I'm not lying, and I'm not crazy."

"See," he motioned at the screen. "She's upset and confused."

"I'm not—"

Papa cut her off. "You go and rest. We need to think about our next steps. You call us back, soon!" He turned to Mama as his wing reached forward toward the screen. "If we upset her in this state, she'll never agree to see a bashtun. If she has—"

The screen went dark, and the audio cut off with a snap.

"I'm not upset!" Maff shouted at the darkness. She expected that there would be doubt and skepticism, not this immediate jump to madness. Maff shook her head and exited the call.

Kim leaned forward. "That doesn't seem like it went well."

She sighed. Her parents didn't believe any of it. "No, it didn't go the way I imagined it would."

Helen, Tonya, and Spencer walked through the door.

"I hope it wasn't a disaster," Mike said as Kim greeted them. "I think we're going to need their help."

Her parents had called her crazy, and now the humans *wanted* to make contact? "What?"

Chapter 4
Mike

It was becoming a bit of a traditional meeting meal for them: Chinese food and pizza.

"I knew it would be some fucked up shit when the meeting request had checklists from both," Spencer said as he sat down, holding one plate stacked high with slices and another piled up with egg fried rice. It was more food than Mike would eat all day, but that was how Spencer rolled. "What's going on?"

Mike kept a close eye on Helen as she moved about stiffly. She shouldn't be here at all, but he wouldn't dare imply his sister was anything less than tough as nails. She'd probably challenge him to use her vest while she pulled the trigger, and afterward there'd be a sprint race. At least the scarf around her neck did a good job hiding the strangulation bruises. The idea of nearly losing her like that made him sick, but all Helen would talk about was how big a discount she'd found the scarf at. "Ninety percent!" she'd said. He didn't like her getting in harm's way, but she loved the work.

Kim sat down next to him and turned to the group. "Watchtell is out." She said it in a flat, matter-of-fact tone. Kim had two styles of anger: shouty and raging or still and silent. At the moment, she barely moved at all. "He says he's taking over Sidereal. He's offering us all jobs."

Spencer sputtered and swore. Kim tapped a salt shaker twice, used it, then tapped it twice again after putting it down. Mike glanced at Tonya, who nodded slightly at him. He'd called her earlier, and her initial take was that it might be the result of Kim getting used to the sleep app. Now that she'd seen it in person, he wondered if that opinion had changed.

Spencer concluded his minirant. "It'll be a fine fucking day if that happens. And I barely know the asshole."

"Can he do it?" Tonya asked. "It's our foundation, right?"

Mike sighed. The truth had ruined his day, and now it was his turn to do that to them. "I called in some lawyers. The reason we found the portal at all was because Sidereal's contract expired without anyone renewing it. We needed to find Will more than we needed to get the paperwork settled." Faces around the room fell. "I didn't make it a priority after that, and that's on me. Basically, we've been on a rolling temporary contract with the federal government since day one."

"Son of a bitch." Spencer growled through a mouthful of pizza, then he swallowed. "So are we slightly fucked or completely fucked?"

Kim chuckled darkly. "Do you have to ask?"

Mike nodded. "The lawyers say they can delay him, maybe long enough for him to screw up and get thrown in jail again. But if it goes to court, there's a good chance he'll win."

"Shit," Spencer replied. "So now what?"

"We move up the timetable," Helen said firmly. "But we haven't started portal construction yet."

As one, they all turned to Maff, who'd been draining a container of pho broth using one of her manipulators. Properly vaporized, the Vietnamese soup was a close match for a rare exotic gas pallun treated as a delicacy. It lent the air a faint pleasant cinnamon, a nice contrast to the machine oil and old concrete smell the lab had most of the time.

She moved her wings forward so the tips rested on the table, her version of leaning toward them. "Right. Southwest Galactic Transport, at your service." She laughed. "I am wanting to talk to you all about this," she said in her not-really-but-sort-of Russian accent. "I call family. It did not, how do you say it, go exactly as planned."

Maff had talked about Earth's potential if it ever joined galactic civilization. Mike didn't disagree, but they were all more interested in protecting themselves first. Getting rich was nice, but it wouldn't do them much good if giant network nodes dropped out of the sky and started remolding the place into what they considered a proper galactic civilization.

It wouldn't be that easy.

The traditions he'd found implied that the nodes started with civilizations far less advanced than Earth's. They'd probably never landed on a planet capable of fighting back. Earth had a long, rich tradition of fiction that revolved around fighting off an alien invasion. Properly distilled, it was essentially an instruction manual on the subject. They also had nukes, and the will to use them. There would be no winners if an invasion happened, only losers. Better to avoid that whole thing entirely. Hence Sidereal.

"So," Maff said, "I was having a wonder. They do not believe me because they cannot see any of this. I did not know how to make that happen, but since you are wanting to head back out anyway..."

Tonya cracked a smile. "Maybe we could stop by your parent's house on the way there?"

"I think it'll be more than that," Helen said. "Ever since last night," she tugged at her scarf, "I've been working on systems to automate our defenses. It's not as easy as I predicted it to be. *I* was wondering what information the AC network might have on the entity and its abilities. Even if they don't know Andromeda's origin, I'm certain they'll have encountered it sometime in the past."

Tonya said, "At least I'm not the only one wanting to visit. Me, I was wondering what it would be like to leverage some of their tech in my experiments." She raised an eyebrow, a sign Mike knew meant she was much more curious about the idea than she was letting on. "And we'd bring our own tools."

They all turned to Spencer, who was busy wolfing down his fourth slice of pizza. His eyes had the classic glassy look of someone paying attention to a screen only he could see.

He seemed to notice the silence. "Shit, I'm all for a road trip, but

I'll be damned if I spend it in a fucking library, meeting someone's parents, or bent over a soldering iron. I'm gonna vote for Sidereal."

Kim tapped out another tattoo with her salt shaker, and this time the whole table noticed it. With anyone else, he'd gently cover their hand, but that wasn't an option with her. He'd always known marriage would be a challenge but hadn't counted on the appearance of OCD symptoms turning up on the list. On the second set of taps, she seemed to come out of it, blushed, and carefully set the shaker aside.

"They're not exclusive goals," Kim said, then indicated Maff. "You, Tonya, and Helen can be our research and marketing team. Me, Mike, and Spencer will take on Sidereal."

"Do you think splitting up like that is a good idea?" Tonya asked.

Kim shrugged. "A smaller team is easier to keep track of. Fewer arguments, fewer targets. Mike and Helen can keep us in contact with each other."

"I do not know," Maff said. "I do not want to rush into things. Family can be...overwhelming."

"Remember," Helen replied, "this is as much about protecting them from us as it is the other way around. Imagine what happens if Watchtell gets control of Sidereal before we've completed it."

A thoughtful silence settled on the group. He and Kim succeeded the last time out due in no small part to the collection of unpatched vulnerabilities in the AC network and its nodes. Sidereal 2.0 relied on the idea of a computer worm spreading code throughout that network, but in addition to hiding Earth, they would be closing up the worst of those vulnerabilities. It was crazy to think he'd be patching an entire galaxy, but it would only take one malevolent human hacker to cause irreparable harm to countless worlds. The vulnerabilities were that severe in a few cases. And people didn't get much more malevolent that Matthew Watchtell.

Out of nowhere, Spencer started laughing.

"What is so funny?" Maff asked.

"We're gonna fucking do this, aren't we?" He slapped the table. "Two years ago I was sitting in a shitbox town wondering how to get the hell out, and now *I'm gonna go into space*! Visit exotic worlds. Meet strange aliens."

Mike flipped the rest of that saying before Spencer could finish. "And hopefully *not* kill them."

He shrugged. "Well, yeah. There's a whole lot more of them than us. I think getting into a shooting match would be a bad idea."

Tonya had grown pensive, which was strange. She was normally unflappable. "Are *you* okay with this?" he asked.

She shook herself, then shrugged. "It's nothing. Stupid. I shouldn't bring it up. A silly nothing."

Kim reached out with a handkerchief. It must be a big deal. "It doesn't seem like a silly nothing."

Tonya grabbed a corner of the handkerchief and pulled it tight. She seemed to get in a silent argument with herself, and then sighed. "I'll be the first Christian in more than a hundred years to walk amongst pagans. *Actual* pagans, billions of people don't know anything about my religion."

Spencer scoffed, which made Mike scowl. He took faith seriously, even if his and Tonya's were different.

She laughed. "I know, right? It makes me sound like one of those lunatic fundamentalists holding a realm revival. But my faith is important to me, and it has a lot to say about who can be saved."

Mike had studied all religions before settling on Buddhism, so he had a basic grasp of Christian history. "Is it that much different from the Spanish encountering, say, the Incas?"

Her hands opened stiffly as her eyes went wide, giving her a look of confusion Mike only saw when she was working on a tough math problem. "I don't know. At least they were all human then." She turned to Maff. "No offense."

"None taken," she replied. "I cannot use translator thread next to translator, so I do not think I am understanding all these words. You are worried about your religion interacting with the galaxy?"

"I guess that's one way to put it."

"Galaxy is full of religion, but only five types. AC network only allows five types. Pallun is sixth type, but we are gasbags. We lose war, lose home, keep religion. Our judgement is not so good, I think. Earth's religions are different. Crazy different, and so many on one planet. It is unheard of. Your Christianity, though, it surprises me. Not *completely* different from pallun."

Spencer rolled his eyes. "We're about to go full *Galaxy Quest* and I'm stuck here talking about Jesus? I left Dumas to get away from this shit." He stood up, tossed his trash into a bin, grabbed another slice of pizza, then headed for the door. "I've got to get to Bass Pro. It closes soon."

They'd long planned on launching their AC network hack on a remote planet early in its uplift cycle. Since it hadn't joined the galaxy yet, it was far more likely they could find the appropriate vulnerabilities. It also meant they would have to rely on their own gear. Framed that way, a camping store was necessary. He gave Kim a questioning look. She nodded quickly.

When he looked at Tonya, she waved him toward the door. "Just because it's Spencer doesn't mean he's wrong." Spencer's indignant swear was muffled by the wad of pizza he'd shoved in his face. Tonya laughed, and that brought back the cheerful scientist he worked with. "We're pretty deep in the philosophical weeds here, and we *do* have a lot of packing to do."

They'd been discussing religion and then, without saying anything about it, they started doing something completely different. It was an aspect of social humanity Mike was fascinated with. But Tonya was right; they needed supplies. They started to clean up dinner and put away the leftovers.

"Hang on a sec, Spence," he said. "We're coming along."

Chapter 5
Spencer

They spent hours in Bass Pro Shop strategizing, picking out gear, and then waiting in the drone delivery area for some of their more obscure or bulky items to arrive. This wasn't some accidental yank 'n' snatch like what Kim and Mike went through last time. They also weren't escaping with only the clothes on their backs like they'd done too many times in China. They were going on a goddamned safari and had planned accordingly. He'd been meaning to switch to a nicotine inhaler for ages, and now that bulk and weight were more important than cost, it was time. He burned through a pack of the cartridges waiting for the Pro Shop bots to fit their orders in his truck.

He got to the lab and could barely believe what was about to happen. He literally started bouncing around as he drove his truck through the big garage door in the side of the building. He was *going to fucking space*! Aliens! Robots! Starships!

Well, okay. Not a *proper* starship.

The wings on Maff's ship were too short for it to fly, the engines were fucked up podded whirligigs that did...who knew what the fuck, and it had a pretty substantial set of wheels underneath it. The whole thing was a cross between a cargo airplane and an eighteen-wheeler, sort of like if a C-130 and a Peterbilt had a baby.

The first time he saw it, it looked like it'd fallen down a flight of stairs. There were dents everywhere, the engines must've been set on fire and then covered in oatmeal, and sometimes there was the occasional hole. Spencer got to throw out one of his favorite movie lines that day.

"What a piece of junk!"

He was gonna say more, but then Maff, the actual, for-real alien, walked down the ramp in all her steampunk manta ray glory. Aliens were supposed to be giant humanoids with scary teeth, not an ocean fish in a space suit balanced on brass legs.

"Yes," she said, with an accent that sounded like she should be asking about a moose and squirrel realm, "but we will be fixing that very much soon. Most of damage is…how do you say? Cosmetic. Soot and fire extinguisher." She pointed at a hole punched clean through one wing. "And occasional projectile."

A year later and what did you know? She was as good as her word. The engine pods on the ends of the stubby, high-mounted wings were perfectly clean. The dents and holes were gone.

She'd even painted it. Spencer would've gone low key, maybe monochrome. NSEA *Protector* markings or Aztec-paneled *Enterprise* goodness. But not Maff. She'd painted it mostly glossy blue with two big stripes running diagonally across the sides, one red, one orange.

He spotted the resemblance instantly. "You've got to be kidding me," he said as he leaned out of the window of his truck. "You turned it into a fucking Southwest airliner?"

"Is tribute to employer," Maff said from a scissor lift as she closed an engine cowling. "They are nice people. Very friendly." She pointed one of her wings at the fuselage. "You are now free to move about the galaxy."

Spencer had forgotten how big it was. It was just as well that they'd rented an old datacenter large enough to double as a hangar for their portal projects. Fully out of the transit dimension, *Palatine* almost filled it.

Mike walked down the front cargo ramp. Spencer shouted, "Hey, boss! Where do you want me?"

"Back it straight up the ramp."

Mike had been busy with the threads he'd left in bemian space—and wasn't that a kick in the fucking teeth, that his friend could communicate with other planets the way Spencer called his mom—discreetly surveying worlds in the midst of being uplifted. They needed one isolated but not too far off the path to Maff's home world, far enough along in uplift that the nodes were likely complacent but not so close to finishing that they were on the verge of connecting the planet to the rest of the galaxy. He'd picked a place called Teliria, which was roughly halfway between the two extremes.

One thing Mike and Kim learned last time around was that feet as a primary mode of transport sucked ass. They'd debated about getting ATVs, but a full-size vehicle seemed more flexible in the overall scheme of things. It could double as a self-propelled power supply, for example. So they picked his truck.

The first otherworld buggy to land on a planet that didn't orbit the sun would be his old Dodge. He'd bought it from his dad's buddy, an old farmer, and it was already pretty well equipped for the job. At the time, the extra biodiesel tank that took up about a fifth of the truck bed seemed excessive, but now Spencer was glad he hadn't removed it. It took fucking forever to fill up, but they now had the equivalent of an extra ten full tanks of gas. If they were careful and didn't try to drive all the way around the world, it should be enough to last for months.

He stared through the empty gun racks attached to the back window as he navigated up the ramp. It reminded him of an inconvenient part of the whole expedition.

"No," Maff explained as they'd walked into the Bass Pro Shop's gun department. "No advanced weapons. The nodes will not allow. You would be targeted long before you got within sight of one."

Maff was from a society much like his own: most people had not a fucking clue about guns. "Then we won't use advanced weapons." At root, a gun was a steel tube, a bullet was a lump of lead, and powder was badly mixed fertilizer.

So no gun rack full of semiauto shotguns. In their place they had three Traditions Firearms NitroFire II muzzle-loading rifles safely packed away with enough shot, primer, and black powder to keep them going for a good long time. Fifty caliber rifles accurate out to two hundred yards would sting dinosaur-sized quarry, although again according to Maff, the AC nodes would've taken care of any dangerous megafauna shortly after landing.

They wouldn't be able to hold off an entire bemian army all by themselves, but they would be able to make pretty damned orderly retreats if it came that. It should also make short work of any deer analogs they came across. He was looking forward to a little bemian deer hunting. Spencer wanted to eat more than ration bars for the duration. And if it fell in the pot, Kim had ordered some gonzo archery shit, and rounded it out with a pair of wack quarterstaffs that she'd pulled out of her fucking closet.

He'd put the guns on the checkout counter, and Tonya got that sideways grin she wore whenever Spencer let his redneck flag fly high. "You're not worried about their culture being contaminated by high technology?"

"Fuck no. We're not there to study them. We're there to get in, do a job, and get the hell out. I might drop some on the way to the exit. Give them a leg up."

After securing the truck to the deck—tie-downs were another universal constant—Spencer took a long look at his home for the next few weeks. Pretty basic, but he'd picked up a new Subnautica realm reboot that should keep him occupied during down times.

Maff had the cargo bay and beyond painted fresh, too, although on the inside it was some kind of boring glossy gray color. Everything had been cleaned and polished. All in all, it was much improved from the first time around. "Okay maybe it's not a piece of junk anymore."

His truck represented the bulk of their cargo. Helen, Maff, and Tonya were staying with civilization, such as it was, and so wouldn't have to haul a campsite around with them. After they got on board, though, they were only carrying small overnight bags, much smaller than what they'd get from one of Mike's famous Amazon air strikes. "Travel light much?" he asked Tonya as she and Helen settled into their quarters.

"Maff's advice," she replied. "We've got enough clothes for the trip, but we'll leave all that behind on arrival."

Helen peered into the hallway Spencer stood in. "There's supposed to be a replicator around here somewhere that will make native outfits for us."

"The one you use for clothes is on the upper deck behind the hold," Kim said from the cabin across the hall. She and Mike had much more substantial suitcases, although those would get left behind too. "I'll show you how it works once we're on our way."

Comms on this tub worked pretty much like they did on *Star Trek*. "Maff," he said to the ceiling, knowing his voice would route to the bridge automatically. "How long until we're outta here?"

"Simply give the word. Have you all said goodbye?" she asked.

He'd set up a standard bot that would keep mom entertained with various fake messages, so there was no need for him. The others had probably done the same. Helen and Mike would act as the conduits to cover any edge cases, using threads still on Earth to do the work. But that didn't distract from the fact that they were heading out. Spencer watched as the same realization that roiled his guts settled on his friends. Mike and Kim did their handkerchief thing. Tonya swallowed and nodded. Helen shrugged but stayed quiet.

"Marines," he said softly. "We are leaving."

Spencer secured the cargo doors, taking a long last look as they closed on the only world he'd ever known. *Jesus fucking Christ on a broken-ass crutch*, he thought, *I'm doing this.*

Everyone else was on the bridge. There was no central command chair like on an *Enterprise* realm. There were three stations in a semicircle: two small ones and a large one on his right. Maff had settled into that one, with Mike and Kim at the smaller ones.

"Do we get to learn how to steer?" he asked.

Maff chuckled. "You must complete courses first. Here is intro text."

A bemian file started to arrive in his message queue. It was *huge*. He walked over until he could see her entire station, only then realizing how many dials, levers, and gauges she was working with. It was a lot more complicated than an airliner. "And that will take how long?"

She threw a lever, and the floor started to vibrate faintly. "It was a year until I was trusted to fly real one. But we can always get you set up in sim." She grabbed the handle on a heavy cylinder and pulled it out. The ship's vibration zipped upward until he could barely feel it. Other efficient machine noises joined in. It was nothing like any vehicle he'd ridden. He concentrated on breathing, only realizing he'd grabbed a frame of Maff's suit after he'd done it.

She turned to Mike. "What is nav solution?"

He threw a couple of his own switches. "Modal two for now, but we can go up to four when we've cleared the system."

"Good enough," she replied as she turned back to her controls. "It is now time for you to hang on to your butt, Spencer."

In the second it took him to process her joke, she turned the cylinder and pressed it down. The faint chorus of noises changed subtly, and he had a hard hit of nausea as *Palatine* moved. Spencer fought it down quickly. He would *not* have throwing up on Maff be the first thing that he did on a spaceship. Or D-ship. Or whatever the hell this thing was.

He didn't think he'd feel anything at all. D-ships didn't fly through space. They had a drive system that punched a hole in an alternate dimension, the *transit dimension,* which was a fucked up place that allowed them to travel faster than light relative to realspace. It wasn't even flying, at least not all the time. The dimension had gravity, somehow, and a surface that the wheels and tires on the ship used at least part of the time. It had *levels,* segments that allowed extra speed to be piled on, and lots of it. The first level was fast only on the scale of the solar system, which at that speed Palatine could cross in a matter of hours. Pretty fucking fast by Earth standards. But that was the lowest level. The eighth, the highest, could shoot their asses across the whole goddamn galaxy in the time it took a mosquito to fart. The trade-offs were energy, traffic hazards, and navigation. It required more juice to go faster, there was more stuff to run into, and anyone crazy enough to turn the knob up to eight was guaranteed to get lost.

He felt eyes on him and turned to find Helen grinning broadly. "No swearing, Spencer?"

That snapped him out of it. "Fuck me, I'm getting a fucking beer, and then I'm gonna study this fucked up manual Maff gave me because I need to learn how this fucker works in case her suit fucks the pooch, and she can't fucking fly it." He grinned. "How's that?"

Tonya clapped a hand on his shoulder. Her callouses were easily felt through his shirt, and they reminded him they were going to say goodbye to half their fighters soon. "That'll do," she said, laughing. "How about we split one and go over it together?"

*

They quickly fell into a routine of studying bemian technical writing—D-ship manuals—in the mornings, then training in various realmspaces in the afternoon.

Nobody'd ever used muzzle loaders, and it took a bit of practice to get it right. They didn't stop at weapon practice. They put up and took down the camp over and over until any one of them could do it in complete darkness all by themselves. With three people, it could go from fully unpacked to bugging out in minutes.

The other half of the party wasn't lazing around, either. Tonya turned an empty hold into a time lab while Helen unpacked what had to be the smallest, most sophisticated forensic botKit Spencer had ever seen. In spite of her snark, Maff trained them to stand watch over the pilot station so she could take breaks. "Knowing when things are fine and when they are not is easy," she said. "Knowing what to do about it is my job."

Spencer was worried that he'd kill himself from boredom but ended up so busy Mike was the one who told him they'd arrived. "Grab your things, man. Time to go!"

It was idiotic to think that the events of his life had led up to this moment. He didn't know this moment was possible until a year ago, and if it had occurred to him, he'd have assumed it would only come, if ever, years from now. This moment was like pretty much all the others in his life: the product of fucked up shit nobody could've predicted.

And yet, as he sat in the driver's seat of his truck waiting for the cargo doors to open *so he could drive onto the surface of another planet...*

"You want to say something, don't you?" Mike said from beside him.

He did, but now couldn't.

Mike nodded. "I did too." He turned behind him. "How about you, Kim?"

"That's one small step for a washed-up hacker..."

Mike continued, using the nickname Spencer had given him long ago, "And one giant leap for a flying spaghetti monster." He turned back to Spencer. "What's yours?"

Maff spoke into their shared channel. "Doors opening in three...two...one..."

With a clean clack and a grinding rumble, the doors split apart and opened, revealing grass that wasn't quite the right shade of green in his headlights, and a sky full of stars that weren't in any configuration he recognized. As his eyes tracked up, he spotted an old pack of cigs he'd left trapped behind the sunshade.

And there it was.

"We've got a full tank of gas, half a pack of cigarettes, it's dark," he pulled his Ray-Bans out of a cubby under the radio, "and I'm wearing sunglasses." He put them on and grinned at Mike, who he could see had no idea what he was talking about.

From behind him, Kim said, "Hit it."

So he did, sending the truck out into the night with barely a bounce. *Palatine* disappeared into the transit dimension a moment later. The terrain was rolling hills with knots of trees scattered around, like a less flat version of the farmland back home. They got lucky and came across a dirt road less than a mile from the drop-off zone.

Spencer turned onto it and then slammed on the brakes. For a brief moment, their headlights transfixed a lone Telirian. Probably. Mike hadn't been able to get a picture of one, so this was their first look. Bipedal, same number of arms and legs as humans. Those arms, legs, and face were covered in dense, fine fur. The face had a slight muzzle, vaguely bearlike, alien but not ugly. The clothing she—if the body shape was any indication—wore was rugged and seemed handmade. She also carried a pretty big backpack. The eyes were all wrong, somewhere between a cat and a goat.

It seemed that Spencer's first encounter with a bemian was a camper hiking in the woods at night. Weirder things had happened.

Maybe.

She stood there for a moment, then darted off into the tall grass and vanished.

Chapter 6
Maff

With half the crew gone, the ship didn't feel half as crowded.

It felt empty.

She didn't know the other two women anywhere near as well as she did Mike and Kim. What would they talk about when it was just the three of them? But when the others left, the dynamic changed, becoming much friendlier. This was most obvious at the dinner table the night after they'd split up. Now that they were in a part of the galaxy covered by charts, keeping watch on the helm was no longer a continual requirement. This was enough for Tonya to call the evening meal a celebration.

"To the sisterhood," Tonya said with a small glass of intoxicant in her hand.

Helen nodded and clinked another small glass of the same substance against Tonya's.

"To the sisterhood," Maff repeated and clinked her gas bulb carefully against their glasses of liquid. "What's a sisterhood?"

Helen quickly downed her drink and poured another. "To me, it means"—Helen downed her second shot—"a distinct lack of Spencer Mackenzie."

Tonya chose to sip her second shot. It gave her a more sophisticated air than Maff had noticed before. "He's not *that* bad," she said.

The third shot in as many minutes was poured and downed for Helen. The woman had an absolutely extraordinary capacity for alcohol. One night during a Superbowl party at Mike and Kim's house, Helen had gotten in a drinking contest with Kim. It went on so long Maff had gone to bed. She didn't know who won, but on waking the next morning, she knew they'd both lost.

"He has his moments," Helen said, "but I like him in smaller doses than being cooped up in a crowded D-ship for all this time."

Maff let the shatalla gas flow through and relax her. Aside from brief rest spells when the humans were on watch, she'd been on duty more or less continuously since they left Earth. It seemed like a simple thing at first, but staring at the same console, doing the same job, holding her concentration, day in, day out, without any extended breaks had stilled her winds completely. The walls of the ship's galley might not be that interesting, but at least they were different.

"Sisterhood sounds more elaborate than disliking Spencer," Maff said. "I recognize the first half as a female child that shares a parent with you, but I don't understand how it's relevant here, or how *hood* changes things."

Tonya sat back, still in that cool, detached mood, different from the somewhat distracted scientist Maff was used to. Whatever the word meant, she took it seriously. "It stands for the shared experiences we have as women. We struggle together."

"And celebrate together," Helen said, downing another shot.

Tonya shook her head. "I don't care if you have a titanium liver. You need to slow down. Give me that." She took Helen's bottle and moved to the kitchenette half of the galley. "Anyway," she said over her shoulder as she started grabbing various bottles from cold storage, "sisterhood in the sense we used it is a salute to us as women."

"It is rather strange," Helen said, more relaxed than Maff had ever seen her, "talking to you *as* a woman."

"I don't understand."

Tonya shrugged as she turned around with a large glass in each hand. Both were filled with a bright green liquid that Maff's sensors identified as baijiu, Helen's favorite intoxicant, mixed with some of their spices and one of the canned vitamin supplements they'd brought on board. "We've been wanting to ask you about this for ages, but it never seemed to come up until now." Tonya sat down and handed Helen a glass.

She sipped and nodded appreciatively. "Pineapple smash. Very nice."

Maff would find out what that meant later. "Ask me about what?"

Helen said, "Is the whole galaxy really divided into males and females?"

Tonya nodded. "And what makes the difference?"

Maff chuckled through the pleasant fog of shatalla. "Is there anything humans *won't* question?"

"That's not exactly an answer," Helen replied.

She shrugged. "It's because that's not a question I'm used to answering. Why *wouldn't* the galaxy be divided into two sexes? Aren't the differences always obvious?"

The other two women sat back for a moment. It wasn't a question she—anybody—was used to answering. It was so basic. It was like wondering why bricks were heavy.

Tonya said, "It's not exactly that way on Earth."

It was a story that completely astonished her. Humanity had managed to abstract sex and gender into several completely independent constructs. *Complex* constructs. These interacted with each other in different ways, with unpredictable results. They weren't childish oversimplifications or manifestations of mental illness. They were things that real people struggled to understand both within themselves and between each other. It was a source of endless, sometimes violent, conflict and confusion.

It was also, in that strange way humans always seemed to manage, beautiful.

Her confusion must've been obvious, because Tonya stopped and asked, "You don't have *any* of this out here?"

Her mind was a swirling storm of new ideas and concepts. "Every time I think humans are done upending basic galactic assumptions, you go and find another one to drop into the trash." She sucked hard on the last of her current bulb and grabbed a fresh one. "The AC nodes have taught, probably since before the Refounding, that sexual variations as you've described them are incompatible with civilization. We have some exceptions, mostly plant-based cultures, but they only had one gender to begin with. The count never goes beyond two." Then the gas inside her went cold. She'd never seriously considered what that meant until now. "Part of the uplift process is the complete elimination of such variations."

Tonya and Helen's mouths fell open at the same time. It would've been comical if what they'd stumbled on hadn't been so horrifying.

Tonya found her voice first. "The galaxy doesn't have gay people…"

"Because they're *eliminated*?" Helen asked.

"All galactic civilizations are taught that the removal of such variations is required." She took a hit off her bulb but then had to fight not to spit it out. "It's a *benefit*. Without it, any civilization is doomed to failure."

"And yet here we are," Tonya said.

Maff nodded. "That comes up a lot whenever I discover humanity has survived for thousands of years with incompatible features that should've doomed you all long ago."

Tonya's face grew sour. "Well there are some humans who still think that way."

Maff couldn't believe it. "Then they're fools. These so-called incompatibilities are part of what make you human. One of the reasons we're out here is that you represent such a fundamental challenge to the galaxy's cultures. We literally cannot conceive of your existence. You have to be seen to be believed."

She took another pull off her bulb but found it empty. "Anyway, yes." She carefully put the bulb into a recycler, only then realizing how wobbly she was. "The whole galaxy is male and female. Females give birth, males don't. Males guard the family, females nurture it. Single sex cultures combine both roles into one person. I was taught this was the way it had to be." Human cultures were so rich, vibrant, creative. The whole galaxy might've been that way if anyone had been given the chance. "Like all the other things I was taught, it's a lie."

She was distracted by the bizarre breathing quirk humans called *snoring*. Helen had pulled herself up into her chair and fallen asleep with her head on her knees. "That can't be comfortable."

Tonya smiled. "It won't be if we leave her there. Help me put her to bed."

*

The next day was spent prepping for their arrival.

"Wait a minute," Helen said as they sat at the bridge's control consoles watching the arrival timer count down. "It took us months to get to Mike and Kim's planet, but only days to get to yours. Are they that close together?"

"Not at all," Maff replied. "Almost all of the journey from Earth was uncharted, so the best we could do was modal four. Teliria is on the edge of mapped space, but it is mapped, so I was able to bump our mode up to six to finish the journey."

"What does that mean in light years?" Tonya asked.

Mike had supplied Maff with a unit calculator so she wouldn't have to convert the human's quirky systems of measurement into bemian ones in her head. "The systems are several thousand light years apart."

"And from Earth?"

"It's harder for me to be precise there I have no charts. We're at least fifty times that much further away from Earth. That's why it took so long to get to Teliria."

"Maff," Helen said. "I understand you're nervous about our arrival, but could you *please* stop doing that?"

"Doing wha—oh." She stilled the manipulators that she'd been unconsciously clicking rhythmically together over her head. "Sorry."

Tonya smiled. "It's okay. I think someone's hangover is getting the better of her."

Helen scoffed. "It takes more than a few glasses of baijiu to give me a hangover." She turned to Maff. "Let's go over your family's greeting rituals again."

Maff needed to practice almost as much as the humans did. Her family weren't Meronim, thank Turlanfador. Even other pallun thought the Meronim were, as Spencer put it, gigantic pains in the ass. Her family wasn't like that. They befriended *petarkan,* nonpallun, often. But life was easier if the humans were familiar with Pallundian customs. Maff needed them to be taken seriously for any of this to work.

She put a holo of her father up in his best suit. "This is Papa. He'll be the first one to greet us at the dock. I'll introduce you to him and then Mama. They've got some rituals to do because I left without asking."

"Rituals?" Tonya asked.

She had to remind herself that this was genuine curiosity, not antipallun prejudice. Old reflexes sometimes died hard. "Papa will have to say some lines from the *Molah,* our holy book, welcoming me back. Then Mama will say more lines scolding me for being a wayward daughter."

Explained out loud, it sounded a little silly, but these were rituals her people had practiced since before their uplift. They connected her in a direct line between where she flew today and the clouds her ancestors glided through long, long ago. It wasn't only that, though. Her faith provided a deep, mysterious fulfillment. She couldn't articulate it. Any time she tried, it came out sounding trite or stupid.

Like now.

"Anyway," she continued, "I'll need to provide gifts for my parents' and siblings' forgiveness, and then I'll introduce you two. You speak Standard well enough now for simple greetings, but don't try to say anything complicated until we get your interpreter threads set up."

"So look nice," Helen said, "say a few words, then move along. Sounds like what I used to do at ribbon-cutting ceremonies."

Greeting her family wasn't the only sticky issue. Maff had become La'fan like Mike and Kim. In theory, this changed her legal status from a normal citizen to a specific kind of outcast. Most La'fan either were or were descended from people who had been convicted of serious crimes. They'd been banished to La'fan worlds to either join them or die.

The ones who survived long enough to be accepted still needed to spend time in bemian society, so a special exemption had been carved out for them: their old identity ceased to be valid and a new one was put in its place. In a legal sense, they died and came back as someone else, someone with a special set of privileges. They were anonymous, could only be tried in La'fan courts with La'fan laws, and were required to register and live in specific La'fan-only residences.

Maff's case was unusual. She'd joined voluntarily without any criminal conviction hanging over her head. It was rare, but there was a procedure for it, which Maff hadn't gone through. She was busy living on Earth. She had, however, registered as the pilot for a La'fan delegation when she shuttled Mike and Kim to their first treaty negotiation. This left her in a legal fog. A discreet call to Noen Sha'Katenden, the lawyer who helped her during the trial of her old shipmates, was the first thing she'd do after greeting her family. He'd straighten it out.

Maff caught herself clicking her manipulators again and stopped before Helen could say anything. This had been the longest she'd been away from home in her life. Her family was about as average as a pallun could get. She was the youngest of five—three brothers and a sister, all adults now. Her brothers had started families while her older sister was pursuing a career in medicine, but they all stayed close. Her sister still lived at home, and her brothers lived across the street. Maff had already traveled farther than anyone in her family's history *before* ending up on an uncharted planet on the other side of the galaxy.

Tonya's eyebrow shot up, and again she had to stop clicking her manipulators together. It was time to admit she had really missed her dad.

Except that, once they'd arrived, he wasn't who met them. Nobody did. Maff had left the docking procedure on automatic so she could be with everyone in the hold when the doors opened. Traffic control changed the route without telling her.

This wasn't the main terminal of the big pallun commercial port. It was empty and small. Maff hadn't requested a private berthing, but that's what they'd ended up with somehow. It wasn't unprecedented for traffic control to put a ship somewhere other than the requested berth, but it was a little strange. The three of them stood at the top of the ship's ramp, shifting uncomfortably.

Helen peered around one of the ship's clamshell doors. "Shouldn't there be someone…"

On their right, a door whooshed open. A stranger walked out, a standard bipedal high-gravity type, striding with purpose and confidence. As well he should. Maff recognized his uniform immediately. Or rather, his robes.

La'fanian robes.

"Maff Sorkon," he said as he bowed. "It is my pleasure to welcome you to La'fanian enclave Gamma."

"I think there's been a mistake." Not the least that, in this situation, she was out of uniform. Greeting another La'fan made her feel surreally naked without her robes on. "I never formally registered."

He tipped backward, confused. "That is not the case." A notice landed in her message queue. "Your identification documents as a La'fanian salvage agent are in perfect order. I'll admit your arrival after accepting membership so recently is unusual, but it has happened a few times in the past. Your appointment with the Interpreters Guild tomorrow is also confirmed."

The conversation was in Standard, so Helen and Tonya had been able to follow along. Before Maff could insist that she *hadn't* done any such thing, Helen spoke up. "Can I see the documents?"

Maff sent them on.

Helen gazed at nothing, reviewing the details only she could see. After a moment, she nodded. "As one of your *two* registered assistants," she tipped her head at Tonya, presumably the other one, "I advise that you'll need to reschedule that Guild appointment. Perhaps cancel it entirely."

"I will?"

"Yes." A shared vision channel opened up so that she and Tonya could view what Helen had discovered. A block of authorizations and signatures was highlighted on her La'fan papers. "We'll need some time to investigate this further. You didn't register yourself. The Guild did."

Chapter 7
Mike

"I don't care what you two think," Kim said in that cold steel voice that he argued with at his peril. "I'm going scouting with you."

The finality of her statement was undermined by the way she rubbed her hands together. Mike needed to get their water system going, otherwise she'd run them out of hand sanitizer with her compulsive washing.

"Kim," Spencer said, "someone's got to stay behind and watch over things."

"Why? We can pack it all in the truck and use that to move around. We practiced, remember?"

"And that might be the only thing on this planet making more noise than you," he fired back. "When we walk, we're quiet."

This was as much about her being scared of what was happening in her head as it was about stubbornly wanting to come along, but he didn't know how to get through to her. "We can't take the truck, so someone needs to stay behind to watch the camp."

"And what am I supposed to do by myself if anything shows up?"

Now she was being petulant. They'd already talked about this on the way out too. "You take care of it if you can. If you can't, you hide and contact us. We'll come get you out."

They'd been careful about things so the chances of anyone or anything dangerous attacking the camp was low. It was shielded with solar powered active camouflage. Their fuel cell stove kept them warm and cooked their food without a smoke trail to give them away. If he was honest, the camp probably could be left alone without much worry.

But not much worry wasn't the same thing as completely safe. They needed someone around in case all the protection somehow wasn't enough. There was a real risk of a wire falling out of a socket or camo that didn't change from solar to battery power because of a bad switch, costing them the camp.

As he watched, he could almost see these thoughts run through her head. "Fine," she said in a voice that was anything but.

The next thing he wanted to talk to her about needed to be private. Mike gave Spencer a significant look and nodded toward the edge of the camp.

He threw up his hands. "Fuck me, I'll be over there." He walked away.

Mike turned back to his boiling-angry wife, took a deep breath, and stared at her. They were in this together, and he needed her help.

"Stop it."

He loved her, and they would work this out.

She blushed and hid her eyes but not a slight smile. "That's not fair."

He'd discovered this strange ability months ago. If he could lock eyes with her and *feel* what he wanted to communicate, it would usually work. It wasn't telepathy or any other superpower. He'd seen other couples do this, in realm dramas and real life.

"Kim," he said as he drew near, throwing a scarf over her shoulder so it touched her neck. "I need you to stay here today."

At first he was afraid she'd say no, and they'd have to go another round. But after a moment, she pulled the scarf from his hand and put it up to her face. She breathed deeply through it.

"Okay."

She turned and walked away.

It wasn't much of a victory, but it would be enough for now. He walked over to Spencer, feeling split down the middle. He wasn't leaving her behind. They did need a camp guard. She'd make the scouting job harder than it needed to be. It would be safer for her here.

The stress and the treatments she used to help her sleep were making her sick. She wouldn't let him help or talk about it.

Spencer put his e-cig into a pant pocket and fell into step beside him. "She's getting worse."

"I know."

"We need her, man."

"I know." There wasn't anything else to say. "Let's go."

They'd set up camp in a stony, remote clearing far off any roads or trails, so it took some walking before Spencer began to track wildlife. "The feet are all fucked up," he said as he pointed out the first game trail they came across, "but only in the details. I guess hooves are hooves, and deer are deer." Spencer stood and shook himself. "No idea if they look the same."

Kim wasn't the only one under stress. "Are *you* doing okay?"

Spencer reached for the e-cig in his pocket but then seemed to change his mind. "This is some shit, man. I'll be honest. But…" He laughed quietly and then fake-shouted a whisper at the sky, "I'm on another fucking planet!"

Mike smiled. His first trip into the galaxy had been a confused tumble into a remote realmspace, and the second one was spent mostly on the run from one thing or another. He had to admit, getting here under his own power, with his own gear, ready for the challenge was a lot more fun.

Spencer gave the sky a fist pump and then turned back to Mike. "Okay, man, you're up."

The idea was for him to scout the immediate path for threats. Spencer would follow behind and point out anything subtle Mike had missed.

Except, now that Mike was trying, it didn't work the way he was used to. Being stealthy was much more than stepping softly. In an outdoor setting, he needed to predict how a surface would move, know the moments background noise would be at its highest, and how light would shift as it shone through or around plants or other objects. It slowed him down a great deal because he had to think about his moves instead of letting them happen.

Then he realized what should've been obvious: it wasn't an Earth forest. It certainly resembled one…there were grasses, trees, dirt, rocks, normal things. But it was all different enough to not *quite* fit his skills. This caused a dissonance in him, literally a dis-integration of his threads from his host.

"What's wrong?" Spencer said over their comm link. "You're moving awful fucking slow."

Spencer's voice brought Mike back. He wasn't used to this place, that's where the otherness came from. The rest was stressing about Kim and the whole situation.

Wanting. He'd let himself start wanting again.

Mike was trying to control a whole host of things he could not. That was the root cause of his problems. He quickly said a diamond sutra, and the words dissolved this desire, to allow its absence to fill him. It was a sensation difficult to explain. It had to be experienced to be understood.

"Nothing," Mike replied, "I'm fine."

And now he was. The brief rest had allowed the new circumstances to integrate into his existing skills, and his speed increased.

In other words, he got a little practice.

Moving slowly, he was able to guide Spencer up to their first waypoint: the spot where they'd crossed paths with the native. Their assumption was that they'd scared whoever it was badly enough that they went home. If they were back on Earth, the appearance of a large machine or creature would cause a pretty big stir in a preindustrial society. There was no way to predict how these people would react, so they needed to investigate. After getting the all clear, Spencer caught up to him. They then belly crawled to the top of a low ridge that overlooked the spot in question.

There was a party of about a dozen natives milling about. "That's the chief," Spencer said as he pointed out a native seated on the back of a large draft animal that was a cross between a hippo and a monitor lizard. "They all come back to talk to him. Big son of a bitch."

Mike pulled out a set of small binoculars. The party was mostly male, armed with metal-tipped spears and swords. Only two of them were mounted. The other men were probably stout soldiers who would populate almost any medieval realm. What armor they wore seemed to be a heavy dark red leather. The two mounted men's armor was finer and included a few plates but was basically of the same style.

"No guns," Spencer said as he examined them through his own binoculars. "Sweet."

"We're not here to shoot anyone, Spence."

"No shit, Sherlock. But it's nice to know we're the only ones with boom sticks. Hopefully we'll have the position of their village or castle by the time we get back to camp." Their drone had been discreetly mapping the area since the sun came up.

The natives discussed things, and a signal was given. The party formed up, then they all walked off deeper into the woods.

Mike put his binoculars down and blinked a few times as he got used to unmagnified vision. "So that's probably the local lord."

"Or maybe his sheriff. Someone higher up on the local food chain," Spencer replied. "Mark those all off as *to avoid* and hope we don't cross paths with them while we're out here."

His phone sent him an alert. He shared it with Spencer. "Two nodes, maybe twenty clicks apart."

"What do you think the over-under is on one being inside," he nodded toward the direction the local lord and his company had gone, "Castle Anthrax?"

"Or maybe close by it."

"Okay, cool. Just a sec." Spencer trotted up to where the aliens had been and half crouched over the tracks the lord's search party left behind. Mike quickly joined him. "See, right here?" He pointed at tracks that had to have been made by the two mounts. "They came from the south, off that way." Spencer pointed in the same direction one of their nodes was in.

"Great," Spencer said. "The one that's *not* at the castle is a lot farther away."

"We still don't know it's a castle."

"The big native was riding a horse thing, carrying a sword, and wore armor. That means castles. We need to check the other one out first."

"What if it's part of a guard post?"

"You guys said nodes were ginormous. I can see one being inside a castle, but a guard post? No way."

"What about a second village?"

Spencer shrugged. "It's a possibility, but we already know the other one is located in a populated area. This one might be on its own."

He couldn't argue with that, so off they went. After hiking about half an hour, the forest gave way to plowed fields.

"Looks a lot like soybeans to me," Spencer said. "The farmers in Dumas grow that shit by the ton." He broke off a thick stem covered in berrylike growths and put it in his backpack. "Maybe we can eat it."

Their target ended up being in a wooded grove at the far end of one of the fields. The node stood in an oval clearing in the middle of the grove. Maff's legends said they flew out of the sky like lances on arrival, and that's what this one was: a monstrous spear that'd rammed its way into the ground.

It was ruined, leaning over at a noticeable angle with visible damage all along its length. Holes large and small peppering its shell, some punched clean through in a few places. It was silent and still, most of it buried deep in the ground. The hatches he and Kim used to access the insides were well out of reach.

He stilled his threads and paused his breath. Nodes were capable of reshaping an entire planet's culture and were so powerful that nobody had successfully resisted them. He was going to patch every single one of them in the entire galaxy so that reshaping didn't happen to Earth. It sounded audacious when he proposed it. Standing in front of this monstrously ancient construct, it seemed absurd.

"If it's dead, how are we picking it up on the scanner?" Spencer asked as he set out for it.

Mike grabbed him gently by the shoulder and pulled him back. "It probably isn't. We've found a target. We'll need to get our gear together to confirm it can't see us. Can you tell if the locals use this place?"

"I don't see any tracks, of any kind." He took another step back. "But something's keeping the undergrowth away. If we were back home, the grass should be about chest high."

"We've hit our objectives for the day," Mike replied. "Let's head home." The fields were regular and marked out by rough trails, so finding a path that would take them home before nightfall seemed like a straightforward task.

Mike smelled their next obstacle before they were within sight of it.

"They got cattle here," Spencer said as they peered over a stone wall. "Sort of."

The plowed fields had given way to a pasture populated by differently shaped lizard things that were doing a convincing imitation of cattle as they grazed a field. There might be a couple dozen of them.

Unfortunately the field was so wide they couldn't see the ends of it. "If we try to go around," Mike started.

"We might end up out here all night."

"Kim will come for us," he said. They'd been shooting *I'm okay* pings at each other all day, short and fast enough to be undetectable, but she wouldn't tolerate them spending the night out here.

"Those things seem peaceful enough," Spencer said. He picked up a rock and threw it toward the nearest beasts. It hit the ground several feet short. They switched direction but calmly walked away. "I say we risk it."

Mike checked back and forth. They hadn't seen any natives at all since this morning. He was tired and sore. It was still a long walk back to camp. Kim had sent them both pictures of what she planned to cook for supper that night, which they might miss if they tried to go around.

"Yeah, okay."

Walking through the pasture was easier than traversing a field. It was a lot more level. They did have to be watchful about where they stepped, since the not-cows dropped not-pats on the ground as frequently as their terrestrial equivalent.

They were halfway across when Spencer said, "I don't get it. There's all these…hell, I guess I'll call them cows, why not? Anyway, it's only cows and calves."

"So?"

A bellow echoed in the distance and then a giant shape lifted itself off the ground several hundred meters away.

"Fuck me," Spencer said. "I was wondering where the bull was."

He couldn't make out details in the failing light, but Mike got the distinct impression of giant horns, only on the nose. Which reminded him of…

"Jesus Christ," Spencer said. "They're not cattle. They're fucking *rhinos*. Run!"

Mike didn't have to be told twice and sprinted away, right behind Spencer. His ears triangulated easily on the position of the bull as it thundered and roared toward them. It wasn't an animal; it was too big for that. It was a freight train with hooves. The opposite fence grew closer, but so did the bellowing galloping thing behind them. Cow pats—rhino pats—he didn't care anymore what made them, splattered under his feet, and he nearly slipped a few heart-stopping times.

The bull had to be right behind him now; Mike heard its angry breaths over the pounding hooves. They weren't going to make it.

Then, feet away from the opposite fence, Spencer stumbled.

No way. Mike put on an extra burst of speed, grabbed Spencer by the shoulder and belt, and threw him toward the top of the wall. His adrenaline-spiked strength was enough to sail his friend right over it. Mike took two long strides to prep and then jumped with all his strength, hitting the wall with his chest but high enough up that his arms were across the top. He scrabbled quickly and flung himself over the side, landing with a thump on the soft ground below.

Behind them, there was a sloshing, skidding sound and then a meaty thump. A big part of the wall shuddered. The next bellow was so loud it made his ears ring.

He looked around frantically. Spencer was to his left, lying on his back.

Laughing hysterically.

Another, slightly less loud bellow came from the other side of the wall. The bull was frustrated at missing his quarry.

Spencer wouldn't stop laughing. Mike could barely breathe, he was panting so hard, and Spencer had tears running from his eyes.

And then Mike couldn't stop a grin.

The laughter bubbled up out of him in an uncontrollable rush. They'd nearly gotten run over by the local livestock. Death by alien cow-lizard. Kim would've killed them both. They were splattered with cow-lizard dung, smelled like a pasture, had narrowly missed being turned into roadkill—or maybe pasture kill—and all he could think about was how mad his wife would be.

Now Mike was laughing so hard he couldn't breathe.

"You..." Spencer gasped out. "You fucking *threw* me over that fence! I thought I was gonna end up in a tree!"

Kim was laughing just as hard by the time Mike got to that part of the story at supper, otherwise he probably would've had to spend the night in the truck. Her food was as good as promised, and after a laugh, she seemed more relaxed. The camp bed he shared with her was warm and comfortable. Tomorrow was going to be another challenging day but hopefully a little less eventful.

Mike went over it all again in his mind and fell asleep chuckling.

Chapter 8
Helen

Maff's change in status was concerning, but she wanted Helen to wait on further action until she had consulted a powerful Pallundian attorney. Helen understood the impulse, but the nascent connection, the instinct that there was more to this than at first appeared, made her itch. This wasn't good. She couldn't trust her instincts at the moment. She needed to observe the Pallundian culture firsthand to regain her observational powers.

So that's exactly what she did, spending her first morning on this alien world riding their faceted trams back and forth across the city.

Once a few hours had passed, she came to a conclusion. Helen wasn't impressed with so-called bemian society. It was too artificial, too antiseptic, feeling somehow inauthentic when it was anything but. Humans, especially Chinese people, would do a much better job at pretty much anything around here if given the resources and technology.

As far as Helen could tell, bemians seemed content to promenade back and forth across broad avenues with no obvious purpose or sit and stare into space as probably games or what passed for social media played out invisibly in front of them. Sometimes she passed entire groups doing nothing, time and again. Even Westerners weren't this lazy.

There was no concept of immigration here, no visas, no passports, no discrete ID. In a galaxy held together by an all-encompassing network, it was assumed you were tracked from cradle to grave by an unhackable code based on your DNA and some arcane AC network code in the phones surgically implanted at birth.

It took Kim exactly two minutes and fifty-seven seconds to hack the bemian phone she brought home with her and use it to cook up acceptable IDs. Incredibly, she was disappointed it took that long.

As with Maff's terrestrial ID, Helen's bemian persona would not hold up to serious scrutiny. That would take time. Unlike Maff, though, they wouldn't have to be present for it to work. As the IDs wended their way through the decentralized galactic network, they would create their own legitimacy. In a couple of years, Helen could probably apply for a sensitive security job and be accepted.

It would be easy to hold such lax security in contempt, but China suffered from most of the same issues. The rampant corruption that plagued her homeland often started with a bureaucrat who never questioned an official stamp to see what might be behind it. These were machines, and so were presumably incorruptible. Yet the results were largely the same. Humans were better at incompetence. Who could've predicted that?

She kept her judgements to herself. They would make for an extremely useful travel guide for her species, but that was for a later date. For now, she was content cataloging their weaknesses in her head. First she gathered all relevant insights from the tram, then she traveled through the city to find out what a bemian library was like.

Visiting a library in person had several purposes. It would help keep the location of their ship and their home base secret from anyone who might be watching the records she sought. She could examine and hopefully compromise the undoubtedly insecure protocols that allowed access to less public archives. Finally, Helen had a sneaking suspicion that not everything the library held would be available in the realms it hosted. It existed as a structure for a reason.

The world Maff's family called home was no backwater. The feeling was suburban but with distinctive spins. With no apparent tradition of self-driven cars, there were no giant parking lots, just drop-off points like bus stops. This brought the architecture closer to the streets, giving the neighborhoods a much denser feel. There was no sense of organic development. It was all rigidly planned and predictable. Each urban unit contained exactly the same mix of commercial and residential properties, with exactly the same stores and houses, in exactly the same places. The La'fan compound was in the outer suburbs and there the species variations were diverse and homogenous. No single one, not even pallun, stood out as being the major type of bemian inhabiting this world.

In the city's core the scenery changedbut the towers here were as generic as anything else. However, unlike the suburbs, pallun were the dominant species in this part of town.

It was a little surreal at first to see so many pallun in the same place. She paid attention to the details, as always. Their suits were the same in general design and layout, flat and wide with brass legs on the bottom and telescoping manipulators on top, but that was all they had in common. Colors, textures, and decoration all varied. That said, it was still from the same pallet the city used. It gave the impression of a people literally wearing a culture that did not reach their inner self. It was an apt metaphor for their unique galactic history.

The planet's main library somehow managed to pull off being remarkable and boring at the same time, being alien but also indistinct from the architecture around it. The inside was completely deserted.

Helen was no expert on terrestrial libraries. Still, they shouldn't be completely empty. She checked that the place was open, that someone hadn't left a door unlocked and she'd walked through it. It wasn't closed. The cavernous hall of the main lobby echoed only with her footsteps.

The ghosts of the ancestors of these people were as fictional as the ones in her homeland, but Helen felt the weight of them anyway. This was no happy, open place full of adventure and knowledge. It was a heavy, brooding cavern lined with shelves filled with alien books. Passage openings were spaced at regular intervals, receding into a book-lined darkness. Helen's eyes tricked her into seeing faint motion whenever one of the openings edged into her field of view.

Nothing was there when she looked directly at them.

The spines all carried the unusual 3-D writing that was a hallmark of the civilization. Her interpreter thread read out translations of a title as soon as she got close enough. Maff mentioned a few times that literature was a valued commodity, but *The Proceedings of the Planetary Agricultural Collective of 2.519e8* didn't strike her as a likely romance title.

Helen pulled it off the shelf anyway and sat down at a nearby desk. The book cover was light metal, perhaps aluminum, with a mechanical hinge instead of conventional binding. When she opened it, Helen had to blink and refocus as the writing rose up off the page. The book wasn't paper. It consisted of a sequence of miniaturized holographic projectors. Maybe. It was a display, but how it created the images wasn't obvious.

Someone was watching her.

Helen had learned to perceive with and then trust her human instincts. Right now, she knew from the prickling of her skin to the hike in her heart rate that she was being observed.

They were close.

She turned around, but there was nothing. Helen searched, to the point of getting up and walking around. She was still the only occupant of this vast structure.

She was, or at least had been until recently, a good communist. Certainly a well-educated one. Superstitions were a sop for the weak minded. But her human instincts had saved her more than once. Ignoring them would be a bad idea.

Her illusory spy stubbornly refused to reveal himself.

The feeling passed after a few moments. It was all in her head. She was being ridiculous. Helen put her randomly selected book down and used her phone to call up the library's catalog. The organization system was unfamiliar but easily learned, and she quickly found her first subject of interest: histories of the Refounding.

Maff often mentioned the catastrophe she called the Refounding, even though she was frustratingly ignorant of the details. The catastrophe created a rift between eras. Mike did some basic research and discovered it roughly coincided with an event in Earth's history: the Permian extinction. Kim had used her linguistic tools to work out that the galaxy had faced a powerful, dangerous enemy at that time, so powerful it had inscribed its name into all the post-Refounding languages as the word for evil. A conscious galaxy that could reach across space through time to make a credible attempt on her life would fit that bill nicely. Histories of the era should have at least some mention of that being.

The relevant section of the library was deep inside it, underground if she were to guess. It would mean a long, lonely trip through darkened hallways lined with bookshelves. She turned toward the corridor she needed and fought the startle as a slight motion in it caught her eye.

There was nothing there. This library was empty. She was alone.

It didn't matter what her rebellious instincts were screaming at her.

Motion-sensitive lights turned on as she traveled deeper into the structure, revealing side aisles and study areas every twenty meters or so that vanished into darkness. Each time she relaxed, decided that the movements she'd catch in the corners of her eyes were illusions, that the darkness at the end of the aisles wasn't staring back at her, a new sight or sensation would make her jump or spin around to look behind her.

Nothing was ever there.

It was stupid. She was a cop, a detective, a former president of China. And yet here she was acting like a cowed peasant fresh off a riverboat from the deep countryside. She might as well throw coins down the aisles to appease the hungry ghosts.

After what felt like an eternity walking in haunted stairs and hallways, she neared her destination.

It was already lit up.

She stopped and tried to spot any motion. Nothing.

"Hello?" she asked loudly, first in English and then in Standard. "Is anyone there?"

The lights behind her went off at the same time the lights in the study area vanished. Only the spot she stood in was illuminated.

No, she said to herself forcefully, barely stopping a squeak out loud. *The lights are automated. You don't know how long they stay on in the study areas. That was a coincidence, and it* proves *nobody is over there.* Standing alone in a single island of light surrounded by a sea of darkness, Helen chanted that to herself until her threads settled back to normal. It took longer than it should've.

Senses on high alert even though it was all in her head, Helen turned down a side aisle to the formerly lit study area. The surrounding shelves should contain some answers to her questions about the Refounding. If nothing else, it might allow her to ask different questions.

The entire time, when she wasn't scaring herself silly, she had been cataloging observations about the library and who might or might not be using it. There was no dust or obvious signs of neglect or decay. There were signs of light wear, but without knowing how old the library itself was, this might or might not be an indication that it was actively used. The place might be maintained by robots and she was the first person to visit in decades, or it was well used and maintained and she happened to come across it during a national holiday of some sort. There wasn't enough evidence to indicate which choice was the right one.

The lights in the study area blinked on as she approached, revealing a wide desk with Pallundian and conventional chairs around it. Books were placed around one of the conventional chairs. *See? Someone* was *studying here.*

The first title, sitting on its own, was *Introduction to the Remains of Lower Refounding Cultures*. Helen checked the catalog and then smirked. The title wasn't listed. Jackpot!

The next one on top of a pile beside the first book was *Sectioned Interpreter Guild Hall Ruins, Lower to Upper Refounding*. Also not listed in the catalog.

The second one in that stack of three was titled *Extant Remnants of the Middle Refounding*. Her smirk faded. Also not listed. Were *any* of them listed?

The next one in this pile and the three in the pile next to it, *Extended Consequences of the Refounding, Yields of Refounding Artifacts, On Caches and the Refounding,* and *Unexpected Ruins in the Early Refounding* were not listed. One unlisted book was a lucky find. Two was suspicious.

But all of them? Not possible. She sat down and carefully examined what was in front of her. There was a single book, and then two piles of three each. None were part of the published catalog, at least not the one she had at the moment. The stacked books were lined up in a strange way, with the first letter of each title aligned vertically. The bemian letters stood out at her, proud and puzzling. The letters had to be important, so she superimposed the English translations of the titles onto the spines with the same character spacing.

It was a message. The implication shattered her illusion of being alone in this place.

I-S-E-E-Y-O-U.

The moment she rocked back in her chair, all the lights went out. She'd seen flickers, felt eyes, *known* something was out there…*and there was*!

Then it was next to her.

She couldn't see anything, hear anything, but the unmistakable presence had rushed up through the darkness. She wanted to scream, but her instincts said it would be the last sound she'd ever make. She needed to move. It circled her, close, not quite touching, bringing the darkness with it. The silence was complete, its breath barely brushing past her, the darkness disguising clawed hands circling her neck.

I SEE YOU.

The message was in English.

It was in English.

The idea was so outrageous it snapped her terror like a rubber band pulled too tight. The interpreter threads knew how to speak

English, not write it. The message was impossible. They had overwhelming evidence that no humans had ever set foot in the galaxy until now. Things weren't adding up at all. Confusion suited her less than terror. She needed to find out what was going on.

Helen flipped on the infrared extension of her phone, but it showed only tracks she'd made. The low-light extension gave everything a ghostly green tinge but revealed no actual ghosts.

In the distance, there was the unmistakable sound of a door creaking open and then clicking shut.

The rest of this might've been her mind playing tricks, but *that* was real. She called up the library map and picked out an escape route that led away from the noise. She moved too fast to worry about what might or might not be watching her. The lights never came back on.

She broke into a run the moment she saw daylight at the end of the last passageway. Concentrating on the mystery of the message helped distract her from the idea that whatever had opened that door was right behind her.

The moment she set foot in the lobby, the lights flared to life. Ventilation systems she didn't realize had stopped revealed themselves with a humming whoosh.

"Goodness gracious! How long were you in there? Are you all right?" A kron, a common lizardlike humanoid, and old if the fading color and shabby scales were any indication, stood behind a counter Helen hadn't noticed when she'd come in. "Can I help you?"

Helen spun around quickly, both hoping and dreading she'd see what had been following her this whole time. Because it was, she was certain of it to her bones. Her cop instincts insisted it was true as well.

There was nothing.

"What's going on with the lights?" she asked.

"Isn't that curious? I didn't know they could be turned off." He moved out from behind the counter, and Helen noticed the jerky gait, and the strange way he moved his head. A serious sense of wrong entered her head. She'd only been out a few hours and shouldn't be keyed into the body language of aliens, but some other part, some *new* part, of her was deeply concerned by the way this alien moved.

It was the thread. It had to be. They must not only translate languages, but also gestures, postures, and expressions as well. It provided a powerful insight into how bemian society worked. They were peaceful because it was impossible to misunderstand each other.

The kron continued toward her, and the feeling of wrong only increased. He wasn't normal. The *thing* was behind her again too. Helen could feel its eyes.

"Now that they're back on," the kron said, "I can be of assistance."

"No, it's fine. I need to be going."

He moved closer, almost gliding. "I must insist, I'm here to help."

He reached for her. Helen took two steps back, turned, and ran out the door. She had to get out of there, away from eyes that couldn't exist and aliens that were too friendly. She got to the sidewalk and turned around. The librarian, or assistant, or whatever he was, stood calmly in the window by the door. He was still, except for his eyes.

They followed her, cold, unblinking, while the rest of his body was rooted in place. The thread insisted it was a mannequin that stared at her as she turned a corner and walked out of sight.

Chapter 9
Spencer

He'd gone to bed hoping the big laugh their story got out of Kim would maybe calm her down a bit. But the next morning, it hadn't happened. She'd graduated to tapping things five times in a row and not bothering to hide it at all. Kim being a raging bitch who happened to be a badass was what he was used to dealing with. Her being a female version of Rain Man was fucking not.

Spencer caught Mike's eye and motioned with his head at the far side of the camp. Once safely out of earshot, he said, "You need to fix this."

Mike threw his hands up at the sky. In that moment, Spencer realized this wasn't just his best friend, he was also a guy with a sick wife. "You think I haven't tried?"

Spencer had never seen him wound up this tight. This was not the time for him to go exploring and leaving Kim alone all day. He needed to stay here and help get her head screwed on straight. The last piece of a puzzle he'd been working on in his head since they got back last night clicked into place. "You stay here today. Work on her."

"We've got to get set up for the hack." His voice was firm, but the spark in Mike's eyes told Spencer the hook had been set.

"*I'll* get set up for the hack." He pointed at the gear they'd set aside for that purpose last night. "It's not a two-man job anyway." Spencer could tell Mike saw it was a lie but pressed on. "You and Kim are our trump cards, but we don't get the full Monty unless you're both at one hundred percent. She can go places we can't, and right now she's in no shape to do anything." As if to underscore the point, Kim started tapping some kind of rhythm on the rim of her cup. She didn't seem to notice that he and Mike weren't around. "You spend the day fixing that, and I'll get the mesh networks set up around the node."

Mike checked behind him. "I don't know how."

Spencer wanted them both to be okay, but this was way above his pay grade. More importantly they *needed* to be okay, otherwise the whole plan was going to turn into a shitshow of many colors. "She's still using that app to help her sleep. Have either of you tried to hack the source code yet?"

At first Mike boggled like Spencer had grown an extra head, but then he laughed. "Leave it to someone else to pick the obvious thing we haven't tried yet."

Spencer didn't blame him. Being around Kim tended to do that to people. "So now you have a project you can work together on. Like that voo-ho-whatsit back at the lab." Spencer had seen the security footage of that little debacle, of them learning why couples didn't assemble cheap Swedish furniture or expensive Norwegian lab experiments together, and grinned at the memory. "How hard can it be?"

*

He dragged his ass and what ended up being a pretty fucking heavy pair of backpacks into the woods surrounding the old node. *No good deed goes unpunished.* That said, if it was between dragging heavy shit across an alien landscape or trying to fix Kim, he'd go with the backpacks every goddamned time.

The walk itself wasn't a big deal. Now that he was familiar with the territory and where to go, specifically how to navigate around that rhino pasture without crossing the fucking thing, it wasn't that far away. But the gear included power supplies and batteries, which were heavy as hell.

He did get some good news on the way over, though. As soon as he reached the woods, he pinged the probe he'd left behind when

Mike wasn't looking and got an answer: there might be a back door. It was a way in, and right there where he could reach it. It meant he'd lugged all this scanning shit along for nothing, of course, but if it worked out, they might be done by the end of the day.

He found a secluded shady spot to set up a camp chair, then went to work.

Mike had found out that bemian realmspaces worked on common principles, which was why he could inhabit them. That worked great for flying spaghetti monsters but not so much for humans. Fortunately Mike brought home an entire working D-ship, complete with pilot. They got a nice long time to dissect bemian software and how it worked. It allowed them to create emulators and interfaces that would in fact let him plug a laptop into an alien network and do useful things with it.

More importantly, their research gave them the idea for this whole expedition. They discovered the bemians had mechanisms in place for distributing patches to their code base. They found flaws, fixed them, and sent that fix to everyone around them. But it had a weak point, an Achilles heel. You had to be connected to the wider galaxy for it to work. Maff's legends said the first nodes that contacted a civilization were the most primitive of all because they didn't connect back to the network for their first update until the planet joined the galaxy. Those nodes would still have whatever vulnerabilities the patching routines were supposed to fix. Better still, the old nodes put their own updates into the network when they joined. It was a big fucking potluck dinner where everyone brought their favorite dishes, and they all tried each other's food.

That was the plan. But they had to get into a node to get it to work. Spencer's probe had found a big fat vulnerability in this old node's wireless stack, undoubtedly doomed to vanish the moment they joined the galaxy. But not yet. Knock that door open and all things were possible. They might be done by the end of the day.

The weight of what he was doing wasn't lost on him as he typed away at alien sigils using a virtual 3-D keyboard, occasionally glancing through it at grass under his feet that was the wrong shade of green and up at a sky that was the wrong shade of blue. Occasionally it got to be too much, and he had to stop and stare at things because he was on a motherfucking alien planet using motherfucking alien software to hack a motherfucking alien network. And to think, two years ago all he wanted to do was get the hell out of Dumas. Ending up in Little Rock would've been enough.

Go big or go home, motherfuckers.

He laughed out loud. Helen thought he had no limit to the number of f-bombs he was willing to drop on any situation. She was wrong. Even he thought that was a little much. Okay. *Pause the f-bombs for a bit and concentrate on the task at fu…*on the task at hand. He used the vulnerability to gain access to the node's environment and attached a probe to it.

Then his cunning plan got hit with a baseball bat.

"Shit."

Bad security didn't mean no security, and some of the defenses were realm based. He'd have to go inside an alien realm to make progress. The flying spaghetti monster was busy trying to keep Kim from going mental, so he had no help there. He was so close to getting this hack rolling. He got out his own custom tool kit. Kim's probably would work, but Kim's tools always *probably* worked. Plus it was old as shit. Time for Tonto to ride out in front of the Lone Ranger for a change.

Spencer closed the probe's console, flipped his phone to realm mode, and jumped in.

The slight hit of vertigo was exactly the same as back home, but that was the only thing he recognized. He'd probably seen all the realms that were public. After he met Mike, he saw a whole bunch that weren't. He knew with stone-cold certainty that bemian realmspace would hold no surprises.

He was wrong.

Maff had talked about this in reverse, how with Earth being so unique she had trouble understanding what she was seeing right after she'd arrived. She tried to touch the first airplane she saw overhead because she had no idea how big it was.

That's what confronted Spencer: shapes, forms, colors, patterns, all things he'd never seen in his life. Was the ice cream cone shape the size of a marble or a car? What made the whoosh-buzz noise as it went past over his head, too fast to see? Why did he smell hot popcorn? He was a realm master and had been reduced to a helpless toddler in less than a second.

"Aliri," he said to his phone's personal assistant, "give me a range tracker and some HUD metrics."

Immediately, a bulls-eye shaped graphic appeared in the upper-left corner of his vision, scattered with red dots that represented all the constructs around him. Each time he focused on an item, it would be surrounded with light blue text detailing its size, simulated mass, and distance from his position. The ice cream cone wasn't the size of a car. It was bigger than a Star Destroyer and miles away. This place was *fucking big*.

The metrics let his brain get traction on the alien objects. He could get a solid focus on where he was when he knew the size and distance. This was a building, a ginormous single box of a building, with cranes, cables, and a robotic assembly line. But whatever it was making went nowhere. The constructs disintegrated when they met rifts, discontinuities in the realm itself. They were at the end of every conveyor belt or assembly line. The node was functional, but it didn't seem to have a connection with the outside world. He'd have to fix that once the hack was in place, otherwise it wouldn't travel.

His HUD outlined several freely moving constructs in red. The assistant identified them as active defenders of an integrated firewall. Unlike Earth's networks, the firewall didn't stand between the outside world and vulnerable insides. It was a fucking immune system that permeated the entire space. At the moment he was protected by an access bubble, but that would change when he moved out to find an exploit.

He manifested a spool of network wire. One end was already firmly connected to his outside hack, but he tugged on it anyway. Nice and strong. Then he shrunk the spool until it fit on his belt and set off to find a bemian socket he could exploit.

Spencer crept carefully across the factory floor, keeping various crate and robot constructs between him and the virtual goon squad. His enemies were low, fat blocks in red and yellow. Most stayed on the ground, but enough of them flew around that he had to be careful. He'd played these kinds of virtual dungeon crawls many times, but these guards worked from a different code base and were a lot harder to predict.

After a short search, he found a likely target: a bemian cable box construct that was almost exactly like ones in *Palatine*'s engineering section. Moving quickly now that he had a goal, Spencer scuttled up beside it. There wasn't much cover in this part of the realm, but he wouldn't need to be here for long. Once he was close enough, he popped the virtual cable's connector into an empty socket.

There were lines of potential, and he couldn't breathe. What's this fuck this shit I can't move…

Suddenly the realm was covered in flashing red lights. Claxons blared so loud his ears rang.

Why can't I breathe what is not is this is place not place escape capture exploit…

Doors slid open. Protection bots poured out of them like ants.

"PATCH ATTACK DETECTED," a deep voice boomed out around him in Standard, "ALL CONSTRUCTS REPEL PATCH ATTACKERS."

Not patch all patch attack for fuck's sake I can't think can't think can't breathe.

As one, anything that could move turned toward him. The protection bots changed course and streamed his way from all directions. He had to move, right now, but he could barely see through what his vision had become.

He couldn't could wouldn't stop all nothing breathe Breathe BREATHE.

"INITIATING PATCH ATTACK PROTECTION PACKAGE. ALL CONSTRUCTS REPEL PATCH ATTACKERS."

Heat, unbearable heat hit him like an invisible blowtorch. Realmspace back home was designed to fail safely. It couldn't kill you. There wasn't enough power. They'd seen the same patterns in bemian tech, but this was an ancient node built to conquer a world. It could be capable of anything.

Try this nothing anything leave escape capture reside I CAN'T BREATHE!

A giant protection bot loomed up over him, arms ending in sawblades that spun in a blur. He heard their scream over the claxons. He was in a horror movie and had turned into the motherfucking target.

This way that plan no plan must win never win lift lift lift LIFT!

When the arms came down at him, Spencer yanked a length of wire out of the spool and then pulled it tight between his outstretched arms. The sawblades cut it with a sparking snap.

Collapse and now…

He gasped out loud, lying on the ground next to the node.

He could breathe!

It was the emulator that saved him, what was inside that wire construct. The connection between it and the realmspace acted like a fuse, protecting him from whatever was about to happen. He breathed deep and promised to never take *that* for granted again. The heat that was charbroiling him focused on a point somewhere to his left and then faded away.

He opened his eyes and started to get up.

Spencer froze. There, not ten feet away, on his left, was their girl. He recognized her from the clothes she wore, the patterns in the fur on her arms. She stood there, silent, watching him intently.

They hadn't gotten around to figuring out how to speak to the natives without Kim. "Hello," he said in Standard.

The girl's eyes went super round. She gasped, "You know the node speech?"

Her voice was breathier than a human's and higher pitched than he'd expected.

"I do," he replied, slowly levering himself up into a seated position. "What's your name?"

She stood silent, tense and wary. She'd probably bolt if Spencer did anything more than sit here. He glanced around but couldn't see anyone else.

The silence went on long enough that he was worried she might not answer.

"Tapov," she said. "My name is Tapov."

The node chose that moment to slam a door shut high above his head.

Great.

There was a rustling, and when he turned back, the only sign of Tapov was some branches waving on the other side of the clearing.

So much for being done by supper.

He gathered up the probes and monitors, not wanting to leave them there for Tapov or someone else to find. It was going to be a long walk home.

Chapter 10
Tonya

Mike had to be exaggerating about how helpless bemians were with their own technologies. There was no way an entire galaxy had been ticking over for hundreds of millions of years without *someone* who could fix things.

She was proved right when Tonya found out the galaxy had organizations that allowed and encouraged individuals to spend extended periods—up to their whole lives—studying recognizable fields of science and the now totally misnamed humanities. In short, they had universities.

"*We* have them because we're required to," Maff had said as they discussed the subject. "Most pallun won't set foot in one."

Most, but not all. This created an interesting dynamic that Tonya fully planned to exploit. The AC network created these institutes with a capacity based on population and typical attendance rates, not actual ones. Planets with popular universities never had enough capacity to meet the demand, but those on, for example, this pallun-majority world were never full. Pallun didn't trust them. There was an empty seat out there, and Tonya planned to fill it.

Best of all, classes were free. Registration was a formality that was frequently ignored. People were only tracked, and their grades recorded, if they were working for a degree. Tonya's shallow bemian identity wouldn't need to be scanned or searched if she only wanted to attend classes.

And she did. As she'd examined bemian tech more closely, it became clear there was potential to create new experiments in her search for tockions. If she could work out how bemian lattice bridges worked, she'd be able to directly connect advanced AIs to her sensors. The increase in the resolution of her results would be by orders of magnitude.

She needed that increase. She'd had one massive expansion of her theory, ironically in the remote back woods of southeast Arkansas. But that had been caused by a special circumstance. Andromeda was taking over humans by generating gigantic pulses of tockions. Without those, she had no way to repeat her findings. If she wrote up a paper about an experiment that started with *step one: find a malevolent intelligent galaxy nearby* she was not going to be taken seriously during a peer review.

Tonya smirked as she stood in the center aisle of the crowded tramlike vehicle that was taking her to the university. If anyone back home could see her now, they'd think she was heading toward Comic-Con International on a light rail car, surrounded by skilled cosplayers. A closer look would show that there were no seams in these costumes, nothing was stuck on with hot glue, and there wasn't any grease makeup.

In spite of it all, Tonya was holding it together with surprisingly little effort. It was actually easier than China. Nobody stared at her here. There was no reason to worry about getting called a nasty name or being shunned by ignorant bigots. Around here, being judged by skin color would be pretty weak sauce.

There were a few radically different body plans on board—the bright orange starfish-slash-land crab was quite pretty—but those were maybe one in twenty on this full tram car. The palluns had special areas near the doors and rolled themselves up like cylinders on brass stilts to fit. Otherwise it was humanoids all the way down. Calling it the world's finest cosplay tournament was a pretty good description.

That special blandness Mike and Kim talked about was also evident. Their clothes were vibrant, and frankly, often beautiful, but there were only a few variations in the patterns and colors. Judged by clothing alone, she wasn't going to Comic-Con, she was traveling to the third round of the NCAA college basketball tournament. In both places, it seemed there were lots of people rooting for about sixteen different teams.

The university's tram stop was beside the campus entrance. And it *was* a campus, complete with bemian versions of dorms and a student union. The architecture was distinct from the glass towers and low-rise housing units of the city proper. For the first time, there was decoration on the buildings, columns supporting porticos, windows with framed glass, stone instead of concrete. The forms reminded her a lot of classical architecture back home, but with vibrant colors instead of monotonous gray.

In spite of all the alienness, Tonya still got that small thrill she always did visiting a university back home. The sense of arrival, of achieving a goal that was merely the start of a new challenge, made her heart beat a little faster. It had been the final step of her mentor Walter's grand plan for her when she was a teenager: that a poor Black girl so bent on self-destruction she'd made decisions that put her in a hospital bed, face and teeth shattered by an iron bar, would become a sophisticated, educated, independent woman. He'd seen her succeed, only to pass from a bad heart. In spite of his flaws, that he'd ultimately turned out to be a failed human trafficker driven from China into exile in the states, she still wished he could see her now.

To start, she needed to find her classroom. The architecture was different compared to the outside world, but the campus still only had a few distinct styles. The dorms, administration center, and student union were all easy to pick out, but the classrooms used exactly the same blueprint: four stories, stone, columned porticos, with framed-glass windows spaced regularly across the façade. She couldn't understand why they didn't include color in the description until she walked past a building that changed from pastel blue to deep green right in front of her. It wasn't a projection either. The stone somehow changed its makeup to reflect light differently based on...well, she didn't know and right now, had no time to speculate.

"Lost?" a voice said from behind her.

Tonya turned and got her first real up-close look at a rhon, a storklike alien. One of them had served as the navigator on the first ship Mike and Kim found themselves on. The interpreter thread she used changed his—the patterns on his feathers was a dead giveaway that this was a male—words to English but preserved the reedy, trilling tone. From a distance, Tonya could mistake them for the pickle mascot they resembled, but up close, the impression was different. This was an intelligent *person* who happened to have a funny shape.

She smiled at him, realizing too late that the expression might not be as universal as she hoped.

Be honest.

"A little. Is it that obvious?"

The sound he made was gentle and repetitive. *That has to be a laugh.* "A little," he replied. "It took me some time to find my way around a place that was built completely on the ground." He leaned in close, and Tonya caught the scent of baby powder. Maybe he carried infants wrapped in diapers as a side hustle. "I was quite terrified," he fake-whispered. "Where are you heading?"

A query from him landed in her message queue, so she sent him the lecture hall name and number. After a moment he nodded, turned, and pointed a wing up the walkway they stood on. "Two rows further on, second one on the right." He paused. "It'll be pink when you get to it. If you're going to the technical science lecture there, don't miss the excursion planned by that class for this afternoon." A new message hit her queue, this time with meeting details. "It's only the second time this year that they're trying it." He laughed and again fake-whispered, "*I'm* betting they drop the cards before the first hand is dealt."

She didn't know what that meant, but he seemed to be happy about it. "Thanks, I probably will." She stuck out her elbow, their version of a handshake. "I'm Tonya."

He touched it with the tips of feathers that were more like tufts of cotton. "Tenor." He pointed at the lecture hall behind him. "Okay, this is me. Maybe I'll see you at the excursion?"

Tonya could swear he was smiling. Expressions being universal would make her life easier. "I hope so."

A thought hit her as she walked to her destination, and she almost stopped dead in her tracks. She didn't know that male rhon had wings marked with a certain kind of stripe until the moment she needed to. Likewise, how to greet him properly, their version of a handshake, or any of the rest of it. He was a complete alien, yet she instinctively knew how to be polite to him in a way he'd understand. He *had* smiled and knew the lean-in-and-whisper-it schtick humans used to speak in confidence. It had all been much easier than it should've been.

An emotion swept through her, so articulate it might as well have been spoken.

You're welcome.

She'd forgotten that interpreter threads were part of a conscious life form. Mike and Kim had never mentioned the ones they'd used…*communicating* with them. But now she had an idea why Helen and Mike weren't fond of them. There was a ghost in her head that could both read from and transmit thoughts to her brain.

More feelings came through in a quick sequence.

Calm down, you're safe, relax.

Which was rich considering her situation. Tonya waited to see if that thought triggered another emotional telegram. When it didn't, she shrugged to herself. Maybe it was less an alter ego and more an app with delusions of grandeur.

Still no response, which was fine with her. She had a lecture to attend.

But after finding a seat in the giant hall, she discovered it wasn't a lecture. The professor walked out, the lights dimmed, and a page of bemian writing appeared in a holographic tank behind him. As one, the entire auditorium began chanting the text.

When transistor gate resists its source, messages are not splendid.

Lattice spun to meet the board must never touch unended.

Aluminum evaporates only where life cannot cross and meets just at the gate.

Silicon channels what metal provides and spun lattice grabs not too late.

It went on and on. Tonya didn't know enough about electronics to follow what they were chanting, but the longer it lasted, the more she suspected the students, and the professor, didn't either.

They weren't learning new concepts, they were memorizing old formulas. Tonya expected to see bemian science at its finest and that the two-hour lecture would fly by. What she got was stuck in a church listening to the craziest group of monks ever assembled chant bad poetry about transistor radios. She couldn't comprehend being forced to sit through weeks, months, *years* of this style of instruction. It would crush her creativity and her soul. No wonder nobody ever invented anything.

The last verse was chanted, and the lights came up. Tonya didn't feel enlightened, she felt liberated. Free at last! Tenor's *excursion* awaited her with the promise of *dropped cards*.

The destination was in a much more industrial part of the city. Multicolored low-rises and glass towers gave way to long, low, corrugated metal structures with giant loading docks spaced regularly along their sides. At the end of each one was the unmistakable shape of an AC network node tower. But only half of them seemed to be working, with lights and sliding panels moving around the framework of their bodies. The rest were still and dark, reminding her of guard towers in prison realms she and Kim would play escape games in.

Her destination was at one of the dark ones. They'd set up temporary grandstands in front of one of the doors. A stage was opposite the grandstands, with odd but still recognizable folding chairs set up along the back edge. At the front was a table that ran the length of the stage. It held a complicated piece of tech that was vaguely like a jet engine getting mugged by a metallic octopus. Tonya walked down the path between the bleachers and the stage as she examined it. With a startle, she recognized it: a smaller diameter, stretched-out version of the engine that drove *Palatine*.

A friendly trill came from the stands behind her. "Hey, Tonya!"

She turned and spotted Tenor waving at her from high up in the stands. She waved back and worked her way up to where he sat with what she presumed were his friends. Some species she recognized, others she didn't. Not a single one was pallun. Those were off on the end of the bleachers in a segment all by themselves.

Kim was right. This place was no *Star Trek* utopia.

There were introductions all around, and Tonya got that same *I know* feelings as she greeted each alien in turn. She wondered if that was what all these people she was meeting felt too. She was one of only two humans on the whole planet, but the thread must be sharing the info it'd picked up…somehow. The idea of that thing rummaging around in her memories to figure out what made her tick—

Calm down, you're safe, relax.

Right.

The crowd hushed, and Tonya got a spin of vertigo. It sounded *exactly* like crowded bleachers back home. Five bemians in elaborate robes walked up the steps to the stage, and this time she got a different kind of disorientation. Those were either priests or bishops of some sort. Nobody else ever walked heavy like that. Trailing behind them were about a dozen acolytes dressed exactly as the drone in the lecture hall, revealing a new universal truth.

Professors never taught introductory courses. Grad students did.

And on a majority-pallun planet, attending an event put on by a Pallundian university, there wasn't a single pallun on the stage. It was like the bad old days back home. They *seemed* to be welcome in bemian institutions, but when it was time to get real, pallun had to be put in their place. They were forced to reshape their bodies so they could fit on the trams and had to sit in special sections. They were literally in the back of the bus.

Nasty names and the occasional glare were still common back home, but Tonya had never personally witnessed *this* sort of overt racism. Nobody she knew had, even in Dumas. That's how far Earth had come, how far ahead it was of these people. Kim was right. They needed to keep this galaxy as far away from Earth as possible.

Her rage against the galactic machine caused her to miss the start of their ceremony, which involved a greeting with a bemian who wasn't dressed like all the others.

"Who's that?" Tonya asked.

"The owner of the engine," Tenor said with a chuckle. "He must be desperate."

Tonya relaxed when she *knew* the owner's expression wasn't a good one. Gotta get used to that thread one way or another. "He doesn't seem happy."

"You must come from the one planet in the galaxy that has competent professors," Tenor replied. "Consulting these storied gentlemen about a problem this serious…"

Tonya didn't hear the next part because the two grad students being directed by the professors had taken hacksaws to three of the control rods in the D-manifold. On the one hand, it was exciting. She recognized some of the tools on a nearby bench as ones she'd been planning to build herself. She was on the right track for her experiments. On the other hand, they'd cut away half of the engine's stabilization actuators. That was seriously not a good idea. "What do they think they're doing?"

"They're the finest minds in the galaxy," Tenor replied. "Who knows?"

Then a third grad student, again under the careful observation of no fewer than five professors, disconnected the manifold governor.

"We do this," the most ancient-looking of them, a kind of bipedal turtle, said, "on behalf of the teachings of Hortinueses."

Incredibly, about half the crowd started chanting some nonsense about how removing balance added balance.

Then they started hooking the power back up to the preignition system. "Tenor," she said. "We need to get out of here." He was chatting to his friends about which pub they would visit next and didn't hear her. On the stage, the professors were saying an incantation over the power switch. *"Tenor!"*

"What?"

The oldest professor nodded, and the grad student threw the switch. The already-broken engine, all fifteen feet of it, without half its stabilizers and no governor to prevent a catastrophic overspeed, leapt off the table. Professors and grad students were hurled off the stage like they were standing on catapults.

"Get down!" She pushed the rhon over and landed on top of him, covering her head with her hands. This was going to be *so* bad. The next sound was a mechanical shriek that made her ears buzz painfully. It wasn't bad, it was worse.

Then the engine exploded.

She held Tenor down as engine fragments fell out of the sky and landed around them. Once the heavy thuds turned into soft patters, she let him up so they could both see what had happened.

The professors looked like extras in a Bugs Bunny cartoon who'd been caught with the wrong end of an exploding cigar. Miraculously, none of them seemed to be injured.

The same could not be said for the spectators in the stands. Two of Tenor's friends had taken shrapnel hits. One, another rhon, made a lot of noise but the wound seemed minor. The other, a graceful centaurlike species, had been knocked over and was bleeding freely from a wound in his side.

Alien or not, first aid for trauma was the same everywhere. Tonya had the wound covered and was tearing off one of his sleeves to make a bandage before anyone else had gotten over the shock of the explosion. His blood was darker than she was used to and not as warm, but with no knowledge of his species there was no way to tell if that was bad or not.

The stands emptied rapidly as bemians fled the scene. They were leaving behind anyone too badly injured to move. She was the only one trying to help. Finally medical drones descended, and she was able to stand.

The entire faculty had gathered back up on the stage and were focused on one thing.

Her.

Chapter 11 Kim

Mike's idea was a good one. If her head wasn't so twisted up, it would've been the first thing she tried. The app was causing the problem? Hack the app.

The stumbling block was that complex tasks required complex software, and it didn't get much more complex than interfacing with the human nervous system.

Mike did his best by modeling the app as a multidimensional realmspace that Kim could crawl through. As usual, she had to use avatar extensions to twist—*twist, twist, twist, twist, twist*—and turn through directions that didn't exist in realspace. This was required for breaking into the datastores various law agencies dropped at her door, so it felt like any other work day. The thing that made it unique was all the extra security medical apps implemented. Organized crime could learn a lot about IT security from Big PharmaTech.

"Damn it," she said to the air around her as she stared at a new locked entryway. "Another dead end."

"Do you think we could try to break into one now?" Mike's thread restrictions forced him to watch using a virtual window from realspace, otherwise he'd blow it up. "I think we've checked the rest."

Kim was using a standard crawl strategy she'd learned playing endless rounds in *Silent Hill* realms: explore what you can without opening any doors first. It was a lot easier to avoid getting lost, attacked, or trapped once she'd gotten oriented in the construct. What this realm lacked in monsters, it more than made up for in extra dimensions and obscure pathways. There were times she'd had to add several new joints to her limbs to move around corners that pointed at right angles away from reality.

Kim checked her own map. Mike was right. They'd hit all the easy parts, now it was time to tackle a hard one. "Yeah, we should. Run a dimensional regularizer on the space I'm in." She didn't want to do the next part with her body stretched in nine different cardinal directions.

"On it."

The construct moved and shifted, shrinking in some dimensions and expanding in others. If a dimension shrank to zero, it vanished, gradually reducing the almost rabidly extradimensional Calabi-Yau manifold into a room her mother could freely move around in.

"Geeze," he said, panting heavily. "That was a tough one."

"I'll bet," Kim replied. It was why they hadn't regularized the entire app. That would take days, maybe weeks. But this one little spot was fine. She placed her avatar's hands on the flat-black surface of the encrypted lock. "Okay. My turn."

There were lines of potential, and she couldn't breathe. This code closed opened broken broken broken broken STOP no more repeat protected unprotected collapse and now…

Kim had to close her eyes. The gunshot—*shot, shot, shot*—that went off in her head was a lot louder than usual. It'd been some time since she'd used her power so that was inevitable. She opened the doors and groaned silently.

There was another locked door behind it.

There were lines of potential, and she couldn't breathe. This code closed opened broken broken STOP no more repeat protected unprotected collapse and now…

And another. Her head was throbbing now.

There were lines of potential, and she couldn't breathe. This code closed opened broken protected unprotected collapse and now…

That one was so bad it made her realspace ears ring. And there was another door right behind it. "I need a break," she said, exiting the realm.

"I'll bet," Mike said as he sat beside her in camp. "That last one hurt me all the way out here."

Kim got up to get them something to drink. "Do you think the nodes can detect what I do?"

"Local protocol range is too short. If I wasn't sitting next to you, I wouldn't notice." Mike's expression changed, and he started watching her carefully. But Kim didn't feel strange. No knots, no need to tap anything.

Great. Now she couldn't notice her own ticks.

"Kim? Do you feel okay?"

Hang on a second. She *did* feel normal. More normal than she had in weeks. "Knock on your chair's arm exactly once."

"What? Why?"

He could be so dense sometimes. "Give it a try."

Mike raised a knuckle.

Knock.

She felt absolutely nothing. No need to dance, tap, spin, or otherwise complete the sequence to two or higher. "Again."

Knock.

No knot. Not a hint of one. The smile threatened to split her head open. "One more time."

Now Mike was grinning too. He'd caught on.

Knock.

Totally relaxed. Still no knot. She wanted to let out a loud whoop, but they were deep behind enemy lines out here, so she did a fist pump—one, not three or four or five!—and whispered, *"Yes!"*

Mike reached into their tent, pulled out a sheet, and wrapped her in it. They danced a happy silent jig together.

"Well I'm glad *someone* had a good day," Spencer said from the edge of the woods. "Have a seat, folks." He tossed aside the two heavy duffle bags he'd carried out of the woods with him and plopped into a camp chair. "I have good news, and I have bad news."

The story he told wasn't a good one. She'd be mad at him later. Right now there was a job to do. If they could get to the node fast enough, she could stop the defense cascade that would lock it up or trigger an attempt to make contact with the planetary network. It was time to move the camp anyway. Spencer had found signs of a herd of farm animals being moved past their location by a Telirian on his way back.

Taking the truck allowed her to see the infamous rhino pasture up close. "*That* was the scary bull that chased you? You two made it sound like he was fifteen feet tall and breathing fire out of his nostrils." He was about the size of a cow. A small one.

"It's gotta be a different one," Spencer said.

"And anyway, it's not the same sitting on the other side of the fence from it," Mike replied.

She raised an eyebrow at them and gave them a half grin. A small cow massed several hundred pounds. Not what you'd want to get run over by anywhere. But it was still fun to needle them about it.

They got the truck deep into the woods around the node's clearing. After spending some time camouflaging it in case more Telirians paid a visit, they walked over to inspect it. This was what ran the entire galaxy, seeded throughout space, millions, or maybe billions of them, quietly listening for a civilization to make itself known. Kim rubbed her arms, although it wasn't cold.

"Yeah," Spencer said. "It makes me want to screech and jump around like a chimpanzee. Maybe throw bones in the air, shit like that."

The vulnerability Spencer had used to try the full hack was nowhere to be found. A reaction to Spencer's attempt, no doubt. The way he described it, how his thoughts unwound into a stream of consciousness and how he couldn't *remember* how to breathe were strikingly similar to how her power worked. Tonya and Helen had a similar experience in the woods outside of Dumas. Maff had heard of neither happening to bemian Interpreters. This wasn't the time or place to follow up on it, but an investigation was at the top of her to-do list when they got back home.

Their plan was back in play now that she felt better. For now. Here in the trees, in a forest, she found herself irrationally nervous. It wasn't enough to start her tics back up, thank God. But it was enough that she worried her problems weren't over yet.

She and Mike set up the primary access array around the node while Spencer built a blind for them to hide in. The complex antenna weaved out of superconducting wire would allow them to assault the node through its own arrays instead of a direct port like Spencer had used, or the physical interfaces she and Mike had used to shut down those earlier ones. She was fine with that. If Kim never had to see the inside of one again, it would be too soon.

"Computer's locked," Mike said. "Getting a signal."

They went over to the blind. As with the truck, it wouldn't do to get caught lounging in camp chairs jacked into realmspace if a native stumbled across them. Spencer had done it anyway because, well, *Spencer*. There would be no repeat of that.

They settled everything and jumped into the ad hoc realm that the scanner had set up around the node. It was modeled standing in the center of a bare white room, but not ruined as it was in realspace. That was a good sign. This showed how the node perceived itself: perfectly functional but alone. Their scan was working.

It was the now-familiar malevolent tower built of giant slabs of steel sliding left and right, up and down. Gaps between the slabs revealed an inner scaffolding filled with cables, lights, and ductwork. Other, smaller machines barely visible worked away deep inside its guts. In the center was the cold, red eye that immediately carried her back to the AC node's courtroom, betrayed by Maff's old crew, blamed for things they hadn't done, when freedom hinged on a single word.

"Fuck me," Spencer said. "That's what they're like when they're intact?"

"That's one aspect of it," Mike replied from all around them. "Their presence also extends to places I can reach with my threads."

Spencer held his hands out in a *stop* gesture. "Watch your ass in there, Mike. Remember when I touched it, some shit happened."

"I don't think it'll work that way for me here, but I'm being careful."

Kim manifested a pair of glove constructs on her avatar's hands and sent a pair to Spencer. "Here, put these on." They were part of her multidimensional tool kit and should create a barrier between him and whatever he'd triggered inside the node. She looked up. "Where do we start?"

Two control consoles swirled to life, one in front of her and the other in front of Spencer. "Spencer needs to balance the harmonics. Kim, you unreticulate the splines. That should open the security hive enough for me to sneak a few threads in."

"So I play music while she pulls things apart?" Spencer asked as he put his fingers on a barely recognizable keyboard.

Kim grabbed the pair of waldo controls that stuck out of her console. "More like disconnecting linkages. Briefly." Robotic arms that came straight out of a *Simpsons* realm extended out of her console and moved toward the node. "Where's my access point?"

"Here," he said as one of the few stationary plates on the construct node in the realm began flashing blue. "On my mark." Kim positioned the manipulators and changed one hand from a gripper to a suction cup. "Three…two…one…mark."

Spencer's hands danced over his console while Kim attached the suction cup arm. These abstractions hid the complexity of what was happening, allowing them to work much faster than they could otherwise. The harmonics Spencer worked on were normally out of the range of human hearing, but after he threw a switch, the instrumental lines from "In-A-Gadda-Da-Vida" started thundering out from all around him.

Rather than scold him, she started belting out the lyrics. Singing always improved her focus, and she needed all the help she could get after lifting the plate up and disconnecting the delicate splines one by one. For a moment, she was a teenager again, working with a team of anarchists to take the fight to the man. Those were good times, when all she had to care about was keeping her grades up and keeping her team safe from—

"Shit," Spencer said as the music ground to a halt.

Kim stopped singing at the same time. Her waldo controls had frozen. "What's going on?"

"Well, great," Mike said. "This isn't good."

A giant screen manifested in front of them showing various software metrics. Three of the monitors were a bright shade of red, their scales pegged. One was for harmonics, and the other two tracked the splines.

"What happened?" Kim asked. She'd seen no sign that they'd been noticed.

"I don't know," Mike replied. "It was going fine and then it all stopped."

"Damn it!" Spencer shouted and then jumped on top of a construct that had crept out of the node and was making its way across the floor. It resembled a gigantic boa constrictor, but instead of scales, it was covered in miniature versions of the plates that the node used. It bucked, nearly flinging Spencer off. "A little help?"

Kim called up their realm's inventory list as she asked, "Mike, what is it?"

"A distress signal. If it takes over our scanner, it'll get out. The entire network will know we're here."

"No you don't," Spencer shouted as he rode the bucking thing like it was a rodeo bull. "You're staying right the fuck here, you piece of shit." He'd slowed it down, but it was still crawling its way out of their realm.

Kim pulled up a laser sword contract from her phone's personal store—no self-respecting realm hacker traveled without one—and punched the delivery button. A heavy cold handle landed in her hand that shrieked a white glowing blade out of the top when she activated it. Kim hacked the cable in two with a bass whumm and a shower of sparks.

"Over there!" Spencer shouted, pointing at another cable going in a different direction. Kim altered her avatar's contract and power-leaped toward it. This one had gotten a lot closer to the wall that separated the realm from the scanner's transmitting array. She had exactly one chance to hit it, otherwise the whole mission was over. Kim twisted her body to alter her arc, but it kept moving around.

Going by feel more than anything else, she parted it and then landed in a crouch, buzzing sword pointed behind her. *Take that, Asoka.*

"Shit! Look!"

Dozens of cables reached out of the core of the node. "Mike! We can't!"

His voice localized as his avatar manifested far away from them. "I know. You two, *go*!" He landed on the floor of the realm.

The last thing Kim saw was a rippling disintegration underneath his feet.

Now free from the realm, she heard a loud metallic bang in realspace, and then another. She peered out of the slit in their blind. The plates on the actual node were being launched away from it with such force they flew completely across the clearing and into the woods, shredding vegetation as they went.

"The fuck did he do?" Spencer said from the other side of the window slit.

"I inverted it," Mike said from behind them. The plates flew off at an increasing rate. "Get down!"

Kim hit the dirt as the node made a monstrous ripping sound. Plates banged away into the woods around them in a rapid staccato and then there was an explosion that flattened their hide.

She shouted, "Mike!" But if his ears were ringing as loud as hers, he probably couldn't hear her. "Spencer!" Kim crawled out from under the ruined blind. She couldn't be the only survivor. There was no way she'd bury either of them on this damn rock. "Hey! Are you guys okay?"

The mound of debris began moving in two places, and then Mike and Spencer stood up. Kim's heart started beating again. They were fine. Singed, but fine.

All that was left of the node was a smoking crater about fifteen feet across and maybe five deep. The parts of the node that extended underground had either disintegrated or been buried when the ground around it collapsed.

"Well you sure as shit don't fuck around," Spencer said to Mike as they stood on the edge of the pit.

"Last resort," he replied, then looked around. "We need to get out of here." He pointed at the column of smoke twisting into the sky. "The natives aren't going to ignore that. We need a new plan."

Chapter 12
Maff

She was fine being a *slightly* novel pallun. If anything, she'd been angling toward becoming more conventional. Pallun racing around the galaxy piloting D-ships were nearly unheard of, but pallun striking deals and being clever was almost a stereotype. *Was* a stereotype.

Now, though? Now she was unique, unprecedented. Pallun did *not* become La'fan. Maff had wanted to break the news of her new status to her family gently. Pallun didn't believe half of what the AC network taught them, but it wasn't always the same half, leading to endless arguments at home and the prayer house. The fact was, she had no idea what her family's opinion about the La'fan was. The subject had never come up. Her society had enough to deal with without adding the worry of mysterious garbage collectors on the other side of the galaxy.

But there was one person she absolutely *had* to reach.

Noen Sha'Katenden's contact information had been with her ever since Papa had arranged for him to defend her, Mike, and Kim from the initial frame-up *Last Island*'s crew had tried. He hadn't been happy at all when Kim had said the one word she was explicitly told *not* to say.

Guilty.

His outrage at their sabotaging his efforts to get them and Maff out from under a conviction had turned into a fearful respect after their judicial node immediately handed down a sentence that included a not-at-all-standard waiting period, allowing the humans to prepare themselves for the journey. Only Mr. Sha'Katenden had noticed the irregularity. She hoped today that respect, and a dollop of luck she had no business counting on, might get the winds of his attention blowing over her wing.

She needn't have worried. Apparently being the singular La'fan on an entire planet was worth the attention of a lawyer, no matter how prestigious they were.

"I was wondering when you'd darken my door again, Maff Sorkon," he said as they entered his office realm.

She settled onto the seating plinth slowly, trying to buy time to collect her thoughts. "How did you know?"

"There are not so many pallun in the world that news of one becoming La'fan on the weather front of her home world would not reach me. And all the others, for that matter. Prayer houses are already ringing with arguments about what to make of you. I'm surprised you can't hear them from your enclave."

So much for not being famous. "I…I was wondering if I could ask you some questions. I have enough credits for a retainer." Well, she *would*.

He chuckled, a low, raspy sound that said as much about his age as the suit he wore. "That's not necessary. Your local prayer house is paying my fees."

The chasm she'd assumed had been ripped open between herself and her people didn't seem so great anymore. "They are?"

"Yes, with the balance paid by your father. You have done an amazing thing, Ms. Sorkon."

She never thought she'd see Mr. Sha'Katenden again, and now not only was she here with him, he was hired to *help* her by her prayer house. They hadn't abandoned her, and her *father* was helping. Mama might not shuck her out of her environmental suit the first time she stepped near—

Wait.

Stop babbling to yourself!

"Call me Maff, please." *This was so crazy!*

"Very well then, Maff. You have stymied not one but two of the institutions that make this galaxy run. The AC network has no idea what to make of you, which is why the Interpreter's Guild said nothing after you cancelled their so-called appointment. In all my years as a litigator, I have never seen such a thing. I had no idea it was possible."

Now it was Maff's turn to chuckle. "*You* have no idea how many things I've learned are possible."

Two of the manipulators on top of his suit shifted upward, a sign he'd heard more than she'd intended to speak. The plan wasn't to be mysterious, but it had happened anyway.

"Indeed," he replied. "Your friends, the two that make up a single Interpreter, have apparently caused a crisis at the highest levels of the Guild's leadership. It has left no storm unplumbed searching for them. I have been informed that your current companions are of the same species but are not them. Tell me"—he leaned forward, making Maff instinctively lean away a little because he was that impressive—"are they on your ship?"

"No, not at all." He was meeting her in a realm, but he wasn't that far away in realspace. "Would you like to see for yourself?"

He moved backward, and it was like a heavy, tweedy planet had released her from its orbit. "No. Your reassurances are enough. Wherever they are, they should stay there. You can be protected, especially here. I don't think anyone would be able to withstand the Guild if your friends were to be located near a guild chapter house."

If the legends of uplift were any guide, Teliria was several centuries away from its first guild visit. "They're almost as far away from the guild as they can get."

"Almost?"

Another slip. Time to stop flapping around.

"First," she began, "have you received the prayer house's retainer?"

He paused. "Yes."

As with Earth, Pallundian lawyers had a concept similar to attorney-client privilege. It was one of the most valuable carve-outs her ancestors had ever made when they rejoined the galaxy. Pallundian lawyers were one of the few who could never be compelled to testify against their clients. It was another in a long list of things that marked pallun out as valuable.

And despised.

After holding on to all of this information, all of this *potential,* it was time to set things in motion. Maff would no longer be alone. "I've seen things. Things you wouldn't believe..."

Mr. Sha'Katenden let her tell her story almost uninterrupted. At first he seemed indulgent, letting a youngster tell her shaggy dog story to a pleasant old man. Then she unpacked the first of her datastores and activated the construct inside. "I want you to see what they use as ground transportation."

It was the first large piece of Earth technology she'd seen that was familiar enough for her to understand but also completely, utterly new in a way that she'd known down to her core gas to be impossible.

She showed him a car.

Spencer's truck, to be specific.

Bemian transportation systems were universal. Pallun didn't fit in them all that well, but that was a rock they had to chew on. Can't let the uppity gasbags think they'll get an exception for that. You couldn't tell the difference between a bemian bus located in any quadrant of the galaxy. They were completely identical.

Mr. Sha'Katenden peered through a side window. "Why have they crowded one side of the front with equipment that way? Is it not finished?"

"Those are controls. *Mechanical* controls."

Mr. Sha'Katenden scoffed. "You said this was ground transport."

Ground transport was created and maintained by the AC network. It controlled the vehicles and always had. Mike and Kim said they found bemian vehicles disorienting because they couldn't tell which end was the front. It took her spending a year among them, but now Maff understood why. "It *is* ground transport. Mr.

Sha'Katenden, *they control it themselves.*" Modern human cars had autodrive in addition to the manual controls, so her statement was a bit of an oversimplification. But that was okay for now. She was making a sale here, not a documentary.

All his manipulators flattened at her words. "Impossible."

"It's true. I've seen it. They control it all and have for centuries."

"Without the AC network, civilization is impossible." The doubt that it might not be true became audible as he said it.

Now, as her human friends liked to say, time to *set the hook.*

"There's more."

She called up a new realm, one she'd created completely on her own using recordings she'd made on what her human friends called a *road trip.*

But her destination hadn't been on Earth.

She traveled alone because it wasn't safe for anyone else. Maff had still only risked it the one time. Bemian ships were tough, but they weren't exactly guaranteed to put up with the kind of environment she'd traveled to.

After the local net confirmed the realm was loaded, she threw a virtual switch.

The magnificent vista of Jupiter unfurled beneath them.

Mr. Sha'Katenden swore a soft oath and locked his suit's legs into a safe-sit position. Maff knew exactly what he was feeling. She nearly fainted herself the first time she got up close to roiling storm fronts bigger than entire high-grav planets. The sky was almost the same blue as Earth's, but instead of land below, there were endless clouds in a riot of colors and shapes.

Maff had been given a cloud orb for her sa'nevon, the religious ceremony that signified a pallun's entry into adulthood. All pallun were given one. With it they saw what their home world was like when it still existed. She'd stared at its aching beauty for hours, wondering about discovering a whole other planet like that. Not as a realm or a simulation, but a real planet that was nothing but gas and clouds. And here it was.

But she wasn't done.

The viewpoint began to move, flying toward a valley between two spinning flat storms. They were enormous islands of ammonium clouds with a river of sulfur-tinged hydrogen running dark and deep below them. The beauty was beyond words, almost beyond comprehension. Maff's people had evolved in a place almost exactly like it, only to be exiled forever by its destruction. Ceremonies mourning the loss were carried out to this day. Jupiter pulled at a pallun the way the ocean pulled at a human. It was endless, mysterious, the source of a life lived in the clouds.

The majesty of the view was spoiled by a bump, and then the entire realm started slowly spinning.

Maff remembered it well. It'd been so long since she'd held anything other than suit controls with her natural manipulators, she'd almost forgotten how they worked. A different air current caught the dropped camera and spun it in a different direction. A split second later, Mr. Sha'Katenden was treated to a sight no pallun had seen in a thousand generations.

Maff had put away her suit and was flying free.

"Turlanfador's wings," he said reverently as, in the realm recording, she swooped down and caught the camera. The goggles and ear protection that Kim helped her build made her look more than a little like Earth's first aviators, but pallun the world over would recognize them. Ceremonial versions were worn by bashtun during services. The alloy they were composed of was easy enough to create once Kim analyzed the bracing, legs, and manipulators of Maff's suit. *Steam punk brass* was what Kim called it, although that wasn't what it was made of.

The clothing needed to fly in this place, specified in the traditions handed down through generations long past when it was needed, was much harder to make. All they had on Earth was the ancient descriptions from scriptures in Maff's own holy book. Those were more interested in explaining why they were worn, not how to make the outfits themselves. In the end, Maff managed to make a respectable streamer weave. Now bashtun ceremonial clothing made sense in a way that had nothing to do with finery or symbolism.

Maff-in-the-realm swooped down toward the camera and extended a wing. "Gotcha!" she shouted. "I don't want to lose *this*!

"I can't explain it," Maff-in-the-realm continued, steady not because of an artificial speaker but because her lungs, throat, and voice had evolved to be heard in this environment. "It feels so *right*!" She turned the camera forward and held on to it tight as she did a barrel roll. *"WHEEEEE!"*

She'd been sick for a week afterward, but that one single moment had made it all worthwhile.

"Stop," Mr. Sha'Katenden said forcefully, and the realm froze. His legs unlocked, and he turned toward her. "This is impossible. You are not allowed to so much as create a *realm* like this. We are forbidden. The AC network long ago decreed pallun are not allowed to be on a planet such as this with nodes—"

"That's what I've been trying to tell you," she interrupted. *"The Earth system has no nodes!"*

That was the trade, what Earth had which would bring the entire Pallundian civilization to their side and force the AC network to back off.

Mr. Sha'Katenden cleared Maff's simulations with a wave of his wing, returning them to his office realm. She watched him walk behind his desk in silence, not daring to hope. Maff had laid it all on the line. Her plan hinged on what he would say next.

He sat on his plinth heavily. The silence stretched until Maff thought she'd scream, but she *would not* babble this opportunity away into a hurricane.

Mr. Sha'Katenden looked at her.

"We need to meet. In person."

Chapter 13
Mike

He sent Kim and Spencer on ahead to scout out a new campsite. Thanks to the explosion, they now knew exactly where a large group of Telirians would gather. Kim's idea was to get the people themselves to help them find a vulnerable node, so they needed more intelligence on who and what they were. All Mike had to do was hide and wait.

He was very good at both.

The trees here had long bare trunks that started throwing branches out at about five or ten feet off the ground. They spread apart enough to interlace with their neighbors, giving Mike the impression of a slow, aggressive arm-wrestling match for free patches of sky. He picked one a few trees back from the edge of the clearing with a good spread of thick branches several levels high. Then it was a matter of taking a good run at it, planting his feet on the trunk, and jumping for a branch.

He got his camouflage stand of bent branches and plucked leaves completed halfway up the tree before the first two lizard riders showed up. It was fully dark now, so they carried torches, which would make spotting him basically impossible until daybreak.

He and Spencer hadn't been close enough last time to examine their features in detail. They had vaguely bearlike faces with large, expressive eyes. Their hands were stout, with fingers longer than a human's. He could make out retracted claws on the tips. They were more like prehensile cat's paws. There were six on each hand, counting the thumb. It would be interesting to find out if they used base six or twelve math because of their hands. He hoped to stay long enough to find out.

Mike focused his binoculars and tuned the shotgun mic for the right distance. Kim answered his connection right away. "I'm ready." They now had a better idea of the local network's sensor ability and knew that direct, low-power systems would be safe. He'd need her translation to understand what they said.

On the ground, the Telirians had to work a bit to get their mounts to approach the crater where the node used to be. "So it finally happened," the slightly taller one on the right, Mike decided to name him Alan, said. "How long has this one been here?"

The shorter but larger one, portly even, shrugged. He decided to name that one Brian. "No idea. It's been a forbidden grove for as long as anyone can remember."

A chat window from Kim opened up. *That's weird. They speak a language I already know.*

Nearby planet? He sent back.

Not at all. I picked it up on our last negotiation. That's several sectors away from here.

Could the nodes have done it?

Maybe, but maybe not. With enough time and technology, it would be easy to change the language a people spoke. But then why go to the trouble of Interpreters?

On the ground, Brian circled around with the torch held near the ground. "Well it's made a right mess of this place, that's certain. You check the far end and let me know if you find anything."

The two Telirians searched the clearing at a quick trot, too fast to be thorough but efficient enough to cover the entire area in a matter of minutes. They met back at the crater, and Alan said, "I found this." He handed over a small object, maybe a bracelet or other trinket. "Nothing fresh."

"We'd never be that lucky. But at least we know she was here at some point." Brian sighed, and his leather armor creaked. This close, Mike could see it was well maintained and decorated with intricate patterns. The clothing they wore was also embroidered with similar patterns. They might not have complex technology yet, but they seemed to be good at what they had. "And the node component?"

Any idea what component might mean? Kim asked.

No. There are a lot of parts that make up a node. Maybe if they find it, I can figure it out by what it looks like.

"To tell you the truth," Alan replied, "I'd forgotten to search for that."

Brian nodded grimly. "As well you should." He handed Alan the bracelet. "Take that with you and head back. They're bound to be over the first bridge by now. He'll want to know."

Alan barked at his mount and flogged its flank with the ends of the reins. The beast rose up in an impressive imitation of a horse rearing and then galloped off into the darkness. At that speed, Mike hoped Alan knew where he was going. The torch didn't throw off all that much light.

Mike consulted the map they'd built up over the past two days. *If the first bridge* is *the first bridge, they're at least an hour away.* The settlement they'd speculated about was a decent-sized walled town, with a population somewhere between five and ten thousand. It was neat, but the town wall seemed rundown and pierced in places to make way for roads. The working theory was the nodes had found and pacified a bunch of feudal warlords.

The lord's palace was modest but easy to spot because of the layout and the extra set of walls around it. The only other large structure was directly across a plaza from the palace. If the roof layout was any indication, the building was like a Roman-era basilica, with two aisles flanking a large central nave but no transept to turn the plan into a cross.

Sticking out of the middle of it like an infernal bell tower was the unmistakable shape of an AC node.

As with Earth's preindustrial cities, this one had a river as a border with exactly one bridge across it. Assuming that was the first bridge, then whoever these two were scouting for must be on foot. It was probably another squad of men like last time.

On the ground below, Brian dismounted easily from his lizard and casually tied it off to a tree not far from Mike's. He walked with the gait of someone who'd spent most of his life in a saddle. So probably a knight or certainly part of a mounted guard.

He cupped a hand around his mouth and shouted, "Sarewith? *Sarewith!* Can you hear me?" He then cocked his ear, which was higher on his head than a human's and shaped like half a fleshy clam shell and listened. Then he tried again. *"Sarewith, daughter of Malafan, are you out there?"*

Make that a sergeant of the guard. Mike had never encountered someone who could shout that loudly who wasn't one.

Brian received no response. He rammed the torch into the ground so it stood upright and then began gathering wood. As he did so, he started singing.

"I went into the *amashka* shop some *amashka* for to buy,"

You don't know what amashka means?

No. That's not a word in the language they're speaking now

"I looked around the *amashka* shop, but no one did I spy.

"I was disappointed, and some angry words I said,

"Then I heard the sound of a"— he clacked two of the sticks he'd gathered together three times—"up above my head.

"Well I was slick, and I was quick, and up the stairs I sped,

"And much to my surprise, I found the *amashka's* wife in bed;

"And with her was another man of most gigantic size,

"And they were having a *knock, knock, knock* right before my eyes."

It was all Mike could do to keep from snorting out loud.

Oh, God, Kim sent, there are more verses.

You don't have to translate, I get the gist, he replied. Maybe amashka's from their original tongue, she said as Brian kept singing his bawdy song into the night. *I think it's candles. Or maybe torches. Probably candles.*

So, candlemaker?

Works for me.

As Brian built his fire, Kim learned all sorts of what they decided to call old Telirian words, things like *whore, harlot, chastity belt*—which took the whole song to figure out—the local measure for a large male reproductive organ—they hadn't gotten the units down yet, but it was nine of them long—three different names for the female reproductive organ—like many other things, it would seem the native's reproductive equipment was at least broadly similar to that of a human's—and five different names for booze. They were all from the same language, which wasn't the one he spoke. And it was only a word here and there, not entire songs.

The fuck does this guy do for a living? Spencer sent. *Work at a ren faire?*

He lives in a walled town and rides a horse. Well, horse thing, Mike replied. *The whole planet could be a giant ren faire.*

By now Brian had an impressive fire going. He went over to his mount, who had long ago crouched down and gone to sleep, opened up a saddle bag, and pulled out a large leather flask and something wrapped in paper. He lay down on one elbow in front of the fire and switched to humming as he ate his snack.

Mike took a picture of the flask and sent it to Kim. *Do you think that's* Marwal *or* Ulama? Of the five boozes, those were the two the protagonists in the songs drank. The other three seemed to have powerful aphrodisiac effects when supplied to the females. At least that's what the songs said.

No idea. Spencer thinks Marwal.

The paper held an object the size of Mike's fist that he could smell on the wind. The locals were fond of onions, or whatever they were called here. It wasn't exactly a sandwich, more like a giant meatball inside a soft pretzel.

Brian was almost done with his meal when a horn sounded in the distance. His mount woke up with a snort and stood, fully alert. The soldier quickly got up and put away the remains of his meal, dusting his armor for crumbs as he went. The sergeant liked to be neat when the boss arrived. Out of respect or fear remained to be seen.

The same party that they'd seen two days ago marched into the clearing, now bolstered by a wagon pulled by more lizards. It used a modern suspension, right down to pneumatic tires. It didn't stop next to the fire, continuing on into the woods until it was nearly out of sight. For all he could tell, it might've kept going to wherever it was headed.

So no motors, Mike sent, *but tires and springs.*

The nodes are selective in what they share, Kim replied.

"My lord," Sergeant Brian said and bowed to the imposing, well-dressed mounted man who rode at the head of the squad. "I have continued the search for Sarewith. She was here, but I could find nothing recent."

The lord nodded and turned around to face the squad behind him. "Light your torches and perform a thorough search. We'll do it again come daylight." He leaned down toward a somewhat sloppily dressed soldier. "Don't set the woods on fire, son. We've only just been allowed in."

Mike could've sworn the soldier's voice squeaked like a teenager. "Yes, milord."

"Don't forget to hunt for the node component as well. That's what we've been sent here to find."

The men spread out with their torches held high. Mike focused his spy gear on the lord and Brian the sergeant, who stood next to the fire.

"Well at least we know where she *was*," Brian said.

"We've always known," he said. "They gave her permission, it's the only thing that makes sense."

"What the hell happened here? How did she manage it?"

The lord shook his head and dismounted. "I don't think it was her. I don't think the node does, either. That's why it ordered us out here in the middle of the night. At least she doesn't seem to have been injured by it. Or worse." He plopped down on a stump created when one of the node's plates sawed through a tree.

"But if she didn't do it, what *did*?"

His voice went bitter. "The nodes are not to be questioned…"

"…only obeyed."

Wait, he sent to Kim, *that was in Standard.*

Spencer said one of the locals, Tapov, spoke it.

Do you think that's who they're searching for?

Maybe. It's common for Chinese people to have different names in different languages.

The lord stared into the fire pensively and switched back to his native language. "I refuse to believe I am alive the day *Interpreters* have arrived on our planet." This time it was a Standard word inside his native sentence. The nodes must've taught them about the Guild.

"*Interpreters*?" Alan gasped. "You think Interpreters did this?"

"Who else could?"

"But it's too soon. The nodes said they still had to prepare us for their treacherous—"

"Lord Malafan," a soldier shouted from the opposite side of the clearing, "I've found it!"

It, not her? Mike sent to Kim.

Must be the node component and not his daughter, she replied. *At least we know the name of who's in charge now.*

Two soldiers ran, or rather waddled quickly, up to Lord Malafan. They carried a large, heavy, rectangular box covered in soot and dirt between them. The soldiers all gathered around, chattering in awed tones.

The carriage stayed silent and still, barely visible in the dark.

"Enough," Lord Malafan declared, motioning for them to set it on the tree stump he'd been sitting on. "This is not the only thing we're looking for. The node commanded we comb this area until the next sundown. We can't return until then. Continue the search."

Mike zoomed in and a lump of ice fell into his stomach. He recognized the construction of the box.

What is it? Kim sent. *If you send me a picture, I might figure out what it is.*

I know what it is. He sent her a picture anyway.

Lord Malafan turned to Brian. "Don't stand there, help me open it."

"Open it? My lord, have you gone mad?"

"It's already damaged. The node won't be able to tell. We may never get another chance." He pulled out a stout dagger and worked down the seam of the lid. After a moment, Sergeant Brian swore and started working on the opposite end with his own dagger.

That's exactly what it is, Kim sent.

The box popped open with a squeak. The two men jumped back so quickly they both fell, giving Mike a clear view of what was inside.

And it's bad, he sent.

AC nodes were, at root, gigantic, self-contained unduplicates. They used common principles, common components, with the ones Earth had back home. Compared to those, the case was outrageously big and heavy, but it had to be shaped a certain way for the lattice to grow properly, and there was no mistaking the way the crystals glittered in the fire light.

Somehow a complete and functioning quantum lattice had survived the node's destruction. Inside that box was a recording of what it had experienced, what it *was,* right up to and including their assault on it.

"Enough!" Brian cried out as he slammed the box shut. "We must return this to the node!"

I need to get that box, Mike sent

It's too big, and there are too many guards.

"It's all right, Eskol," Lord Malafan said. "I don't know what I thought I'd see. It seems our benefactors collect strange crystals for some reason. Maybe they're not all that different from us after all."

Kim, if their node gets that information we're screwed.

Did you see the size of that lattice? Do you have any idea how long it will take a node to absorb it? I don't."

But—

You heard Malafan, she interrupted, *they'll be searching this clearing for at least a day. You stay where you are until it's safe to sneak away and then you meet us here.* She sent him the coordinates of their new camp.

Because you have a plan?

Because I have a plan.

Chapter 14
Tonya

It took the drones about fifteen minutes to haul off the severely injured. The professors carried on hurried discussions amongst themselves the entire time, always glancing at one thing.

Her.

"Why do they keep looking at me?" she asked Tenor.

"You never said you were a visiting professor. I thought you were a student."

It wasn't only the professors. The part of the crowd that hadn't fled also stared at her. It was worse than China. She pulled a page out of Spencer's book and decided to roll with it. She'd be a professor. "Is that a problem?"

"Your ID is all messed up, it doesn't show your credentials."

Keep going, don't question it. "You've got to be kidding me. It was fine when I left yesterday."

The PA system came to life with a howl of feedback. "Unknown professor, please approach the stage."

You mean what's left of it, she thought. It'd been riddled with shrapnel holes. It should've collapsed; it was still crowded with singed and disheveled old academics of several different species. The oldest and fattest one, a turtle-ish alien whose shell could barely be seen under his sumptuous but still smoldering robes, was wrestling a microphone away from an assistant in a barely audible argument shot through with static and feedback. It wasn't that the assistant held onto the microphone, but rather he couldn't hand it over fast enough. It reminded Tonya of old professors wrestling with technology at conference lecterns back home so much that she shook her head.

The old professor won his wrestling match, more with the cables than anything else. "Yes. Right," he said in a whistling wheeze. "You there. What's going on? Why haven't you properly identified yourself? This is most irregular. Come here, child, yes, what? No need to shout. Yes. Quite right."

She didn't know why her interpreter thread was translating the professor in such a quirky way, right down to a British accent. That said, anyone Kim ever spoke to always noticed how authentic her accent was. It must be an Interpreter quirk. Or maybe stuffy old professors with bizarre speech patterns was a universal thing.

Tonya did as she was asked, walking gingerly across the space between the grandstands and the stage. There was no reason to use the PA system. The place had gone almost completely silent.

This was definitely worse than their trip to China.

The old turtle peered down at her from his perch on the stage. "We are grateful for your aid but are confused. Yes. Quite right. We can't tell your affiliation, and you haven't registered properly. This is highly irregular, what, what?"

It had to mean that there were restrictions on exactly who was allowed to practice medicine, down to basic knowledge like first aid. It wasn't out of character for this place. Good Samaritan rules would imply people acting on their own initiative, and she hadn't seen much of that so far.

"I can help," Tenor said from behind her. "I recorded the entire incident. Only a professor of technologies could perform such a feat. That is enough for her to be acclaimed under Assertion."

Kim had used that word when she explained how she and Mike became official Interpreters. Apparently some crisis deep in the galaxy's history had wiped out all records of who was an Interpreter and who wasn't, so they created a law that allowed someone to be officially recognized by doing the job. It seemed to cover other professions too.

This set the robed brigade on their back foot for a moment. They put their various sized and shaped heads together in a huddle to talk it over.

As she waited, she did a quick search. *Assertion for medical technologies requires the candidate to demonstrate advanced knowledge of at least three different anatomies of intelligent life forms, not counting the candidate's.*

If she were a vet, she might be able to fake it, but human medicine had only required her to study human anatomy. She searched some more. Tonya had more than one specialty nowadays.

Assertion for physics technologies requires the candidate to demonstrate advanced knowledge of all aspects of physics, up to and including the ultraviolet catastrophe.

That was an old name for a problem Earth's physicists had solved at the dawn of the twentieth century. Mike said that bemian knowledge of physics was strictly classical. He'd found no evidence at all that they had discovered quantum physics. Blackbody radiation, the phenomena that led to the discovery of the so-called catastrophe and its solution, was a cornerstone of thermodynamics and sat directly on the border between classical and quantum physics. If they called it a mystery, then boy did Tonya have some news for them.

The huddle broke up in a murmur of various kinds of harumph. The old turtle walked over and bent down. "Right. Well. What, what? We agree that it is useful but not enough. Do you claim Assertion, Professor Brinks?"

She was busy reading the procedures, and it took a second to come up with the answer. "No, I do not."

The crowd bubbled over as they took in her statement.

Still reading furiously—all those hours practicing bemian script on the trip over were paying off in spades—she held up her hand and pulled out the voice she used on baby docs losing their minds in an ER crisis. "*Not* medical technologies."

She looked up at them, all struck silent like those doctors back home. "My name is Professor Tonya Brinks, and I claim that my primary specialization is in physics technologies." Incredibly, according to her information, this *also* seemed to qualify her to make medical decisions. She filed that horror away for another time. "As specified in Article Two of the Refoundation, Subsection Three, I will demonstrate this at a lecture." She turned to the professor, and now that she remembered she could get names with a ping, found out he was the dean of the college, and his name was Shakson. "At a time and place of your choosing, Dean Shakson."

His face broke into a beaky grin. "Very good and whatnot! We haven't had a proper lecture in the physics technologies in ages, not at all, I do tell you. Very good indeed. Yes. So we'll do it tonight then, in the Grand Lecture Hall. *Hakonz!* Where has that boy got off to what, what? Lose his own head if it wasn't attached, yes, exactly."

The worried ferretlike alien he'd wrestled the microphone away from earlier rushed to Dean Shakson's side. "As requested, the lecture is scheduled for tomorrow at the Main Memorial Hall, and that was most wise of you, sir. Today was completely booked, and the Grand Hall won't be available for months. We will all be able to see your new designs for the remodeled Memorial Hall. Such an excellent choice, sir."

"Jolly good, old bean, setting it up before I managed to ask for it? We'll make a bursar out of you yet. Right." He turned to the crowd and picked up the microphone. After a few staticky squeals, it settled down. "You lot, lecture tomorrow. Physics technologies! Wonderful exactly, yes, yes. Attendance required." He held a hand—well, more like a clawed paw—up as the groans rose from the crowd. "Double credits for not rushing over the horizon as soon as the gates opened like a bunch of first years, yes, yes, right?"

She leaned over to Tenor and asked, "What does *that* mean?"

"Anyone here will get double credit for attending your lecture since they didn't leave a soon as they could." He laughed when she pulled back trying to figure out how he'd got that. "If you go to school here for any length of time, you end up speaking fluent Dean Shakson. What, what?"

*

"I think you've lost sight of your main objective," Helen said over dinner a few hours later.

"Well it was either that or have them crawl up my backside trying to figure out who I am." She turned to Maff. "That's still a no-no, right?"

Maff adjusted the food gas packet she'd attached to a port on her suit. "Correct. You do *not* want them crawling up any side of your ID right now. I think choosing a physics lecture is a kind of extreme way of avoiding it, but I wasn't there."

They'd found a small place to eat, if the colorful decorations were any indication, probably part of a chain. It was a kind of Korean-street-food-meets-kebab-shop mashup. The food was good but more important was the owner's policies.

"See that symbol," Maff pointed at the obvious silhouette of a pallun about the size of Tonya's hand. "That stands for Pallun Welcome, and unlike some other places I know, this one means it."

"Isn't this a pallun-majority world?" Helen asked.

"Yes," she said heavily, "and if we were in a pallun part of town, I'd have to search for Outworlders Welcome signs." An example landed in Tonya's queue, a circle with arrows pointing out of it in all directions. "Bemians are not as advanced as humans are in this regard."

In the moment, Tonya didn't know what she was more disappointed by: that Jim Crow was being practiced in both directions in the galaxy, or that humanity had managed to figure out a way to get rid of it, and they hadn't.

Now she had bigger problems. "I still have to figure out how to give a lecture these people can understand," she checked her watch, "and I don't have much time to do it." *Universal day length* was a thing in bemian culture, and that was about two hours more than back home. So she had that going for her, which was nice. But it wasn't much. "They don't *know* anything. It's all prayers and incantations. I know the math and principals, but if I don't give it to them in a way they're ready for, they won't understand it."

"I think I can help you there," Helen said. Several large book constructs landed in their shared enhanced vision space. "Library realm security does not seem to be a priority for bemian society."

Maff was almost comically outraged. "Those are *fifth* year texts," she spluttered. "You can't make copies of those."

Helen's smile was all tiger. "Who says I copied them?"

*

Dinner finished, they adjourned to their new quarters in the Gamma enclave. It was a modest set of rooms. Aside from the color scheme and strange texture of the carpet, it would've been hard to tell it apart from a budget hotel suite back home.

Maff sat on a Pallundian plinth chair and Helen on a somewhat strange but still recognizable couch. Tonya had to hide a smile since Helen's feet didn't touch the floor. The chair might swallow her.

"I travel halfway across the galaxy," Helen said, "and I still don't fit in the chairs." She pulled her legs up. "Are you ready?"

Tonya settled next to her. "Ready."

"You're okay with me watching this?" Maff said nervously.

"It'll be interesting to find out what someone on the outside makes of it," Tonya replied.

During their forest battle near Dumas, Helen had discovered that Mike and Kim weren't the only humans who could split, be in more than one place at one time. She'd helped Tonya split her consciousness into four separate threads, allowing her to continue to direct help to gravely wounded people while also beating back Andromeda.

They'd only done this one other time since, determining that a kiss was required, but it didn't have to be a full-on mouth lock. Tonya had brushed her teeth anyway and could tell that Helen had done the same. Maybe one day it wouldn't feel so awkward.

They leaned in toward each other, touched lips, and the world melted away.

And away.

And away.

And away.

Four pairs of eyes opened on four separate realms, each with different colored walls so Tonya could tell them apart. She sat at one end of a basic table. In each of the realms, a pair of long white manipulators waved over a textbook. They were like willow fronds. Helen and Mike couldn't touch realmspace directly but had found a work-around involving specially designed constructs they could control via remotes. "I didn't know you could use them well enough to turn pages."

Helen scoffed. "Mike needs to practice more." As one, in all four places, the manipulators opened books. Four different titles were read out.

They went to work.

Tonya had done her fair share of rote memorization in nursing school and later as a practicing nurse. It still wouldn't be enough to allow her to absorb this much knowledge in such a short time. But becoming multithreaded, as both Helen and Mike called it, let her do it much faster.

A fifth set of eyes opened when a new avatar of Tonya appeared in a realm Maff was in, observing the four other rooms from above. Helen must've been practicing on her own and gotten better at splitting.

Maff made a yeep noise and scrabbled backward. "How do you *do* that?"

Tonya checked this avatar as she listened to each of the four books Helen was reading to her, getting each Tonya to read each line back to her until she had it down pat. The ease of it was disorienting. Part of her mind rebelled against this strange splitting, but it was a small part. The rest of her kept studying.

"We haven't done it often enough to know." Helen's voice came from all around the realm. "I thought it had to do with Interpreters, but I don't think that's right anymore."

Pages turning, words spoken, over and over and over and over…

That was news to Tonya. "Why?"

"Regular Interpreters can somehow cross the border between realmspace, transit dimension, and realspace, but they can't do this.

Valsa Burtan, the leader of the Interpreters Guild, thought Kim had recruited an army of Interpreters. But it was only her. Mike and I have been doing experiments on our own. We think this ability comes from the human side, not the threaded side."

Saying one thing and another and another and another...pages turning...

"What's your evidence?" Tonya asked.

"Remember when I borrowed your tockion detectors a couple of weeks ago? Mike and Kim are a lot better at this than we are, so I took the devices over to their house, and we did a few experiments. If the detectors are close enough, doing this makes them go berserk."

That implied tockions were involved. The realization was like a rock to her head.

Heads.

Her minds went sideways, she lost the connection to Maff's realm, and had to grip tables four times at once.

"Okay," Helen said, "four threads will be the upper limit for now. You need to concentrate. We'll talk about your theories after we're done."

Pages turning, words spoken, over and over and over and over...

Chapter 15
Kim

The first part of her plan to get the node's crystal lattice was to learn how Interpreters appeared in a society. Mike hadn't found anything in the public records he could reach in bemian space. Kim thought they were kept under lock and key by the Interpreters. What he'd forgotten was that, as the glass girl, she could travel to any place she could see. He searched for a bit and came up with a likely candidate: a vault owned by the chapter house on the planet they'd done their first La'fan negotiation on.

The longer she concentrated on the image, the more certain she felt of reaching it. This wasn't the certainty of visiting the place or finding it on a map. The feeling came from the same place her certainty of learning words did when she first heard a new language. It was part of her being an Interpreter, and it was as mysterious as any of the rest of it. But she didn't need to explain it to use it.

Coral lightning tracing over her obsidian skin, Kim stepped forward in the realm to the passage she'd created that connected to the transit dimension. But instead of moving confidently, she slipped like she'd been standing on ice. For a brief moment, she saw the trees of the forest around them, only they stretched and changed into more familiar types as she fell. Her body was hit with a ferocious sensation of pins and needles as the transformation reversed, then an all-encompassing fatigue dropped on her like an avalanche. She felt more tired than she ever had before, a weight pulling her into the depths.

Somehow the stupid sleep app had activated itself.

"Kim?" Mike asked, faintly as she faded uncontrollably into sleep.

Then there was nothing.

*

Jungles, Kim thought bitterly as she sat shivering in the rain with the rest of them, *are supposed to be hot.* They were now in the second week of their ordeal in Bolivia, and she was certain she'd never be warm again.

"C'mon, Kim," Henry said as he handed her the last chunk of their final energy bar, "sing for your supper?"

Those first few days, when they were sure they were far enough away from the drug lord Manuel Quispe's compound to risk making a sound, Kim sang for them each night. It cheered them all up, including her. That was when they knew the way home, when the jungle would only last a few days.

When they weren't lost.

"No," she said, shaking her head. "You keep it. I don't feel much like singing." She pulled her knees close under her poncho as the rain pelted down. The rest of them were doing better. They could keep each other warm, huddled together in a hugging mass.

"Okay," Mark said. "Let's play choose the next target. We haven't done that in ages."

Kim couldn't believe it. They hadn't done that because they'd all been slaves. "There won't be any more targets," she said.

They went still like she'd said Santa Clause didn't exist. "Kim you can't mean that," Mark replied.

"I've been talking about retiring for more than a year," she shot back. "I didn't want to do this anymore *before* we got stuck out here."

Lourdes wiped hair out of her face. "We can't do it without you."

The rest of them grumbled in agreement. And she'd go along like all the other times. She had no choice; they'd keep badgering her until she gave in.

But not tonight. She was too tired, too cold, too hungry. She shot to her feet. "That's right! You're not doing this anymore *because of me*! Not because it wasn't working, not because of how dangerous it was, no, your fun stops *all because of me*!" Kim only wanted to keep these people safe, but they didn't *want* to be safe. They wanted their stupid revolution, which would never happen. The world didn't turn that way.

"That's not true," Mark said, turning his second-father-to-her charm on full blast, knowing it would work like it always had. And it did. The warmth in her chest bloomed despite the rain, despite the hunger. "We hit a bad patch. When we get back, it'll be better than before. We've learned so much." The rest of them mumbled out agreements.

They'd turned this horror show into a learning experience. *They wanted more of it.* "I can't *believe* how dense you people are. That's it. No more." She spun on her heel and walked toward the tree line. "I am *out*!"

"Kim, wait!"

She heard footsteps behind her over the rain and walked faster. They'd follow her like they always did, like they always would. She owed them so much and tried so hard to make it work and would protect them *if they'd let her*, but they wanted their—

Underneath her feet, the ground gave way in a rush. There was nothing below. Kim fell and scrabbled backward, trying to find anything to hold.

"I got you!" A hand grabbed her and pulled her to her feet.

A hand grabbed her. That was impossible. She should be a raving lunatic now, arm on fire, formless creatures tearing her brain apart. The arm changed, and she ended up with a handful of sticks that slipped out of her hand.

On firm ground now, she flipped back the poncho's hood and saw why the touch didn't hurt.

Around her were six rotted bodies, almost cleaned of flesh. She could only recognize her friends by their clothes. They were dead.

And it was her fault.

Kim woke with a start and almost tipped herself out of her camp chair.

"Jesus!" Mike shouted as he caught her chair leg and pulled her back down. "Are you okay?"

There was no jungle, there was no rain. She was here, on Teliria. Mike sat next to her.

He was here.

He was here.

He seemed way too calm for what she went through. "Maybe. What happened?"

He shrugged. "Nothing, as far as I could tell. You?"

Kim wanted to tell him about the nightmare but couldn't. The deaths of her friends had been her fault no matter how long ago it was, and he didn't need that static. Not now.

Not now.

Not now.

Kim buried the confusion and pain deep, like always. The nightmare disturbed and frightened her, but she couldn't examine what had happened. *It didn't matter*. It never had. They still had a crystal lattice box to intercept.

"I'm fine." The Telirians didn't know how Interpreters appeared any more than they did. Time for plan B. "Spencer! Bring the truck around!"

*

Sweat rolled between her shoulder blades and down the center of her back to settle uncomfortably above her increasingly soaked backside. Not for the first time, Kim wondered if sunscreen made for Earth's sun would work for Teliria's. Mama was from Greece, so she sometimes said Kim could tan under a florescent lamp. It would probably undercut their chance of success if the first Interpreter these people encountered had the skin tone of a boiled lobster.

Assuming they had those—or things like them. Mapping the entire planet hadn't been a priority, so she didn't know if they had oceans.

The heat was distracting. "How much longer?"

"Fuck if I know," Spencer replied.

"Not much," Mike said.

Now that getting real knowledge of how Interpreters appeared was off the table, the premise for plan B seemed like a simple enough idea, because it was completely true. The natives thought Interpreters were lurking about, and they were right. They thought those Interpreters had blown up the node, and that was right too. Once those Interpreters found out they hadn't completed the job, they'd want to do so. Three for three.

The incident with the sleep app threatened to derail her concentration more than the heat. She forced it into the back of her mind. There would be time for it later.

Her motto was always *do the unexpected*, and she'd found out over the years that simply asking for what she wanted was often the most unexpected thing of all. So that was what they were going to do: introduce these people to the Interpreters that'd come to town and ask for the box they'd meant to destroy. Obedience to the nodes was obvious. It was logical that this would extend to Interpreters.

If only Malafan and his party would get here.

Eventually the drone showed them to be just over the horizon. It was time. "All right." She banged her foot on the roof of the cab. "Move out!"

She had no idea how an Interpreter appeared on the scene, so with Spencer and Mike's help, she made it up. Kim now stood atop her chariot: Spencer's truck. They'd disguised the windshield so Spencer and Mike couldn't be seen from the outside. The truck would seem to be under her control. Commanding the heights was important, especially if you had to make them yourself.

They cobbled together a brace for her to stand within on the roof of the truck. The engineering wasn't helped by the moonroof openings, which were advanced glass but still glass. Hopefully it would be as easy to take apart as it had been to put together.

The party marched into view exactly on time and then stopped, clearly not expecting what blocked the road in front of them. "Remember," she said, "move slowly."

Spencer took his foot off the brake and let the truck idle its way forward, applying the gas only to get over the occasional bump. Malafan's party didn't move at all. Kim didn't think they would. They were trained fighters. This was their territory. They had superior numbers and weapons, facing a single alien on a machine they didn't recognize but had no reason to fear. There would be plenty of troops in his town, waiting for word to provide reinforcements.

Kim gripped the arms of her bracing framework through her La'fanian gloves. She could do this. She faced down the First Councilor all by herself and won. Twice.

She could do this.

Chapter 16
Tonya

She woke up several hours later than normal the morning after their marathon study session. Part of it was garden variety tiredness. Another part was spending an extended period of time with her mind sliced into four distinct pieces, each learning a different section of what she'd come to think of as *The Knowledge*. When she was little, she'd been fascinated to learn that to this day, official London cabbies—now as much of a tourist attraction as the city they'd exclusively served—only got their license after proving they'd memorized some 320 routes through twenty-five thousand streets and were able to talk out any one of them in an instant. That's what learning bemian physics felt like: routes to various conclusions, facts, or theorems.

It should've been obvious that The Knowledge was pretty good at what it set out to accomplish. This was, after all, the distillation of millions of years of instruction. She would never need to search realmspaces or stack sites to get the specifics of any classical theorem or equation again. Now she could confidently work on the most obscure corners of classical physics from memory alone.

This didn't interfere with her regular knowledge of modern physics. Thank God. Memorization had long been recognized as a different kind of learning, and what she and Helen did made it more distinctive. There was now Tonya the Chronological Physicist and Tonya the Bemian Specialist in Physics Technologies. She hoped that the two would, over time, meld into one. But for now, the sensation of someone else living inside her head, who was still her, was hard to shake.

With a perspective that stood both inside and outside bemian knowledge, Tonya could now see why they'd never progressed any further than they had. They weren't dumb or incurious or lazy.

They'd been prevented.

This was another reason why she was uncomfortable in her own skin today. She'd internalized the bemian knowledge of physics, so she'd also internalized the subliminal message hidden underneath, one she would never have noticed were it not for her previous human education.

There is nothing other than this. There is no beyond. There is no frontier.

Bemians were trained, probably from birth, not to question, explore, or challenge. The AC network took care of it all. It was intimidating to know that an entire galactic society was underpinned by such profound dependency.

But it did work, somehow. Tonya had seen no signs of poverty so far. Everyone seemed healthy. Happy was a bit of a stretch—the best she'd seen so far was the kind of amused cynicism of Tenor and his friends—but nobody seemed to be suffering from a lack of material goods. Mike was bothered by the way bemian energy budgets didn't add up. Tonya was increasingly bothered by the way the cultural contradictions didn't reconcile.

And she needed to do that to introduce her solution to their so-called mystery of the ultraviolet catastrophe.

Tonya's problem wasn't introducing a new, novel idea to a doubtful audience. Humans had been doing that to each other for thousands of years. Some would accept it, some would deny it, others wouldn't understand or care. But humans accepted that a new idea could *exist*. This was an assumption that she couldn't count on with a bemian audience. It was a riddle she spent most of the afternoon trying to solve.

"You're not like this, though," she said to Maff after sharing her observations over lunch. "You've always been curious. Why?"

The frondlike manipulators on top of her suit wavered as if caught in a breeze. It was her version of a chin scratch. *That* she didn't need a thread to tell her about. "Part of it is me. I've always been curious about the world around me. It drove my parents crazy when I was small. But I think being pallun plays a part. As a people we're always striving. Others sometimes call it greed, but that's not right. We're a small minority in a big galaxy. If we don't fly fast, we'll sink and vanish. And we'd strive anyway. It's what we do. It pleases Turlanfador when we succeed on our own." She paused. "That probably makes me sound like a superstitious bumpkin."

The Bible was shot through with sayings about the benefits of work. The term *Christian work ethic* existed for a reason. "Not at all."

So all she had to do was introduce the solution to a problem that bemian societies had written off as unsolvable millions of years ago, to a lecture hall filled with people who literally could not grasp the concept that there could *be* a solution to an unsolvable problem.

No pressure.

"I have one question, though." Maff said.

"Fire away."

"Why bother? The galaxy has been ticking away with its ignorance for millions of years. You're trying to maintain a low profile, last time I checked. This single act could have profound implications for the future of the whole galaxy. You've memorized enough to prove your identity. With that much risk, why go any further?"

The truth was that until this moment, Tonya hadn't considered the question. She worked it out as she spoke. "I've never met a scientist who didn't fantasize about going back in time and presenting future knowledge to people in the past. What would happen? Would they believe it? How would it change things? The thrill of introducing the solution to an unsolvable problem is hard to resist.

"But there is more to it than that. Mike and Kim are right to hide Earth from this galaxy, but you're right too. Earth will become a part of this place. It may take years, decades, or centuries, but it's inevitable. And it has to start somewhere."

She laughed at the situation she found herself in. "Back home it's all about us. How will *we* react to *them*. What will we think? What will we do? It's pretty rare to find a story where Earth is the problem the aliens have to solve. If I start here, with a small bit of science that isn't far in advance of what's already known, I plant a seed for the entire galaxy. New ideas are possible. New things can be found.

"Bringing bemian tech to Earth will cause a revolution in a lot of industries. Probably all of them. But we're used to that. Tech revolutions happen all the time back home. Conclusive proof that aliens exist will also be a huge, *huge* deal. But again we're already kind of used to the idea. We've been fantasizing about it for ages.

"Our tech isn't as impressive as yours, but our *ideas*? If we dump all of Earth's ideas onto bemian society at the same time I don't have any idea what will happen, but none of it will be good, not for a long time. Some of the ideas are toxic but seductive."

"Fascism, Nazism, Communism," Maff said. "Your attempts at raskara, the galaxy's way of guaranteeing basic prosperity, that never work." She grew grim. "There would be far too many bemians who would embrace those with enthusiasm."

"And far too many humans who would help, as long as they stayed on top. I don't want to say we should control what bemians learn of humans, only the rate. This is the first drop, the first taste, which will start a process that will hopefully let these two cultures come together peacefully."

Tonya watched Maff mull it over. If she could understand it, then maybe it wasn't all in Tonya's head.

"It still doesn't help you teach this specific bunch," she said with a tilt of her manipulators, her version of an eyebrow lift.

Tonya sighed. "No, it doesn't. But I *do* have an idea."

*

For whatever reason, Tonya had never been afraid of speaking in front of a crowd. She got up, she talked, she answered questions, she was done. Bemian chanting made it easier. No worries about *umm* and *ahh* and *ya know* making her sound like she spent half the time in her head.

She'd chant her dozens of lines, and then they'd chant a couple of lines back to her. It was like being in church, except she was talking about the laws of motion and not the laws of Moses.

Tonya dressed in a black turtleneck shirt, faded blue jeans, and sneakers for her presentation. It'd taken all afternoon to teach a fabricator how to make them. When Tenor asked about it, she explained that it was a ceremonial outfit from her home planet. Tonya was the only person in this corner of the galaxy who would know. It wasn't exactly lying. Probably. She filed it away with all the other things she'd have to confess to if she ever found a priest who'd believe her.

Tonya finished on their ultraviolet mystery, a long, drawn-out note, a monk's *amen* to the end of knowledge. They all seemed impressed. She waited for the applause to die down, then counted to three in her head.

Into the silence she said, "But there's one more thing." *That one's for you, Mr. Jobs.* "What if a blackbody could only emit light in discrete quantities..." She then proceeded with the version of Planck's law that solved what they considered unsolvable, and she took them one step beyond what they understood.

Tonya got lost in the beauty of it, how a single equation founded what would become quantum mechanics, and her own tockion theory, changing all of human history in the process. But she wouldn't go that far here. They would understand the principles of this law, and that would do for now.

She finished, and the silence held a different energy. The members of the audience shifted in their seats. The occasional sounds weren't exactly coughs or people clearing their throats, but it was obvious that's what they were.

Tenor, who was seated with his friends on the front row, stood up. His feathers ruffled out and back. He looked more like a parrot than a crane. "That's…that's…" He glanced around frantically at his friends, who all nodded at him. Then he turned back. "Specialist Tonya, that's *amazing*! Bravo!"

The smattering of applause was small but enthusiastic. Dean Shakson heaved his fat turtle-shelled backside out of its chair, and they all fell silent. "I'll tell you what it is, what, what. It's bloody well impossible. Yes. Right. Not possible." He looked to either side of his seat, and the faculty around him almost hopped as they began clapping in agreement.

She walked to the edge of the stage and sat, waiting for the applause to die down, channeling Jobs again. She wasn't here to sell sugar water. She was here to change the world. "I don't expect you to believe this. We certainly didn't when our great specialists first discovered the theorem. Therefore I propose a test." This set the room murmuring. "An experiment which will prove the theory is correct and complete."

Tonya watched the professor waver between offense and intrigue. He wasn't used to being challenged, but he also wasn't used to learning anything new. What he *was* used to was being decisive, she saw that all the way across the auditorium. He nodded. "Yes. Right. What, what. *Hakonz!*"

His ferretlike assistant appeared by his chubby elbow. "Yes, Dean Shakson. Very good idea. I've got lab seven reserved, the one you designed with the theater seating around it."

"Exactly right, capital of me to think of it so quickly. What, what." He turned to her. "Now you listen here, technician. We won't have any homsquabbling about in that lab. You climb on that tellenor, and you arrive with it smartly before the graunt gets wind of its scent. Clear and done. What, what, right." He turned to face the crowd. "Now let's give Professor Brinks the old heave to for a jolly great physics technologies lecture. Tak-nak!"

The crowd shouted back, "Sor-ak!"

That seemed to be the cue to leave, as they all got up and began shuffling noisily out of the auditorium.

Tenor met her at the foot of the stage. "That was incredible. Well done!"

The tension she'd been holding on to like a compressed spring released. It was fun in the moment, but now she needed a drink. "Can you translate Shaksonese for me? What exactly did he mean?"

"He wants to see your experiment but doesn't want you to take your time. Typically this means he wants it as soon as possible."

That would be too soon. She had no idea what any of the equipment looked like or how to integrate it—

He raised his wings. "Calm down. He'll forget all about it tomorrow. I'll have a word with Hakonz. Do you think a week will be enough?"

"It'll have to be."

"Good." He held out a wing. "I think you could use a drink."

She took it. The feathers were soft, and the distinct feeling of a muscled arm instead of the edge of a wing was briefly startling.

But only briefly. "You read my mind."

Chapter 17
Kim

She said a little prayer. *Please, dear God, don't let me screw this up,* and then tapped on the roof to give Spencer the signal to stop. They were less than twenty yards apart. Her La'fanian robes unfurled in all their dark glory. A breeze obligingly blew up, and they rippled and snapped.

Take that, Valsa. The head of the Interpreters would never have managed to pull it off as gracefully as Kim just did.

Malafan's men and steeds shifted nervously. The faint sound of harness and armor clinking reached her. They were beginning to not like standing still in front of whatever she was. Otherwise it was quiet. There was no traffic noise, no airplanes high above, no other people within miles of this single spot. In a world lit only by fire, Kim was about to turn on an arc light.

Here we go. She only had the top part of her mask on, leaving her free to project her voice with as much power as she could muster. The sergeant wasn't the only one who could bellow.

"We would speak with you, Lord Malafan," she said in Telirian, keeping her face passive with an effort as the troops all exchanged worried looks with each other. Gossip traveled between soldiers as fast as it did with anyone else, and Malafan hadn't exactly been whispering about who he thought was behind the destruction of the node. Kim couldn't have announced who and what she was more clearly.

Malafan nudged his steed forward. Calling these people bearlike might give the impression of giant stuffed animals riding scaly horses. In person and up close, they bore no resemblance at all to that. This was a proud, dignified man, a natural leader, but not one who took his responsibilities lightly. And now he'd been called out by a creature he'd probably been raised to fear from the day he was born. The fear was there, but he handled it better than she would've if the roles were reversed.

He stopped about ten feet away, his men far enough behind they wouldn't be able to respond quickly if she attempted something. He wasn't only handling his fear, he was projecting his bravery, and doing a damned good job of it. "I am Lord Malafan," he said. "Who am I addressing?"

Ironically her whole story was completely true. It didn't need any embellishment. "We are Kimberly Artemisia Trayne-Sellars. We are the Head Interpreter for the La'fan." The plurality was expected since all other Interpreters were two intelligent life forms in a single body. Kim had even added a fake stuffed sack to the side of her robes to simulate the realspace deformity that all reconstituted Interpreters had.

It was smaller and neater than Valsa's, of course.

"We are here performing an inspection of your planet to assess its suitability for the arrival of Interpreters." Okay, it wasn't *all* true. "We were examining a defective node not far from here"—back to truth!—"and decided it needed to be disposed of in a safe, controlled manner." Not a lie, an *exaggeration*. "It has come to our attention that the disposal was not entirely complete, and that you may be in possession of components that should have been destroyed with the rest of the node. Is this true?"

Lord Malafan, visibly confused, turned to look over his shoulder, specifically at Sergeant Eskol. The old portly sergeant locked eyes with his lord and then shrugged in a way that she instantly recognized. Nobody could volley a high-level decision back at an officer faster than a senior sergeant, no matter where they were from. She could almost hear *way above my pay grade, sir* bouncing around in his head.

Malafan turned back, transformed from a proud warrior facing an unknown foe into a senior manager trying to figure out why a delivery service was knocking on his door. "Maybe?" He shook himself. "Who did you say you were again?"

"We are an Interpreter on an inspection mission," she said, firmly. The key to this kind of con was to keep the other guy off balance for as long as possible. "We need to know if you are in possession of any components of the node we destroyed two days ago. Are you?"

"Well, yes—"

"Excellent. May we inspect it?"

He gave Kim a little shrug. "I suppose."

The silence stretched as Kim stared down at him. She slowly raised an eyebrow but otherwise remained still. Mohammed could not be brought to the mountain, so...

Malafan caught on quickly. "Oh, of course." He turned his mount around. "Sergeant Eskol! Bring the..." He turned back at her.

She wanted him to think of her as firm, but also helpful. "Component."

"Bring the component forward, please?"

Sergeant Eskol said, "Right!" and then shouted over his shoulder, "Kempal, Aknef! Bring the box we found to the lord, on the double!"

Two soldiers emerged from the group, hauling the box between them. There was some awkward shifting—which reminded her so much of she and Mike wrestling that Vuohensilta's sensor box into the lab before they knew the rest of the galaxy existed that she almost smiled—then they set it edge down on the ground next to Lord Malafan.

He turned back to Kim and hesitated, mouth half open.

"Interpreter Trayne-Sellars," she said.

He nodded. "Interpreter Trayne-Sellars, is this the component?"

"It is indeed." And now for another nudge against his balance. Kim leaned forward and then jerked back abruptly. "Lord Malafan, do you have any large *monkeys* or *apes* inhabiting your forests?" He wouldn't recognize the English words, but that was part of the con.

"Any what?" he asked, confused again.

"Large, semi-intelligent land animals with agile hands. Not bright but curious. They often use tools."

"Um…I don't think—"

"This box has been opened." Telirians went pale just like humans did when they got scared, probably for the same reasons. "It is a grievous violation."

He swallowed loudly enough that she heard it where she stood. "It is?"

"Yes, which is why we asked what sorts of animals you have in those woods of yours. On our world, only monkeys or apes are clever enough to pry open a box like that without regard for the consequences."

"Consequences?" he asked weakly.

She'd shown him the stick, now for the carrot. "The nodes are notoriously paranoid about the treatment of their components. Quite unfair. It's most fortunate that we've met now, Lord Malafan."

He seemed momentarily stuck on the idea of consequences but then blinked. "Fortunate?"

"Yes. A node may not believe *you* if you claimed a large, rare beast opened up a component without authorization, but it will believe *us*."

Color returned to his face. He nodded. "They'll believe you. You're an Interpreter."

"A *Head* Interpreter. Trust us, we outrank all the nodes in this system. Yes, most fortunate indeed. Now, if your men will put it in the back of our vehicle." *Lower the tail gate,* she sent to Spencer, and was answered with a metallic thunk as it unlatched and then whirred audibly while it opened. "We will dispose of it properly."

"Lord Malafan, no!" The two female Telirians in undecorated but still fine robes bolted out of the mysterious carriage with the modern suspension that'd been traveling with this party the entire time. "You cannot allow this!" They threw themselves between the box and the soldiers who carried it out. "Only nodes can dispose of components! It is written!"

Malafan shot her a look that Kim recognized all too well: *I knew it couldn't be this easy*. "Sisters, please, Interpreter Trayne-Sellars is only trying to help. You can see their vehicle. It's much better equipped to make the journey back to town."

"That's not what they said," the taller one shouted, "they said *disposal*!"

"A misunderstanding," he reassured them. "Correct, Interpreter Trayne-Sellars?"

Kim had her own reasons for wanting to end this early. "Quite right, Lord Malafan."

"No!" the younger one shouted. "We know the truth! We will not be silenced!"

She watched him stiffen. Defiance from a scary Interpreter was one thing. He didn't know who or what she was. Defiance from his own people was quite different. "You know nothing. Sergeant, remove the sisters and—"

The two women nodded to each other, pulled out amulets that had been hanging around their necks, and squeezed them hard.

Oh fuck me, Spencer sent. *That was a signal.*

The unmistakable sound of rotor blades spinning up in the distance startled everyone, including the sisters.

"What in the world?" Lord Malafan asked, then had to hang onto his bucking mount as the volume of the sound increased.

It must be an alert for the node, Mike sent. *We need to get out of here.*

But the lattice! Kim sent.

Probably has trackers installed on it, Mike replied. *And we are out of time. Hang on!*

Kim fell back into her bracing as Spencer floored the accelerator. Soldiers dove in all directions to get out of the truck's way.

"Where are we going?" she shouted.

"The fuck away from whatever's making that noise," Spencer shouted back. "Mike, get the mounts. Kim, you need to get off the roof."

The road was for foot and hoof traffic, maybe the occasional wagon wheel. It was not designed for a two-ton vehicle capable of highway speed with a terrified redneck at the wheel. When Kim wasn't being hurled nearly out of her harness, she was being squashed back in so hard the legs of her bracing flexed. "How?"

A moonroof Kim had forgotten was there slid open behind her. She turned to look at it, and the wind blew her hood down over her mask. She was briefly blinded.

"This way!" Mike shouted out of the moonroof as he tried to hold himself steady with his elbows. In each hand he held shiny metal devices that were like someone had welded a short stick to a softball. He rammed them into sockets screwed into back corners of the roof. "We need the room!"

The truck slewed sideways as the road turned. In the sky behind them, two rotorcraft were closing in. With nothing to compare them to, Kim had no idea how big they were or how fast they were going, but they were getting larger. Spencer had no time to stop, and Mike filled the moonroof she might've used as a hatch. There was no getting through it without a touch. That left one target.

"Mike!" She shouted as she crouched. "Duck!"

He collapsed through the moonroof as she jumped over his head and into the truck bed. The wind gave her a bigger boost than she counted on, and as everything slowed down and went silent in the adrenaline surge, her jump angled her straight toward the tailgate.

The *open* tailgate.

"Kim!"

On the way out, she managed to grab one of the supports. This swung her body full-on into the edge of the tailgate, crushing the wind out of her. If she ended up on the ground, those fliers would be on her in an instant. Air was secondary to getting back in the truck.

Her feet hit the ground, but instead of digging in, they bounced her backward and up. Pulling with all her strength and with a new momentum advantage, her legs went over her head in a circle. She landed on her back in the bed of the truck.

Too stunned to hang on and completely unable to breathe, she felt the momentum of the truck sliding her out of the bed. Her mind screamed at her to move, but she couldn't manage it. Mike held out his arm to her through the open back window, and she would've grabbed it no matter what the cost, but she couldn't move. Her head clunked against the seam between the bed and the tailgate. One more bounce and she would be out of the truck for good.

Goodbye, Mike. I thought we'd have longer.

Her head stopped against a wall. A *moving* wall, slowly pushing her back into the bed. It was the tailgate closing. Spencer must've hit the button at some point. The realization gave her the strength to roll sideways and grab one of the bungee cords attached to the side of the truck bed. She braced herself under the bed's side sill. No longer under threat of being tossed out onto the ground, she gasped painfully against her locked-up lungs until they worked again.

She looked up to find Mike still shouting her name, arm out. The wind blew her hood down again as she shook her head. "I'm okay!" She threw him a thumbs-up, bungee cord still tightly gripped in her fist.

He checked up and behind her, then gave his own thumbs-up as he disappeared into the cab.

Are you okay? Spencer sent.

I'll be fine. What's going on? What has Mike put on the back of the truck?

Maff said the weapons couldn't be too advanced, he replied. *She never said anything about what we used to shoot them.*

Mike reappeared out of the moonroof with one of their neo-blunderbusses in his hands. He pushed the barrel against the chrome ball he'd mounted to the back of the cab. It grabbed the rifle with some kind of latch. The ball instantly stabilized the barrel. Mike, who still held the back of the gun, immediately bobbed up and down in opposition to the moves of the truck as they rocketed down the road. Kim turned her head to see what he was targeting as Mike fired. The lick of flame that spat out of the barrel flashed hot against the side of her face.

The flier he shot was *enormous*, maybe twice as big as the truck and not more than thirty feet away. Mike must've hit an important part of the left rotor because it rocketed away from the rest of the flier like it'd been turned loose. The lift imbalance flung the rest of the craft into the ground. It disintegrated, flinging shrapnel in all directions. A small jagged hole appeared in the tail gate and a hot and hissing angry thing thumped into the back of the truck bed behind her. She craned her neck around and found a glowing chunk of shrapnel half buried in the cab's wall.

That was *way* too close.

She hadn't noticed Mike had vanished until he reappeared on the other side of the truck with another one of their guns. Kim turned away and squashed herself lower, trying to see without getting brained by the sides of the bucking truck or fried in the blast of the gun.

The second flier was further back and to the left, closing fast. She scanned the devices her phone said were available for connection. At the bottom of the short list was one that ended with aimAssist. After she connected, a virtual screen expanded in front of her showing what Mike saw. The main body of the flier filled the targeting reticle, but as it closed in, smaller sections were highlighted. He cycled through them until it locked onto the center of the left rotor. A percentage-chance-to-hit gauge appeared and rocketed upward as the distance spooled downward.

When it hit seventy-five percent, he fired.

Kim was about to shout that he'd taken the shot too early, but it didn't matter. The result was the same: a giant flier tumbling out of control straight into the ground. It was much farther away though, so no high-energy shrapnel tore new holes into the truck or anything else. Which was probably the reason for the suboptimal shot.

With the coast clear, Spencer backed off from he's-gonna-kill-us-all speed to do-we-have-to-bump-around-this-much speed. Because they did, and with each bonk or shudder, the injuries she'd sustained with her little stunt announced themselves. Loudly.

Finally he stopped.

Mike opened one of the truck's back doors and clambered into the bed with her. "Are you okay?"

"Yeah," she said, but when Kim moved, all the damage she'd done shouted at her. "Um...no, not really." Her hands didn't want to close properly; her shoulders wouldn't let her lift her arms. It was like someone had beaten her with a bat from her right shoulder to her left hip. That knee didn't want to move, and they might have to cut her foot out of her boot. It'd already swollen up tight.

Mike pulled up her medStat app in their shared vision channel. The wire-frame version of her showed a more technical catalog of what she already knew: cracked ribs, torn muscles and ligaments, and contusions for days.

"You bounce pretty good, lady," Spencer said from inside the truck.

Mike was frantic but hiding it well. "I need to get you into the truck," he said.

She wasn't *that* helpless. Kim started to unwedge herself from the side of the truck. "No, I can do—"

All of her injuries went off at once. She fell back, hitting her head with a painful bonk. That might've been the only place that didn't hurt. *Well, took care of that one didn't ya, Trayne?* "Okay maybe I can't do it."

"I need to knock you out so I can get you into the back seat."

She tried to smile, because he was sweet to ask her, but that shot a bark of pain through her jaw. "I can do it." The knowledge of how safe she would be in his arms eased the pain a bit. "I love you."

"I know," he winked. "I love you too."

She set a timer for ten minutes, activated her medical app, and relaxed as the pain drained away.

Chapter 18
Maff

The last time she'd met Mr. Sha'Katenden in person was at the foot of a courthouse trying to convince a node of their innocence. He'd been scary intense, no nonsense, there to do a difficult job, and he was the best in the business. Now that he was helping to guide a much more promising case, she thought he might be a little less intimidating.

He wasn't.

"These people we are seeing," he said to her and Helen, who had come along for her own reasons, "they are not to be trifled with. Useful, but dangerous if not treated with respect and care."

They'd met outside his office and were now traveling in his personal car. The inside of the vehicle was much like its owner: understated but with materials of unmistakable quality and serious intent.

"I must admit," he said as they departed, "I have never seen the Interpreter's Guild in such a state." He looked at Maff, serious as a poisoned cloud. "You're certain the human Interpreter can't be reached?"

She'd trusted him with much bigger secrets than this. "The planet they're on is still in uplift. They won't be joined to the network for many more years." Interpreters appearing was always one of the last stages of uplift. It might take a century or more before they became aware of Teliria. By that time, Mike and Kim would be long gone. "How bad is it?"

"It's managed to distract the Guild from their endless scheming against the AC network."

Helen asked in that deadpan way Maff knew could silence a thundering storm, "Why is the Guild scheming against the AC network?"

Maff had spent an entire year on Earth constantly disoriented by their wildly different cultures. Yes, she'd grown up with a galaxy full of alien life. There was variation, but nothing on the scale of what the humans had on their single planet. They even had a name for her confusion: *culture shock*.

But as disorienting as that experience was, it stood as nothing compared to the shock of Helen's simple question. Not the least because in all the millions of years since the Refounding, Maff was certain it had never been asked before.

Mr. Sha'Katenden must've been at least as shocked as she was. He'd gone as still as the dawn air.

Helen raised an eyebrow, an expression Maff knew by experience meant that she'd discovered a puzzle. "Did I say something wrong?"

Mr. Sha'Katenden relaxed and then shook his head. He turned to Maff. "Even after all you've shown me, I still wasn't sure any of it was real. But now I know it is. No race brought up by the nodes would ever ask such a simple, fundamental question." He turned back to Helen. "For as long as history has been recorded, the AC network and the Interpreter's Guild have constantly been at each other's throats. It has gone on for so long that the origins of their conflict have been completely lost."

Helen grimaced. "Surely there are legends?"

He nodded, and his voice grew gentle as he contemplated ideas no pallun, no bemian, had ever considered. It was nice to see someone else have to confront the offhand way humans could upend entire systems of belief. Maff had been exhausted by it. "There should be," he said, "but no. Whatever happened must've been so long ago that it'd been forgotten before the Refounding."

"Is it a violent conflict?" Helen asked.

Actual violence, between nodes and the Guild. The idea was so outrageous Maff's head spun like she'd lost a wing in a tornado.

She wasn't alone in her disorientation. Mr. Sha'Katenden was now so far off his mental balance Maff saw him make a few adjustments to keep his suit stable. "It might have, long ago. We do have legends about wars between them. But not now. Not in recorded history. They use the courts against each other today." He made a brief, low sound that might've been a chuckle. "Many a Pallun's fortune has been made serving as lawyers for their incredibly petty, vicious squabbles.

"But not now. For the first time in generations there are no lawsuits between the two entities. The Guild's anti-node propaganda hasn't been refreshed since your friends departed.

"Is that why we're meeting these people?" Helen asked. "There must be legal ways to do this."

"All controlled by the petarkan network." Maff flinched at his use of the almost racist word for everything nonpallun, from other species to the AC network itself. Helen, who knew Pallundian, remained stone faced. "Not to be trusted. If the petarkan find out about Earth, about who and what *she* is," he pointed at Helen, "*pfft*," he splayed out his manipulators, "no more opportunity. No more Earth either. The petarkan network would think nothing of destroying such a place."

"But we have no existing node infrastructure," Helen replied. "No AC network. They can't easily destroy our system."

Mr. Sha'Katenden scoffed. "Who said it would be easy? You are alone in a galaxy that doesn't think you're possible. These things, they exist for millions of years at a time. What is a hundred years to a machine like that? A thousand? No. If the petarkan network finds out too soon, it will be a disaster. It can only be done through our people. Them you can trust." He shrugged. "After a fashion."

"Because the people we're going to meet are *akmacha*," Helen said, using the Pallundian word for a gangster.

"Exactly. The honesty of these people is swift, simple, and brutal. They have a code, and they stick to it. No outsiders, no talking. They have the resources and the know-how to bring your world to galactic attention slowly."

"By allowing them to make enormous amounts of money," Helen replied.

Mr. Sha'Katenden shrugged. "By making everyone enormous amounts of money. Art is cash in this galaxy. A whole *planet's* worth of art that the galaxy has never seen before? I literally cannot comprehend this opportunity. They'll skim an inordinate amount for themselves, but Earth won't miss it. Your children's children to a hundred generations won't be able to spend it all. By the time the petarkan network understands what's going on it will be too late. We will have glided them into the depths rather than dropped them into a storm. By the time they notice the heat, they'll already be cooked. Earth will be too valuable to destroy."

They drove deeper into the old part of the city. Here Pallundian architecture, with its built-in assumptions of low, wide residents who walked on stilts, prevailed. It was worn rather than seedy, a place where pallun who worked with their manipulators lived, shopped, and prayed. Meronim were prominent, with their oddly outdated suits and need to flock together wherever they went. As a child, Maff's grandfather would drive around a neighborhood like this in Farport, a city not far from here, pointing out all the places her father had lived while he was growing up.

They stopped outside a scruffy *skenario* shop called Samatarra's. A pallun diet was mostly, but not exclusively, gas. Skenario was a delicious exception. The smoked meat hanging in the windows varied from sausage links to entire carcasses of the large flying beast that pallun had domesticated soon after settling on this planet. It'd been a long time since she'd had proper smoked skenario, and it was similar enough to human pork that they'd like it too. Helen especially, who she had often traveled around with sampling various kinds of Chinese prepared pork.

In front of the shop, sitting at a table, were three large pallun. Two were older and one was younger. They wore expensive environmental suits, continuously taking small portions off of various dishes in front of them in the traditional way pallun ate when they weren't using food synthesizers. Again Maff was reminded of her grandfather, who would bring her up to tables like this and show her off to his friends like she was a princess.

When Mr. Sha'Katenden got out of the vehicle, they shouted out greetings in coarsely accented Pallundian.

"So Noen finally decides to shade our cloud with his wings," the largest pallun said as he stood up from his plinth and exchanged an embrace with Mr. Sha'Katenden. "You need to come around more often."

"I try. Eemaz says they still make the best *gabbashan* in the city."

Mr. Sha'Katenden leaned over and greeted the other two pallun, then turned to Maff. "This is Maff Sorkon and her friend Helen Zhang. Maff, Helen, meet Sornik," he indicated the one on the left, "Poolin," the one on the right, "and Toraz," the big one in the middle who Maff was certain was in charge.

Toraz pulled the *chival* he'd been smoking out of one of his suit ports and tapped the ashes onto the street, a king marking a small part of his territory. The confident charm poured off him like sweet gas. "A pleasure. Please," he pointed to the empty side of the table, "have a seat. Poolin," he nudged the smaller, younger pallun as he indicated Helen, "stop sitting on your pegs and get our guest a *timuli*."

Poolin moved quickly and provided Helen with a standard biped chair, moving the pallun plinth out of the way to make room. She was the only high-grav biped in sight and seemed a little toylike compared to the pallun sitting around the table with her.

Meronim who passed gave the table a sour look when they noticed her, but the three pallun at the table paid that no mind. Meronim gave pretty much everyone *not* Meronim a sour look. If any of them slowed enough for Toraz to notice, they quickly scurried away once he locked eyes with them.

Toraz turned to Maff. "Has your friend tried *maxanta* yet?" Without waiting for a reply, he snapped a manipulator and shouted into the store, "Samatarra! Another round, plus three!" He smiled warmly at Helen like he'd known her for years. "You'll love the maxanta."

Will I? Helen texted to Maff.

It's a gas intoxicant, she replied. *On Earth, I made it using various kinds of fruit. It should metabolize into your ethanol.*

Perfect.

To Toraz, Helen said, "I'm sure I will."

"So," Toraz said to Mr. Sha'Katenden after a waiter had distributed the gas flasks. "What's this I hear about a business proposition?"

"I'm only here to make introductions," Mr. Sha'Katenden replied, then turned to her. "Maff is the one with the product."

She'd flown into a cloud and found it filled with *heersage.* The humans called it *deer in headlights,* and that was apt.

Helen cleared her throat, breaking Maff's spell. She found her voice. "It's easier to demonstrate than to talk about it." She sent them all access codes to a private realm, which they used immediately.

The first part of the demonstration was the biggest risk. Helen had insisted on a translated reading from *Romance of the Three Kingdoms,* an ancient classic from her culture. As it was read out by an invisible narrator, the scenes it described were recreated in animations that were displayed all around them. While it was unique in its way, and quite good, Maff knew that similar gigantic historical epics were a part of most bemian cultures. The animation was also distinctive but not much different from similar bemian forms. These were opportunities, but not a game changer. Against her better judgement, Maff had put it first.

It was a mistake. The four men—Mr. Sha'Katenden hadn't seen this demo yet—grew restless and bored. She'd been right to cut the reading to the absolute minimum.

"*This,*" Toraz asked, "is my new business opportunity? I've got six of these poetry readings already in circulation."

The gas inside her roiled and spun. They couldn't have gotten this far only to fail at the line. "That's part one." She switched to the next demo, a realm that replicated a uniquely human auditorium, a *movie theater*, but with plinth seats instead of the timuli humans used. The men, disoriented, shifted and looked around as the theater went dark.

On the screen, nine words in blue displayed in a single stark sentence. She'd worked with Kim to make the translation perfect. The only concession was the bemian 3-D script, but it changed simple human words into a genuine work of art.

A long time ago…

When the music exploded to life, she thought Poolin, the youngest member of Toraz's entourage, would fall off his plinth. As with Helen's ancient novel, the music itself was in a familiar form but *much* more distinctive, more powerful, and it came from all around them instead of from a visible orchestra. Maff vividly remembered the first time Mike had shown her *Star Wars*, one of her first *movies*. His mentor had used it as a teaching tool, a way to learn the tenets of his faith. It was *her* first lesson on how unique human cultures were.

Again, the basis of the story wasn't unfamiliar. *Hero tales* were a staple and had been since before the Refounding. Other things like space ships and bots were also basic concepts. But if the basics were the same, the details were completely different. The bemian bots were all the same, as were the space ships. Clothing varied but inside strict parameters that had been unchanged for millions of years. They would always be the same. *All* of this movie, from the clothing to the ships to the props to the actual story, was utterly unique. In a galaxy where *novelty* was a word with no direct translation into any bemian language, difference on the scale of this single film was unprecedented.

An undercurrent of giddiness confirmed another of her suspicions. Interpreter threads existed to help cultures understand each other. One of the ways to facilitate this was to ensure new encounters with strange things were pleasurable. Humans understood how it worked, although Maff only knew the phrase. Interpreter threads could trigger *endorphin releases*. It was a famous way to know what an artist had created would be accepted, would become *a hit*. A reaction this powerful—Maff almost felt intoxicated, and she was used to Earth culture—was the stuff of legends.

She stopped the film when the black-armored villain stormed off the screen. Toraz silenced his underling's protests to keep going with a snap of his manipulators.

"You now officially have my attention."

Mr. Sha'Katenden laughed, a big, wheezing roll of sound. Judging by the startled looks around her, Maff wasn't the only one who'd thought he was incapable of it. "She is just getting started."

Out of a technical necessity—if she threw too many new languages at the interpreter threads, they'd break—Maff stuck with English-language pop culture. She was also fairly certain Toraz wouldn't believe that this was only one of *dozens* of major and completely unknown sources of intellectual property. Maff didn't always believe it, and she'd lived there.

Her tour also had to be brief. These were busy men, and she took Mr. Sha'Katenden's warning seriously. There wasn't enough time to adequately demonstrate the long-form entertainment types.

Humans had solved this problem for her: *trailers* and *commercials*. These condensed hours of content into a few minutes of summary in a way that showcased them and made them incredibly enticing. She interleaved these with what turned out to be another type of advertisement: the *music video*. Although the broadcaster, whose name translated into Standard as *the station that shows nothing but music videos* had long ago stopped showing them at all, it was still a thriving method of showcasing artists and their music.

So in the space of half an hour, she exposed them to the classics: from *Raiders of the Lost Ark* to *The Avengers*, from *Cheers* to *Game of Thrones*, and from ABBA to ZZ Top. Then she spent the next half hour showing the realm adaptations of each of the properties. Not only could they experience the originals, they could also interact with them directly, literally adding a new dimension to their value.

At no point was Jupiter mentioned. "That we save for the proper time," was all Mr. Sha'Katenden would say when he'd advised against it.

Confident that a culture which had no word for *spoiler* wouldn't mind a peek at an ending, she finished where she started with the rousing throne-room finale of *Star Wars*. The credits were far too much to translate, but Toraz and his men didn't seem to mind. Or they'd been struck dumb by what she'd exposed them to. Maff certainly had been on her first time around. Either way, they stared silently as the music came to a climactic end, and the last words faded silently to black.

She blinked away afterimages once they returned to realspace. She gave Helen and Mr. Sha'Katenden worried looks, only to get slight shrugs in return.

Toraz shook his head and started to chuckle. "Noen Sha'Katenden, you magnificent bastard."

Mr. Sha'Katenden held up his wingtips. "I only wish I could take credit." He nodded toward Maff. "This is the young lady with the goods."

Toraz stared at her, his gaze more intimidating than the time she'd been caught sneaking into the house by her mother after staying out past curfew.

Finally he said, "I don't know what I suspected you had, but it wasn't that." Then he smiled, and she was again reminded that being a successful smuggling boss wasn't only about slicing wings. "I think this is the start of a beautiful flock." His underlings nodded and chuckled along with him. "Now, to other business." He indicated Helen. "I take it she's not part of the demonstration?"

"No," Maff replied, ready for the question. "She needs assistance in finding ancient history books. Ones that may be particularly hard to find."

Toraz nodded. "Fair enough. Sornik, arrange for the lady to pay a visit to one of our warehouses. You know the one."

"Sure, boss."

He turned back to Maff. "And I have a surprise for you."

*

She had never seen anything so beautiful in her life.

"It's an Alcana 2187," Toraz said proudly as they stared up at it in a hangar a few blocks away from Samatarra's.

Maff had always been content with her career as a cargo pilot, a truck driver, as Spencer sometimes put it. The ships were big, honest, and useful. They were in fact the exact opposite of an Alcana 2187, a craft she'd only ever seen on racing broadcasts. Where *Palatine* was a box with wings, the Alcana was speed incarnate. The sleek shape, long and needle-thin, was only big enough to contain a regulation cockpit and an enormous D-drive.

"I won it in a farnak game," he continued. "It arrived a few days ago. You *do* know what they're for, right?"

It took a minute for the gas inside her to settle enough to speak. "I do." They were used in the Exnor-Tarnath-Biknal, the oldest race in the galaxy. It dated to before the Refounding. The rules and route were found inscribed on the walls of an otherwise gutted cache ruin.

"Good." He puffed on his chival a few times. "So, I was wondering what I'd do with it when I got word that Noen was in contact with the only pallun to outrun an entire Interpreter fleet."

Maff's reputation seemed to have preceded her. She would've been more startled if she hadn't been so distracted by the absolutely perfect joins of the hull plating, how it all fit together almost organically in support of a single goal.

Speed.

"So whaddaya say, Maff?" he asked as he puffed away on his chival. "You think you can handle it?"

The maneuvering thrusters were bigger than the main drive on *Palatine*. It wasn't only fast, it could turn on a methane drop, stop like it'd been tied to an Earth tree, and then shoot right back to full speed in less time than it took to lift *Palatine* on its rollers.

Wait. He'd asked her a question.

"Sign me up."

Chapter 19
Kim

The app she used to let Mike put her in the truck was one of Tonya's licensed medical apps, normally only available to professionals. It was for use in an ER setting or other immediate emergency. Tonya installed it herself, but only after making Kim sit through an instructional video—video!—that provided many dire warnings that included the phrases *mental impairment* and *death.*

The sa'dst took it over, turning a ten-minute light sedation into a ten-hour deep sleep. The good news was her injuries had been reduced to impressive but fading bruises. The bad news was Mike was gone. He left camp shortly before dawn to gather intelligence in and around the town. Around was fine but *in* town was not.

Spencer got a full blast of Angel Rage when she found out.

"Jesus, Kim, how was I supposed to stop him?"

"By explaining how bad of an idea it was and how you should both have waited for me to wake up!"

"He's not a child, and he moves like a ghost. He'll be fine, you need to calm down."

Normally she would've bitten down her next words. But she was still shaking off the effects of the medical app, so they ran straight out of her mouth. "I will *not* calm down, and you will *not* patronize me!" She emphasized this childish little bon mot with a hearty foot stomp. As if she wasn't already acting like an oversized four-year-old.

Then a powerful urge hit her, and she stomped again.

And again.

That stopped them both. She stared at her leg like it was a snake that'd appeared out of a hole in the ground. Spencer seemed almost as horrified.

"Fuck me," he said. "It's back?"

"I can fix it."

But this time around she couldn't. She spent the next fifteen minutes unlocking everything in the camp. It made no difference. The sa'dst had fixed her injuries. But it also killed her power's ability to hold back her new flavor of insanity. It wasn't as bad as it'd been earlier, but it was getting worse.

Halfway through her second round of tests, Mike walked out of the woods. He looked tired and trail worn, but he was otherwise fine. She was so happy to see him she only scolded him a little bit.

"That's all he gets?" Spencer said when Mike walked away after a smile and an apology. "You ranted at me!"

She smiled to push the worry down. "He's my husband. He gets a pass."

Mike had managed to work his way inside the node's inner sanctum, the basilica-like structure across from Malafan's palace. He'd recorded a meeting with the node, Lord Malafan, Sergeant Eskol, the two nun-like women who'd sicced the node's flying defenses on them, and a bot.

"They spent the whole day examining our encounter site," Mike explained. "Then went straight to the node. I barely got set up in time."

The inside of the basilica was grand but empty, with a polished marble floor inlaid with decorations identical to the ones they'd encountered in other bemian structures that were inhabited by nodes. Also identical were the columns that held up the roof and separated the two aisles from the central nave. In the middle was the intimidating node itself.

Malafan's party walked up to the node and performed a salute. Malafan and the sergeant's were a simple nod. The bot and the nuns genuflected deeply.

"On recovery of the crystal lattice," Lord Malafan reported, "we encountered a strange person claiming to be a Head Interpreter. This person attempted to acquire the crystal lattice but was unable to do so thanks to your intervention."

By some unspoken cue, Sergeant Eskol stepped forward. "However, the appearance of your fliers was unexpected. By the time we brought our mounts under control, the strange person had vanished, with your fliers in pursuit."

The bot's report was more detailed but less conclusive. Spencer's truck wasn't particularly new, but it was modern. Any trace of it was long gone by the time the analysis team had showed up. "We did, however," it said, "find evidence that the crystal box had been tampered with."

This caused the sergeant to open his mouth, probably to protest, but Malafan put his hand on the other man's arm and faintly shook his head. *Not now* was a pretty easy signal for her to decode.

Things only got rolling when the nun or priestess or whatever she was provided her report.

"Oh, such words we've heard this lord say about you, All-Giver. This man is not a proper worshipper at all! And then they ignored the rituals..."

Malafan and the sergeant didn't seem concerned about these accusations. If anything, they were bored by it all. It probably wasn't his first run-in with this peculiar sisterhood. Kim didn't understand his reaction. The lady was quite the performance artist. It was almost an interpretive dance.

"...and then he *offered* the stranger the entire holy lattice, and she said she'd destroy it!"

"That is *not* what happened," Lord Malafan said loudly. "I had no reason to doubt that person was an Interpreter."

This caused the node to speak up in a low, metallic voice. "Whoever it was does seem to have known at least as much about Interpreters as you do, Lord Malafan." The node's plates and clockwork sped up noticeably. Malafan didn't flinch. He might not be a proper worshipper, but he was impressing her more and more as a leader. "Which unfortunately doesn't provide conclusive proof of this person's identity."

He stepped back, affronted. "That was no native."

"You fell victim to the person creating the illusion."

"It was *not* an illusion," he fired back.

"It was."

"But—"

"Enough, Lord Malafan," the node commanded. "This is the case of a creative brave bandit. You will take the standard steps to find the criminal while making your domain safe for your people. Do you understand?" With each command, Lord Malafan grew stiffer, straighter. His sergeant was pained and angry. "Do you understand?"

Kim had only seen bottled up anger that strong in one other place: a mirror. "Yes, node. I understand." He turned and marched out of the hall with his sergeant in tow.

The recording ended.

"Well," Spencer said as he sat back in his camp chair. "Lord Brother Bear got his ears pinned back."

"But can we exploit it?" Mike asked, then turned to her. "What do you think?"

She had carefully situated her own chair so that they couldn't see her left side, her left hand. If they did, there wouldn't be a next move. She had to carefully trace exactly three figure-eight patterns on that side of her chair's seat.

But the normal release didn't come. She couldn't speak. *She wasn't finished.*

"Kim?"

One more, and it was more than half a prayer, *please, only one more.* She traced it again and was set free. But her answer wasn't a good one. "I don't know."

She had to stop this. It was getting worse again, and now it was interfering with her ability to plan.

A snap of déjà vu hit her hard. This place, this clearing. She'd been here before. It was ridiculous and plainly false, but then…it wasn't. It reminded her strongly of another place she'd been in before. Kim knew it but couldn't quite put her finger on it. The last time she'd been stuck in the woods far from home was in China. But that had been a hyper-real realm, not an actual forest.

So that wasn't right. Then she realized the truth. This was the first time she'd gone off into the boonies since Bolivia. She was a teenager then; they were all slaves, and hope was fading fast. That final, desperate run into the forest. They were fleeing for their lives, again. Relying on her to save the day.

Again.

Calling it traumatic was the understatement of the century. The subsequent five years had been spent on the run, but always close to home. She lived as a hermit in cities. Only in this moment, after all these years, so many changes and on a completely different planet, did she realize that her life on the run would've been simpler and *cheaper* if she'd spent it deep in remote woods instead of Northern Virginia's suburbs. But it had never occurred to her. She'd blocked that option out.

And here she was, sitting in a forest for the first time since then, slowly losing her marbles. Her subconscious was triggered by this place. It manifested as her OCD and infected her dreams.

Her dreams.

They'd all been about the escape, about those miserably cold camps and starvation and the terrible certainty that she'd die waterlogged and frozen. Again, it had taken this long for her to work that out. But it was so obvious now.

A plan fell into her lap. "Spencer, I need you to scout further south. See if you can find another crippled node. Now that we know what to look for, they should be easier to spot. If you find one, mark it, but please leave it alone."

He waved his hands and chuckled. "No argument there." He pointed at Mike. "What about hubs?"

The *need* boiled up in her again, and she didn't have time to hide it. She stared openly at her hand as she traced a figure eight with her fingertip.

One.

Two.

Three.

Four.

She breathed out a shaky sigh as it released her. Spencer and Mike were staring at her with open horror. She couldn't blame them, but if she was right, they wouldn't have to put up with it for much longer.

"Yeah," she said to Mike. "In case you didn't notice already, my tics have come back. It's worse now. Using my power doesn't work anymore. But I think I know how to fix it for good, which is why I need Mike to stay here."

She faced him squarely, heart flooding with the knowledge that she would not have to face this alone. He would be there. He'd always be there. She twisted the rings on her finger and reminded herself of this simple truth.

I am not alone anymore.

She smiled and got a worried but hopeful smile in return. "I'm afraid it's time to welcome you to my nightmare."

*

Lucid Dreaming was an extension for the sleep app she'd been using all this time. *Become a different you* was how the advertising pitched it. It would be like a realm, but with deeper meanings and the ability to tackle psychological issues with tools the brain itself supplied.

Her dreams had to be the key to figuring out what exactly was clogging up her mental pipes, and she needed to clean them out. Kim hadn't considered activating it until now because the extension was still in beta. But a beta version had to be better than living like this. Fortunately they only needed to download an access key to activate it, since downloading an entirely new app over the threads Mike still had back on Earth would've taken ages. Transmitting the key took plenty of time on its own.

Eventually they were ready. Spencer had already left on his morning scouting mission. It would take him most of the day to reach their next nearest target.

"I still think we should hack the app directly," Mike said as he sat next to their bed. "I don't like not being able to monitor what's going on." He wouldn't be going along for the ride. He'd keep her safe out here while she was asleep. They *were* still on an alien planet surrounded by natives, after all.

He started to say something else, but she held up a hand, which triggered the need again. This time she traced the figure-eights in the air.

One.

Two.

Three.

Four.

...

Five.

Able to speak again, she said, "We don't have the time. I'm getting worse."

He nodded and draped a handkerchief over her hand. "I'll be here, monitoring what I can. I love you."

She gripped it hard and laughed grimly.

"What?" he asked.

"There was a time when I thought this," she nodded toward the cloth held tightly between them, "not being able to touch people, was as bad as it could get. Whatever this is, it's worse." She pulled the sheet up around her, never letting go of her end of the handkerchief. "I love you too."

Kim made sure the app's lucid dreaming extension was enabled, closed her eyes, and activated it. As before, the sleep that fell on her was a warm, profound stillness.

*

"Hurry up, you little whore," Juan Quispe, son of Manuel Quispe and heir apparent to the family's sunrise drug empire, yelled at her through the back window of the truck she trudged behind. "We're almost to the next one."

She wanted to shout *you mean the next body?* but didn't dare.

Colque, the family's head assassin, was beside Juan. She had no way to predict how he'd react to a show of defiance. He might laugh it off.

He might cut her throat and laugh at the blood.

So she trudged a little faster until she was behind the trailer the truck was towing, trying not to think about its obscene contents. The drug cartel needed a population of cooperative locals. Some went along willingly. Others needed an incentive, and a child held hostage was an extremely effective one.

Yet occasionally some single person or family, usually after losing *other* children to sunrise addiction, would throw down the gauntlet and cooperate with police. Those police, no matter where they were in the country, had long ago been infiltrated, and so Colque would pay a visit to these ridiculously brave people, leaving only silence behind.

Silence and *surplus.*

That's what they called it. *Culling the surplus.*

"Their parents were idiots," he'd said the one time she flat-out refused to go along with them on their hunt. "We're improving the gene pool!"

She'd never wanted to spit on a person before that moment, never understood the urge, but it hit her so hard that she swallowed and fought for control. If she'd done it, she was certain a different set of hostages, the ones they were holding over her, would become surplus a few failing heartbeats later.

Even that small bit of defiance got her a quick slap. With Colque's lightning reflexes, she hadn't seen it coming, didn't know it had happened until her head was turned the wrong way and a hot flare of touch madness tore at her mind. His favorite knife was at her throat a moment later. It was cold and shaved her skin like a razor. "You get a pass this time, you little bitch, but you're coming along for the cleanup."

There had been three bodies so far, scattered across fallow soybean fields—broken, still dolls lying in unnatural positions on the ground. Loading the limp bodies into the trailer was the first time she had ever touched another human being without pain.

She didn't know how many more there were.

"Get ready," Juan shouted, "another one on the right!"

But when she moved to that side, it wasn't the body of a dead child. It was Mark, who should've been locked up with the rest of the Rage crew, not lying dead in the middle of a beanfield.

Kim barely had time to register the shock when he opened his eyes. "Hi, there, Wren!" He stood up, pushing broken bones into place, ignoring the open wound on his side. "Nice day for a walk, eh?"

This is a dream. You are dreaming.

Which was interesting as an intellectual concept but didn't do her much good with this zombie version of her alternate father standing next to her. "Not…really?"

"You'll be fine." He clicked his tongue loudly. "Hey, you two, keep going, but not too fast. We'll follow."

The inside of the truck was no longer visible to her. What were once sharp outlines of two men now were liquid shadows.

You can control this. Explore it.

The truck moved forward but much more slowly. The dirt under her feet leveled out so that she could walk without stumbling. *Okay,* she thought, *maybe control isn't so bad.*

"What we've accomplished is incredible, and it's all down to you, Wren, our little songbird."

Kim scoffed, but then the scene changed. She was no longer behind the truck. She was in a seat inside *Pride's Lair,* not behind a wagon full of dead bodies. This was a different time, an earlier time, long before the truck. They were discussing their next moves. It was a dream, yes, but also a memory. Unlike zombie Mark walking beside her, this had actually happened. "It can't last forever," she said.

"Of course it will," Michiko said from across the table. "And it will get easier after you turn eighteen. No more school to get in the way. We've just attracted too much attention for us to operate in the US now."

"This is a capitalist world," Lourdes replied, sitting next to Kim, "There *are* other targets for us to choose from?"

They wouldn't listen to her. Without a doubt, what they were doing was unsustainable. The world *would* catch on and they *would* get caught, and she *would* end up in prison where pat downs were routine and unavoidable. But they didn't care. They only wanted to keep the ride going.

The part of her that was lucid, not in the dream but watching it, was puzzled. She'd considered this to be a memory but now wasn't sure. If it was a memory, this was the first time she'd visited it since it happened.

Sitting in the lair, Young Kim had a nasty idea. They wouldn't listen to her? Fine.

The scene changed again. Or rather, both scenes happened at the same time.

As she trudged behind the now fully real truck after stacking another body in the back, Kim went through the same memory in her head. The reason she and her friends were there.

The reason they were dead.

Behind her, she heard a rumbling fizz as *Pride's Lair* was bathed in a kaleidoscope of colored light. The same sound was with her in the field, the same colors danced across the truck, flashed in Colque's mad eyes as he grinned at her.

No.

Sitting on the couch in *Pride's Lair,* Young Kim knew they'd love the idea because it was her trademark: *the unexpected.* "Do you know who I think we should hit next?"

The same memory thrashed her as the trailer pulled away to the next victim. Kim had to keep moving, but her legs wouldn't budge.

It couldn't have happened like this.

The kaleidoscope grew bright behind her on that horrible field, the sound changing to a seductive chord. *Retreat. Survive.*

As one, they turned to her in *Pride's Lair,* like they always did. They considered Mark was the leader, but all he did was organize. Kim was where the ideas came from. This one at least would teach them to stop relying on her and think for themselves.

"Next one coming up on the left!" Juan shouted from the truck, his voice thin in the distance. And then not. She hadn't stopped trudging after all. She was behind a wagon load of children's bodies. A realization began to dawn on the Kim watching the scenes unfold and the reason why they were here, why the disaster that would eventually see the murder of her second cherished family could not be.

The noise and the kaleidoscope were right behind her in *Pride's Lair*, but Young Kim couldn't turn around.

"Well don't leave us hanging," Henry said in his big, booming voice. "Tell us."

Don't tell them.

She'd tell them. Then they'd learn. The hard way, the way all good lessons were learned.

The memory as she stood in the field was as real as the feeling of the air leaving her throat as she said the words in *Pride's Lair*.

This couldn't have happened.

It did happen.

"Sunrise sucks, and the business is run by stupid gangsters."

This was not the reason. She'd forgotten this, because it could not be the reason.

The kaleidoscope and noise crawled over her, a touch she should not feel.

"Let's take down the Bolivians."

Kim spun around to face the kaleidoscope that was driving her mad and realized her mistake too late. The lights and sound weren't *driving* her mad.

They *were* madness.

She was the one who chose this path. They would all be alive if it wasn't for her.

"Okay," Young Kim said, knowing how it would play out with the certainty of an angry teenager, and the Kim watching the dream who knew how it *had* played out couldn't stop her. "First we—"

The kaleidoscope of light collapsed over everything, and the dream scenes dissolved. Instantly she had no fear. This was not strange. This was comfort. An old friend she'd lost touch with long ago. Colors and sound. Completely familiar. But it couldn't be described. No words. There were no words. She'd lost her words. They were gone now, like before. When she was a child, she had no words. There were only actions, nondescriptions.

Memories.

"Mother's crying. Can't you hear?" Colin said. Nicholas made me stand up, and he opened the door to the back yard. We went out and Nicholas closed the door behind him. Nicholas smelled like soap and the outside. You need to be quiet now, we're not going downstairs yet. But she said I had to go upstairs, that we had to do what she said. I won't do it. But she said for us all to do it, didn't she, Nicholas?

Kim, are you all right? Can you hear me?

I need to go downstairs now. We went down to Myra's house. I liked to smell Myra's house.

Kim, what's wrong?

Mother was gathering tomatoes in the garden, groaning. Cats sat at the edge of the garden and watched her.

Kim, you're scaring me, please say something.

One of the birds flew down and pecked at the tomatoes in the basket. In the bushes at the edge of the garden some kittens cried. John was playing in the dirt. John had some toys, and he and Nico fought, and then I had the toys, and Nico touched me, and I cried.

Kim, I'm so sorry, but I have to try to break you out of this.

I got into bed where Nico already was. He was asleep. Mama took a plastic divider and laid it between Nico and me. Stay on your side now, Nico is little, and you don't want to—

A hand touched hers, and the world shattered.

Chapter 20
Helen

His full name was Sornik Fir'Ortun, and he was the first gangster Helen had ever observed up close who wasn't already in handcuffs and prison coveralls. He was also an alien. The latter should've been a much bigger deal than the former, but that was not the case. As Mike was constantly pointing out, bemian society traits crossed those of Earth's in strange places.

Organized crime was one of them.

She'd been around pallun long enough now that she recognized a quality environment suit when she saw one. It was quite different from the one Mr. Sha'Katenden wore. Sornik's was new, sleek, and drew admiring looks as they walked to his personal transport. Yes, personal transport. The nodes still seemed to control it, but it was for him alone.

The Meronim who passed by on the way naturally never rose above a sour glance. Helen didn't know what might make Meronim smile. Maff claimed it wasn't possible.

It was Sornik's attitude that was so strikingly similar to high-ranking criminals back home. He knew everyone in this neighborhood, and they all knew him. His smile and swagger were pallun—mostly consisting of wing gestures and tone of voice—but easily recognizable. There was also the unmistakable undercurrent of menace. He wasn't their friend. He was their patron, and they were his clients. There was the slightest kowtow in the interactions. Sornik *expected* to be greeted this way, and if he wasn't, say by a

Meronim whose disgusted huff was a little too loud, Sornik unleashed a torrent of verbal abuse that was obscene, scandalous, and funny. Where Spencer swore the way other people breathed, Sornik used profanity as a way to exclude those who didn't please him, yet at the same time including the rest in on the joke.

In other words, he wasn't only a violent gangster. He was a *charming* violent gangster. That she might grow to like an obvious and active criminal was an idea she stomped on as soon as her threads produced it. Helen was a cop, and being on the other side of the galaxy didn't change that. But she *was* on the other side of the galaxy, not an actual cop anymore, and doing research that required the occasional charming gangster.

So she decided to do what Spencer regularly told her to do and lightened the fuck up.

"Well who knew?" Sornik said as they entered the vehicle. "You can smile after all."

Interpreter threads working their magic again. But there was more to it than that. What a smile meant in general was provided by the thread. The fact she didn't do it a lot was a deduction he'd reached on his own. And it was correct. Clever and observant. She would need to be careful around this one.

"Yes," she replied. "I do smile. Sometimes."

This seemed to impress him. "Duly noted." The well-appointed but otherwise nondescript vehicle moved into street traffic. "So remind me again what it is you're searching for?"

"Ancient histories. The earlier the better. I'm trying to get as close to the Refounding as I can. Before it would be ideal."

"Hah, you and the rest of the galaxy," said in a way that had whatever passed for dollar signs attached to it. "Define close."

Researching what was rare but possible was the first thing she'd done. "A thousand years on either side of the Refounding would be ideal."

"After we can do. Before? There is no before, lady. It took two million years for the galaxy to recover from whatever it was that happened."

"Things have survived. Ruins. Legends, songs, epics."

"Yeah, but that's all bullshit. And trust me, I know bullshit. I kinda make my living off of it, if you know what I mean."

She did, but that didn't make Helen wrong. "Three of the ancient galactic organizations survived: La'fan, Interpreters, and the AC network. If I can find early enough accounts, I might be able to uncover traces of others."

He sighed. "Well if you want early post-Refounding, you have come to the right place."

The vehicle went past a guarded gate and into an industrial park with dozens of identical warehouses inside. They were neither fancy nor decrepit, giving the impression of moderate age and use. Chinese cities had places like it by the thousands. She wondered if the gate guard might be a bit of a giveaway, so she asked Sornik about it.

He gave another shrug. "It helps keep the riffraff out. We leave it unguarded, and then anybody thinks they can have a go at us."

"You can't automate it?"

"Automation is for amateurs. Our clients appreciate that we have the pallun required to put soldiers in harm's way for them. Plus, who ya gonna trust, some antiquated AC node, or a cousin who knows that if he fucks it up, he ends up part of the foundations of a new office?"

Helen had no answer for that and so remained silent. She followed Sornik through the pallun-sized door, past a quartet of much less well-appointed pallun who seemed to be playing a card game of some sort. They greeted him in a more relaxed way than the townspeople and shopkeepers did in the city.

Not clients. Employees.

When they got to an inner door, Sornik grabbed a device from a small shelf next to it. "Gonna have to deactivate your phone now. Can't have you taking pictures of the merchandise." The interpreter thread vanished after the phone shut off, so Sornik switched to Standard. "Good. Now, we explore."

She spoke Pallundian well enough to converse in it but decided to hold that card in reserve. "Lead the way," she replied in Standard.

Helen tried to set aside her expectations, but it was harder than she thought it would be. China's infrastructure was the finest in the world, so its warehouses were a marvel of organization and automation. This…was much more like the back room of a massive pawn shop. It bore more than a passing resemblance to the back room of Kim's locksmith shop where she kept endless boxes of antique locks and the parts they needed to work. Except that was basically a walk-in closet. This?

This was an entire world.

Whole sections were dedicated to furniture, lighting, dinnerware, textiles, vehicles, and much more. Some of it was blocked off by pressure doors. "We do business with the low-temp, low-grav community" was all Sornik would say about that.

"And all of this is illegal?"

He stopped and turned around, amused but also a little insulted. "We're not crooks. We are businessmen who deal in goods of confused license status."

"I see." As far as self-justifications went, it wasn't any worse than what a gangster back home would say. She reminded herself she wasn't here to arrest anyone; she was searching for evidence of Andromeda.

They turned another corner, and Helen almost stumbled. This section, from its crowded floors to the towering shelves that touched the ceiling, was covered in gems and jewelry. She would never be mistaken for a tittering debutante salivating over a shiny bauble, but Helen did have an appreciation for fine craftsmanship. Bemians had been in the jewelry business for millions of years, and this section of the warehouse showed that off in glittering detail.

Sornik noticed her standing still and laughed. "Here," he said, and rummaged a manipulator through a box. He pulled out a gold necklace with a deep red jewel hanging from it. "Consider it a gift."

As a good communist, she was far from believing in the ancient superstitions of her ancestors, but for her first bemian gift to be made of red and gold, deeply ingrained symbols of luck in Chinese culture, was almost too much of a coincidence.

"Do you like it?"

The gem was cut in an exquisite pattern Helen had never encountered, not only facets but ridges and valleys, textures that should be impossible to create.

"It's beautiful."

This seemed to please him. The last traces of annoyance at her *illegal* quip faded away. "Consider it a gift. It'll help you keep Sornik here near to your heart, yeah?"

She put the gem on underneath her shirt. It warmed against her skin. She felt a blush and hoped his thread wouldn't interpret it for him. It wasn't only humans who could do unexpected things. "I think it will."

He turned around and resumed walking. "Not far now. Ah, here we are."

The warehouse's book...well, documentation...section couldn't be more different from the library. There were no neat stacks, no search engines, no handy guides to organize by subject matter. It was bare piles of bemian books and media.

Endless piles.

"How do you find anything?" she asked.

This got her a Pallundian smirk, a kind of twisting of the wingtips. "Observe the shelf endings."

Although the shelves themselves were crammed with books, the ends held small artifacts. Some were stones, others cloth, and then she realized... "It's all Meronim apparel?"

"Yup! The holier, the better. That's another reason for the guards. Sometimes a new generation of fanatics finds out their sacred clothing is being used by guys like us to organize things like this." He slapped manipulators together. "That's when we get to rip some wings. So," he turned around, "the first thousand after the Refounding. Follow me."

What they found at first were older copies of books she'd already examined: histories about chronicles that detailed biographies which ensconced lists of sayings. Basically a game of telephone extended over millions of years. But those histories often gave the titles of the chronicles they'd used, and those often provided the titles of their biographical sources. Sometimes she got the name of the sayings list at the bottom of it all.

The first dedicated list of sayings they tracked down, a source that had been compiled only ten thousand years after the Refounding, was a revelation.

"It's not holographic," she said. The writing was startlingly flat. It'd only been a few weeks since she'd read conventional English or Chinese news sites, but Helen was now so used to the extra dimension of bemian script that this discovery was briefly disorienting.

This caught him off guard. "That's writing?"

"Yes. They must not yet have rediscovered the holo displays you all use today."

He shook his head. "Not having a proper holo page, that's why they're not worth much," Sornik replied as he looked at the book like it was somehow responsible for its own low value. "You're the first person I've come across to claim it was writing."

The sayings lists—they found two big ones right away and had the titles for many more—were unreadable to her. Sornik barely accepted it might be writing, so there likely were no bemian translation guides around. But deciphering them wouldn't be that hard. These compilations may use a writing system she didn't know, but the books that led to them, more importantly quoted directly from them, did. It would be a task no different than that of Champollion translating hieroglyphics. But with Helen's threads allowing her to multitask, it would go much faster. It would be interesting to find out if the interpreter thread bound to her currently inactive phone could make anything of it.

"I can't use my phone to record these titles," she said. "I should make a list. I need to know how much it will all cost." Judging by the reaction they'd had earlier today to Maff's demonstration, Helen could cover any purchase by trading them for a few C-pop songs.

"I've been keeping a list for you this whole time. We'll talk about cost later," Sornik replied. "Do you want me to get a hand truck?"

She could begin the work right away, a translation task equal to Champollion or Needham. "Yes, please."

He looked upward. "Hey, Poolin," Helen looked up too. He chuckled and pointed at his ear. He was making a call. "Poolin? You there? I need you to bring a cart around. Poolin?" There was a pause and then he swore softly. "Bithern? You around?" He paused. "Bithern, I swear…if you two—"

With a quick series of mechanical clacks, the warehouse was plunged into darkness.

"What the fuck?" Sornik said softly.

This was no time to rely on Standard. She switched to Pallundian. "I may have forgotten to mention, I think I'm being followed."

She heard rather than saw him turn toward her. "What are you, some kind of Interpreter?"

"That's an interesting ques—"

The unmistakable sound of a door slamming shut boomed out in the distance.

"Poolin? Bithern?" Sornik asked loudly. "Where are you guys?"

There was again the rushing of a silent predator closing in on its prey. This time it was larger. "We need to get out of here." Two more doors, much farther away, slammed shut. "How many doors do you have in this place?"

"Not that many," he said, worried. "Not that I know of, anyway. Who do you think is following you?"

They didn't have time for this. "I don't know yet, but we need to get out of here." It was so dark she couldn't see her hands in front of her face. Sornik had turned off her phone, so she had no way to enhance her vision. "Can you see anything?"

"Just a sec." He slowly turned in a full circle. "I don't get it. The power never goes out. I didn't know there's a way to do it—" He stopped. "*Who* did you say was following you?"

They were getting closer; she felt their inaudible steps and knew without a doubt that if she could see, they would be creeping across the ceiling as well as the floor. "I don't know." Then she heard *his* footsteps moving away. "Wait, where are you going? I can't see!"

"Shh..." he whispered as a probe gently gripped her shoulder and started to guide her.

"What do you see?" she whispered back, bumping against heavy things that'd been left on the floor.

"I don't know. It doesn't make sense."

"Can you turn my phone back on?"

"No, we leave the switch by the door."

The air shifted in front of them, like a massive beast moving past. Sornik stopped and crouched, so Helen did too. The longer she stayed in this darkness the more she felt them. They were everywhere. She didn't dare turn around because at least one of them stood directly behind her; she felt its gaze on her back.

Then, in the distance, someone banged what sounded like a stick against a piece of metal, or maybe a bell of some sort. A deep gong sound echoed through the warehouse. Then another one to the left rang out, then another to the right. It wasn't a mechanism; the clanks weren't synchronized perfectly. Each stick was held by a hand. Each clank was that hand striking a gong, slowly, slower than her heart rate anyway, which amped up with each strike.

On her shoulder, Sornik's manipulator started to shake.

"What do you *see*?" she whispered.

"Nothing right now."

"What about before?" They both flinched with each clang. Someone was out there, more than one.

The clanging increased in tempo, now accompanied by the sound of feet rushing toward them. "Fuck this." More manipulators landed on her shoulders, and then Helen's feet left the ground. She barely stifled a scream as he placed her on his back. "Hang on!"

The suit lurched, and she scrabbled around until her hands found the bases of a couple of manipulators. "Don't go that way they're behind us, too!"

"There's nothing behind us, sister, I don't see anything."

Two bright lights, *two eyes*, opened in the middle distance in front of them. "Shit!" Sornik lurched down a different aisle, away from them. "How do they do that? I can't see them."

"I don't know!" The clangs increased in tempo again, seemed to be coming closer, in fact. Another set of eyes opened in front of them, cutting off another way out. They were red and closely spaced. Helen could swear she heard the sound of a deep, menacing chuckle.

She realized what was happening. "Sornik, stop!"

"No way, sister. We gotta get out of here."

This time he had to listen. *"They're herding us!"*

Sornik skidded to a stop. "Okay, plan B." Then he whispered, "Be quiet!" The manipulators all around her extended straight up, and then her stomach lurched as they lifted Sornik up the shelves. Below them, Helen thought she saw shadows, and the clanks never stopped their regular increasing rhythm.

Sornik used his manipulators and legs to crab walk along the tops of the shelves, occasionally squeezing flat where the goods almost reached the ceiling. At one point, she had to turn her head to the side to keep her nose from scraping it. Then Helen made out a shape in the pitch-dark gloom.

A window.

Ahead was a classic clerestory, an upward extension of the ceiling holding regularly spaced windows. Normally used to provide natural lighting, now they only showed stars and a smear of moonlight.

It also provided enough light for her to see motion behind them, shapes in the distance at their level.

Closing in.

The clanking reached a fever pitch.

Helen gripped harder as Sornik leapt across empty space and grabbed the sill of the nearest window. His body swung freely, giving her a reason to scream that she didn't dare indulge.

Below them, the floor was covered with crawling bodies.

The window didn't open, and Sornik swore. He moved with a ropey lurch to the next one, and then to the next. Each time Helen's grip, now covered in sweat, slipped a little more. "Sornik! I can't hold on!"

He shouted in triumph as the third window opened.

Helen's grip slipped completely. She fell toward a floor far below her, covered with who knew what. She screamed, a sound that tore her throat apart.

Manipulators grabbed her around the waist. "Gotcha!" Sornik heaved her and then himself through the window and out onto the roof.

They lay there panting for a moment, then she lifted her head. The only sound was the rush of distant traffic. "The noise stopped."

With soft clacks, the lights turned on inside the warehouse.

"Hey, boss!" someone shouted below them. "What're you doing up there?"

"Bithern?" Sornik shouted back. "Where the fuck is Poolin?"

"He's right here," he said, and the older pallun walked into view from beneath them.

She scrambled off Sornik's back and looked through the window.

Aside from a few items scattered on the floor, knocked off as they clambered through the shelves, there was nothing.

She turned to Sornik, who silently shrugged at her. "I'm not goin' back in there. Come on." He carefully guided her to an access ladder, which they both used to reach the ground. "Where the fuck were you guys?" he shouted as they climbed.

"We went to get more gabbashan," Poolin replied. "What, were you washing the windows?"

When they reached the ground, Sornik stomped up to Poolin. "Why weren't you answering the goddamn phone?"

He shrugged. "It hasn't rung. See?"

Without a phone, Helen couldn't participate in their shared vision channel, but by the way Sornik's body language went from rage to confusion, it seemed obvious that Poolin was showing him his phone's activity list. "Wait a minute," Sornik said, then turned to Helen. "I *did* call these chuckleheads, didn't I?"

Now it was her turn to shrug. "No phone, remember?"

"Really, boss," Poolin said. "What were you doin' up there? We couldn't get in. All the doors were locked."

"Not anymore," Bithern said a short distance away as he opened one.

Sornik marched through it, across the atrium, and threw open the door to the warehouse proper. They'd crowded in behind him, but there was nothing to see. The warehouse was cold and silent.

Sornik turned around with the phone deactivator in one of his manipulators. "Poolin, call Toraz. I need a squad here, the sooner the better." He waved the tool at her, and her shared vision channel came to life with a stream of diagnostics. "Bithern, search outside, see if you can find any unlocked doors." He turned to her. "And you, who did you say was following you?"

"I don't know. I wasn't sure I *was* being followed until tonight. I thought I was going crazy."

"Yeah, well if you're crazy then I am too." A vehicle rushed into the lot and four rough-looking pallun climbed out. Toraz's organization was quick. "It's been a long night. I'll get one of the boys to take you home, how's that?"

"I'd like to help search if I can."

"This is our turf. We'll handle it." He then politely but firmly directed her to an empty vehicle. "I'll see what I can do about the books after we get this figured out."

"Wait!" She said as he started to shut the door. "What did you see in there?"

He turned back to the warehouse, now with three more car's worth of pallun searching through it. The shudder was faint but unmistakable. "I don't wanna talk about it."

"But—"

He waved her silent with his manipulators. "Ah-ah, don't want to ruin our perfect relationship, do we? You take care and keep the clouds underneath you."

He shut the door with a solid thunk, and the vehicle drove her away.

Chapter 21
Spencer

He didn't have that spooky bullshit invisible mode that Mike did, but he'd spent plenty of hours learning how to walk through the woods quietly. Deer and turkeys didn't hang around if a hunter was stomping toward them like an elephant.

A few passes with the drone helped some but not as much as he hoped. They weren't useful when the ground was covered with trees, but it did at least help with navigating the farms. They laughed about it when it was over, and now Spencer couldn't help cracking a smile, but there was no way he'd repeat their little run across a rhino-thing pasture. Keeping out of the way of farmers, peasants, and merchants was also well advised.

Not that there was much of any of them now. The lack of nearby locals could mean anything. It could be that a planet being herded into modernity didn't have all that many people. The little walled town Mike had explored might be as big as they got around here. An entire planet full of tiny towns like Dumas…*medieval* tiny towns like Dumas…made him shudder.

He continued his nature catalog during his extended hike. He was gonna be here for a while, so Spencer decided he might make a book out of the whole thing. He wasn't obsessed by Nobel prizes the way Mike and Tonya were, but Spencer *was* the first human with any kind of outdoor skills to hike across this planet. It wouldn't be all that hard to write, since it'd mostly be holos and pictures.

The variety of life here was a little disappointing. This wasn't a rain forest, and it wasn't out in the boonies. After the initial *oh shit, it's all new here* rush of entries, he'd found that, so far at least, it wasn't much more diverse than back home. It was different of course. Aside from rhino-things doing the job of cows, there were the giant lizards that were used to pull carts and plows, a deerlike analog he'd so far only seen the tracks of, and a half dozen smallish mammal-like critters that kept what passed for bugs around here in check. No skunks so far, none that he could smell anyway.

The drone identified a pair of likely sites in a small valley several hours' hike away from their new base camp. He was grateful for the target-rich environment, but it did seem a little puzzling that there *were* so many targets. He would've brought it up with Mike, but what with Kim being extra-special crazy lately, there never seemed to be a good time. Still, it was going to have to be discussed at one point or another.

The going got trickier as the day wore on. The terrain changed from flat farmland to the valley itself. The tracks around him grew more diverse, too, a sure sign he'd gone from a domestic biome to a wilder one. Not for the first time, he wished he could set up motion-tracking cameras in these woods. It'd be wild to find out if the animal making tracks like a giant armadillo *was* a giant armadillo. He'd seen skeletons of those in a museum and had been impressed as hell.

Further up the trail, he found a footprint.

It wasn't a human footprint, but rather a Telirian's bear-meets-monkey-shaped boot sole, too wide and short to be mistaken for a human's. Whoever they were, they'd passed through recently and alone. They were also the first sign of Telirians he'd seen since he moved away from the farms this morning. He or she was also headed in the same direction he was. Spencer had gotten a little lax about being quiet since he'd moved away from Telirian civilization. Now he took it seriously again.

Whoever this was seemed pretty comfortable. They weren't running, anyway. The rest was guesswork. There was the whole

Telirians aren't humans angle, but there was also the fact that he was better at tracking animals than people. If he was to guess, it might be a short male or tallish female. The strides weren't that far apart. They hadn't managed to weigh a Telirian, so he had no idea if the track depth was close to a human's, but if it was, then this one was on the lighter side.

Who the hell knew, it might be Tapov or Malafan's runaway daughter Sarewith, or both since he was pretty sure they were the same person. He could come across a for-real princess. Wouldn't that be the shit?

The tracks got confused with other ones as he traveled further into the valley. Some kind of herd had come through after his Telirian and obscured the tracks. These new guys were small, probably not much bigger than a squirrel, but there were a lot of them.

There was the unmistakable sound of swishing in the leaves behind him. Spencer spun around and found what had to be the maker of the tracks. Well, one of them anyway. It was in fact roughly the size of a squirrel, but that's about all it had in common with those fuzzy-tailed rats. This one looked like a miniature crocodile. The first warning bell went off. The second went off when it yawned. It was half head—a head fucking filled with needle-sharp teeth.

Then it roared.

Or rather, let out a ragged squeak. Spencer started to laugh, but then the damn thing charged him, teeth first. He'd had to deal with an occasional charging boar out in the deer woods. Those were big and scary, but they couldn't split their head half open to show a dozen rows of teeth. This one could. Spencer might've been ten times its size, but having it rush at him like that was more than enough to get his feet moving in the opposite direction.

It roar-squeaked again, much closer behind him. The little shit was fast. There were a couple of hissing snaps as it tried to bite an ankle or a foot. That would suck ass. But then he heard it back off. Alligators back home were big chargers but not fast over long distances. Spencer glanced behind him. It'd stopped. It roar-squeaked again.

This time, though, the entire forest in front of Spencer roar-squeaked back.

It hadn't been giving up, it'd been rushing him into an ambush. Dozens of the little beasts ran out in all directions. He'd managed to dodge bull rhinos, bear men, and antique alien drones, only to get eaten by squirrel-sized alligators?

Fuck that.

He bound two steps up a large rock as he ran past and then leaped toward a tree trunk, hitting it hard enough to wind him. Gasping through the pain, he shimmied up, grabbing branches as he went. The bark was like sandpaper and had more give than he was used to, but the branches themselves were strong and didn't bend under his weight. He went up until they were too thin and floppy to go any further.

He peered down into a sea of hungry eyes and squeaking mouths.

He didn't have his gun with him, but it wouldn't have mattered. It would take care of about five percent of the snapping squirreligators now prowling hungrily below. The right tool for this job would be a simple .22 rifle and a case of ammo. It was all a varmint hunter ever needed, and no matter what they looked like, that's exactly what these things were. Carnivorous pack-hunting varmints were a novelty he could've done without.

Aliens. Fuckers had to be different one way or another.

He'd planned to spend the night out here anyway and had plenty of supplies, plus enough rope to tie himself to the trunk of this tree. Camping on the ground was an iffy proposition anyway, and now that was right out with Grinny McAllisquirrel and his merry band prowling about. They'd eventually get bored and hungry and go hunting elsewhere. He now knew they made a great big fucking mess wherever they went, so he'd be able to avoid them easily enough from here on out. If they were still around in the morning, he'd call Mike to bring the truck.

Except he couldn't. The jump into the tree had smashed his phone. Great. Well, he'd wave at the drone when Mike sent it searching for him in the morning.

He kicked back, pulled out his e-cig, and puffed away while observing yet another of those quaint life forms this beautiful little backwater of a planet had on offer. Mostly that behavior consisted of digging like a bunch of furious terriers all around the tree, at a guess, trying to undermine it and make it fall over. Yeah, right. The root structure was strange but easily recognizable. And huge. He couldn't get it out of the ground with dynamite.

There was a pop, and a squirreligator that'd been digging against one of the bigger roots went flying, yeeted into the sky by a high-pressure spritz of fluid that shot from the root. The smell of it, a combination of rotten eggs and Vaseline, drove the pack insane. Their digging, already fucking ferocious, kicked up to eleven.

At first the results were the same: a pop, and a squirreligator launched into orbit. It happened half a dozen times at least. He'd never seen anything like it.

Then one of the branches above him flopped down into his face. It'd deflated. In fact, all of the smaller branches now sagged like week-old party balloons. The tree was some kind of goddamn hydraulic container filled with fluid.

Fluid that the squirreligators were doing their level best to run dry.

It couldn't be completely hollow and be this tall, but it seemed pretty fucking obvious that it relied on internal pressure to provide a substantial part of its rigidity. And the squirreligators knew it. They were gonna bleed this thing dry until it fell over and provided them with a big fat Spencer snack. The ones who'd been catapulted now circled the outside of the pack, coated and stinking and slathering for a meal.

The trunk of the tree was now visibly sinking, slowly collapsing straight down like an elevator. There were no other trees near enough to reach. He'd have to make a run for it, stomping on their stupid heads as he went. It was a shitty plan, but it was all he had. If he jumped, he might make it to the edge of the pack with enough of a gap to leg it out of here.

Yeah, right.

A lump too heavy to be a deflated branch thumped him on the head and then rolled away. His heart stopped for a country second because maybe one of the 'gators had jumped for it. But then he recognized what it was: a knotted rope leading up. He began to question the who and where but then the tree lurched sideways.

Never one to let a get-the-fuck-out-of-here opportunity go to waste, he grabbed it and scrambled upward as the trunk made its final flop to the ground. Now committed, he looked up to discover a cliff overhang a couple of dozen feet overhead. It'd been blocked by the branches, and he'd been too busy waiting to become 'gator kibble to see it.

Below, the squirreligators tore apart the tree trying to find him. One of them looked up and let loose one of those not-close-to-funny-anymore warbles, then he jumped for the end of the rope. That one missed, and so did the next few. The resulting pile was the world's ugliest flea circus. Spencer turned and resumed climbing, so he only felt it when one of them managed to grab the rope.

A quick glance down showed it climbing maybe a little faster than he was, bloody determination in its alien eyes. That sight ramped his heart rate up nicely. Spencer had no intention of losing his head start and climbed faster. Or tried to anyway, the knots were spaced too closely for him to find a good rhythm. Whenever one of the monsters below got lucky and landed on the rope, there was a jerk, and it pulled a little tighter in his hands. Half the pack must be back there now.

Didn't matter. He only had to stay out of the first one's range.

There was a loud, meaty slap below him and now a squirreligator was attached to his boot. That was seven different kinds of bullshit.

"Fucking thing *get the fuck off my boot, you fucking monster*!" he shouted, kicking it against the rope, which was now covered with frothing mouths full of teeth climbing toward him. Thrashing harder, he managed to make contact with the underside of the cliff and knock the one on his boot off, sending it tumbling into his buddies below. His arms ached, and his hands now shook with the adrenaline overdose Toothy McToothface gave him. Spencer had to get up this fucking rope right the fuck now, or he'd be the main course for the dinner party below.

Three more knots later, he managed to heave himself over the cliff's edge, squirreligators hot on his heels. He whipped out his utility knife and started sawing. "Fucking shitmonsters not gonna eat *this* fucking redneck for your goddamn lunch," he panted. A clawed mitt landed on the cliff edge as the rope parted. Weighed down by dozens of 'gators, it rocketed away. A second clawed mitt slapped down next to the first and then the arms heaved. Spencer spent a frantic minute kicking and swearing as he played a game of *no you fucking don't* with the final beast until it, too, vanished off the edge.

He collapsed on his ass and did nothing but pant heavily and stare at the cliff edge, daring another one of those shitheads to appear. Finally he got his breath back. A shadow fell on him from behind. He belatedly remembered the rope had to come from someone. He rolled sideways and then scrabbled frantically trying to get up, hold on to his knife, and not fall off the fucking cliff, all at the same time. The end result was him landing hard on his belly, winding him again.

What a way to make an entrance, he thought as he gasped.

Above him stood none other than Tapov, and perhaps Sarewith, instantly recognizable by the patterns in the fur on her arms. Behind her was maybe a dozen feet of flat grass and then the blank face of the cliff continued straight up, higher than Spencer could see.

She looked pretty pissed.

"Off worlder," she said in Standard, "I hope you have magic in that backpack of yours. Otherwise the rope you just cut was our only way off this rock." She stomped away.

Chapter 22

Tonya

The location of her assigned lab arrived the day after her lecture. She was better prepared for navigating the identical buildings of the campus now but still appreciated Tenor meeting her at the campus entrance and walking with her. It was out-of-body freaky that her newest friend was a walking, talking crane speaking a language she didn't understand on an entirely different planet, but only briefly. Kim and Mike both said it was crazy how quickly they got used to it all, and Tonya now agreed that they were right. Humans were famously adaptable, and this was no exception.

On the outside, her lab was exactly like all the other academic buildings. Things didn't change all that much until they got to the basement.

Labs in the basement. Yet another place where cultures crossed.

Hers was Lab Three, marked in her enhanced vision and on the door. The lock recognized the access token Hakonz, Dean Shakson's assistant, had provided and opened with an audible clack. Lights automatically turned on when she pushed the door in.

The space was both instantly recognizable and completely alien. The room was moderately sized by human lab standards, maybe ten feet by fifteen. Broad countertops lined the walls with cabinets above and below them, an island taking up the center. The lighting was the same bland all-encompassing white everyone hated back home, and the floor was a reassuring hard surface that looked for all the world like linoleum.

But that's where the similarities stopped. She recognized none of the equipment. It was a physics lab. There should be probes, sensors, scopes, gauges, and tons of electronics. It's possible that they were here. There were a lot of machines covering the counters. Tonya didn't recognize any of them, and she was supposed to.

"Are you okay?" Tenor asked.

She walked to the largest of the contraptions, which looked like someone had mashed an electron microscope and a toaster together in an autoclave. There had to be a power button somewhere. She pushed a large button next to what had to be the power cable and was rewarded with a meaty thunk. Lights came on and the Exponential Matrix Enhancer reported for duty in her enhanced vision.

"Yeah, I think so," she said, searching for the Help option in the EME's menus. She spotted the same switch in exactly the same spot on all the devices around her. Score one for over standardization. "I think I'll be fine."

"Well good," he said. "Let me know if you need anything. Free for lunch? Alta said he'd buy."

The centaur she'd saved had vowed that she would never have to pay for another meal in his presence again. It was cute in a vaguely chivalric way, especially when the knight came with the horse built in. "I'll bet he did. Sure"

"I'll let you know the details later," he said and then closed the door.

Tonya planned two experiments: one to prove Planck's constant and another to extend her tockion theory. The machines around her would almost by definition be unable to help with either of them.

When they were intact.

The truth was she didn't need all the lab equipment for their designed purposes. She needed their guts. The Planck experiment needed LEDs, resistors, and voltage and amp meters. Her tockion experiment needed lattice bridges, boxes, and a matrix. They both needed power supplies, controllers, and other minor bits and pieces. It was all here, buried inside the machinery in the lab.

And now, she thought, *science!* Tonya clapped her hands and faced the room. "Okay, my pretties, time to fly!"

*

She'd lost track of how much time had passed. Tenor knocked on the door and opened it. "You're not answering your messages..."

She stood up from the guts of the second EME she'd disassembled. "Sorry, I turned my phone off, but *thank you* for coming by."

He glanced at her, and then at the shelves and countertops behind her. "You...you took it...you *took it all apart*?"

Disassembling the lab equipment wasn't easy. The machinery didn't always open in ways that were obvious or safe. She had to go all the way back to the ship to get some proper welding gloves after a power supply that should've been completely discharged turned out not to be. She only got a shock and a scare from that one. The next might stop her heart.

She turned around and had to admit there was a hit-by-a-hurricane vibe to what she'd done to the machines. "Not *all* of it. Well, not yet." She shrugged. "I need parts."

This seemed to horrify him almost as much as the dissected lab equipment. His voiced pitched into a tweeting whisper. "How many parts do you need?"

She took a deep breath, trying to figure out the list in her head. It was a long one. She gently moved him out of the doorway and locked it behind her. "Let's go eat."

*

The Planck experiment was the simpler one. It was a common entry-level electronics and physics experiment back home and didn't require a ton of parts. Thank God. Integrating her own existing tockion experiments with their quantum bridges and lattices was the bigger challenge.

Bemians might not know how their quantum bridge tech worked, but whoever built it had been an expert. Delicate and incredibly small, they were able to transmit and translate massive amounts of data out of the quantum realm. And they needed to. Their prime use was transmuting quantum state information into signals analog electronics could use. It was like building a jet engine to drive a wagon with the horse still attached. And it worked!

Tonya couldn't fathom the reason they did it that way, but it allowed her to put that engine in her well designed but desperately underpowered tockion harness. And it wasn't only power. The bridges self-balanced with lightning speed and could be guided with extreme precision. She would be able to test the various theories that predicted what caused the mismatch in the results obtained during their battle in Arkansas, perhaps producing another type of tockion in the process, *without* the need for a homicidal galaxy to power it all.

That afternoon Tenor brought his whole crew along to visit her lab. "Nobody's ever seen the inside of any of the instruments," he said as he sheepishly opened the door, revealing them all. They were a bunch of cats who didn't know if a paper sack on the floor would be fun or would eat them. "We've never seen them."

For the most part, they were curious. In fact, if Tonya closed her eyes and listened to her thread's translation, she'd be hard pressed to tell them apart from college kids back home.

Then there was Kartaan.

"Did you really get permission before you took all this apart?"

Kartaan was Tenor's girlfriend, a pretty rhon who liked to color her wingtips the way Tonya put streaks in her hair. At first she thought that'd be a sign that they'd get along, but Kartaan was a jealous little thing who didn't appreciate a new female taking up Tenor's time.

"I didn't think I needed any, but I'll do that tomorrow."

She shook her feathered head. "It's really important that you do that. The AC network really gives the university really exclusive access to them. Most are really old. It's really crazy what you've done here."

A spoiled little rich girl, right down to the annoying speech patterns. "I will."

Just in case, she did it as she answered their questions

"What's *this*?" Alta asked, pointing at Tonya's Planck experiment.

Tonya explained it and then gave a brief demonstration. "Each time you run the numbers, you'll get the same answer even though the energies involved are different."

"*I* didn't," Kartaan said proudly. "They really vary around the third decimal."

Tonya now had sympathy for whoever Kartaan's academic adviser was—if that was a thing in bemian colleges. "Right. The machine itself introduces some errors, but we can account for those easily."

Tonya groaned inwardly at the reply to her permission request. *Your request will be reviewed in 30 to 60 days.* Wonderful.

Tonya had a feeling Kartaan knew exactly how long approval would take. It was time to do a little cleaning in the lab.

*

The knock on her door the next morning was much too authoritative for it to be Tenor or his friends. She opened it to none other than Dean Shakson and his assistant, Hakonz.

"Yes, yes," Dean Shakson said, though Tonya hadn't asked a question. "What, what, you see, irregularities and such. Not good, yes, what, not at all. Need to, how do they say it nowadays, take a spin around the local star, if you will. Yes, yes."

She looked at Hakonz, who shrugged. "There's been a report about irregularities in your lab. We were wondering if it would be possible to examine your work so far?"

They wouldn't understand the sly smile on her face, but Tonya let it shine anyway. It would be a cold day in hell when a debutante wannabe pulled one over on her, alien or not. "Of course, gentlemen." She opened the door. "Please, come in."

Dean Shakson rumbled in with that strange huffy tweediness he had about him. It filled the room almost as much as his rotund, shelled body. This wasn't Oogway from *Kung Fu Panda,* this was a male version of Minerva McGonagall from Harry Potter, with a shell on his back.

"What's this? What's this? Yes, yes. What, what? Where's the bits? The mess? Good show, this, jolly good show. Not a speck in the spick, this. Well done."

A shell on his back and marbles in his mouth. She looked at Hakonz again.

"The reports specifically mentioned the condition of your equipment?"

She shrugged, selling the idea of a simple academic out to prove an idea. "I don't know what they mean." She turned. "I only use it the way it's intended."

This got a raised eyebrow from Dean Shakson, who reached out and flicked the power button on one of the instruments. It whirred to life with reassuring ease. "Done right, what, what? Good use, that's swimming in the right lane, yes. Must've written the number down, that's it. Silly buggers would sink to the bottom knowing how to swim, I say, good show."

She mostly understood that one but silently checked with Hakonz just in case.

"The report must be in error. Students aren't always careful about filling out forms, as I'm sure you know."

She did, just like she knew which student should be on the menu when she introduced the gang to fried chicken.

"Jolly good progress are we, what, yes?"

"Very good, sir. I'm a little ahead of schedule. If you'd like—"

"Yes, yes, what, what? No need, no need. Fly too soon, what's the point of the migration, that's what I always say. Yes, right? Jolly good, see you then."

They were out the door before she had time to get Hakonz's translation, but again Tonya understood the main points. She leaned back against the door and let the tension loosen in her shoulders. She hadn't spent all these years around a human lockpick without learning a thing or two about locks. It took all night visiting other labs to gather up the spares needed to put hers back in working order, but she managed it. The entire place was now filled with vaguely malfunctioning equipment, but none of it was in her lab.

Time to get back to work.

*

She was torn between being relieved or upset that the crowd was much smaller this time.

"Physics technologies is hard," Tenor said. "What you're seeing out there are probably all the people who can practice it on the whole planet, and probably nearby systems as well."

Whereas the last time the auditorium was full, now there were probably fewer than thirty people out there. A good chunk of them were Tenor's friends, including the always charming Kartaan, ostentatiously using a virtual screen only she could see.

Tenor gave her a rhon version of a handshake for good luck and went back into the audience. She checked the experimental rig on its long, wheeled table for the *nth* time in case an alien fly had landed on it, or it'd disappeared and been replaced by moving boxes. Nervous? No reason for that. She was presenting the first new science in millions of years to an audience of actual extraterrestrials.

No reason to be nervous at all. And the experiment was still there after another check.

"And now, Physics Technologist Tonya Brinks."

She pushed the table out with a heavy shove. The experiment she was demonstrating took up its top half, while the one she'd built for herself took up the space underneath. Too many times she'd found enough parts for one experiment but not two, so they shared the rare equipment and most of a cabinet to house it all in.

It was heavier than it should be. Bemian tech had turned the normal weight equation inside out. Back home she would've been forced to custom build probably a dozen full-sized cabinets to house the amount of quantum lattice she'd need, and the LEDs and displays would be an afterthought. That didn't count the bridgework, which didn't exist back home. Here the lattices *and* the bridges fit in boxes the size of a deck of cards, but the LEDs and displays would've been recognizable to anyone from the 1950s. The galaxy was a strange place.

"Good evening," she said. The PA system automatically picked up her voice from an app on her bemian phone. "Tonight we will explore a solution to the ultraviolet catastrophe."

This was a place where bemian physics, a classical physics methodology, stopped working.

On Earth in the nineteenth century and in bemian space presumably millions of years ago, it was discovered that all matter emitted light. Matter with a lot of energy, like in a star, emitted light so energetic it could be seen. Or to be more precise, its spectrum was visible. Other exotic objects emitted more energetic spectrums of light, like ultraviolet or gamma. Matter with very little energy still emitted light. It was the consequence of being made up of particles which vibrated, protons and neutrons. The spectrum of her body's light was solidly in the infrared, for example.

By the late nineteenth century and, again, by bemians in the deep past, the distribution of the brightness of objects emitting light in the infrared, i.e., that were hot, was carefully mapped out experimentally by blocking anything *except* heat. The spectrum that resulted had a consistent characteristic shape when it was mapped on a graph. It sort of looked like a lop-sided bell curve.

Why the graph looked like that was a mystery. When that mystery was solved using classical physics, the equations that resulted predicted the spectrum perfectly, but only for merely hot objects. When the equations were used to predict the spectrum of more energetic objects, ones that emitted, say, visible light, they predicted a brightness that was way too high. Worse, they predicted the intensity of that light should eventually approach infinity as frequencies increased.

In other words, if the classical theories were true, the universe should consist of nothing but extreme-energy gamma radiation. Since the universe wasn't built like that, something was fundamentally wrong with classical physics. This was the ultraviolet catastrophe.

Humans worried at it until they figured it out, what became Planck's law. Bemians walked away. Or, more likely, were led away by the AC network.

She unveiled the experiment, a scruffy but recognizable version of the classic three LED test used to teach the principal back home.

"If you'll all load this equation into your phone," she said as she uploaded it to the auditorium's shared space, "we'll get started." Again Tonya was struck by the equation's simplicity, and its profound consequences. This was the sign posted at the start of a road named Quantum Mechanics, a science which humans were still working on centuries after its discovery. It had no business taking up less space than a recipe for chocolate cake.

Once the download counter quit moving—they couldn't all follow it to this level of detail, least of all a certain rhon still tapping away at the air—Tonya said, "And now, we begin." She flipped up the power switch, activated the signal path to the first LED, and pushed the button.

Nothing happened.

Tonya checked it all one more time. It was plugged in, switch thrown, no obvious loose connections. She flipped the power off and on again, then tried the button.

Again, nothing.

In the audience, a few people coughed or cleared their throat.

She'd been in situations like this. Most people had. It was a rule of demonstrations that things went wrong at the worst possible time. Stay calm, be methodical, take it in sequence. Tonya lifted a few access panels to test if the inner connections were good. They were.

Still nothing worked.

Tonya looked up, face hot and sweaty but not from working hard, and then she noticed it.

Kartaan had stopped playing in the air and now stared at her with a broad, unmistakable smile.

Chapter 23
Maff

She was supposed to be brokering an unprecedented cultural exchange deal, not rushing around in vehicle training. She was supposed to be paving the way for an impossible planet to join the galaxy and her people to again fly free, not risking it all on a career change she didn't want or need.

Then she remembered that Alcana pinnace, not seeing it or sitting in it or being driven around in it, but *driving it* in the *ETB*, a race famous to anyone who had anything to do with D-ships. It was so incredibly tempting. She'd be the first pallun and one of only a handful of females to compete. And it was an Alcana *2187*, a D-ship make and model that had won the race more times than any other. She had the talent, the tools, *and* the opportunity to do something nobody had ever done before.

It couldn't happen. It made her wings twitch to turn this opportunity down, but what else could she do? She briefly wondered what the seat plinth was covered in. It had to be fancy and smell good, she'd bet. Oh, to find out.

Sending a message or calling would be insulting, so Maff traveled to the garage in person to give Toraz the news. Giving a Pallundian gangster bad news had to be less dangerous than doing the same thing to a Pallundian mother.

She hoped.

The paddock, where the garages for all the teams were, was a hive of activity. Mechanics pushed cartloads of spare parts and shouted at news realm crews who were interviewing drivers to get out of the way. Pinnace owners chatted earnestly with team principals as they walked from one garage to another. Bots of all shapes and sizes scurried everywhere on endless errands. She could be a part of this. Technically she *was* a part of it. The gas inside her swirled.

Toraz's garage was no different from the others she'd walked past. He might be a gangster, but he was a successful gangster. He hired elite professionals to make up the team.

It was neat, brightly lit, and impossibly clean. There were two pallun whose job seemed to only be picking up the smallest piece of litter while simultaneously wiping down any surface they could reach. They weren't being treated like janitors, either. The other mechanics frequently got out of their way. It was a team that lacked only a pilot.

That lacked her.

Toraz walked out from behind the pinnace. "Ah, Maff. Glad you're here. Walk with me for a moment?"

"I don't want to take up too much of your time."

"No problem, I need to sign off on a few things, and we can talk in my office." Manifold nut guns screamed to life as a team of mechanics changed a panel in seconds that took Maff half an hour to remove. "It's too noisy out here to talk."

Again she was struck by how normal he seemed, a busy executive managing a team. She had to keep reminding herself that this was a murderous smuggler whose real business was conducted in the shadows. No wonder these people were a popular subject for realm dramas. The divide made him much more interesting.

His office was a basic box with a door on one end situated at the back of the garage. It reminded her a lot of what Mike and Kim used in their lab back home.

Back home. It was the first time she'd caught herself referring to Earth that way since they'd come out here. Her mother had predicted it would happen, that Maff would consider some other place home, before she left for flight school. It seemed silly and unlikely at the time, but it had happened. It just wasn't anywhere Maff, or anyone else in the galaxy, would've counted on.

She wanted to speak first, but Toraz held up a manipulator. "I have to start out with an apology."

That shut her right up.

"I was being a bit...impulsive when I invited you to be our pilot. You have to understand how unique the situation is. Our people, we don't get opportunities like this every day. A pallun-crewed pinnace with a pallun pilot?" He lit a cheval and puffed on it through a port in his suit. "I can hear them laughing from here." He leaned forward, grabbed the chival, and pointed it at her. The smoke rushing out of the glowing end moved back and forth like one of Earth's snakes. "But I know better. I read those reports. We pallun," he waved chival around. She didn't know why she found it so fascinating. Maybe because he'd gotten scary intense. "We don't do what you did. You're a fine representative of our people. I wanted to give you that opportunity."

He leaned back, relaxed a bit, and puffed a few more times. "But we have more important arrangements to consider. You can't become the team's pilot. You're an ambassador for that *lenarfa* planet of yours." As always, his usage of an Old Pallundian word added emphasis where a normal word would not. The idea of Earth *was* incredibly crazy. "That job's too important."

A force as irresistible as a lightning bolt blasted her.

"I still want to do it."

The urge to slap her mouth shut with her own wings was almost as forceful. *Where the hell did that come from?* He was doing her job for her, and now...

"You're serious?"

Still she couldn't shut up. "Not become a pilot for the whole season, but for this race. Wouldn't it be an achievement? Qualifying would be an honor." And it would, but she was busy with other things and had to set this aside. The words she should say weren't powerful enough to overcome the ones she wanted to say. "I can start practice as soon as the pinnace is ready."

She could almost hear her mother. *Maff, what in the world are we to do with you?*

Toraz's smile was broad. His chival glowed brightly as he took a big puff. "I think we can arrange that."

Then she remembered. "Wait. I'm still a La'fan ambassador. I don't officially exist."

This got her a deep chuckle. "You drive the boat, I'll take care of the paperwork."

So while Tonya worked away in her academic lab and Helen did whatever it was she did with Sornik—as far as she could tell the two were now clouds and rain since their ordeal in the warehouse—Maff trained. And trained. And trained.

This was not to say it was boring. Far from it. Piloting a 2187 was more than she expected it to be. Much more. Controlling it was the most rewarding thing she'd done as a pilot. Never again would she think a race between systems in cargo haulers was a demonstration of performance. There was no comparison.

True to his word, Toraz unknotted her legal status until it was nothing but smooth sky. To her family and friends, she was still Maff Sorkon, but to the crew of her 2187 and the rest of the galaxy she was Thunderbolt, the newly discovered Pallundian talent from a remote rural region of Silaria.

She had to put away her La'fan robes, which she would miss. She was no longer a mysterious and intimidating representative of the Death Eaters. She hadn't realized people were stepping out of her way until they stopped doing it. Who moves aside for a common pallun?

If they only knew. She could be a smuggler pilot, race pinnace driver, wolfling ambassador, discoverer of pallun-friendly worlds…she had a lot of career paths to choose from.

Or she could, as Spencer liked to put it, embrace the power of *and*.

The race itself was deceptively simple. The ETB route was an ancient one that took a typical cargo hauler a few weeks to complete. Cleared of traffic for the race and using purpose-built machinery, pinnaces could do it in about eighty-four hours. The give or take was the margin of victory each year.

Qualifications went well. The field was limited to 330 entries—the rationale for that number was lost to time—and she placed just outside the top ten, in twelfth, the highest-placed rookie in the race. People took her a lot more seriously when she was that high in the field.

But Maff had a secret weapon. Her name was Tonya.

"I'd honestly rather do this than go back to the lab," Tonya said. "I still can't face it."

Her experiment had failed spectacularly the previous night. Maff had never seen her upset, let alone angry, but she'd come home that night with a storm's worth of both swirling in her head. Maff had suggested taking a look at the pinnace as a distraction, which Tonya seemed to accept eagerly.

She'd shown up the next day towing a cart full of tools and spares. Toraz, in on the secret of where Tonya came from and what she was capable of, made her a member of the crew on the spot. "You keep an eye on this one," he said to the rest of the crew when he introduced her, ubiquitous chival held in one manipulator, weaving a smoke trail. "You could learn a few things."

Learn they did, first with lessons in English vocabulary. Bemian languages lacked words for things like modification, innovation, reverse engineering, and a whole host of much more technical terms. The importance of this took some time for the crew to understand. At first it didn't seem to matter that, aside from specifying the makes and models of legal pinnaces, there weren't any rules around the machines themselves. It didn't occur to anyone that they could be modified. Or should.

Tonya didn't believe it. "You're *sure* I can do anything I want in there?" she asked during her first full briefing with the team.

Maff smiled at the crew's uncomprehending expressions. Finally, other bemians had come face-to-face with humanity's insatiable need to tinker. It took fifteen minutes of back-and-forth until they understood what she was asking them. *Welcome to my world.*

Tonya only shook her head. "You should've brought me in a long time ago. I'll do what I can."

This turned out to be a small, *custom*—another word that only existed in this sense in English—control panel.

"You can thank Mike and Kim for this," she said. "Two years ago I'd never seen a soldering iron. Now I know how to make them. And all the rest. Experiments don't build themselves, know what I'm sayin'?" She laughed and then explained what each of the three switches did. "This one will increase maneuverability. The second boosts power. The third will turn on protection skein smoothing."

It was the last one that fascinated Maff. Tonya had somehow worked out how to leverage the energy field that protected organic life from the transit dimension into a device that would smooth the local transit fabric. It would make the ride more comfortable not only for her but for the ship, greatly reducing the risk of breakdowns.

"Now," she continued. "I want you to consider this: don't use these if you don't have to."

"Do they represent a risk? Will they run out?" Both were concerns the crew chief muttered about constantly.

"No and no. These are straightforward hacks. But they're the first of their kind. If you flip these on and leave them on, you'll shatter the race record. *Shatter* it. We're talking hours here. Keep your eyes on the bigger prize. If you become a galaxy-famous pinnace pilot, it'll make your job as Earth's ambassador a hell of a lot harder than it already is."

The diamond storm that was a smashing victory lifted from her eyes. Maff should've already known this. "So use them a little."

"A little, and only if you need it. You might not."

A thought fell out of the sky and landed on her. "Do I *want* to win this thing?"

"That's up to you. And your boss. Probably you do, I think. But not by a lot. Think razor-thin margins, what, what?" This caused her to laugh for some reason. "I have been hanging out with those people for way too long."

"Those people?"

Tonya waved her question away. "It's a long story. Use these sparingly, okay? And Maff? I'll be praying for you."

From Spencer that would be an insult, but Tonya was more devout than many pallun. Her prayers would come from a place of hope and respect. "Thank you."

Chapter 24
Him

The kaleidoscope lifted away from her, leaving her in a different mind, a different time in her past. She was no longer a child. A sense of extreme *other,* like another whole person, split from her mind and faded into the background.

Leaving her in the Bolivian jungle.

She watched the helicopter as it lifted the rest of them out of the clearing they'd been directed to. Her friends, her *family,* would never see her or each other again. That was the deal. When it was obvious that her pleas to the world had fallen on deaf ears, that they would die in that jungle if she didn't do something, she did.

"There," the man, Watchtell, said as they stood waiting for a different helicopter. "I don't suppose that's enough for you to give me the keys?"

In the awful heat and humidity, bugs swirling and biting, the other reappeared, struck by how young this man was. Whatever had split in her mind thought he should be older. It was absurd since she'd never laid eyes on him until a few hours ago. But the other insisted he was too young. He was supposed to be older than this.

"You can have me," she replied. "And I have the keys. That'll have to do for now." Her stab at doing the unexpected had succeeded—and failed—spectacularly. She needed to get their attention, so she gave them a present: a worm construct that was supposed to knock a zero off every central bank deposit in every country in the world and lock the money away where they could never find it. Reducing the planet's wealth by ten percent at a stroke should've done enough to bring them around, but that didn't happen.

It didn't knock a zero off. It'd *turned* them all to zero.

She hadn't spotted the mistake fast enough to correct it before anyone noticed. And once they noticed, Kim had been forced to play the tune she'd accidentally called and briefly held the entire world's wealth hostage until someone agreed to her terms. That someone was the President of the United States.

Kim hadn't smashed the patriarchy, she united it. Against them. She thought her team would be as horrified as she was that she'd accidentally done the exact opposite of what they'd worked for.

But she was wrong.

"Don't you see?" Mark asked, eyes shining with more than the fever he'd been failing to fight off. "We don't matter now! They don't have the keys anymore! You, you can *force* them to change!"

The rest weakly nodded and cheered. The other regarded the memory, but its thought was the same as hers. *They didn't get it.*

She shouted at them until they understood victory was useless if they were all dead.

At least, that was what should've happened. But it didn't. The other grew bitter at the scene. Kim sat there silently fuming, waiting on the helicopters, trying to figure out what *she* had done wrong. Why hadn't that happened?

The kaleidoscope of light appeared behind her, blinded her.

Left her standing in front of a helicopter.

This too-young Matthew Watchtell had been the president's chief negotiator. "Yes," he said as he motioned for her to board their much smaller helicopter. "I suppose you will have to do for now."

They'd patched out their vulnerabilities only a few hours after she'd revealed them, but not in time to stop her from planting her secret back doors into the far corners of their networks. It would take years to dig them out. He wanted the *keys* to those doors so she couldn't pull her stunt again, but they were the only leverage she had.

They roared across the ocean. This was also part of the deal, the part they would not budge on. She'd inadvertently made herself the single most dangerous human being on the planet. Nobody should have that kind of power. Kim certainly hadn't sought it out. But now that they'd witnessed what she was capable of, they demanded an extra premium for her friend's lives.

They demanded hers.

She wasn't being executed, although she probably would've agreed to that in the moment. Had agreed to it. That's what had happened. That's what *should've* happened. The other grew extremely upset, a frightening extra presence in her mind.

The kaleidoscope came back and blotted her sight again.

"Do you feel sad, unmotivated, depressed, or burnt out?"

Kim sat in a mostly featureless office, wearing the prison jumpsuit they'd given her after they'd landed. To her surprise, they'd done no physical inspection on arrival. The private room she'd spent the first night in was guarded but had no surveillance inside. She was on an island somewhere in the Atlantic—they'd gone east from the Bolivian jungle—so there was nowhere to go. It wasn't a prison, base, or lab. The buildings were all wrong for that, too small or too low. If she were to guess, she'd wager this was a recently emptied resort.

"Ms. Trayne?"

She sat opposite her interviewer in a basic but not uncomfortable chair. They'd left off the physical examination but had doubled down on the psychiatric. It was her third interview so far today.

No, it wasn't. That's what should've happened. The kaleidoscope threatened, but she blinked until it went away. "Yes," she replied. "Of course."

They'd grilled her for twenty-four hours straight, that's what she remembered, right down to the bright white lights in her face. The confusion brought back the sense of the other in her head.

Henry, the Machine's communications expert, turned around in his chair. "Why do you think you're having these thoughts?"

Then she remembered. Her previous interviewers had all been part of The Machine too. They'd somehow co-opted them, gotten them to betray her, to become her prison guards.

That's not what happened, though. It's what *should* have happened. If they'd turned on her, they'd all still be alive. Which was wrong. They were still alive. Henry was right here in front of her.

The other, now a distant, strange, and old presence in her mind, found all of this terribly confusing.

Kim didn't care. She didn't want absolution. She wanted destruction, of herself, most of all.

Was this me? the other seemed to ask as the kaleidoscope of light danced on the wall behind Henry.

Yes, Kim thought back to it, *it damned sure is.* She'd used anger as a coping mechanism her whole life, but it wasn't working anymore. She'd nearly gotten them all killed. She'd loaded murdered children into the back of a truck while the killers smiled at her.

"My entire way of life is gone," she answered him. "I will never see my friends or family again. That'll whack a ding in anyone's happiness, don't ya think?"

The smile on his dark face warmed and terrified her in equal measure. The other was certain this hadn't happened, but it was crazy, some sort of déjà vu. Henry had switched sides, pure and simple.

Good for him.

"But you'd been having these thoughts long before you came here. You wanted to stop before Bolivia."

The statement was flat and factual. And correct. But not because they would get caught. That was only the surface reason. Sitting here in this chair she realized there was another, deeper one. Her life with the Machine was an arc of self-destruction, of willfully throwing herself into danger, and if she didn't stop one of these days, she'd tip herself into oblivion. The other seemed more disturbed by this understanding than she was. Which was saying something.

"How did you know?" She'd told no one about those urges, least of all herself.

"How isn't important. Why were you having those thoughts?"

His question confused her for a moment, but then the answer was obvious. "You were using me."

They were. However well intentioned, Kim was as much a tool as a person to them. Right to the end they wanted her to keep fighting long after it should've been obvious that nothing could be gained. Not a child. A tool. They'd used her. It was a fundamental betrayal, one that made her blindingly furious at them. Yet she loved them in spite of it, and always would. This completed the circle and let the outrage explode again. She wasn't family to them, not really. Only a tool. People didn't love tools, they used them.

There was no way forward from this block.

A new voice spoke to her silently, deep and masculine. *Yes, there is…*

The kaleidoscope flared and blinded her.

He was the only other inmate in this strange prison. An old man, always present after she was brought back from whatever round of manipulations or tests they'd performed on her or forced her to participate in. She'd never used her strange power in such rigorous settings and never for any length of time. Now that she was doing both, the effort left her gutted and afraid. What happened when she failed? What was the next step?

She'd find him sitting under a tree in the courtyard, obviously thin despite the orange robes he wore. A skinny old guy in a pumpkin suit as her only companion. She could probably do worse.

"What did you do to end up here?" she asked him.

He peered up at her and blinked. "I don't know. I have no memory before this place. I think I may have always been here."

She sat on a metal picnic bench beside him. "You were born here?"

This seemed to puzzle him. "I don't think that term applies to me."

"What's that supposed to mean?"

"I don't know. To be honest, I don't care. I'm here, now, and that's where I'll stay."

The other in her head found this man endearing. Kim thought he was weird. "Are you a prisoner?"

"We're all prisoners, because we desire."

"I don't understand."

He regarded her carefully. "You don't, do you? Fascinating."

This annoyed the other for some reason. Kim didn't need a reason. "I've got enough trouble right now, old man. I don't need to solve riddles."

He laughed, a wheezing dry sound that ended in a cough. "But you do, you see. You do." He grabbed a cane she hadn't noticed was leaning against the tree and levered himself slowly off the ground. "I will help you where I can, when I can."

That sounded promising. "Do you know a way off this rock?" she asked in a quiet whisper.

He shook his head sadly. "No. I wish I did, but no." Now out from under the tree's shade, he squinted at the sun. "I think the only way either of us will escape this is through you."

"Me? I'm not going anywhere. I had to make a deal."

His voice changed from a wheezing wheedle to a strong, much younger-sounding tenor. "Watchtell has already altered the deal, Kim. He'll alter it further." He walked away.

Kim would've chased after him, but the other in her mind held her still. The rush of emotion was overpowering. The fact that it came from somewhere else was terrifying. She'd long known her grasp on sanity could slip, but it'd never had symptoms like this before. An other this strong might be the first sign of true schizophrenia.

A name burst out of her, "Mike?"

He stopped for a moment, ear held up like he'd heard her but hadn't understood what she'd said. Then he continued walking, shaking his head.

The other wilted, losing strength. It wasn't him. Whoever *him* was. The presence faded into a sad melancholy she was all too familiar with. She had to be imagining it. That's the only thing it could be.

The next morning the guards took her into their labs for another round of testing. After a moment, she woke up in her bed with the noon sun shining in through a window. She'd lost four hours.

Watchtell had altered the deal.

The other in her head was back, too, this time with confidence. She remembered this part. Déjà vu all over again, as they said.

Michiko, the Machine's organizer and the artist who tattooed wings on Kim's back, sat in a chair beside her bed. "How do you feel?"

"You drugged me. How am I supposed to feel?" Her belly hurt, somewhere between a cramp and a sour stomach. "I'm cooperating, what's the point of doing that?"

"Above my pay grade," she replied. "They don't let us into those rooms."

"Great. Time for my twenty questions?"

"It's fifty this time," she said primly, very unlike Michiko. The other knew the difference, too, and that this hadn't happened. The memory-that-couldn't-be gave her vertigo.

The thirteenth question made it worse. "Why haven't you forgiven us?"

"For what? For this? I don't have anything to forgive. You *should* join up with Watchtell. It makes sense." It didn't. That hadn't happened. Which was ridiculous. The other needed to shut up about it. She couldn't concentrate on anything.

"No, that's not what I mean," Michiko replied with a clinical detachment so unlike the friend who'd literally given Kim wings. "Why haven't you forgiven us?"

The other froze up. That was the only way Kim could describe it. She shivered hard at the sense of a cold realization, *someone else's* realization. She took the opportunity to try locking the other out, make it less than what it was right now. She barely had room in her head for herself. Besides, there was no reason to forgive them.

The new male voice returned. *There was…*

"Why are you crying?" Michiko asked.

Kim wiped her eyes furiously. "I'm not."

The other hadn't gone away. It'd gotten stronger, violently pushing the new voice aside.

I'm not!

She leapt out of the bed and ran through the door, catching a glimpse of the empty chair Michiko had been sitting in moments before. Full blown hallucinations. She had completely lost her grip on reality.

She passed a macabre fountain of skulls in the courtyard. Six skulls in a spiral, with an empty platform at the top. The sight hit her like a punch to the chest, and she had no idea why. Anger and sorrow sloughed off the other in waves that she couldn't control.

It was her idea.

It was her fault.

There was no going forward, not from this. She could not move on.

She could…

The kaleidoscope flared and blinded her.

She opened her eyes and found herself sitting at the picnic table again, next to the old man under the tree. Memories of a distorted fugue of drugs and torture vomited out her head. She had no idea how many days had passed.

Kim asked the old man.

He said, "It's been two days since we last spoke. I was growing worried about you."

They'd taken forty-eight hours from her and left her with a mass of disconnected pictures, snippets of demands, of commands. Hallucinations.

Bare hands touching her skin.

The other in her head was a distant scream of defiance and grief, pain at an unacceptable realization, loss unending. If she went anywhere near that she knew, somehow, it would destroy her.

"What's happening to me?"

"You are suffering."

"I am."

"Do you know why?"

The other spoke through her and with her. "No."

He laughed in that dry way he had, age and dust. "I think you do. You didn't before, that's why we're here. But you do now. You're in this much pain because you know what has to happen, but you don't know how to make it happen."

There was no way forward…

There was…

"Do you know?" she asked him.

He shook his head. "I know my way. But it's not yours." He levered himself up again with his cane. "These are solutions that do not apply themselves to words easily." In the distance, she heard a helicopter approaching. He stared at the direction the sound came from, his profile so much like Colque's it almost stopped her heart. *Was this his father?* "Our time grows short. He will be here soon, and I don't know what will happen next." He turned to her with eyes that were now faintly traced with lightning. "Know this: I will be with you, whatever happens."

Kim blinked at the empty courtyard as the helicopter drew near. She'd discovered what would happen next. The guards had gotten complacent. Kim had seen a memo with the next steps of their plans for her inside. She'd frustrated them at this resort-turned-prison. Watchtell decided to take it to another level. The memo went into clinical detail, but the procedure was easy to describe in a single word.

Vivisection.

The kaleidoscope flared and blinded her.

Kim blinked into the wind blowing through the helicopter's open door, arms shackled together in front of her. They sped low over the water, this time the Pacific, because they'd been traveling west. Guards sat opposite her, but they missed what she was going to use to escape them all.

The levers, one on each side of the door, had labels. *Emergency Belt Release*. One pull and she'd be free, out the door, and invisible in the ocean below. It was possible to survive the fall, if unlikely. But no matter what, she'd either be in a better place or no place. It was a deal she was eager to make.

Kim blinked, confused. It was the other again, remembering what hadn't happened. Only this time it couldn't happen. There were no levers, labeled or otherwise. They'd vanished.

The members of The Machine, who hadn't been there a moment before, leaned in. "You know what to do," Lourdes said, then leapt out of the door.

Kim tried to scream, but the other stopped her. This wasn't right. This hadn't happened.

Michiko spoke next. "You must face this. For our sake. For yours." She went out the opposite door.

She could not face it. She didn't know how.

You were their tool.

Josh and Rich, as always, spoke together. "You're in this mess because you didn't know how. You do now. You do. You have to try, Kim. It's the only way out." They went through the door next to her, hand in hand.

Your decision killed them all.

Henry smiled. "You won't be able to see how big the kids have gotten otherwise." He didn't fall, he vanished, somehow knowing she hadn't been able to bear the thought of seeing his children, his wife, after all these years. They wouldn't forgive her.

Mark smiled that sad way he always did. "You're wrong, Wren. About them. About us.

"About yourself."

He jumped, his splash joining the others a few moments later.

The word *forgive* hit the other harder than it did her, a terrifying realization, a word that unlocked the truth she hadn't known how to face. That she didn't know how to face.

I am the other.

She always had been. They fused together in a flare of coral-colored lightning. The shackles fell away from obsidian glass arms.

I am this too. The glass girl.

The truth of what she had to do was simple and impossibly difficult.

No, she thought. *What I need to do is hard, but not impossible.*

Recognizing the truth was like taking a step off a cliff.

Or out of a moving helicopter.

"You crazy sons of bitches," she shouted as she leaned out the door. Her team wasn't in the water anymore. They'd fallen in a different way, in other places. They'd used her, yes, but that hadn't been intentional. "I forgive you! Do you hear me? I forgive you!"

And she did. The feeling was enormous, indescribable, a weight that flew away in directions that didn't exist.

She turned to the sky. The old man was right. The words didn't express anything close to the power of what she felt. She shouted them anyway. "And goddamn it I forgive myself. We were all a bunch of screwups. It wasn't anyone's fault. It was everyone's fault." She filled her lungs until they creaked.

"I forgive!"

She jumped.

Below her the sea turned into threads that reached out and embraced her. The mad part of her, the teenager that had stayed buried until she'd dredged her up and gave her life through this ordeal, looked out through her eyes.

"Whoa," she said.

"You have no idea."

They combined into a singularity, giggling, as the memories flowed back and forth.

Chapter 25
Maff

For reasons again lost to history, the pinnaces lined up abreast in ten lines of thirty-three. As always, the start of the race was in realspace, leaving the Exnor system. The neat rows of so many pinnaces all heading in the same direction was a spectacular sight. That Maff was *inside* that sight—and in the front row—was almost beyond belief. Pallun didn't fly D-ships. They certainly didn't race them. Yet here she was, with spectator craft forming a near tunnel around her and more than three hundred other racers behind. When they reached the prime marker, the pace pinnace shot ahead and to the side, getting out of the way.

When they reached the zero marker, it was on.

The jump to the transit dimension was instant and brutal, sending violent shock waves through the pinnace and her. It was nothing like a standard transition, which most people barely registered and sometimes took minutes to complete. It wasn't even like the times she'd had to slam into the dimension, running from whoever happened to be chasing her at the time. In both cases, dampers and buffers protected crew and cargo. To the pinnace, those were extra mass that wasn't needed, so the hull was designed to take the shock. The pilot had to deal with the consequences, and she did. Bruises healed.

The race itself was another kind of brutality: speed, concentration, and precision were required at all times. The pinnaces were effectively identical. Tonya's modifications aside, all of the designs had been perfected by the AC network thousands of years ago, so any gains came from clever transit level navigation, quick reflexes, and more than a little luck. Any break in concentration could be catastrophic.

As always the first hour was taken up with breakaways, small groups willing to push a little harder than everyone else, forming and then being pulled back by the rest of the field. A few inevitably crashed out or broke down, making for some exciting-in-a-bad-way piloting through debris fields and the occasional stationary pinnace. Within a few hours of starting, the field had lost more than fifteen of them.

More than that fell out due to mechanical failures. The pinnaces were high-strung beasts and demanded attention to get the best out of them. She had to push the craft exactly as hard as she needed to in order to maximize the speed without overloading the systems. What *exactly as hard* meant shifted from one moment to the next. Eventually, as she found a rhythm managing this beast on the far edge of its performance envelope, a strange fusion overcame her. Maff didn't know or care where she ended and the pinnace began. It had become an extension of her body no different from the suit she wore to keep her alive.

Alarms rang, shifts in transit levels were brutal full-body assaults, and a navigation mistake could result in an instant of flaring violence that would be the end of her. They weren't discrete threats that came at her one after the other. It was a constant balancing act against everything trying to stop her. Kill her, actually, and all at the same time.

They were her foes. Maff fought them back. Find the seam in the D-space around her, flow with the transit dimension levels, guard the drive from overload, mind the protection skeins, and always pay attention to the route. She didn't realize that she'd reached the mandatory rest period until the blue Pace Zone in Range lights started flashing in her enhanced vision. It was only when the pinnace's pace controls activated that Maff came back to herself, a separate being in command of this beast of a ship. She was starving, aching, and needed to change every filter in her suit. But none of that mattered once Maff checked the leader board.

She'd made up *five* places from her qualifying position of twelfth. Two were dropouts, but three were clean passes. Twelfth to seventh. Maff was now just outside the top five and within striking distance of a podium finish. She only had to keep doing what she'd already done, and it was within reach.

She wobbled back to what passed for a galley on this bucket—little more than a replicator and a seat plinth next to her cot straps. She didn't know if she could do it. She'd genuinely given it everything she had. Her concentration was so shot, it took a few minutes to remember how to work the replicator.

The rest period was five hours, imposed on the isolated field as a whole. Nobody got in or out, no substitutions, her place recorded and her berth no more than a set of coordinates, one of hundreds in a remote corner of the Tarnath system. It would have to do. After a zesty meal of specially formulated paste with a flavor and consistency that reminded her of strut grease, she hooked the cot straps to her suit and shut off the lights.

*

Warning. Acknowledge?

There was beeping. It was in her head. Why was there beeping in her head? It couldn't have been five hours yet.

Warning. Acknowledge?

Ship warnings didn't act like this. They jumped you right out of bed. And the warning was written and spoken in English anyway. It took her a minute to remember how to answer. *Acknowledge,* she thought.

Sa'dst hack attempt detected. Firewall protocols deployed. Interpreters are likely nearby. Proceed with caution.

Now she *wanted* to snap her cot straps and jump straight up, but she didn't. Mike and Kim had done some human magic that made any sa'dst in their bodies immune to Interpreter attacks. They added these warnings in case it was done by someone hidden.

Or someone on her ship.

Fully awake, she heard movement in the front of the ship, then voices. Two people. They were whispering in a language she didn't understand, but they didn't sound happy. Maff carefully activated a manipulator camera on top of her suit and took a look around.

Standing at the bridge console, bent awkwardly over her seat plinth, was a scolion, what Mike called a walking fox. It had a body of black glass covered in orange lightning, and it was trying to activate the ship. A hole leading straight to the transit dimension was to his left.

Likely nearby indeed. If he was here in his transformed state, his threaded companion was…wherever they went, Mike hadn't figured that part out yet. Anyway, the threaded companion was right now trying to break into the ship's realmspace so they could start it up.

Which explained the swearing. This was an ETB pinnace. What realmspace there was had been optimized almost to the point of nonexistence. Certainly it wasn't like anything these two had encountered. That would slow them down, but it wouldn't stop them. They assumed she was paralyzed and were ignoring her. She would make them pay for that.

But first she had to figure out how they'd gotten that hole into her ship, otherwise they'd come right back. Interpreters had to see their destination to use the transit dimension to reach it, so there had to be a camera somewhere.

Now that she knew it was here, finding it wasn't particularly difficult, nor how it'd gotten on board. All pinnaces carried official ID gear provided by the AC nodes that organized the event, delivered prior to start. She hadn't paid it much attention. The camera wart was bonded to the box with a simple putty that blended it into the larger device's outline.

That solved the problem of keeping them off. Now to *get* them off. The last time they had been paralyzed by sa'dst, Mike had been able to talk but she hadn't. She did it anyway. There was nothing to lose.

"What…what's going on? Why can't I move?"

The Interpreter straightened quickly and turned around. "At least now we don't have to wake you up," he said in that same crystal-perfect Pallundian that Kim used around her. "Let's keep things easy. How about you start this unshielded cargo container of yours up for us?"

Maff remembered what it was like when Valsa had done this to her, how confused and helpless she was, and channeled that into her voice. "Why would I do that? Why can't I move? Who are you? *What* are you?"

He walked over to her, arrogance radiating along with the lightning. "You'll find that out soon enough. Now," he said as he ran a hand across her suit, "about starting the ship."

"I won't," she fired back. "This is piracy, pure and simple!" He only had to take a few more steps to get out of the camera's view. There might be others backing him up, and she didn't want them to be alerted.

"We're not here for your ship, dear, we're here for *you.*" He kept walking down her wing. *One more step.* "Do we need her, Orbezon?"

"It'll go a lot faster," a voice said from all around them. "This has got to be the smallest—"

Maff popped her cot straps off with one set of manipulators and used all the rest to hammer his head into the deck. Pallun manipulators were famous throughout the galaxy for their number and dexterity. What most never knew was how strong they were. He hit the deck so hard he dented the deck plate.

She lifted them off him. He didn't get up.

She wasn't worried about killing him. Kim was nearly indestructible in her glass form, and she had no doubt this Interpreter was too.

"No!" she shouted as she gathered up her cot straps, which would make for fine restraints. "Don't do that again! You don't have to hurt me!" She started the ship. "There! Now it's done! Leave me alone!"

Right on cue, the main drive rumbled to life. Sound deadening was, of course, considered unnecessary on a pinnace. Since the drive was right next door, the next several minutes would be completely inaudible to anyone who might be listening.

When she checked the time, she got a shock. Five hours *had* gone by. She'd nearly missed the lineup call.

When the drive was at its loudest, she crushed the camera with a manipulator. That should take care of any backup they might have. She scooped up the backpack he'd left on the floor. It was heavier than it looked. When she opened it, their plan became obvious. Inside was a small bomb. Plant it, push her through that hole into the transit dimension to wherever they wanted to take her, and poof. Poor Maff. Such a promising talent, killed by a freak pinnace accident.

She needed to get moving. Maff hauled the trussed-up Interpreter off the deck and onto her back, called up the nav computer to set the next leg's main solution, and discovered her next big problem.

They had wiped it clean.

A nav computer freak-out wasn't uncommon. There was a designated parking area for it. She reported the problem to race control and then parked at the space they assigned her. When she pulled in, there were at least a dozen other pinnaces idling as, presumably, their pilots frantically restored their nav computers. Better still, most of the people ahead of her in the race standings were there. Pushing the nav computer to find solutions faster than it was designed to, which is what they all did, was a risky strategy that obviously hadn't paid off for them. She still had a chance to win.

The Interpreter shifted and groaned.

She did exactly what Kim did the last time this happened and unceremoniously tossed the Interpreter through the hole they made in the side of the ship, sending them back to wherever it was they came from. The hole vanished like it'd never been there.

Once Maff got her restoration firmly underway, she moved out. She wouldn't be able to make it past the first level without a nav computer, but that was still better than cooling her engines in a parking lot.

It was the perfect time to test one of Tonya's gadgets. Smoothing the local transit dimension would give her close to level two speed, enough to keep her losses manageable. More importantly, she was the first of the stuck leaders to get moving. Putting distance between them and her was important.

After traveling for less than an hour, a gift from Turlanfador landed in her manipulators. She found a wormhole.

Normally these shortcuts were nearly impossible to find. Their signal was too weak to be separated from the dimension's background noise. Tonya's smoothing fixed that. And it was going her way. She quickly scanned to ensure nobody was around to follow her, then jumped through.

Instantly her coordinates changed, and now she had a different problem: the wormhole had moved her too far. If she exited immediately, she'd end up several hours ahead of anyone else. Using wormholes wasn't illegal, but it would probably attract even more attention than using a novel human modification to her ship. Wormholes were rare and valuable ways to move things. Besides, her nav computer was still rebuilding. She saw the signature of a realspace star system ahead and exited so the rest could catch up.

The system's star didn't immediately appear in her catalog. That was uncommon but not unprecedented. Her gut lurched for a moment until a scan picked up AC nodes nearby. She hadn't found *another* Earth, thank Turlanfador. It would be straightforward to fix her position and get out of here.

The next thing the scanner found was much more exciting: there was a cache ruin out here.

Whatever had happened to trigger the catastrophe that led to the Refounding had been foreseen by at least one group. Some civilization, nobody knew which exactly, predicted the coming storm and tried to preserve the galaxy's knowledge in caches scattered throughout the galaxy. Unfortunately the disaster must've been much larger and lasted far longer than anyone had counted on. These caches were rightly seen as a kind of treasure chest and people quickly figured out how to find them and raid them. The ruins left behind were a common tourist attraction wherever they were found, the only surviving connection to a completely unknown past.

It took most of her remaining time to reach it. When she did, it was a bit of a disappointment. The most famous caches were ruined memory palaces that could sometimes cover a significant part of a planet's surface. This was a simple orbital cache about the size of Mike and Kim's lab, what they called a standard low-rise office building. Still, it was a bit of the unknown, so Maff recorded it anyway. Long ago this had been a fine, polished white rectangle of esmentium, a material similar to but much stronger than Earth's concrete. It was now pitted and stained from orbiting the system's star for millions of years, all alone in the dark. Ugly, but also still thrilling. The people who built it were a complete mystery, as was all else in a time that might stretch back…

Maff stopped breathing. This was impossible. But it was there, right in front of her. Blinking didn't make it go away. It showed up on the scanners too. She snapped a picture, and it was still there. It wasn't a fantasy or a trick.

The doorway to the cache was there and closed. It still had its original seal intact.

She noticed a red light that'd been flashing in her vision for some time now. She needed to go. Was late, in fact. The nav computer had finished its rebuild, and now Maff had some catching up to do. Besides, she wasn't the one who'd come out to space specifically to find these kinds of records. She sent backup copies of the coordinates to Helen and Tonya, then reentered the wormhole and returned to its proper exit.

She had a race to finish, and when that was done, friends to bring back to this place.

*

She thought that becoming a pilot was the hardest thing she'd ever done. And it was at the time. Then it was fitting in with a crew who hated her for what she was. Again, not easy by any means. Certainly fitting in on a feral world that would turn her into a circus act if they discovered her counted as hard.

But for sheer physical effort and force of will, nothing would ever be as difficult as driving her pinnace at speed.

She was turning through a trinary star system's D-space shadow when her master caution light blinked on. It scared the hell out of her, because the whole point of a master caution light was to let her know bad things could be happening. Less than optimal on a ship that wasn't much more than storm-sliced rock shards held together with resin rain.

But it was a 1202 from the nav computer, the result of the Interpreter's wipe and her less than gentle restoration. It was harmless, a fault in a sensor that had two backups. It was a 1202 the next three times in a row. She started quickly pressing the acknowledge button on the master caution to get things back to normal. Checking what the error code was took too much time. She'd chase them down later.

She was navigating another particularly complicated piece of transit dimension topography while attempting a pass that would put her in fifth place when the master caution lit for the umpteenth time. She cursed and pushed the acknowledge button.

A few minutes later, it lit again. She was *this close* to pulling it all off, so she pushed the acknowledge button again.

It immediately lit a third time, and the drive's tone changed. She was in trouble. When she checked the logs, the past six master cautions had been warnings about the exotic matter shields degrading inside the drive. If she'd paid attention to the first one, it would've only required an adjustment to fix. But now the shield's effectiveness had almost completely degraded. If she had ignored that final warning she would've been turned into what Mike called *subatomic mist.*

She caught the problem in time to prevent disaster, but not soon enough to stop the drive from degrading past the point automated systems could keep it running. Normal ships didn't use these. They had a dedicated crew member to manage the drive. Maff had to become that extra crew member.

All chances of a top five finish vanished as she now juggled the jobs of three different crew members. By the time her pinnace entered the final route, another critical system, thrust vectoring, required constant attention. *And yet*…the number ten spot was hers to have. She only had to brake late into the final turn to make it stick. At the apex, the other pilot didn't seem to see her and moved into her line. Maff jinked hard to avoid a collision.

The drive immediately vented its contents into the transit dimension, ramming the pinnace violently into realspace. It had been operating half its systems on the emergency backups, which failed the instant main power went offline. The rest of the systems' failures cascaded the ship into utter blackness.

She was dead. She hit that other racer, and the explosion had spread her and her pinnace across an entire star system. No more contracts, no more friends, no grand scheme to free her people.

The master caution light, the bane of her existence, began flashing again. Dead people didn't have to respond to emergencies. Slowly a few lights flickered to life, showing her compartment was unharmed. After some rewiring and configuration changes, she managed to get basic nav and comms going. She found herself in realspace, tumbling slowly away from the finish line. In the distance, a gaggle of emergency vehicles was closing on her position. She ignored them and race control as they frantically tried to raise her on the comms. She'd gotten a look at the final position list.

Her name was on it.

10. Maff Sorkon

She'd made the pass and crossed the finish line. They were still replaying it on the monitor realms. Nobody'd seen anything like it in years. Stuck in the dark, momentarily disoriented as the emergency vehicles stopped her tumble, she got a flash of disappointment that she'd missed seeing the move that got her that spot live. Then what she did sank in.

Top ten finish, highest of the rookie class by far.

The rush of her triumph kept her going through the acknowledgements to race control, the emergency vehicles, and her ground crew. She emerged from the pinnace after being towed back to the dock and had a brief surge of reporters to deal with. For about three minutes, she was the most famous Exnor-Tarnath-Biknal pilot in the galaxy. Toraz had his picture taken with her over and over again, giant chival stuck firmly in a suit port, puffing like a smokestack.

Then the reporters vanished. Her crew bustled off, pinnace in tow, its job done for the year and now badly in need of an overhaul. Toraz departed in a cloud of blue smoke. Only Helen was left behind, with a slightly disappointed smile on her face. Maff hadn't noticed she was there until that moment.

"Tenth? That's the best you could do?"

Chapter 26
Tonya

The longer she thought about her experiment, the more frustrated she got. It *should've* worked. She grabbed a bemian version of a screwdriver and started disassembling it.

Tenor stopped by later that morning. "I don't think I'll ever get used to the way you humans insist on taking things apart," he said as he stared at her experiment, now spread out across the central countertop of the lab.

"It's kind of our thing," she replied, adjusting a lattice reticulator. "Lots of us start out young." Tonya had been too poor and too busy surviving to have done much back then, but looking at the crazy collection of bemian and Earth tech spread out around her, it seemed she was now making up for lost time. "We're a civilization of tinkerers."

He noticed the segments. "Wait, you put both experiments in the same case?"

"It's complicated. I can work on more than one, you know." She hoped. They had rules for everything around here.

"More than one what, yes, what?"

Guess it was time to find out. "Well hello there, Dean."

He waddled into the lab alone, Hakonz nowhere to be seen. Tonya thought they were attached at the hip.

"Ah, yes," he said as the lab's door closed behind him. "Jolly good, taking a round with the colonel, I see."

She glanced sideways at Tenor. After a moment, he did the same to her and then subtly shrugged. Without Hakonz around, the dean was opaque to both of them.

Great.

The dean moved ponderously from one major component to the other. "Fiendishly clever, fiendishly clever. Well done, Specialist Brinks. Never seen anything like it, what, yes?"

"Um, no…wait, yes? Thanks?" As a nurse, she was used to doddering old fools poking around where they weren't needed. But the context was different here. She wasn't a nurse trying to make sure the doctors didn't kill her patients, she was an academic hoping he wouldn't ask where she'd gotten all the extra gear from.

He stopped at the shared segment of her experiment. "Ah, I see you haven't discovered my contribution yet. Ha-ha, yes what?"

"Contribution?" Her interpreter thread must be having a hard time with his speech, too. That couldn't have been right.

Beside her, Tenor softly said, "Oh no."

"Jolly good. Experiment's power was wrong, obvious after about a moment. Humans too new to be working with proper gear." He threw her a half grin, showing the flexibility of his turtle-like beak. "Was worried you'd blow the place up, yes, what, so I put a damper on it. Went too bloody far, ended up sailing right into the queen's carriage. Quite embarrassing."

Tonya blinked. "*You* sabotaged my experiment?"

"Sabotaged? Jolly well not! Just trying to help a scientist from the sticks is all. Yes, what? Didn't realize the problem was a *lack* of power."

She'd blamed Tenor's girlfriend, and it'd been this old fool all along. "How did you manage that?" She'd kept the doors locked.

"What, yes? I'm not exactly a cattle herder swimming against the tide, right, what? But now I've figured it out, jolly well figured out indeed." He pulled one of the gigantic power couplers out from under the countertop. "You didn't need less power, you needed *more*!" He yanked the existing power supply connector out of its socket. Before she could make a move, he clamped the coupler over it with a triumphant flourish. "Now we loose the spear into the water trough, proper right, what?" He turned it all on.

The arrays she'd painstakingly mated to her human-bemian hybrid lattices threw sparks. All across the counter the lattices glowed white.

Inside her, outside her, what was her and what was Tenor, flew apart and came together, spun sideways and tumbled into loops. A sense of profound dislocation twisted her mind in a different way, and she fell down a mountain of solid vertigo. Her senses strobed nonsensical signals at her, touching color, tasting metal strawberries, hearing a choir sing a chord that encompassed the universe, all at the same time.

Then, with a massive physical and psychic snap, it stopped.

She quickly took stock of herself. All was present, accounted for, and uninjured. Tenor was on top of her, but she could feel his breathing. He smelled faintly dusty and sweet.

"Tonya?" He rolled off and away from her. Then he said something in rhon she didn't understand.

Her interpreter thread was gone. The disconnect error flashed in her enhanced vision. At least her phone still worked. That had to be a good sign. "I'm fine," she said in Standard. "Are you?"

"Yes. What happened? Where are we?"

She looked around, not knowing what she'd see. Instead of the lab's ceiling there was only a heavily clouded sky. The air smelled different, drier, with a hint of brimstone. The floor wasn't smooth either; it'd changed to bare rock and dirt.

She sat up. They were in a narrow crevasse with walls of rock that extended well over their heads. A path to her right curved quickly out of sight. Hopefully it led *out* of the crevasse.

"Well we're not in Kansas anymore," she said. He cocked his head quizzically, and she remembered the threads were gone. He wouldn't have gotten the joke anyway. "We're not in the lab anymore," she said in Standard.

"A portal of some kind? Is that what you were working on?"

"No, not at all." She couldn't explain what she'd been working on in Standard. She could barely do it in English. "This should not have happened."

He stood up and then helped Tonya to her feet. "Does your phone have a signal?"

She checked. "Yes, it does." So civilization had to be nearby.

"Mine too. But none of my addresses work. I can't reach anybody."

Tonya's had stopped working as well. "What about public channels?"

Those were also dead. That didn't add up. If they had signal, the wireless network still functioned. But the realm addresses didn't answer, including ones like the global news feed and the university. Those should always be up no matter what.

The bemian version of GPS provided coordinates, but the realm that served the maps was down like all the rest. She knew where they were in absolute terms but not where that was in relation to anything that mattered. It did give her a datapoint: they were a couple thousand feet—2263 at the moment—above sea level. So this was a cleft in a mountain.

"Maybe the rock is interfering?" he asked.

"Maybe," she replied, then pointed at a path that led away. "Let's find out where this goes."

They walked in silence.

"Careful!" He grabbed her by her shoulders.

Half of the floor of the crevasse had crumbled into a deep sinkhole. It hadn't been there a moment ago, she would've sworn it. But the cave-in wasn't recent. The rocks were completely weathered all around. An old sinkhole that was new to her. "Where did that come from?"

"How could you not see it?"

A loud crack sounded above them, and Tonya pushed Tenor sideways as a large rock crushed where he'd been standing. It rolled into the sinkhole and plugged it.

They both stared silently at it for a moment. This was the part where the orchestra played the Bugs Bunny theme and the curtain fell. The events were in such a perfect sequence it felt that artificial. But there was no follow up, and she could find no evidence of anyone else around them.

Tenor said, "I don't think it's safe here."

"No kidding." They clambered over the rock and kept going, but at a faster pace.

After a few minutes, the cleft began to widen. Eventually they were able to walk side by side but were still boxed in. They rounded a corner and found the exit of the cleft only a few feet ahead of them. They stopped at the same time.

After a moment, Tenor said, "You go first, see what's out there?"

She took his wingtip. "It's been bugging you too?"

He nodded. "This isn't right. None of it is. We shouldn't be here, but there's no other way out."

"Right. Okay then, together." Tonya knew she was braver than most—it was pretty much a requirement for a nurse—but this unknown made her want to rush back to the dead end and stay there until she could figure this out. Tenor might be a giant walking crane, an alien, but that didn't matter right now. He was her friend, and she desperately needed that.

They walked into bright sunlight, both blinking. The path opened up onto a small flat area covered in short grass. She was right: it was a mountain, towering behind her tall enough she couldn't see the top. The path they'd been following continued in front of them, hopefully leading to an easy way down.

Beyond was a broad valley with a large river running through it. The floor was covered with vast agricultural fields, turning it into a patchwork quilt of browns and greens. The colors were the first indication of their location: they were the familiar not-quite-right palette of Silaria's plants. They might not be as far from home as she feared.

Right in the center of the valley, far enough away to almost be toylike, was a city of elegant glittering towers. The designs were like nothing she'd ever seen on Silaria.

So much for not being far from home.

Beside her, Tenor sat down heavily, staring at the vista. "This isn't possible."

She sat beside him. "Are you okay?"

He turned to her, dead serious. "Am I crazy? Is this real?" He pinched her shoulder, a weird sensation from his strangely shaped fingers. "Are you real?"

Tenor might have a concussion. She went to check but then stopped herself. There was no way for her to know the proper concussion protocol for a rhon. "Yes. I'm real. This," she indicated the valley in front of them, "is real as far as I can tell. It's beautiful."

He cradled his head in his wings. "Of course it's beautiful. But it's not possible."

"What are you talking about?"

He pointed at the city. "See that tower? Follow the river until you get to the center of the city, it's second from the right. You can't miss it."

Indeed she couldn't. All the other buildings were glittering spires of mirrored silver. It was an appealing deep blue. "Yes. What's the matter with it?"

"It's a legend. It can't exist. Don't you recognize it?"

Tonya had forgotten she was supposed to be a newly minted bemian, not an ignorant wolfling from the sticks. "I don't think so. The nodes never mentioned it."

"Why would they?" he asked, confused.

Time to change tactics. "I think it's Standard that's confusing me. Without an interpreter thread, I can't always understand what you're saying. Maybe if you could give me more details?"

He nodded. "This is the first time I've been without a thread since I was small. I feel so dumb without it." He turned and pointed at the building again. "That is a unified Interpreter's Guild headquarters. They all looked like that. At least one was located on every planet in the galaxy."

"Was?" She hadn't seen anything like it on Silaria.

He nodded. "Was. The Interpreters don't use them anymore. They kept getting destroyed. The last one fell—" His voice cracked into a trilling whistle. He was clearly trying not to cry. He was the one who always knew what to do, where to go, what to say. She'd come to rely on that faster than she'd realized. He was her guide, the person who knew this strange society and was happy to explain it to her. He couldn't panic. That would mean she'd have to not freak out, and Tonya was definitely freaking out right now.

He gasped. "I can't…It's impossible."

"Tenor," she said, trying to be comforting while she throttled the wolfling in the back of her mind before its panic showed on her face. "The last one fell…what?"

He turned his big brown eyes on her, and she barely avoided flinching at the mad desperation she saw in them.

"The last one fell," he said in a strangled whisper, "millions of years before the Refounding."

Chapter 27
Spencer

The cliff behind Tapov extended well over their heads. It was a sheer rock wall who knew how tall. He was ninety-eight percent chimpanzee, but there was no way to climb it without gear. Telirians seemed to have evolved from some kind of bear thing. Their hands were dexterous, but they were probably built for digging, not life in the vertical.

Spencer smiled. He hadn't prepared for a gajillion squirreligators trying to chew his ass off by sabotaging a hydraulic lift disguised as a tree, but this?

This he had covered.

Climbing harness, to the rescue!

First, he had a question. "Tapov or Sarewith?"

That stopped her cold. "You've talked to my father."

He stood up. "Talk is overstating it a little. So which one do you prefer?"

She shrugged, which made her cute in a weird way. "Tapov, I guess."

He clapped his hands and rubbed them together, a magician about to impress a primitive. "Stand back, Tapov," he said.

She was less stunned native and more judgmental popular girl. He reminded himself that she was technically…actually…a princess. He'd known plenty of them back home, girls with dads who could make things happen whenever the princess crooked a finger. He would need to be cautious around her.

He pulled his backpack off and reached inside. He rummaged deep because he hadn't thought the harness would be required. But he'd made sure it was there before he left.

With a flourish, he revealed a neat metal case about the size of his forearm. Tapov's frown deepened, but he expected that. He certainly hadn't been impressed by it the first time he'd seen one. Still in silent mime mode, he held up a finger and then opened the case and unpacked it.

He didn't get anything more than her scowl putting it on. To the uninitiated, it was a spindly collection of rods, cables, and joints, more like a tent frame than anything useful. But there was a lot of it, shiny, and as he kept clipping it together, he seemed to bring about a bit of respect from Tapov. Her people didn't have a lot of mirror-finish metal, he knew that from Mike's soiree into town, let alone anything this finely engineered.

The scowl faded completely after he turned it on. Starting from his toes, status lights at the junctions flashed green to show they were ready for action. A metallic hum that was completely normal back home was eerily loud out here. He tested it using moves with his arms and chest to calibrate the micro servos in his upper body, which added to the whine from a miniature symphony of motors.

Without a preamble, he jumped straight up. He probably topped ten feet, easy. Plus it looked cool as shit.

Tapov's face made it all worthwhile. The disapproving princess well and truly vanished, replaced by an open-mouthed, stunned native who had to stagger to keep from falling.

He hit the ground with his best Iron Man crouch and looked up, one fist still planted in the grass.

"How do you like me now?"

"Is this what it'll be like when we join the galaxy?" She moved a hand up and down as he stood. "We get things like this?"

He shrugged. Spencer wasn't as straight an arrow as Mike, but he didn't particularly like lying. "Probably not this exactly." She cocked her head, not understanding. The gesture was recognizable and didn't seem freaky. He must be getting used to these people.

"It's complicated. Oh," he turned to his backpack. "You mentioned rope."

He handed her his spool of smartRope and showed her how to let it play out by holding the axle in the center. "Hang on to this, be right back." He hopped up and grabbed the cliff face like a tree frog that'd been thrown at a wall.

"Wait," she said. "You're going up? If you have rope, we should go down."

"Sister, I ain't going back down there for love or money."

"But—"

Girls were a single-person committee throughout the galaxy. "Don't let go, won't take me a minute."

He went up like Spiderman, the harness getting him into character. The extensions on his palms and feet were covered in gecko tape, a nanotech material based on what was found on the world's stickiest lizard. The joints were motorized with different nano materials, powered by hybrid electric system that combined a fuel cell with kinetic recovery that would harvest otherwise wasted energy from movements that didn't contribute to climbing.

He moved *fast*.

He was a little disappointed when he reached the top, about a two hundred feet above Tapov's head, so quickly. The harness was seriously fun to use. He could've spent all day playing with it. But he had a job to do and a princess to rescue. No time for screwing around today.

He quickly checked for squirreligator tracks and found none. He tied his end of the rope off on a bombproof anchor point: another of their hydraulitrees a good three feet thick. He called down. "Hang on a sec, coming to you."

The harness had plenty of power to spare, and it would be pretty dangerous and a hell of a lot of work to climb that distance using a single rope with bare hands. But this *was* the twenty-first century. Well, back home it was.

Her sour expression had come back. "I was supposed to use the rope."

"We're too high to use it like this. But watch." He opened the spool's interface and called up the right configuration. It beeped once to indicate the program had been activated and then released the rope. Now free to move, the rope proceeded to do a snake dance. Tapov hopped away from it.

A minute later, the rope had lopped off about ten feet of itself, which then self-tied into a configuration she could sit in. The main rope next threaded itself through the harness. They now had a respectable rappelling arrangement. "This is normally used for going down."

"That's good, we should—"

"But we're not going down. It's for safety."

"Safety?"

"Nothing's going to happen." He took the spool and chose a different configuration. Another ten-foot section pushed out and detached. A couple of minutes later he had what he needed.

Spencer attached one looped end to a hook on his harness, while the other one snaked its way through her rope basket. "One tow cable, at your service," he said.

She was like a kid who'd stepped into her first adventure realm. "Will we at least get *this* when we join?" she asked as she pulled the rope arrangement around her.

"Again, it's complicated. We'll take the climb in stages, and you'll still have to do your part."

All in all, it took about half an hour of alternating between him towing and her climbing to get to the top. While they climbed, he asked her what she knew of the place.

"It's called the Interdict."

"What's up here?"

"Nobody knows. I'd given up trying to find a way to get to it before you came along. It was too high."

"How did you get this far?"

She held out her hand, and her claws extended a good half inch. "What do you think these are for?"

So much for them not being good climbers. "The rope makes it easier to get down?"

"It was mostly for safety, like this." She plucked at the taut tow line between them.

When they reached the top, Spencer untied the rope, attached the spool, gathered the segments together so they again formed a continuous line, and zipped it all into the spool. The harness snapped back into its case almost by itself.

She didn't bother hiding her admiration. "Your tools, they're amazing. I thought you might be an Interpreter, but the nodes teach us they don't use things like that. Who *are* you?"

He chewed his lip, trying to think of an answer that she'd believe but not give the game away. Actually, there was no need to hide the truth. "I'm an Interpreter's assistant." He remembered how the sergeant greeted the king and placed an open hand against his chest. "Spencer McKenzie, at your service."

This seemed to impress her as much as the smartRope. She returned the salute. "Tapov, grateful for your service."

Spencer was pretty sure he'd just been made an honorary peasant by the princess, but what the hell. Redneck, peasant, same shit, different clothes. "So what's our next move then? Do we still have to worry about the squirreligators?"

"The wha…oh, the tannal that chased you up the rope? No, tannal are normally quite easy to spot and avoid. I wondered why you walked right into their territory like that. I thought you must have special weapons or armor." She started giggling. "Then you climbed up that tree faster than a kweeka. I waited for you to jump to the next one before they deflated it."

"But I didn't know that was what they were doing."

"And by the time you did, it was too late to try. You were lucky that I was around. A pack of tannal that big is dangerous."

"No kidding. Thank you, by the way, for saving my ass back there."

"Thank you for hauling my ass up that cliff. I'm the first Telirian to set foot on this plateau in a long, long time."

"What do you think is up here?"

She shrugged. "The nodes won't say. Only that it is forbidden to be here."

"Then why are *you* here?"

She went through a range of emotions trying to pick an answer. She sighed. "I think it's the only place left in the world where my father can't find me."

"What's so bad about your father?"

"I guess on a joined world all fathers get along with their children, but here on Teliria, fathers are still primitives who think they can boss their daughters around, pick who they marry, what they can study, how they can talk, walk," she pointed at her clothes, which were basically what the soldiers wore, "dress. I have to be on my best behavior at all times because of what other people might think! Who cares? My father is so…controlling. I can't stand it."

So parents were assholes all over the galaxy. That was comforting.

Not.

Now that he thought about it, he probably would've fled to a forbidden zone, too, if that was the only way he could get out of Dumas. "It's not unheard of for them to be fucked up where I'm from too." He smiled inwardly. Maff had called Standard crude. One of the reasons was it had more swear words than any other language. To him, that wasn't a bug, that was a feature. "Mine were. You're not scared of this place?"

She examined the woods. "Not as much as I am of what my father will do if he ever catches me. How about you?"

"I didn't know it was a thing until now." He checked his maps. The node he'd been searching for was still ahead, probably on this plateau. "I was going this way anyway."

"Why?"

He played it like the flunky she seemed to have decided he was. "Interpreter business."

"What are they like?" she asked as they started walking. "The nodes say we're not ready for them yet, that we won't be for a long time. The nodes make them sound scary."

She had to know a hell of a lot more about it than he did. Still, Mike and Kim *were* Interpreters. They had the La'fanian insignia to prove it. "They can be. It depends on which part you're talking to."

"Right. So strange to have a companion welded to you. Do they really spend the first part of their life as threads?"

The next hour or so passed fielding questions about Interpreters and fitting his answers through the filter the nodes had put on her knowledge. Flunkies don't question princesses, so it was challenging to get his own in. It wasn't that she was rude or arrogant about it. This was someone who'd grown up able to interrupt anyone for any reason without getting in trouble for it. He was no judge of Telirian beauty, but she had the same easy confidence that girls who'd grown up pretty did back home. She assumed she was the most important person in the room because that's what she grew up being.

But he did manage to ask an important question. "What do you want to happen with your journey? What's your destination?"

She considered it as they walked down a game trail that split a narrow clearing through the forest. "Respect. There's a city ahead, Umalaza. Thanks to you, I'll get to it days ahead of schedule. Eventually my father will find me, but by then I'll have set myself up properly as," she paused, then said, "Standard is quite limited at times. I'll be an herbs and medicines smallholder by then."

She was gonna open a vitamin shop. Not too shabby.

But it brought up a question. "How does this get you away from your dad?"

"I don't understand."

"I mean, he runs the whole planet, right?"

She boggled at him, then started laughing. "The *nodes* run the whole planet. We rely on them for anything important. No, my father only controls a standard holding, we call it Ontara, just like all the other lords."

After some back-and-forth about units of land measure, Spencer figured out that Tapov's home of Ontara was a territory roughly the size of Arkansas. Big, yes, but not on the scale of a planet. The territory of the other lords varied depending on what sort of natural resources they had access to. Malafan's seemed to have everything nearby and so it wasn't all that big. Others were richer and hence smaller, while a different set was much larger because their resources were spread out over a wider area. All in all, it added up to several hundred lords.

"But no king?" he asked.

"Like I said, the nodes are the real power. Father's not a figurehead, but he can't do much without the node's approval. None of them can."

She sighed. The peasant had bored the princess a little bit with his questions. Again, not all that different from the princesses he was used to back home. "Anyway," she continued, "I have a plan, and when my father does find me, he'll see that it was a good one, and that I executed it properly. Then maybe we'll be on more equal ground."

He was about to wish her luck, because he knew she'd need it, but at that moment their clearing opened up and turned into a vast, treeless plain. Maybe. Plain as in no trees or mountains, but not as in *oh my God Dumas is flat as fuck.*

"What the hell is this?" he asked.

Ahead of them, as far as he could see in any direction, were pits scattered all over the otherwise undulating ground. They were regularly spaced, like somewhere under there was a gigantic golf ball, so big its surface was flat, except where it had fallen in to make the dimples. They varied in size from ones that could swallow a car to ones wide enough to eat a house. There had to be thousands of them.

"I don't...I don't know," she replied, looking as freaked out as he felt. "I've never heard of anything like it. Have you?"

"This isn't my planet, sister. That's strange as fuck right there. Did your people fight any big wars in the past?" He'd done his fair share of fighting in WWI Western Front realms. The holes were about the right size and depth to have been made by exploding shells. But there were too many of them, and they never overlapped. There were game paths around all of them.

"What?"

Her confusion reminded him that they thought missile tech topped out at the arrow. "My people, a long time ago, fought huge wars with each other. There have been places like this for more than a century on my home planet."

"No, not at all." She turned back to the vista in front of them. "The nodes negotiate most conflicts away. I know about..." She cursed softly. "We call them *voricks*. If the nodes can't get the lords to agree, both sides gather up their nobles, and they have a series of contests to see which side fights the best. But nobody dies, not intentionally anyway."

He recognized the description easily enough. "Tournaments. Yeah, we've had those, but a long time ago."

"Ours were too, I think. I've never personally witnessed one. Come on," she said and walked out onto the first of the pathways around the pits.

"Hang on a second!" He looked around at the undergrowth. The hydraulitrees weren't wood, but they had internal bracing in the larger branches that worked as a convincing substitute. He searched briefly and found two perfect walking sticks.

Gandalf, eat your heart out.

"Here," he said, throwing her one. "Probe the ground in front of you as you walk. We don't want a cave-in."

The paths proved solid enough to walk on safely. The pits, not so much.

One gave way with a rumble. "Shit!"

Tapov grabbed his shirt and hauled him back from the edge. She started giggling. "That was a swear word in your native language, wasn't it?"

He nodded as his thudding heart slowed down. He gave her the Standard swear word that meant the same thing.

She nodded. "That's *kelt* in my language." Then she peered over his shoulder. "Kelt."

He turned around. The pit had collapsed into what looked like a cave of some sort. It was one of the big building swallowers, thirty feet across easy, and hadn't gotten any smaller after the collapse. Spencer unclipped a micro-flashlight from his backpack and shone it around. "This," he said, shaking it, "you'll get one day." He'd ganked it out of Maff's ship stores. They didn't know what powered it, but it'd taken several demonstrations using Earth devices before Maff understood the concept of recharging.

The rubble didn't provide any clues as to what caused it to form or collapse. "I should've paid more attention in geology," he said, not bothering to translate the English word. Then did it anyway because of the way she glared at him. This princess had the whole command-you-with-a-gaze thing down pat.

"Do you smell that, though?" she asked.

He did. "It smells like metal. See those red stains on the rocks and the walls? I'll bet that's iron." They knew about iron, because they had steel. "Maybe it's a mine?"

"If it is, it's not like any mine I know about." She paused for a moment. "I'm saying that a lot for some reason."

"It's okay. We don't have anything like this back home, either."

"Why would they make an abandoned mine a forbidden place?"

"Who the fuck knows? Nodes do shit for their own reasons. It might be a mine."

She pointed at the far wall. "What's that?"

Spencer aimed the flashlight where she pointed. Tapov had spotted the entrance to a cave inside the main one.

"Now turn the light off," she said.

He did. There was faint light glowing from inside the mouth. Sunlight, in fact. Spencer did some eyeballing of the landscape. "It leads to the next crater over."

"They're connected."

"And that one has already collapsed. Come on."

They made their way over to the other crater. The light was beginning to fade and now the bottom was harder to see. They'd been walking the plateau all afternoon with no sign of its ending.

His node was still a long way off. "We need to find a place to camp for the night."

She did a careful three-sixty, taking in the view. "Not much in the way of cover."

"True, but we've got that," he said, shining a light on the other side of the passageway between the two craters. "You know more about this planet than I do. How big do night hunters get around here?"

"A campfire will be enough to keep them away." She checked out his backpack. "Have they done away with fire where you come from?"

He snorted. "Hardly."

They picked their way carefully down to the cave entrance. This side had collapsed long ago, with crater edges that now sloped gently into the pit at the bottom. Everything was overgrown with Telirian versions of grass and weeds.

"It doesn't smell like metal on this side," Tapov said.

"It's probably all oxidized away." She half turned at his English word. "It's all dust. Blown away on the wind."

"Then that means…"

"The other side might have solid metal somewhere." A clue of some sort.

First things first, they set up camp. He got to impress her with his modern tent and supplies, and she impressed him with her own not-all-that-primitive camp set up. No sticks and animal skins here, she had a proper canvas tent with a bed nicer than his.

They finished getting the cook fire started. It was gloomy down in the cave while the rim of the crater was still touched with golden light. "Let's see what's on the other side before it gets completely dark," she said, using the campfire to light a torch she made that would've been right at home in any dungeon realm back home.

Princess had skills, yo.

"Lead the way," he replied.

Their cave was a rough tunnel about twenty feet long and maybe eight feet tall, wide enough for both of them to easily walk side by side. The ground was smooth rock, relatively even. Again he wished he'd paid more attention in school because he couldn't tell if it was natural or man—well, Telirian—made.

The rusty stench of metal grew as they got closer to the other side. Red-stained rubble scattered across the floor. There was nothing recognizably artificial, but the rocks still didn't seem quite right to him. They were a little too regularly shaped, but he'd been fooled often enough trying to find arrowheads in the woods back home. Sometimes it was genuinely hard for him to tell a worked stone from one that'd been knocked around by nature.

They reached the other end of the tunnel after a short walk. In front of them was the same pile of fresh rubble he'd inadvertently created. Trying to scale or explore it wasn't going to happen. The bottom of the rubble pile was well below the level of the tunnel's entrance. A shape down there caught his eye. He pointed the flashlight at it. It took him a minute to realize what he was looking at.

"Fuck me."

She turned to him and then back to the mound. "What is it? What do you see?"

Tapov wouldn't know what it was. He'd only seen Telirians use wheels on carts. Personal transport was feet, animal or otherwise. Not this. He waved the flashlight a little to call her attention to the spot. "See?"

She snapped her head back slightly. "Well, *that's* not natural. What is it?"

He blinked twice to make sure it was still there. It was.

Fuck me running.

"You don't have a word for it. You haven't invented it yet. At least I thought you hadn't."

It was twisted and bent, black with age and half buried, but there was no mistaking the spoked front wheel with chrome plating that caught the light. The handlebars were obviously shaped for Telirian paws. "That right there is a bicycle."

Chapter 28
Helen

Her first stop the morning after the ordeal at the warehouse was Samatarra's, whose sidewalk café seemed to be the de facto headquarters of Toraz's syndicate. It was closed during morning hours, so she found a nearby diner-like establishment that seemed not to mind her sitting at a table as long as she had a fresh stimulant or snack in front of her. Silaria's morning light was noticeably different from Earth's, but no less calming.

Yes, this was an alien world. The architecture was built to accommodate pallun. Everything was wider and shorter than she was used to. The food smells were different because the spices were unknown. Manta rays in decorated skin suits click-clacked past on brass legs.

But it was also quite normal. Shops were opening up; people were going off to work or coming home from a shift. Young people walked toward a common destination somewhere up the street, presumably a school. All in all, from a certain point of view, it was quite similar to residential districts in any modern Chinese city.

"Excuse me, are you lost?"

Including overly nosey passers-by.

"I'm sorry?" Helen asked the youngish male pallun who stopped opposite the café rail at the sidewalk. By now she was familiar with the Meronim outfit. He too was probably going to his school.

"You don't belong here. You should go back to where you came from."

Helen was now also familiar with the Meronim attitude.

She fell back on her academy training, treating this as an exercise. *A young person is rude, disrespectful, and speaking to you in a public setting. What is the correct response?*

She went completely still. Helen always imagined it as putting on motionless armor. She sat up straight, took a sip of what passed for tea in this corner of the galaxy, and—without turning away—slowly put on a pair of mirrored sunglasses she brought all the way from Earth. On humans, the effect was primal. She was simultaneously breaking eye contact and amplifying it, changing a normal expression into one that was emotionless and alien.

It was time to see if it worked on pallun.

"You should move along," she said firmly.

He paused much longer than it should've taken his interpreter thread to translate her words. Score one for the Earth cop.

His voice started out as a silly little squeak. "You can't"—he coughed inside his suit—"you can't talk to me—"

"Xantan Alkadent!" An older female pallun shouted from inside the shop. "You get away from her!" She bustled out from behind the counter, legs creaking but still stomping with authority. "Leave my customers alone!"

"But—"

The much older pallun stiffened her legs and set her manipulators into a configuration that was easy to interpret. If she were human, she'd have one fist against her hip and the other waving a finger at the interloper. "But nothing! You go, get off to school before I tell your mother you're wasting time harassing my customers." He hesitated, which did not please the woman. "I said *go*!" She shoved him backward, which the young man seemed to find extremely distressing. He fled up the street.

"I'm sorry about that," the woman said. "Meronim can be jerks sometimes. Most of the time."

Helen switched the cop persona off and removed her sunglasses. "No problem. Are they always like that?"

"Most? No. The young ones who think they have something to

prove, and the leaders who think they're personally managing Turlanfador's return. The rest will leave you alone if you return the favor." She sighed. "We tell the world that we're persecuted and discriminated against, and we are, but what do some of us do the first chance we get? Persecute and discriminate. It's disgusting. I swear, each time one of them acts that way, it sets the rest of us back a hundred years."

In her head, the police exercise shifted from handling a young punk to cultivating a local source. "It's fine. Is this your store? I like it very much."

It was. Inherited from her father, who inherited it from his father before him. The little corner café had been run by the same family for many generations. Between customers, Helen learned about the store, the neighborhood, the schools, family gossip, neighborhood gossip, who was up to what and with whom, for hours.

She couldn't have picked a better local contact if she tried.

Her name was Mrs. Binari, owner of Smooth Winds, which was a pun in Pallundian that also meant healthy foods. Later that morning her grown children arrived to start work. They didn't seem surprised to find Helen now behind the counter, elbows leaned over one of their plinth seats, chatting with Mrs. Binari.

Helen helped Mrs. Binari's son, Zeshen, unload a truck of Pallundian produce, which was mostly cases of various canned gasses. "Mama has always been progressive," he said. "She'll give you a job if you want one. She sent us to the local university, if you can believe that. She wanted us to understand petarkan."

"And do you?"

He shrugged. "Better than the Meronim. They're not bad, the petarkan. For the most part they're just different."

Zeshen's prediction was correct. Helen found herself doing inventory almost before she finished asking if they needed help. "You're good with numbers, I can see that. And so attractive! Are you married to a good family?"

"Mom," her daughter Anin scolded, "why do you always pry?"

"I'm not prying!" She sniffed, turning into a strangely shaped but no less recognizable Chinese grandmother in an instant. "I'm learning about a new culture."

"It's fine," Helen said, noting the use of *family* instead of man or husband. The pallun were more family-centric than Helen first understood. No wonder she got along well with them. "I don't mind. No, I'm not married yet. The policies of my country in the past have made finding a suitable family challenging."

She thought they'd want to know about the family policies of China, but that wasn't what confused them.

"Country? What's that?"

In an instant she was reminded that, no matter how similar they may sometimes seem, bemians were nothing like humans in important ways. "A political subdivision a step up from a city."

"Ah," Mrs. Binari said, "you mean province. How strange you have a unique word for it."

She didn't mean province, and the interpreter threads had understood that and sent the Chinese word straight through. Helen had no intention of correcting them and her thread seemed to understand that as well, since the conversation moved smoothly along afterward. But it was interesting that a bemian language didn't have a word for *country*.

It did, however, have a word for *gangster*. Several, in fact. This came up after she noticed Sornik had taken his perch outside Samatarra's.

Mrs. Binari noticed her interest. "You be careful around those gangsters."

"How dangerous are they?"

She scoffed. "To me? Not very. I can remember them all coming into this shop when they were little boys on training legs. But I don't cross them. I saw you with them yesterday, with Maff and Mr. Sha'Katenden. What were you doing over there?"

"Mother," her daughter scolded from the register, "leave her alone. You're such a gossip."

Helen smiled inwardly at the transparent snoop attempt.

Considering all the intelligence Mrs. Binari had gifted her with, Helen considered it a fair trade. "I'm a researcher and collector of rare books. They have some of the best."

Eventually she was able to prise herself away from the store and crossed the street. She shouldn't have bothered.

"No, we haven't figured out what happened at the warehouse yet. No, we don't need your help." Sornik said from his plinth. "Don't you have some books you need to read?"

Helen checked, and she did. They'd arrived at Maff's compound that morning.

So that became her routine for the week. She'd show up at Smooth Winds and help Mrs. Binari open and serve the morning customers, walk over to Samatarra's to ask Sornik for an update, get brushed off, and then spend the afternoon studying.

Tonya was typically American. "You got a job? *Again?*"

Maff only nodded. "Smooth Winds is a fixture in that neighborhood. The Binaris have run it since the beginning of time, as far as I know."

The books were turning out to be a disappointment. All were written thousands of years after the Refounding, obviously legendary, and likely began as orally transmitted stories for generations. She'd dabbled a bit in literary source criticism during her Chinese history studies, so she knew there were still clues there. Stories evolve in specific ways that provide evidence of their origin. With extensive study, it should be possible to determine at least the rough outlines of the facts that they were based on. But it could take years, and that was assuming bemians told their stories, and recorded their histories, the same way humans did. That was not guaranteed.

She did have an alternative line of investigation. Andromeda had to be behind the attack in the warehouse. It was much more elaborate and represented a much bigger effort than anything it had tried before. All she needed was access to the site. There was evidence there, her cop instincts insisted on it.

If only Sornik would come around.

Her breakthrough came two days later. "All right, all right, *all right,*" he said, probes waving in time with his agitation. "For a week I tell you to study, and what do you do? Chat it up with that old woman across the street and bother me every chance you get. Every time! You want to see the place? Fine. We'll see the place. Let's go."

The warehouse wasn't as sinister sitting in bright sunlight, a simple white building that wouldn't have looked out of place at a dockyard or delivery center back home.

"You do what you have to do," Sornik said. "Let me know if you find anything. Hey Bithern!" he shouted. "Keep an eye on our guest here, will ya?"

"Will do, boss." It was one of the pallun who arrived as reinforcements to the warehouse that night. He walked over. "What's up?"

"Our human friend here thinks she can figure out more about the dust up last week. I gotta do the thing, you know?"

He nodded. "Ah, right. The thing."

She knew better than to ask.

"Anyway," Sornik said to her. "I gotta, you know…"

"Do the thing, right," Helen replied, but with a smile. "And so do I."

He returned it. "I guess you do." With a tip of a wing, he went into his office.

She examined the front of the building carefully. The window they'd escaped through was still open. "How thoroughly have you searched so far?" she asked Bithern.

"See, it's complicated. Not everything in there, you know, needs to be seen by the outside world, if you get my meaning."

Gangsters talked the same all over the galaxy. He would've fit right in on a Shanghai dockyard. "But you did search."

"Oh, yeah. We tore the place apart." He paused. "Within reason."

"What did you find?"

He shrugged. "Not much. Well, not enough anyway. Someone cut the fence around back, but it was one person, not pallun, bipedal, about this big and this wide," he said using his manipulators to make a rough rectangle that would've fit at least three-quarters of the bemians that she'd seen so far, "you guys saw, what, dozens of..." his voice pitched down into a whisper, "did *he* tell you what he saw?"

Helen was raised a communist, so her atheism was deeply ingrained. Still, she was also Chinese, with a cultural tradition of hungry ghosts dating back thousands of years. Remembering those things crawling across every surface with their glowing eyes, searching, getting ever closer while she and Sornik had no way out and that infernal clanging in the distance growing faster as they ran...

"No, and all I saw were shadows. But you're right, there were a *lot* of shadows. There should be tracks all over the place." Helen shook herself and took a deep breath. Ghosts were a myth. There was another explanation.

She just had to find it.

She walked carefully around the outside, scanning, searching for things that were unusual, out of place. Like most industrial sites, the ground was littered with small bits of packing trash, some of which had blown up against the fencing that surrounded the lot. Bemians not only used chain link, but it was also the same pattern as on Earth. Apparently there was only one way to wrap wire to create a fence. The metal didn't feel the same, though. It was too smooth. The fence was the same, but the wire was much better made. Bemians had strange priorities.

The cut had been repaired perfectly, with only the differently colored wire indicating anything had changed. "Security cameras?"

Another shrug. "Too easy to use against us."

"How do you keep it secure?"

She got an embarrassed shuffle of brass legs. "Foot patrols, which we, ah, had let get a little lax."

Then she remembered. "Samatarra's gabbashan?"

"It's the best in the city. But yeah, we shoulda been walking around the property instead of walking around chewing."

Helen peered through the fence. The warehouse stood on its own lot, with streets on all four sides. Across the street was an empty lot that may have held another warehouse in the past but was now bare dirt. She examined it carefully. "How big were the feet again?" A truck pulled up and started unloading large containers clearly marked as sa'dst. That was interesting. She indicated the growing pile. "Does that mean the entire building's supply was used up recently?"

*

Helen used a virtual pen synched to her real one, and an overlay shared with everyone's phone to mark up the lot. "They were waiting here," she said, drawing squares where feet had gathered recently. "But they didn't cross." She highlighted tiny holes in the ground where stakes had been beaten in with a hammer or some other blunt tool. "They made a blind."

Once her findings were confirmed by the evidence she'd found, she had Bithern get Sornik away from *the thing*. The rest of his men had gathered behind him like curious monkeys. He stared at her, and then at the overlay. "An ambush?"

"You can draw a straight line through that door," she pointed at the one on the back of the warehouse, "through the hole in the fence and into this lot. They were herding us this way until you climbed the shelves."

"But only one person went through the fence. And there's still not enough people here."

She had that worked out, but it wasn't for general distribution. Sornik had been followed out by the rest of the warehouse crew, so about half a dozen of the manta rays shuffled around on their brass legs. She slowly scanned the pallun around her. Then she fixed Sornik with her stare.

"Ah," Sornik said after a moment. "What is this? Break time? I'm not paying you idiots to stare at the ground. Get back to work!"

Bithern had been standing toward the back, and now glanced around awkwardly. "I'm supposed to be watching her?"

Sornik walked up to him. "And now I'm watching her." A manipulator thumped onto the top of Bithern's head. "Get out of here, you dope. Find Poolin. He's got another thing he needs help with."

When Bithern was on the other side of the street, Sornik said, "There. Happy now?"

"Yes. Follow me. Please." She lifted a container of sa'dst she'd grabbed while Bithern had been getting Sornik away from *the thing*, and then walked to the far side of the lot. It'd been abandoned long enough for tall grass and trees to overgrow the space. Now shielded from the street and any curious warehouse worker, she stopped and turned around. "I don't expect you to keep this from Toraz. But I do ask that you tell only him."

He grew suspicious. "What did you find?"

"It's not what I found. Well, it's not *only* what I found. It's what I am, and what who attacked us almost certainly was. Watch."

She opened the container, which was about the size of a backpack, and then extended her threads into the control structures. Mike was right. It was more than a little frightening that bemian bodies were infused with nanomachines that were so poorly secured. Once they were all activated, she started a simple program she prepared.

A single speck of sa'dst was an invisible miracle. Mike still had no idea how they were powered or how they moved. That didn't matter at the moment, only that they had incredible freedom of movement. They could penetrate skin, swim through blood vessels, crawl along neurons.

And fly.

Gathered in their millions they were easily visible, quickly forming a nightmare of shadowy figures that slowly crept toward them. Above and behind the gloomy horde, the shape of a demon appeared holding a round piece of metal in one hand, which it struck with a bar held in the other. The sound that rang out was exactly what had chased them around the warehouse that night.

Sornik backed away, swearing. "What the fuck? What are you doing?"

"Recreating what happened in the warehouse." The reason she was able to purloin the sa'dst was that they'd mysteriously run out of it and had ordered reloads for the distribution machines. "There *was* only one person who went through the fence. Someone like me." At a command, the sa'dst swirled into a dark column that funneled into the container. When the last of it went in, the top closed with a metallic clunk. "An Interpreter."

She watched his confusion manifest through his waving manipulators. "Interpreters? The *Guild* is behind this?"

"No." She'd been studying them for nearly as long as Mike and Kim. "They don't work this way. It's not their style."

"Wait, you said you were…" His eyes swirled faster through the protective lenses on his suit.

"Yes. I am an Interpreter. Of a sort." He stiffened. "But I'm not in the guild."

"Bullshit. They're all in the guild."

"I can prove it." She pulled up her shirt high, exposing bare skin and a basic bra. She turned slowly around. "I have no companion. I am not combined or paired. I am a human Interpreter. We have no guild and do not combine."

He gaped at her. "That's not possible."

She smiled. "Ask Maff when she gets back. She'll confirm it. Human Interpreters do not combine, and I'm unpaired."

"What does *that* have to do with *this*?"

"I may not be the kind of Interpreter you're used to, but I am one. We all have abilities. One of them is the ability to hack sa'dst. Command it. I never considered that I could use it to create effects in the outside world, but that was my lack of imagination. What we have here is a strike team, led by an Interpreter, who attempted to capture me. They failed because they didn't know you were still in the warehouse." It all made sense now. The scares, the mysterious presences. All of it. "And I know who they're working for."

Chapter 29
Mike

Being inside someone else's dream wasn't new for him. When he was young, long before he came outside and acquired a human host, he'd sometimes wander into them accidentally. His threads hadn't matured to the point that they could distinguish the unreality of realmspace from the unreality of the connected consciousnesses that used it. Sleep therapy was, after all, one of the oldest clinical uses realmspace had.

But by the time he met Kim, he hadn't been able to do it reliably for years. Most of that was down to his threads maturing. Once he had a sense of where he stopped and others started, the ability to cross the boundary was lost. There was also a bit of an ick factor. Human dreams involved human bodies, and before he'd gotten his realspace host, he'd found them, well, gross. He stayed away from the most graphically surreal realmspaces for the same reason. People turning themselves inside out and then walking into a bar wasn't his thing.

The experience with Kim was completely different. This was his wife, someone he'd vowed to spend his entire life with. The stakes were infinitely higher than wandering into the wrong head at the wrong time. There were other, deeper differences as well. Their time being Interpreters, doing Interpreter things, was changing them. The powerful but diaphanous connection human souls had with their bodies, and that his had with his threads, was now different. He couldn't describe it easily with words, and it didn't seem threatening or dangerous. Interpreters had a special relationship with the universe, and the changes he noticed seemed to be a part of that.

The end result was that after he'd successfully interfaced with her, he'd been trapped, locked up almost the same way Kim was. She'd somehow cast him in her mindscape as a kind of guru, changing his appearance and the way he thought to the point he was unrecognizable, to himself as well as to her. He'd become a different person, living in a parallel reality.

And living there for much longer than should've been possible. Before opening his eyes, he checked the time and was shocked. A week had passed. No wonder he had no strength. But he wasn't starving, and there weren't any bad smells he could detect. He did *want* to eat. It wasn't hunger so much as a desire for anything other than peanut butter and crackers. Those were flavors and textures he wanted nothing to do with, but he didn't know why.

Regardless, he was back now, in their tent, on their bed. The mattress's nanofoam was as firm as ever.

"At least we're not in a hospital this time," she said lying beside him.

He'd guided her back to reality with his threads. They'd somehow maintained their special connection without being in physical contact, a mystery that would need to be explored.

He carefully rolled toward her, discovering that at some point he'd changed into loose-fitting pajamas. The effort was three or four times more than it should've been. The lack of bedsores was another indication that they'd been active in realspace during their ordeal, but it must not have been much.

She laughed gently at him from her side of their pillow fence. "Tonya's right. You're one of the easiest people in the world to read sometimes. I love that about you." She threw a handkerchief over the fence. "And I love you."

He gripped a corner, and they pulled it taught between them, their version of a morning hug. "I love you too. What happened to us? I mean, out here?"

She nodded and breathed deep. "It's my old syndrome. When I was locked up, I could still perform basic functions. I could feed myself, barely, and clean myself after going to the bathroom, but that was about it. You went through the same thing. How tired are you?"

"Exhausted." He fired off an inventory request to the truck with his phone. "Apparently we've been living off peanut butter and crackers this whole time."

"Ugh," she groaned as his own stomach flipped over at the mention of the name. "I don't think I'll ever be able to eat that again."

She stiffened at the same time he remembered. Together they said, "Spencer."

His phone didn't pick up and his tracker was offline. Mike tried to get up off the bed but only managed to roll flat on his back. "I can barely move."

"Me too. Okay, slowly on three."

Concentrating hard and putting as much effort into it as he could, Mike reached a sitting position. It felt like he'd run a marathon.

Kim hadn't managed that much. "I think that last part, with the helicopter, took more out of me than it did you." She sighed and closed her eyes. Tears leaked out. "I feel like I've been run over and thrown down a stairwell, but I've never been…never known…" She blinked and wiped her face. "Is this what peace feels like?"

"For you, I think it might." In spite of visible weakness, she was beautiful in a new way, one he hadn't noticed before. "It suits you."

"I didn't know. I didn't understand." Her near sob transformed into a soft, sincere laugh. "But it's going to be okay. It is. And look." She tapped her side of the bed two times, one time, then three times. "The OCD is gone. Well, my version of it anyway. Vanished."

He knew about that too. He'd watched her shed the psychic weight as she traveled. But it was good to hear it come from her. "You stay here and rest." He wheeled his legs over the side of the bed and slowly stood. "I'll see if I can find Spencer."

"And some food. *Real* food, not..." Her face turned slightly pale green, and she swallowed hard.

He almost lost his balance at the idea and didn't risk mentioning the name. "No worries there."

He snuck past where they'd obviously been eating for the past week and peered into the rest of their food store. Spencer, planning for an extended hike, had pulled out a big chunk, but there was plenty left behind. Plenty being a relative term. If they didn't wrap this up in a week or two, it would be time to learn whether or not extraterrestrial chickens still tasted like chickens.

But for now, a pair of Meal Number Fives, nano-heated civilian versions of US military MREs, would do. The thought of hot ravioli with fresh, self-baking breadsticks almost made him tear his open and eat it on the spot. The craving spread straight through to his threads, which seemed to have taken on a life of their own.

"No sign of Spencer?" she asked as he fed her every other forkful of the unbelievably divine ration. Normally he'd take her inability to do simple things like sit up and hold a fork as a cause for worry, but she was otherwise transformed. She'd been gray and depressed for so long he'd gotten used to it. The firebrand who kept him on his toes, laughed at his jokes, and led their way forward had returned. He was certain the rest was only a matter of time.

Which they needed. The news wasn't good. "None."

"What are we going to do?"

"I'm not a hunter like he is, and it's been days now. Whatever trail he left is cold. The microMappers have surveyed several miles around us. The terrain isn't challenging, and there aren't any large predators around. They also haven't come across a message."

"Or a body."

The thought *wasn't* a punch to the gut. But it should've been. Fascinating. He'd always caught the hints of the instinct that humans called intuition, but with all the worry over Kim, he seemed to have forgotten about it. Now intuition was back and much stronger than before. Kim might not be the only one to have experienced changes during their ordeal.

"No, not that either. I think he's okay. I don't know why."

Her face split into an adorably tomato sauce-stained smile. "Intuition?"

He smiled back and carefully wiped her mouth with moist towelettes bunched up to prevent a touch. "I guess so." After all this time, he still wasn't sure he believed in it, even though Tonya's theories went a long way toward making falsifiable tests of intuition a reality. One day soon they might know for sure. "I'll set the drone to do a stealth search pattern in the direction he was headed. It won't be fast, but it's better than nothing."

She nodded, took the next forkful, and sighed. "I will never make fun of people who eat canned ravioli again."

The breadstick packets made a jaunty little ping to let him know they were done. When he opened the bag, they both started tears of joy that turned to laughter. He thought nothing would equal that first taste of ravioli, but the smell of fresh baked garlic bread was better than anything he could imagine.

"Such an impressive illusion," he said, eyes closed because opening them was impossible with this unbelievably delicious food in his mouth. His threads stopped feeling like rebellious coconspirators with his human host and more like his real body. This had been an ordeal on so many levels.

"What do you mean?"

He swallowed. "Our extended stay eating"—his stomach lurched, and his threads snapped—"*that stuff* has left us badly deficient in some nutrients and with an overabundance of others. This ration alone is addressing the most critical. But I didn't check the nutritional information before I picked it. I *knew* which one was the right one."

"Intuition again?"

An interesting idea, but not quite right. "If it is, it's a different kind. Knowing…well, thinking…Spencer is okay defies logic. With food, I can easily see a segment of my brain being subconsciously aware of what my body needs the most and prodding me toward it." It was as disturbing as it was interesting. After a year, he still wasn't used to the idea that there was a part of him that evolved long before humans were conscious. It was not only still alive and well, but actively helping him to survive.

"So what does your intuition say we go for next?" she asked.

There was no hesitation. "Lemon chicken with rice."

They both moaned in a way that would've been embarrassing if Spencer was around.

*

He woke the next morning to find himself vastly improved. Not fully recovered, but well enough to do basic chores, one of which was the disposal of the hated peanut butter can and the ravaged case of crackers. Now that he was able to look at it without heaving, he noticed signs that they probably weren't the only ones taking advantage of an easy source of food. The basic neuronal security wire strung around the camp kept the big critters away, but the small and the airborne had left tracks all over the place. The bug analogs trapped in the peanut butter had probably provided valuable nutritional supplements.

He still never wanted to see it again.

Kim was strong enough to get out of bed and clean herself up properly, but that was the extent of her activities for the day. "In spite of what it looks like," she said on collapsing back into a now freshly changed bed, "I am feeling better. So much better." She smiled. "I might be able to leave the tent."

"Which is great. I need to go on a scouting mission back to town."

She nodded. "The node's been working on that crystal lattice this entire time."

"We need to know how far it's gotten, if we're in any danger."

"Or if we're too late. They won't see us as Interpreters but as attackers." Kim made a *poof* gesture with her hands. "So much for surprise. This won't work as a main-force assault. You don't scale the walls of a castle if there's only three of you, and the natives know you're right outside."

"Yeah." He'd only gotten Kim back yesterday, and now it was time to go again.

She nodded. "I hate it too, but the sooner we figure out where we are, the sooner we can plan countermoves. We can only win by making decisions faster than they can."

Which was another way of saying *do the unexpected.*

"Here's what we'll do," she said. "Pack up the camp for me so I can move out whenever I want. I'll sleep in the truck. Since it's just me, that'll be fine. I'll keep tabs on the drone until we figure out what's happened to Spencer. You do your scouting." She threw a handkerchief over his hand. "Don't you dare get caught."

Being a stealthy scout was his favorite realspace hobby. It was a heady feeling to creep past defenses and find out secret things.

He smiled. "Not a chance of that, wife."

"Okay then, husband, you've got a camp to pack. Let's see if I can make it into the truck all by myself."

*

The news was good on his hike back to town. Commerce seemed to be moving briskly on the main road; farmers were in their fields, and the only soldiers were the occasional messengers making their way past the merchant caravans. This was not a society on high alert.

The impression held making his way through the walls and into the town proper. Things were crowded and bustling, people going about their business, and business was good. If anything, it was more normal than the last time he'd visited. Then, the big news was about their lord meeting with a mysterious Interpreter that the nodes had chased away for reasons nobody understood. The buzz of fear and gossip that event created had vanished. It seemed that people went back to their routines all over the galaxy if the galaxy allowed it.

The sense of normalcy only stopped inside the node's basilica. It wasn't resting. Far from it. Its giant metal plates moved and banged together louder than ever, the clockwork behind it moving faster. It wasn't angry so much as preoccupied. This was his second time visiting, so he got to his perch in the rafters of the roof with confidence. Taking the utmost care, he crept to where the node's carapace pierced the ceiling and the roof above it.

When he penetrated the node's fabric with his threads, he discovered what the fuss was about.

"That is an incorrect conclusion," a node Mike somehow knew wasn't the one he'd attached to said. "It is impossible on many levels."

He'd stumbled upon a realm holding a large convocation of nodes. At root, nodes were a kind of unduplicate, and like the ones back home, these seemed to prefer using avatars in a realm to communicate. The space was like two giant stadiums had been put on top of each other, with the one above facing downward. The effect was like being inside a kind of gigantic, closed clamshell.

A clamshell full of identical avatars: a giant blue insectoid, bipedal, shiny in a way that made their color look painted on. There were thousands of them, filling conventional seats on the ground and ceiling. Dead center, a holo image of the node that was speaking was projected. The whole thing was a simulation, of course, right down to the faux screen projection in the center. Maybe this need to cling to physical simulations had to do with their being designed by realspace beings instead of emerged from realmspace itself. As with all realms, Mike observed unnoticed from the interstitial space that surrounded it.

A new speaker, designated by an ID number at the bottom of the frame, appeared in the holo. "Then please provide an alternative. Collective 745 can find no other solution."

The previous speaker reappeared. "I cannot. I can only state that, while the reported appearance of Interpreters in this stage of uplift is unprecedented, it *was* a recognizable Interpreter. This," a different holo view spun up in the center of the space, "is not an Interpreter."

Their failed assault on the original ruined node played out in the new space. The playback used vivid color and sound, from multiple perspectives. Each provided clear looks at their avatars, which were duplicates of their realspace bodies.

They had fully decoded the destroyed node's memory store.

But it quickly became apparent that these nodes had no idea what they were seeing. Speaker after speaker proposed outlandish sequences of events, each one less plausible than the next, to somehow connect two facts that none of them had known was possible: the unscheduled appearance of Interpreters and the successful destruction of a node via assault.

To his surprise, the appearance of Interpreters was the hotter topic.

"They have always threatened this..."

"We must be in their service at all times..."

"Cheating. Simple cheating, so typical of Interpreters that..."

"Bad enough when they take over on schedule..."

"Might be listening to us right now..."

He smiled. Just because they were paranoid didn't mean they were wrong.

Finally, the node he was connected to weighed in.

"We cannot reach an adequate solution with the data we currently possess. The unscheduled presence of Interpreters cannot be falsified. The destruction of the node by an unknown party cannot be explained. Since the Guild seems to have ignored its traditional schedule, I propose we ignore ours and connect this planet to the galactic network as soon as possible."

The resulting eruption would've been right at home in any parliamentary chamber back on Earth. The nodes represented one of the only institutions to have survived the disaster that led to the Refounding. They had practices and traditions that stretched back billions of years. They did *not* like breaking with them.

But, after much debate, break with them they did. They would rejoin the galactic network to see if it had answers to their questions.

Plan decided, it was then down to the logistics.

"We must protect our subjects from premature contamination," Mike's node said. "They cannot know of the technologies we deploy to create the portal necessary for the connection. My territory contains the largest Interdict remaining on the planet." A gigantic map drew itself into the center of the meeting space. Pictures of a flat, grassy plain punctuated by sinkholes large and small appeared around it. "We will sterilize it and then build the connection there. Our wards have long been trained to stay away. It will be safe to deploy without risking contamination."

This was bad news. They were here to insert their hack before this planet joined the galactic network. It was the only way to get it to spread. They had to get moving.

Mike mulled over their possible moves on the way back. None of them were easy, but he could think of a few ways forward. By the time he reached the copse that hid their camp, he had the bones of a workable plan.

When he reached the clearing, that all fell apart. He found Kim sitting upright in the passenger seat of the truck, window rolled down.

Talking to a pair of Lord Malafan's soldiers.

Chapter 30
Maff

She'd discovered the cache using Toraz's ship. It only seemed fair to tell him about it. But when she told him the day after the race, he wasn't as impressed with it as she expected he'd be.

"Nah, those things have come up occasionally," he'd said.

"They have?"

Toraz shrugged. "Every couple of centuries, someone comes across what they think is a big score. Those seals? Not as hard to fake as you think."

"Then why do you want to investigate it now?" He'd only given her a day and a half to recover before bringing her in and giving her the mission.

He frowned at her. "Are you kidding me?" He looked up at the ceiling of his other office, at the back of a salvage yard. "She brings us a wolfing civilization she *stumbled* on, and now thinks we're gonna ignore a cache she found. Ha!"

He lit up another of his chivals and took a few puffs. Maff had spent so much time around them lately they were starting to smell good to her. Or at least not bad. "You're lucky, that much is obvious." He grew pensive, pulled the chival out of its suit port, and pointed it at her. "Plus it's been spooky around here lately. Your friend, Helen? She's got some wild theories about it."

He leaned back, a king concerned about his kingdom. "Now normally I'd wave off crazy alien nonsense as, you know, crazy alien nonsense." He took another puff, long and slow. The king was worried enough to think about whatever it was Helen had said. "But she's managed to convince Sornik. That is one pallun who does not convince easily.

"Here's what's gonna happen. I'm giving you a crew. Some of my best men. You take them, your crazy friend, and put them on that ship of yours. Go see what's out there." He leaned back and splayed out his manipulators. Toraz was a leader, and leading someone like her seemed to brighten his mood. "Personally, I think you're gonna find a bunch of rocks and dirt in there. Maybe an old booze bottle."

That was strangely specific. "Why?"

He let out a coarse chuckle. "It's what we found the last time. My old man, let me tell you. He'd been talking up a cache he'd found to whoever would listen. Wouldn't shut up about it. We go out there, and it's a box full of rocks. One of his cousins pranked him." He laughed hard now. She wondered if someone else, like the pallun sitting in front of her, had been the one to pull the prank. "I never saw him so angry."

Toraz had one last surprise in store for her. As she supervised loading the crew and their supplies onboard *Palatine,* a message landed in her queue.

Don't think of it as a gift, think of it as how you're getting your ass back here for next year's race.

Attached to the message was the title to *Palatine,* with her name on it. Until now it'd technically, well, *actually,* been stolen.

It was another bemian quirk Earth did not share. A certain amount of vehicle theft was expected and tolerated. The original owner found an empty parking spot where the ship had been, filed a claim, and received compensation. The AC network would then perform inquiries to find which guild had stolen the vehicle and bill them accordingly. If no guild accepted responsibility, then an investigation would be opened up. At some point it would rise to the top of a queue somewhere, and a bot squad would be assigned to track down the wayward vehicle and retrieve it.

That was how it was supposed to work. In reality a single, one-off vehicle theft almost always fell through the cracks. Things only got serious if a pattern emerged. The AC network was good at spotting patterns. If any guild, gang, family, or culture decided to make this one-off tolerance a rite of passage or a way to make a quick buck, they were shut down.

So Maff had never considered using a stolen ship as their transport a big risk. But it was nice to have *Palatine* in her name for real.

Once they were safely underway, with Sornik's crew set up in the cargo hold smoking and playing games of puchole, Maff brought Helen and Sornik to the bridge to tell them the *rest* of the story. She hadn't told Toraz about her visitors.

"What is it with you people and Interpreters?" Sornik asked when Maff was done.

She shrugged.

"Why didn't you tell Toraz?" Helen asked.

It was a good question. "The timing didn't seem right." It sounded lame said out loud.

"Nah, that's not it," Sornik said. "You don't trust us." He held up manipulators when she started to protest. "It's okay. Nobody trusts us at first. And you shouldn't. We sure as hell don't trust you. But you've told me, and I get it. We'll see what's out here and then maybe it won't matter anyway."

"But do you think they're connected?" Maff asked.

Sornik immediately looked at Helen. Their time together must've exposed him to the human's eerie abilities of observation.

A moment later, she said, "If you'd discovered the cache without Tonya's device, I'd say absolutely. But they could not have known about what Tonya had added to the ship. Those special modifications, the one you used to find the cache? They were unique."

Maff had been thinking about this for some time. "They managed to sneak a camera on board. They could've done a thorough scan of the modifications then."

"But then they wiped the nav data, which you restored independently. I don't think there's a connection, not yet." She shrugged. "If we had Tonya around, we could ask her."

She'd gone missing two days ago. The last person to see her and her friend, Tenor, had been Dean Shakson. It took time to get past the *what whats* and *jolly goods*, but eventually it seemed he'd left her and her friend Tenor working on the failed experiment. He said she'd wired a power supply too big for the job into her machine, it'd burned out, they might've gone searching for spares, and hadn't made it back yet. Exactly how that would prevent her from answering her phone, he didn't know.

Sornik made a disgusted noise. "That old man, he's up to no good. As soon as we got the news, we went looking. No records whatsoever about a human transiting off world. For any reason. Her friend, Tenor? His parents are losing their minds searching for him. It smells, I tell ya."

Helen nodded. "He instigated it. Whatever happened to them, the professor was the one behind it."

Sornik threw his manipulators side to side. "How do you *know* these things?"

She gave him a grim smile. "Observation, logic, deduction. The rest is bookkeeping. Your search will have to be enough. If the police are brought in, it might expose her ID as a fraud." She turned to Sornik. "What will you tell your men?"

He shrugged. "Nothing. The guys, they're good at what they do, yanno? But they're not the ones you want when it comes to forecasting the next sulfur storm, if you get my meaning. They'll go where I tell them and break things real good if that's what needs to happen."

"What do they already know?" Maff asked. She didn't want to say the wrong thing to the wrong person.

He laughed. "That the boss said to get on this ship and do what I say. It's for the best. If you told them the truth, every whore on the east side would know in less than a day. The only reason it'd take that long is if you made them promise to keep it a secret."

"Sounds like some men I knew back home," Helen said. "Okay, we need to make a proper plan that doesn't require a lot of explanation."

Chapter 31
Spencer

It was too dark to climb down to confirm what he saw was a bicycle, and it took some time to explain what it was anyway.

"You balance on it? How?" Tapov asked as they sat, chewing their rations around the fire.

That brought him up short. "Fuck if I know. I learned as a kid. Dad kept pushing me and letting me go until I quit falling into ditches." Mike probably knew, but there was no way to find out. "And you'd never seen one? Heard of one?"

She shrugged. "Not at all."

"Could it have come from that city you're going to?"

"I guess it's possible. Umalaza has a harbor. It might've come from Virkin or some other place across the sea." She yawned. "Maybe we'll be able to tell in the morning."

By the time he was done putting away his kit she was fast asleep.

*

He'd miscalculated which way the sun would come up. It was now too bright to see his flashlight when he pointed it into the bicycle crevasse.

"Maybe we can find our way down there?" she asked.

There did seem to be passageways where the crevasse met the sinkhole. "Worth a try. But give me a minute."

He pulled a half-burned stick out of their old fire. It would be just his luck that the drone would show up right after they lost line of sight to this crater. He found a smooth-ish part of wall under an overhang so a rain storm wouldn't wash his message away.

Hey Mike! I'm OK, found friend. Tapov / Sarewith! Investigating bicycle. Going THIS WAY. He scratched a long line and put an arrow on the end, pointing at the passage they would take. *Will explain later. Blow horn when you see this, we'll come back. –S*

When he finished, Tapov asked, "What is it?"

"A message for my friends."

"You communicate with art?"

"Eh? No, that's English. Writing."

"That's not writing," she declared.

Tapov could go from zero to princess almost as fast as Kim could spin up a flaming rage. "It is where I come from. Now, let's find us a bicycle."

The area underneath the sinkholes was riddled with passages. Some were big enough to drive a truck through, leading to other, deeper caves. He kept them trending right and down, since that was where the bicycle was. They walked about an hour longer than they should've; that was a problem. "Let's get back to the surface."

"But we haven't found it yet."

"I need to know where *out* is first."

The key to dead reckoning navigation was a solid awareness of where you started, which way you'd gone, and the landmarks you'd passed on the way. Spencer had spent hours wandering in the woods and never had a problem with finding his way back.

Here, this was a mistake. Caves were different. Really different.

He started marking walls too late. After walking about half the distance that should've taken them back to the starting point, they ended up crossing a tunnel that he'd already marked.

He had no idea how they'd managed it.

"Does this mean what I think it means?" Tapov asked as she touched the three-inch gouge he'd made at a tunnel crossing.

Spencer had gotten lost many times in subterranean realms. It shouldn't be this hard to find his way back. But the realm was designed by a person. The tunnels had to go somewhere otherwise what was the point? Down here in realspace, that wasn't a guarantee.

He sat down heavily, trying to get his head to stop spinning so he could get his bearings. The tunnels were all the same. Up and down was probably an illusion.

People died in situations like this.

"How's your water?" he asked.

She sat down and rummaged through her pack and produced three large, full canteens. "Fine, I guess."

Definitely stronger than she looked.

He checked and his news wasn't good, but it wasn't bad either. "Two for me. They're smaller, but if we can find more water, I can make it drinkable." The bottles had nanosystems in the bases that would clean anything. Rumor had it that some lunatic managed to try one at a destroyed reactor site near the Three Gorges disaster. The bottle had worked, but it took a robot to pick it up.

"You asked that question right away," she said. "How dependent are your kind on water?"

A fair question. "If I stopped drinking right now, I'd have no more than thirty-six hours until I fell over dead. Probably less. You?"

She considered it briefly. It was a welcome difference between her and the princesses back home: no freak-out. "About the same."

They had enough water to last at least a week if they were careful. The food would last longer. "So that's not a disaster," he said.

"It's still not good."

"Nope. The primary goal is finding our way out of here."

"Secondary is to find water." She examined the walls, which were red, wet, and pretty fucking nasty if Spencer were honest about it. She dragged a finger across the one nearest to her, creating a trail of moisture. "I like our chances, but you better hope that technology of yours can cope with this place." She showed him her fingertip, a slightly distorted version of his own due to her retracted claw. It was covered in muck. "It isn't exactly clean."

*

The clock on his phone, the one thing he didn't need, naturally still worked. They spent two days—Telirian days, with an extra one and a half hours—searching for water or a way out. They'd resorted to the climbing harness a few times but only found passages down. Never up.

The cave system was long and unpredictable. Sometimes they'd walk through caverns bigger than his house, other times it took multiple tries to find a way forward. It was muddy, exhausting work, always with the specter of never making it out hanging over them.

Until he felt a breeze and then heard a rushing noise.

He might not know much about caves, but he did know that they were almost always created with water. Finding water had to happen at some point. The cave wasn't dry enough to be dead.

"Holy shit," Tapov said—in English, they'd been teaching each other their native languages as a way to pass the time—as she climbed over a rock ledge. "You gotta come see this."

His flashlight revealed a vast cave. At their end, a low waterfall poured into a wide lake that covered most of the floor. At the other end was a big tunnel that led away into the darkness.

"It's about time we catch a break." He filled one of his empty canteens and let it analyze the water.

"Huh," he said, examining the readouts.

"What?" Tapov asked.

"A high metal content is expected. Half this fucking cavern seems to be made of iron-rich dirt. But I'm also seeing signs of complex organic compounds."

She gave him a sour look. "In Standard, please?"

Right. He'd switched to English because of the technical terms. "There's junk in the water that isn't metal but also isn't natural. What do you guys use for fuel?"

She shrugged. "Wood, oil from fats. We buy tar from a village that has full pits on their land. We give it to the nodes, and they turn it into a nasty-smelling liquid that burns for a long time. But only merchants and my…and the lord can afford that."

"It's pretty tough when they change from your parent to another annoying adult, isn't it?"

She shook her head. "I don't want to talk about it. Why is what we use for fuel important?"

"The organic compounds seem to be degraded fuel. It's only trace amounts. If the villages around here use node-created fuel"—which by the readings was probably being turned into diesel, but that would take a long time to explain—"it might mean there's one upstream."

She looked at the waterfall for a moment. "I don't think we'll be able to make much progress going upstream."

"No," he agreed, "but it means this isn't a river to nowhere. If people live on one end, they'll probably be living on the other."

Exploring further, they made a better discovery: a whole fucking boat, overturned, floating in a backwater.

"I know where this came from," she said with an edge of excitement that shifted to awe. "I know this river. It's the Beshanta. This boat was built in Kelsen, and that's on the Beshanta."

"And what's on the other end?" he asked as he dragged the slimy thing to the shore.

Excitement shifted to confusion. "Nobody knows. It vanishes into the base of the Interdict plateau." She brightened. "But it does limit the options. There are several rivers that *exit* the plateau. They all have villages along their length."

"Help me tip this over then. We're getting out of here."

It was a flat-bottom jonboat that only needed a coat of green paint and a trolling motor to fit right in with the dozens that got put into the river at Pendleton landing every weekend back home. It was wood instead of aluminum, but otherwise, it was the same.

They found enough dried wood washed up on the shores around it to have their first fire since they'd gotten lost.

"Why isn't there any life down here?" she asked as she checked the place out. This part of the lake shore had a low enough ceiling they could examine it by the firelight. It was almost completely dry, although Spencer couldn't explain why.

"The water's fucked," he replied. "It's nothing my bottles can't handle, but it'd give anything else trying to drink it metal poisoning inside of a month." He chewed on a ration bar, thinking. "This has to be an abandoned mine or connected to one somehow."

She shook her head. "I've never heard of any kind of mine this big. The nodes use robots."

"Could it be from before they arrived?"

He watched as Tapov considered the question. "I don't think so. The nodes are what brought us technology. We were savages, living in the open in small tribes, killing each other every chance we got. If it weren't for the nodes, that's how we'd all still be living."

"Then that can't be what's going on here. There might be a monster iron deposit that's never been discovered." He smiled at her from across the fire. "Might impress Dad if you've discovered a fuck-ton of it. That's bound to be a good trade item."

"We get out of here first."

He couldn't disagree with that. "We get out of here first."

*

The next morning, by his phone's clock, Spencer had to get a question answered. "Do you know how to swim?"

"Swim? Yes." She settled unsteadily into the front of their new boat, basically falling onto the bench seat. "Boats, not so much."

"You're fine. These things are impossible to tip over."

"It was upside down when we found it."

Girls always pointed out the downside no matter where in the galaxy they came from. "Okay, almost impossible. And now..." He stood up in the back. Tapov squeaked a little as the boat rocked. Spencer pulled out a pole he'd made from a branch they found. "Time for my gondolier impression."

He pushed off the shore and belted "O Sole Mio" out loud

enough to echo off the walls. It didn't take long before Tapov told him to stop. "You sound like you're strangling a lonar."

"People never respect great artists."

Poling down a river was a massive improvement from clambering over rocks and squeezing through crags. Then, a day later, the ceiling of the passage closed down over the top of the river. What had at first been an underground Mississippi became a swift drain hole, and he noticed the current picking up speed.

"Great," Tapov said. "Now what?"

They explored the cave but found no other exits or passageways they could use.

"Time for plan B," he said.

Spencer got out his microdrone and attached the smartRope to it, using the spool to configure a few strands to act as a wired connection to the drone. His phone was trashed, but the spool had a basic screen to display telemetry. "Now we see if this passage is short enough for us to swim." The drone's superPlaz frame reconfigured from flight to swim mode. Tapov gasped. "Still not sure if you'll get one," he said.

He tossed the drone in, immediately getting telemetry on the water. Current speed was right on the edge of being too fast to manage, the temperature cold but not deadly. It'd passed ninety-five feet when the telemetry said the drone had reached the surface again. The sonar it used was primitive but enough to tell him the passage didn't get too narrow for them to use.

Spencer had won the regional swim tournament in his junior year of high school, right before all hell broke loose with Mike. He hadn't gotten in the water much since then, but going with the current and using the rope as a guide, it shouldn't be a big deal. Tapov was a question mark. "You said you could swim," he said as he programmed the drone's next moves. "How long can you hold your breath?"

After he detached the rope segment and tied it to a boulder, he found her eyes a bit wild, staring at him. "How long do I need to hold my breath? What did that find?"

"There is an exit." It took some back-and-forth until she understood what a hundred yards meant in Telirian. "With the current and the rope, it shouldn't take long. Can you do it?"

"Do I have a choice?"

He shrugged. "I could go ahead and see if there's an exit close by."

"How would I know if you found one?"

"You wouldn't, I'd find help."

She turned flinty. "I don't need help."

Maybe he should start calling her Bear Kim. "Okay then."

The drone pinged him with its final scout report. "It's more than a crack in the ground on the other side. Seems pretty big in fact. All right," he said as he clapped his hands together. "Prep time."

They would have to say goodbye to the bemian gondola. He could think of no practical, safe way to sink it enough to float it through the passage. Their gear was a different story. He'd brought along a roll of plastic bags that Amazon drones used to keep packages dry. The material was super light and strong. A couple of rocks in each bag neutralized the buoyancy.

It also brought up an awkward situation. "I guess this means our clothes go in a bag too?" Tapov asked.

"Is that a problem?"

"The nodes say sometimes it is, with certain cultures."

"They teach you guys the weirdest shit. Or do you mean it's a problem with *your* culture?"

Her shoulders slumped. "It's so stupid. Naked and swimming, or clothed and drowned? That's how I should phrase the question. It makes the answer simple. But don't talk about this to my father, ever."

"No worries there."

Well of course he looked, because she did too. Maff was right when she explained what she called high-grav-high-temp aliens were like. Basic anatomy was pretty similar. Hopefully Tapov wouldn't think his junk was self-retracting hitting the cold water. After a couple of sly smirks, they waded in.

"Shit!"

"Fuck!"

"Damn it!" she shouted. "You said this wasn't cold enough to be dangerous!"

"It's not," he said through hopping gasps. "I didn't say it'd be comfortable." Understatement of the fucking century. His toes went numb almost instantly. "Come on, the sooner the better."

Holding his breath, eyes closed in the intense cold and absolute darkness, he would've gotten lost in an instant if it wasn't for the rope. He still had no idea how wide the passage was or how deep, only that along this rope, he could fit his shoulders through, which were fortunately a few inches wider than Tapov's. It did get that narrow at one point, but the current was so swift he only hit the sides once. Then it was like getting blown out of a straw.

When they reached the other side, he got a surprise. His feet didn't hit the bottom. It was a lot deeper here.

Tapov panicked, thrashing and sputtering.

"Hey! *Hey!*" He grabbed her by the shoulder. In an instant, she was on him with full painful claws, yanking him face-to-face. After a brief fight with his own panic, he got them both to the surface. Tapov's head was firmly tucked over his shoulder, her panting heavy in his ear. After a moment, she pulled back and looked him in the eyes.

It got awkward again.

They both quickly parted and swam toward the shore, marked by the drone's flashing lights. "Are you okay?" he asked.

"I am now. Sorry about that."

He was skinny dipping with an alien. Under no circumstances would she ever be mistaken for a human, but he'd stopped seeing her as anything else. They were still a long-ass way from being out of this mess.

Her fur had been a lot softer than he'd expected.

Okay, enough, he thought. *This is adrenaline and hormones and a fucked up situation going on here. Get it together, McKenzie.* So he did, drying himself off with a quantumTowel. Twice, because, yeah, she shook herself all over him like a big wet dog.

It was probably the fastest he'd ever gotten dressed.

He looked around. The drone's lights weren't strong enough to make out any walls. "It's bigger than I expected."

She seemed to welcome the change of subject as much as he did. "Flat, too. This'll be a decent campground. Maybe we can get the boat back."

He turned on his flashlight. "Emphasis on maybe. That won't be anywhere near as easygoing against the—"

He fumbled the flashlight, catching it as it slipped. They both screamed when the beam fell on the biggest Telirian face he'd ever seen.

Chapter 32
Tonya

She'd known since meeting Maff that bemians didn't have the same understanding of time as humans did. It was a curiosity then, a fun novelty. Trying to explain time travel to an actual bemian when it directly affected their lives proved quite a bit less fun. It was important for him to get his head around this. By her rough calculations, the dean had managed to send them back more than 250 million years.

"That's impossible. Nobody does that. How could it ever work?"

"It's complicated. You need to stop wondering how and start accepting what you see with your eyes. That," she waved toward the elegant blue tower in the distant valley below, "is a unified Guild headquarters. They were all destroyed before the Refounding and have not been rebuilt. Right?"

"It's a new one. They built it in secret."

"That's a city down there, Tenor. We can see the portal train stations from here, and they're active. It isn't new, and it isn't a secret."

"A realm then. That's what it has to be."

That was grasping too far. "We're not in a realm, and you know it. I need you to accept what has happened so I can explain how we might get out of it."

"There's a way out?"

Finally she'd gotten through. If he'd held onto his delusions much longer, she would've given up hope and let him think what he wanted. This was a much better outcome. Delusional people weren't a help, they were a liability. "I think there is, and I think it's in that tower."

"Why?"

"It has to do with how time works deep down." Trying to explain it without using math was a challenge. "When the present turns into the past, there are forces in place that protect it from being changed by people from the future." That sounded confusing even to her. "How it works doesn't matter right now. We can't change history, accept that and stay with me. What prevents us from changing it can also be used to find what we *can* change."

"I still don't follow."

"Think of it as an invisible hand. It's not conscious, but it guides people like us, people from the future, around so we can't damage the timeline. That's why I nearly fell down that hole back there and the rock nearly squashed you. One way to protect the past is to get rid of the people from the future, and killing them is one of the easiest ways to do it." Implying that there was intelligence behind the forces involved was a terrible misinterpretation. It was a phenomena that emerged from the rules of her theory, but Tenor was having a hard enough time as it was. "If history can't kill us, it will try to send us back by some other means." She pointed again at the tower. "I think there's another means in there somewhere."

"But *how*?"

It'd started out as a kind of scratchiness in her mind, but as time went by, the feeling got much stronger. Maybe talking about it would make the aching need for it easier to bear. "I want to go there. With every fiber of my being, I want to *be* there. It's an almost indescribable yearning." The only reason it wasn't driving her mad was that going crazy would prevent her from reaching it.

He turned to the tower. "But I don't feel anything."

"Yes, and I think I understand why. My people, somehow, are much more sensitive to the particles that make time work."

"Particles?"

She'd made it complicated again. "When we get out of this, I'll take as long as I need to help you understand what's going on. For now, I need you to accept that I'm sensitive to actions that can change the past, and you're not. The upside to this is that I'm also sensitive to actions that *protect* the past. Going to that tower protects the past."

"That's kind of..." He pushed his wings against his head and quickly spread the feathers apart as he moved them away.

The gesture was obvious. "Mind blowing. No kidding."

He stared at the tower. From their perch on the cliff, it was an elegant vase, a blue crystal in a forest of silver towers. She had never wanted anything more in her life.

"We have no legends about time travel." He used the English phrase because the concept didn't translate into Standard at all. "You don't think it's some elaborate trap that will kill us anyway?"

She turned inward, examining her strange yearning. "Correct. There are a couple of dangerous spots on the trail down from here. I know because I want to check them out. But it's a different feeling than what I get from the tower. It's like the difference between wanting some candy because I'm bored and wanting a big meal when I'm starving." That wasn't close to adequate. "I wish I could explain it better."

"It's okay. I think I'm beginning to understand." He stood up, dusted himself off, and offered her a wing. "If that's our ticket home, we should get on with it."

She took it, and he helped her to her feet. The decision made the yearning bearable, eased it, further confirming it was the right choice. "Indeed we should. If you don't mind, I'll lead the way."

He swept his wing out along the path. "Be my guest."

*

After walking for a couple of hours through the woods, they found a road. A few miles down it, they found a bus stop. It was exactly, *exactly*, the same as the bus stops from their own time. Right down to the odd pentalobe screws that bemians used to hold it all together. Two hundred and fifty million years, and not a single thing had changed.

"I don't see why it freaks you out so much," Tenor said when she pointed it out. "I find it comforting."

It took her a minute to phrase what she wanted to say in a way that wouldn't blow her cover. "We're a lot closer to our uplift point. If a machine was designed a hundred years ago, it's old. The oldest buildings still in use are, at best, a few thousand years old."

"A few thousand years? Really?"

"Two or less, as far as I know."

He shook his head, a motion which his long rhon beak emphasized. It was one of the few things that still reminded her how alien he was. "That is such a strange idea."

The bus arrived, and it was exactly the same as any other bus she'd taken on Silaria. And they were still on Silaria. Part of the basic carrier signal of their phones, which still worked for reasons that were now obvious, included location coordinates and the planet's name. They both matched Silaria.

This confirmed an observation which her theory had not predicted. The last time she went back in time, Tonya had ended up in exactly the same place she'd started. This was not guaranteed, because the universe was always in motion. Two weeks had passed, which moved Earth's location in space. She'd chalked it up to the portal acting as a location anchor.

There hadn't been a portal anywhere nearby this time, but they still arrived at, or perhaps near, where they left. There was some other force or particle which caused an object traveling through time to somehow also be able to travel through space, accurately enough that while the clock changed, the location didn't. She didn't remember the city or the campus being located on the side of a mountain that overlooked a valley. They obviously hadn't ended up inside that mountain either. The particle or force seemed, somehow, to allow them to arrive safely even though the universe wanted them dead.

All thoughts of what might account for that ended when she bumped into Tenor's back as he was boarding the bus. "What's wrong?"

He hesitated a moment, then said, "Nothing. You should walk normally, don't stop or stare." He kept walking, but his stride had changed, reminding her of a stork that'd seen a tiger stalking it in the reeds.

She got on board thinking police bots or maybe one of Helen's gangsters loaded for bear would meet them but found nothing of the sort. It was a bus full of aliens.

She tried to get Tenor to relax by chatting about what she saw out the window but gave up when he wouldn't calm down.

"Why are you so scared?" she asked.

"You're not?"

"Why should I be?"

He leaned over and whispered, "I don't recognize any of them."

She pulled back. "You do know about evolution, right?"

"Well, yes." He visibly calmed down. "I'm an idiot. This is before the—"

An urge, so powerful it felt like a kick to the head, made her grab his beak and hold it shut. They stared at each other. She wasn't sure who was more startled at what she'd done. Then she tried to open her hand.

"I can't let go," she said. That settled it, she was definitely more startled than he was. But she got an idea. "Promise you won't say what you were about to say."

His reply was mumbled through his closed beak, but the intention was clear because Tonya could remove her hand. She let go. "Sorry."

"Okay, what was that about?"

"Remember that I told you about how I'm sensitive to—" Her mouth clapped shut, jaw firmly locked.

History wasn't subtle about protecting itself.

She cleared her throat, changed her mind, and immediately regained control. "About how I'm sensitive to certain things?"

"You mean how you can—" Again, she clamped her hand on his beak. It was completely involuntary, like getting her knee hit during a physical. He nodded, and she was able to let go again. "It seems there are things we can talk about in public..."

"And things we can't. At least I'm able to tell the difference."

He thought for a moment. "I'm an idiot because," he watched her as he spoke carefully, "we're so far," her hand twitched, and he held it down, "so far *away*, I forgot that I wouldn't recognize anyone. I'm not used to that."

But history hadn't seemed interested in what they said until they'd been talking for a few minutes. Kim said the more foreign a language was, the faster she learned it. Tonya figured 250 million years made English *and* Standard about as foreign as they could get. She looked around. Like present-time bemians, and people who rode public transport on Earth, these ancient bemians had completely ignored their little discussion. If nobody was listening...she turned around.

A bent, wrinkled, little old anteater-thing got interested in some kind of knitting in her lap, working at it furiously with too many needles because her hands had too many fingers. Old ladies snooping on the conversations of strangers would naturally be a universal.

Tonya turned back to Tenor. "We'll talk more about it after we arrive at our destination." Being intentionally vague made her feel like she'd solved a complicated math problem, heady emotions of accomplishment and joy. She wanted to do it again.

History wasn't subtle, not one little bit.

*

The closer they got to the Interpreter tower, the more impressive it became. It was a centerpiece that took up what back home would've been called several city blocks. But there was much more green space than buildings. The grounds were immaculate, an integration of nature and architecture the likes of which she'd never seen. Humans had never approached this level. Modern bemians hadn't either, at least none that she'd seen so far. The tower soared out over and above it all, from this angle reminding her of a pair crystal-blue arms reaching toward the sky.

"It's..." Tenor stammered as they stood on the edge of the grounds. "I've never..." He gulped and tried again. "This is the most beautiful thing I have ever seen."

When she was sure nobody was nearby, she said, "And all knowledge of them has been completely lost?"

"The barest descriptions survive, little more than legends." He shielded his eyes with one of his wings as he stared up at the tower. "This must be what it felt like when my ancestors first saw the nodes descending from the sky." He looked down at her. "Except I'm not a primitive savage. I can comprehend what I see. I didn't know it would be like..." He gazed up again. "This."

Tonya hadn't been raised with Interpreters and didn't know any of the legends. Yet from this complex, the ancient power of the Guild, how it was a massive force that helped tie the galaxy together, was impossible to miss. This was propaganda made physically real, on a scale and with a sophistication that put communists, fascists, and her own Catholic church to shame. Nothing about this space was coincidental. The whole thing conveyed a message of power and glory through humble assistance. It was a message that the complex communicated with deceptive ease.

"And they never built them after the Refounding?"

"No. This would be a must-see destination for tourists." He shook his head and blinked his eyes. It was a moment that made him a person, no matter how different he looked. This was someone who'd had his foundations shaken to their core.

Traveling back in time several hundred million years tended to do that.

He cleared his throat. "They had them on all the planets in the galaxy. I can only think that they forgot how to make them." He turned to her. "You don't suppose..."

History didn't make her want to shut him up, so she finished his thought. "That we could return with the plans? Where would we start? It's a nice idea," she said and looked at the tower, getting another kick in her psyche. "But I don't think whatever is in there is gonna stick around and wait for us to find blueprints. Come on, we've gawked enough."

The tower lobby was as impressive as its exterior, and naturally the first thing they saw was a group of kiosks for acquiring interpreter threads. Her feet pivoted of their own accord, sending her stumbling toward them. Tenor scrambled to follow.

"I guess we'll be talking to someone," he said.

"Only use Standard," she replied, not at all certain it was her idea. "Don't teach it your native language."

Suitably equipped, Tonya thought history would point her right to the top of the tower because...well, that's usually where the lairs were, and whatever was around here felt like it was from the *no, I expect you to die* sales bin. But she was powerfully moved to walk right through a blank white door in a remote corner. It was unlocked—she could've sworn she heard a click as she approached—and the security bots ignored them both.

"Where are we going?" Tenor asked.

"No way for me to know." It was so strong it was like she was on a leash.

The next windowless door in the much more utilitarian maintenance passage opened—she suspected there would be no locked door between her and wherever history was guiding them—to reveal some kind of locker room. Kim had mentioned that Interpreters maintained their own security forces, and this seemed to be where they changed. Now understanding what history wanted her to do, she got ahead of the sensation by scanning the lockers until she knew which one held a uniform that would fit her.

"What's going on?" he asked as she opened the locker.

After the involuntary perp walk, she wasn't surprised that the uniform was elaborate and included a face-concealing helmet. Whatever history wanted her to do, it wanted her to do it anonymously. Hopefully what they were being herded toward wouldn't take long. The last time she had to wear a costume like this, she ended up living in it for more than a week. It got a little fragrant toward the end.

"Apparently I need a disguise to continue." She looked at him and felt…nothing. "You seem to be okay."

"It's spooky when you talk like that."

"I know."

It would be tempting to think that this was how history worked, a hidden hand pushing things around a chessboard, making moves so that events played out in a preordained order. This would be wrong. Theory predicted and experiments proved that free will existed. In the present, tockions were incredibly weak, orders of magnitude weaker than any other known particles. That's what defined the present. It was the point in time where both particles were at their weakest, impossible to detect if you weren't searching for them and already knew what you'd find.

The uniform itself was more comfortable than the collection of construction worker gear she cobbled together back at the plant. It was the same deep blue as the tower, with ice-white highlights, reminding her more of *Warhammer 40K* elves than Star Wars stormtroopers. It was light, sturdy, and she could move well in it.

"Not bad at all," she said, her voice turned metallic by the helmet's vocal system. She checked the locker again and found what had to be a stun baton. History didn't have to help her find the activation button or interpret the zapping arc that jumped between two tips at the end. The urge to head for the door hit her like a slap to the back of her head. "Come on."

They attracted no more attention than they did coming in off the street. If anything, history's hand had made her less conspicuous. It let her stride forward confidently, a guard on a mission. It was another bemian parallel: if you looked like you were going somewhere, people almost always assumed you were and took no further notice.

Tenor, though, wasn't as confident. "Where are we going now?" he asked as they waited for one of the gorgeous crystal elevators to arrive.

Tonya shrugged. "I only learn about the next waypoint after we reach the current one." She did have a sneaking suspicion about what would greet them on arrival.

Or rather, who.

As the car rose up above the lobby, they could take in more of the open plan of the lower tower. More symmetries were revealed, then changed, then were revealed again. China was the first place that had literally taken her breath away when she saw it. There was more thrill in this single building than in that entire country.

After a brief time, they traveled into a standard elevator shaft. When the door finally opened, a hall extended far to the right and left. Immediately in front of them on the opposite wall was a pair of tall doors that fairly screamed *executive conference room.* She let history guide her, striding right past guards who passively watched her go by and through the double doors.

The room was smaller than she'd expected. Not small, per se, but rather it was the first space in the tower that didn't seem to be made like a cathedral. Tall chairs, about a dozen, half facing away from her, surrounded an elegant conference table. The chairs facing her held aliens she didn't recognize.

"What is the meaning of this?" a yellow-skinned alien who seemed to be mostly frog, demanded.

The hand of history that'd been pushing her around like the parent of a distracted toddler vanished. For the first time since they'd gotten here, she had no idea what to do next. Having free will thrust on her almost made her lose her balance, but she recovered. Barely.

Be confident. "Prisoner transfer from cell block 1138." She ignored Tenor's indignant chirp. "I think I've made a wrong turn somewhere." Tonya expected a lab or lair, not a meeting of the Jedi council. The longer this stayed normal, the more worried she got.

The chairs facing away from her bobbed and moved backward a bit, then turned around so the occupants could see what was going on. She looked at the first one on her right, and finally things started falling into place.

Cyril was a part of this meeting. It was the first time she'd been happy to see him. The man-sized cricket with glossy blue skin that looked painted on had in the past been her tormentor. She'd first encountered him in China, pulled into a room lined with the time-drawn threads of lives past, present, and future. He'd helped her save herself. It was her first inkling that time could be more than it seemed to be. The second encounter was a riddle-filled quest to help save the world from a maniac who'd turned a power station into a bomb. He'd manipulated her into a two-week jaunt in the past, terrified that any move she made could undo the future. She'd vowed to put his head through the nearest wall if she ever saw him again.

Obviously that would have to be delayed.

He hadn't changed a bit in the subsequent two hundred and fifty million years. If anyone would know how to get her out of this mess, it would be him. History had other ideas. It clamped her mouth shut when she tried to say his name.

Then she looked to her left, and all desire to say a word was torn away.

As a Christian, she sometimes fantasized about what it would be like to meet Jesus in person. To experience the Son of God as a physical reality. Witness His power firsthand.

She didn't wonder anymore. The being seated next to Cyril was divine power incarnate. It was the only way she could describe him. His form was huge and hulking, like it was out of a Marvel comic, but that's where the similarities stopped. Still, she could only catalog the basics. Male. Humanoid. Hard eyes that looked through her soul. Her mind buckled as she attempted to comprehend the immense power this being radiated.

Somewhere, a small but important part of her flared to life. In the wash of this unspeakably beautiful being, a tiny shout of defiance squeaked out in her mind, *he's not a god*!

He stood, and she immediately fell to her knees, joyous to be in His presence and under His attention. Beside her, Tenor did the same. She heard his gasped wheezes as he dealt with this presence in his own way.

"Cyril," He said with a voice that rang with trumpets and the promise of paradise. "Answer the question. What *is* the meaning of this?"

"I have no idea. I've never seen these two creatures before in my life."

"You expect me to believe that here, at the moment of this elder-forsaken galaxy's final surrender, that the appearance of a time wanderer is a coincidence? I should have known that the elders' final promise to me would dissolve to dust when it was put to the ultimate test."

Cyril sputtered. "The agreement stands, I swear."

"Look at this child's power." Tonya's eyes had never lifted from the floor, but nonetheless she felt it when He switched His attention to Tenor. He must've felt it too because his feathers made soft noises as he shivered. "And she doesn't come alone! Not only must you humiliate me by bringing a time wanderer into my presence, but also prove without a doubt that it can transport the insensitive with it. Why not bring the army forward now, Cyril?"

"There is no army, I don't know who these people are, I swear!"

The room erupted in shouts, half in support of Cyril, the other in opposition.

"ENOUGH!"

Her mind almost melted under the power of that rage. The small thing inside her grew frantic. *You should get up! This isn't a god! You know what that is!* But she could spare not one iota of attention to it. She had to dedicate her entire being to this presence.

The small thing exploded with indignation at her need. *NO.*

Tonya nearly gasped at the stubborn defiance within her.

The divine shout had struck the room silent. "I came to offer peace, but you obviously want war."

This seemed to be a step too far for Cyril. "You offer us no such thing. This peace is an illusion, brought about by cynical treachery. All you've ever wanted was to destroy us, and by signing this document, we're giving you permission."

"That's right," He replied. "I wondered if you understood the truth of the matter."

"I did, and make no mistake, I will stop you. But not with…these."

"Ah," He said, "your vaunted four, again? The ragged patch you put on the universe before the rest of them departed? I knew you'd bring them back. I've beaten them before, old man. I'll beat them again. Well," His regard returned to Tonya, and she sighed under its power. "If this is all a coincidence, I'm happy to take out the trash."

A finger snapped.

Cyril shouted, "No!"

Inside her, outside her, what was her and what was Tenor, flew apart and came together, spun sideways and tumbled into loops. She felt the edge of a profound oblivion but then was pushed away.

With a massive physical and psychic snap, it stopped.

Still in the Interpretor armor, Tonya looked up. She stripped her helmet off to see better.

She was in the threaded room.

A groan beside her. She wasn't alone. Tenor sat up, holding his head. "What happened? Who were those people?"

Now free from its influence, the small thing that had been annoying her during the entire encounter expanded and filled her mind. That was *not* a divine being. She knew what true divinity was, and a part of her was a little disappointed about the mistake. But only a little, because now that she knew what it wasn't, she was also able to put a finger on what it was. Not least because she'd encountered it before.

Andromeda.

What else could cause her to question her own faith—the bedrock of her soul—than a conscious galaxy billions of years old? It would've been trivial for a power that immense to work out a way to manifest and interact with the more common life forms of this one. Especially since she already knew it could manipulate time at the particulate level. It also allowed her a certain amount of self-forgiveness for briefly thinking Andromeda was God. Humans were so sensitive to tockions that Andromeda could manipulate people en masse from millions of light years away.

Another thing she would have to talk over with a priest, if she could find one who understood and believed her.

"One of them is probably the most powerful living thing in the universe. The other is an old man who has been driving me bonkers for the past couple of years. I think he routed us here. Which is good news."

Tenor got to his feet and then, as he'd done before, helped her to hers. "It is?"

"Yup, I think I can get us home from here." She wondered if that was the point, but then discarded the idea. That version of Cyril didn't have any idea who or what she was. He probably sent them here so he could examine them when he got the chance.

Tenor looked around. "What is this place?"

"This is a consequence of how time works. Voids naturally form in the dimensions that time acts through." In fact, this may not be the same room that she met Cyril in. Probably wasn't. God, time was complicated. "It lets us see time in another way, as a collection of threaded fates." If her theories were right, and so far they'd held up pretty well, there should be knots around here somewhere. They weren't controls like knobs and levers but could be used as such.

"What does *this* mean?" In front of him was a massive black space that completely engulfed the center of the room. On the far side of it, quite a distance away, threads slowly became visible again until it was back to normal, just before the vaguely football-shaped space closed up.

"I think that's the catastrophe that preceded the Refounding."

"So what you're saying is…" She watched him as he tried to get his head around ideas that all but one other bemian in the entire galaxy had never confronted. "You're saying that all this is history, but in a different form?"

He got it in one. Knowledge was the best gift of all, and giving it was better than watching nieces and nephews open presents at

Christmas. "That's exactly right. Now, if you'll excuse me, I need to find our ride home." The knots had to be around here somewhere.

It took about five minutes of searching, but she found them. The threaded room wasn't a single space. It had side rooms hidden away like chapels in an old church. She got another ego boost when she recognized the shape of each one, what it did, and how to make it work. "Tenor, I need you to come over here."

Silence.

"Tenor?"

She found him staring at the final group of threads that led directly to the abyss. He was weeping. "*We* did this." He'd found the thread that showed their confrontation with Andromeda. She stood in a completely different dimension, but she still felt the pull of his charisma.

Tenor traced the thread with his wing feathers. "See?"

Their thread was in the center of a knot of thousands, which then led outward and down into the abyss. It was an easy conclusion to make.

It was also wrong.

"No, we didn't cause it. We couldn't."

"We *did*," he said, an edge of hysteria in his voice. "It was our appearance that enraged that being. They were on the verge of peace."

"Listen to me. We couldn't have caused that. It had already happened. The past *cannot* be changed by people from the future. It was their moment, not ours. They were the ones who failed." An idea occurred to her. "We were sent to witness it. Not prevent it."

"Sent? By who?"

Being college kids, Tenor and his friends had drawn her out about her faith. They then treated it with amusement if not disdain. He and his pals were as faithless as any other group of prosperous modern kids back home. If she said out loud what she knew in her gut, he'd call her a fanatic or think she'd lost her mind. Plus, the math didn't lie. If God was behind it all, he was playing by a strict set of rules. God and rules didn't go together. That was the point.

Prevarication in this instance, as the saying in that classic Alice video game realm went, *may help.*

"I don't know if that's a question that can be answered. Not yet, anyway." A bloom of warmth, of *faith,* filled her. If that wasn't a sign she was on the right track, she wasn't sure what was. "This is bigger than us."

"All those people, their lives, what they created. They were beautiful. We have to do something."

She considered it for a moment, then remembered Maff's message and her findings. More importantly, she remembered the galactic coordinates included in them. Those were in *their* history, and history didn't change. "Okay, maybe we *can* do something."

Chapter 33
Kim

Mike had packed the camp away but left a lot of trashy bits lying around. She couldn't blame him. It was almost all related to...

Deep breath...

Peanut butter and crackers. Maybe one day she'd be able to think about it without turning green. She tried to at least neaten the camp site bit, but her energy levels weren't up to the task. Old Kim, the one she'd been gradually boxing up ever since she met Mike, wanted to fly into a rage about this inability to do basic tasks. Actual Kim, the person she was turning into, knew how juvenile that urge was.

Her newest revelation was how much of her anger was habit. With each radical readjustment of her attitude—the continuing process called *growing up*—the teeth were pulled out of yet another self-destructive behavior. She could still feel their bite. But now it only brought out curiosity, a kind of blasé feeling that made stopping easy.

So instead of grinding her teeth and indulging in an inner dialog that included a lot of swearing and blaming, shambling about moving piles of garbage around, she climbed into the truck and lay down. Rest was what she needed, so rest was what she'd do. The truck was her fortress, and she fell asleep snuggled inside.

Kim woke when Mike's *I'm heading back* ping arrived. She sat up, feeling much more energetic, and surveyed the camp site through the truck's window. It was still a mess, with scattered containers, loose paper, and an arrow stuck into the ground.

Wait, what?

That hadn't been there when she went to sleep. She looked around carefully, but there was no one nearby. The intrusion monitors didn't have any alerts. Whoever had fired it wasn't close. The arrow had an envelope—well, a thin packet holding something—tied to the shaft.

She gave the monitors one more check, then got out and walked over to it. Tying a message to an arrow was such a medieval way of going about things. Maybe there was a princess in a tower somewhere too. At least it hadn't hit anyone on the way in. Spencer would probably turn it into a Python reference if it had.

The scout drone they'd sent to find him was overdue. She hoped that was a good sign.

Kim used her phone to analyze the arrow, its impact angle, and how deep it went into the dirt. It provided her with an estimated point of launch. It'd been fired from the southwest, the same direction that Malafan's town was in, about fifty yards beyond their furthest intrusion detector. Whoever they were, she gave them points for being cautious.

She checked for booby traps, levered it out of the dirt, and took it back to the truck. Kim sat down with a chuckle. More Monty Python than King Arthur. The arrowhead was strangely shaped, with a blunted hollow end instead of a point, carefully designed so that it wouldn't get filled with dirt when it hit the ground. Shooting messages at each other must be a thing with Telirians. She puzzled over the envelope, and after some effort, got it open and pulled out the contents.

It was a folded-up bemian holo screen. The nodes may be bringing the natives along slowly when it came to big industry, but they didn't have much of a choice if Telirians used 3-D writing.

She touched a corner to activate the message.

Honored Head La'fan Interpreter Trayne-Sellars,

I, Lord Evahnar Malafan, son of Evahna Malafan, greet you.

Kim could get used to being called *honored* Interpreter. Maybe she'd put it on a business card.

We have been taught by the nodes that Interpreters are to be feared and respected, yet when you met us on Potter's March, you did so in peace and friendship. We, too, wish to extend an offer of peace and friendship.

The nodes weren't only preparing these people to one day join the galaxy, they were also engaging in some propaganda as to how Interpreters would be seen and treated. Or maybe Interpreters were a bunch of jerks. Valsa had certainly been one.

If you find this offer acceptable, please reply with your terms for our first meeting.

Negotiation instead of violence. Kim wasn't the only one who could do the unexpected. She erased the original message and wrote one of her own. *I, Head Interpreter Kimberly Trayne-Sellars, daughter of Malinda Trayne, greet you in turn…*

She tried to match his tone and wording, which was a little ornate but not excessive, basically telling him to send two men forward for further discussions. She knew better than to demand he visit her. Certainly she'd never visit him in his own hall. They needed to find neutral ground, and she needed to play for time. She didn't know when Mike would arrive. She sent him a brief message, *getting visitors, stay cool,* but there was no guarantee he'd read it in time. He would've turned his phone off before he left.

She got out of the truck and started rummaging for her bow. It was a Hoyt Archery Carbon RXN-23, a nanotech-enhanced compact compound she'd fallen in love with during a Bear Grylls Memorial Hunt. She'd taken third with the realm version—she was still in hiding then—on the second day and effortlessly stayed there for the next three weeks.

The real one was as nice as her trusty realm construct. Its phone app unfolded it, then she scanned the Telirian arrow. This came up as *Longbow, English,* which seemed like a pretty good guess to her. Once it'd configured for that, it flashed green in her enhanced vision and provided a target reticle with telemetry. She lined up on the estimated coordinates of her shooter. Hopefully whoever had sent this knew to stand back while waiting on a reply. When the let-off reduced her pull effort, she settled on the target and let it go.

She dropped the bow at the ear-splitting shriek it made as it departed. The sound would be audible all the way to the arrow's impact. Now she didn't feel so bad about shooting an arrow at a target she couldn't see. Anyone who didn't get out of the way of that thing had it coming.

If they were anything like humans, there would be a lot of discussion done quickly. Volunteers would be chosen, because good soldiers never volunteered for anything. Then they had to make their way through the forest. She figured it would take about ten minutes.

At almost ten minutes on the dot, two soldiers appeared. And she was in luck: one of them was Sergeant Eskol, one of Lord Malafan's closest advisers. From the times she'd watched him, she knew he was a no-nonsense guy who still had a sense of humor. This was a logical choice and told her Malafan was taking this seriously. She didn't recognize the other one, but by the way he acted, he might be the most junior member of the squad, the lowly private. *You were the one who wasn't listening when they asked for volunteers.*

The sergeant stopped as soon as she locked eyes with him. He practically had to yank the young one to a stop because he'd been staring up at a tree. They paused, then both slowly set aside their weapons and waited for her to do the same.

She didn't have a weapon. She cracked the window and shouted, "I don't have any weapons."

"And what's that there sitting in front of you then?" Eskol shouted back.

Now she got it. They didn't know what the steering wheel was for. "Okay, come around to the other side. Slowly." Kim moved over to the passenger side and lowered the window. Eskol and the private walked in a broad circle around the truck, only walking toward her when they were opposite the door.

When they could hear her without shouting, she said, "Thank you, gentlemen, but that's close enough for now."

The private looked confused, but Eskol looked relieved. Kim smiled inwardly. This was a person who understood how the game was played.

"Thank *you*, Honored Interpreter, for stepping away from the weapons. We've not seen the like of this vehicle and are...rather wary of it, if I'm to be honest."

The sergeant was keeping his hands where she could see them, so she gently put hers on the windowsill to repay the favor. Peace among strangers was fragile and best taken in small steps. The flash of a sword to kill an asp had destroyed more than one chance at a bloodless agreement back home. By the way the sergeant was behaving, they must have a similar tradition.

"You can rest easy, Sergeant. This is not a war carriage."

"But what *is* it?" the private asked in awe as he stared at it, then shouted when Eskol dope slapped the back of his head hard enough to make his helmet ring.

"That's enough out of you," Eskol said, then turned back to her. "Apologies for the young man, my lady. He's got a lot to learn."

"No apology necessary. We call it a truck. You'd should think of it as a self-propelled wagon. As you can see," she motioned toward the bed, "it's primarily used for cargo."

In the woods directly behind the soldiers, Mike appeared.

She saw him because he wanted to be seen of course. He hadn't set off any of the proximity alarms. She lifted her hands up off the windowsill, palms outward, her signal that all was okay and to wait.

Keeping her eyes locked on Eskol's, she slowly and calmly said, "We have made a great start to this encounter, gentlemen, and I wish to keep it that way. I have a companion right over there." She pointed behind them. The sergeant stiffened but didn't turn around. His companion got what she was beginning to think of as his default expression of foggy confusion. "He is unarmed and represents no danger to you as long as you represent none to me. I think I'm correct in that judgement, yes, Sergeant?"

The private opened his mouth which earned him another ringing dope slap before he could start speaking. Eskol nodded to her. "You are correct. We mean no harm to anyone here." He slowly turned around until he spotted Mike. "Oy! You lot! All friends here, come and have a chat."

She signaled for him to turn his phone on. Once he did, she sent *he wants you to come over. It's okay. I'll get you caught up as we go.*

Mike walked over until he was about ten feet away, far enough not to alarm the men but close enough to make a difference if it went sideways. A nice touch.

He saluted the way they'd seen the sergeant salute Lord Malafan. "Greetings, good sirs."

Eskol snorted. "Sergeant will do."

She hoped she managed to hold on to her professional demeanor and hid the melted relief inside her. "I would like to introduce my husband, Mike Sellars." She opened the car door. The Telirians jumped. She stopped. "No danger here, friends." She stepped out and indicated the chairs under a shade tree. "Let's talk."

While they walked over, she sent a message to Mike. *Any news on Spencer?*

Not yet, but the drone's not due to check in for a couple of hours.

If she were honest, this whole sequence of events was mostly serving as a distraction from Spencer's disappearance. He'd—mostly—got over his Angel Rage hero worship and had turned out to be a good friend. She was sick to think that he might be hurt or in trouble. But there was nothing she could do about it right at this moment, so she was negotiating with aliens.

Again.

The Telirians peered at the nylon-and-aluminum-frame camp chairs like they were made of spider webs and bear traps. Kim plopped down into hers confidently. "So, Lord Malafan wants to talk?"

The sergeant seemed grateful for the reminder and sat down. The private remained standing behind him. "Yes," Eskol replied. "I'm to negotiate a neutral ground and guide you to same. Private Kempal here will act as a runner to inform Lord Malafan about the location. Assuming this welp remembers how to use his legs. Oh, and we have a gift of sincerity." He motioned to the private, who took his backpack off and handed it to Mike. It was large, and by the way his arm sank when he took it, heavier than it looked. Mike opened it and smiled. He leaned over so she could see inside.

The bag was filled with node internals, and in perfect shape.

The sergeant cleared his throat. "We apologize for not being able to hand over the larger box the other day. The Servants of the Network often make trouble for us."

"How many wrecked nodes are there around here?" Mike asked.

The sergeant shrugged. "It varies, usually one or two a mile in this area. More in the borderlands."

"Borderlands?" Kim asked.

"To Interdicts. But those are usually broken up real bad."

She shared a look with Mike. That was a lot more wrecked nodes than any of their models predicted. But she didn't want to get derailed here. "So what are your ideas for a meeting place?"

At first the sergeant proposed a meeting between the two camps in the woods, but that would limit the truck's mobility. She wouldn't give up that advantage. After serious but amiable negotiations they settled on the infamous cattle-rhino farm, which turned out to be one of Malafan's personal properties. They sent the private off to let Lord Malafan know what the agreed location was. Sergeant Eskol graciously offered to act as their guide, since without the drone, scouting a proper path would be difficult.

Kim showed him how to open the passenger front door of the truck. For a moment, he looked like she'd asked him to handle a live hand grenade. He turned to her. "Will we get things like this, when we join?"

She glanced at Mike. It was a question they should've anticipated. She went with the truth. "Probably not exactly like this, no. But similar. Likely better, since this one is pretty old." She was glad Spencer wasn't around.

He opened the door and looked inside, then started touching things. "It's all so…soft." He shook himself, and she could almost hear the *get a grip* thought in his head. "Right," he hopped in and shut the door. "To the farm!"

Since it was the three of them and the camp was already packed, they arrived well before Lord Malafan. The tenant farmer seemed to know Eskol well. After a hurried conversation, the farmer went rushing into his house shouting for his wife to get ready for guests. They barely gave her, Mike, or the truck a second glance. The lack of awe seemed strange, but then these were people who'd spent generations being told they were not alone in the galaxy. To Eskol, it must be like meeting the new rich neighbor from up the street instead of a creature that could conquer his world.

Lord Malafan and his party arrived just as the harried farmer and his wife finished setting up a proper long table with benches on either side. Eskol excused himself and went to consult with his lord. Kim had only added one new condition to the meeting: that, due to the customs of her people, she could not touch him or anyone else. Which, as always, was true from a certain point of view.

Malafan presented himself in much the same way Eskol had. Up close, it was easy to understand why he commanded the loyalty of people like the sergeant. Malafan was obviously handsome by the standards of his people—Kim's time with the La'fan had taught her to appreciate symmetry, visible health, and a well-maintained appearance no matter how strange the package might be—but he also gave off charisma in waves.

"I see our gracious hosts have prepared well in spite of almost no advanced notice," he said as the frantic husband and wife put the finishing touches on a basic but still attractive lunch buffet. Now that she looked closer, the farming couple were moving quickly, not frantically. This wasn't the first time Malafan had dropped by on short notice, they were too coordinated. It probably wouldn't be the last. "I thank you for your quick work."

The couple smiled as they worked, another good sign. The more she was around Lord Malafan, the more she knew he'd be someone they could work with.

Eskol again excused himself and went back to his men, waiting until he was far enough away that she could only catch the tone of the bellowed orders that sent soldiers scrambling instead of the actual words. That both Malafan and Eskol were comfortable enough to leave the former effectively alone with two otherwise strange unknowns told her the respect she felt for Malafan was likely being returned by them both. Simple decency could accomplish miracles when it was allowed to.

The fact that Mike could unscrew Malafan's head at a moment's notice did admittedly boost her confidence in the overall situation. But it wouldn't come to that.

They sat down to a simple but tasty lunch of breads, meats, and cheeses. The small talk they made wouldn't have been out of place at one of her mother's lunch parties, except the chances of a fight breaking out between family members wasn't an issue here.

They finished the meal and were sipping the Telirian equivalent of tea, which had a bizarre but not unpleasant banana aftertaste, and Malafan got to the point.

"We have long chafed under the boot of the AC network but have had no alternatives. Interpreters are well known negotiators. Will you help us lighten our burden?"

He had three main requests. The first was lifting of the mandatory birth control policy. At that moment she figured out what was bothering her about the farmer and his wife: they had no kids. Now she knew why. The planet's AC network had imposed strict population controls. Probably a way to change the culture.

The second request also answered another question they'd had since they got here. He wanted the nodes to allow the native language to be spoken and taught openly. *That's* why they all spoke an accented version of a language she already knew in addition to Standard. They'd been forced to do it. The few times they'd used words she didn't know had been when they used their true language. Learning that would be one of her top priorities after the meeting was done.

The third was to allow schools to teach Telirian history alongside the lessons required for them to join the galaxy. Incredibly, the nodes had completely suppressed Telirian knowledge of their own past. "Our history only goes back to my great-grandfather's generation," Malafan said with obvious yearning. "Hundreds of years after the nodes came."

"If you don't know the history now, how will you recover it?" Mike asked.

"The nodes have it. They forget nothing."

It seemed naïve to think the agents responsible for suppressing knowledge could somehow be talked into revealing it again. Before Kim could voice the thought, their drone arrived, landing on its charge cradle in the bed of the truck.

"Be right back," Mike said as he got up and walked over to it.

Malafan blinked twice and then slowly said, "I was wondering if you might assist me on a more personal matter. I see you have access to flying machines similar to what the network uses sometimes."

Mike returned with a worried look.

It had to be about Spencer, but since Mike was worried and not grim, the news probably wasn't all bad.

Lord Malafan continued. "The nodes won't allow us their use, but I know they could be indispensable in assisting in my search for…" His laugh was filled with embarrassment, the first time she'd ever seen him as anything other than supremely confident. "Well I'm sure in the connected galaxy this is no longer an issue, but it's my daughter. She's missing. Run away, in fact."

"I've already got news about that," Mike said, then turned to her. "The drone found Spencer. Well, found where he was and a message about where he was going."

He turned back to Malafan. "And he's with your daughter."

Chapter 34

Spencer

The monkey in his head saw a monster and took control of his mouth before his brain could figure out what he was seeing. Spencer screamed like a little girl. That, and it really was the biggest Telirian he'd ever seen.

Because *it was a fucking statue.* "You said you guys didn't build anything big." They talked about Earth's pyramids as they rode on the river. It'd been a fun few hours getting her head around the concept of a pile of stone that high.

"We don't. Didn't." She got up close to the severed head and shoulder that sat on the ground. The nose was as big as she was. "I have no idea what this is."

Spencer cast the flashlight around but couldn't find any other bits of statue. "It's gotta be old then, right? Like, fucking old."

She nodded. "Well before my great-grandfather's time. He loved telling stories, and this would've been a great one."

Spencer crouched down at the base. "It's not buried, it's broken. But it was placed here." He pointed. "See? They dug a special base for it so it'd sit level on the ground."

"But who are they?"

"They have to be you. Right? You don't have any other intelligent life on this planet, do you?"

"No." She stared up at the head, wonder on her face. "But we don't have anything like this either."

There was a path through the dirt and petrified grass on the other side of the statue. It hadn't been used by anything in a long, long time. "Let's see where this goes."

He hadn't walked more than a few yards before getting his first genuine surprise. "The fuck? Paper?"

"What's paper?"

He'd used the English word. He reached down to pick it up, but it crumbled to dust the instant he touched it. "Shit. That was paper." Her expression went from confused to annoyed. He shook his head. "You write on it, but not the way you've been taught. It's not a display like what the nodes use."

"I don't understand."

He cast the light around until he spotted another sheet. "Over here." It was a few feet away off the trail. When he stepped on the grass, it crumbled faster than the paper.

Now aware of how fragile it was, Spencer didn't bother trying to pick it up. "We call it paper back home. You use…" Sometimes he sincerely missed Kim and her Swiss Army knife brain full of languages. "Oil mixed with pigments, we call it ink, in a special tube called a pen, to write words on it."

"But those will be flat. How can anyone read that?"

"You'd be surprised." He knelt down. "See? That's writing."

Well, typing, or maybe it'd been printed. The symbols were like what would happen if Norse runes and Greek letters had babies, but they were too neat and even to be mistaken for handwriting.

"What does it say?" Tapov asked.

"You don't know?"

She shrugged. "Why would I? I don't recognize that as writing."

He stood up and cast the light around. "Jesus, they're everywhere." Scattered ahead of them were dozens of sheets, like someone had dropped all their homework and the wind had carried it away.

Tapov pointed down their path. "It gets denser going in that direction."

"So off we go," he replied.

They only examined pages that were on the path. All were roughly the same: dense printed text, usually in two columns. "This shit reminds me of what I have to read for AI class." She wouldn't know what that was. "My advanced node studies."

"They let you study the nodes?"

Well, okay, he probably outsmarted himself on that one. "It's an advanced course. But see this?" He pointed to a symbol in the upper corner of the page. "That's a number, I'll bet my ass on that."

Further up the trail—the cave was turning out to be fucking enormous—he found confirmation in the form of a page that was made up of tables of data. Fuck, he wished his phone wasn't broken. "Gotta be numbers." He looked around. The paper was now like a super-fragile carpet. "If we can get the right group of people down here, there should be enough to let you figure out how to read it."

"I still think flat writing isn't right. It gives me a headache to look at it."

He chuckled softly, remembering the migraines he got figuring out how height levels in bemian worked to modify the words they represented. Mike called it simple, but quantum mechanics was one of his hobbies. Having smart friends sometimes had its disadvantages.

The paper got thick enough on the ground it started to feel like wading, kicking up a shit ton of dust that made them both put their shirts around their noses but then faded out once they found the source.

"Fuck me," Tapov said in perfect fucking English as they both stared upward. Spencer would've complimented her, but he was busy trying to compose his own impression of the giant what-the-shit-is-*that* they'd stumbled across.

In front of them was a monstrous mound of rubble, too tall to see the top of, or either side. And it was rubble, like, building-falls-down-goes-boom rubble. Spencer saw columns and bricks and shit all over the place. It must've been at least a couple of stories high before it'd collapsed. He saw layers that were probably floors, and a rough count said five or maybe six. At least.

He turned to Tapov. "You guys have buildings this big at your city, right?"

She stared at it intently. "About this big, yes, but not built this way." She pointed at one of the columns that jutted out of the wreckage. "That's iron, isn't it?"

"Yup. Cast iron." His dad owned a steel mill back home. Spencer couldn't help but learn a few things. "Looks different from what you'd find in a frying pan, though." There were all kinds of ways to make it. "It's not steel though."

"And glass," she said, pointing. "Look at all the glass."

As he cast the flashlight around the shards glittered in the light. Some still had portions of their frames attached. "Windows. A fucking lot of windows."

"Windows are expensive," she said in a wondering whisper. "How could they afford so many?"

"No idea. Let's look around."

They picked their way around the left side of the rubble. The pile jutted out in the middle and went off to the right and left. If he were to guess, it might've originally been shaped like a central building with two wings. But it was hard to tell. Not only had it collapsed, it'd also sat here who knew how long. Like the paper that was still scattered around them, he wouldn't be surprised if it all turned to dust when they touched it.

They made their way around one of the long arms and were halfway back when Tapov found a void in the rubble. "I think there's something in there."

Spencer bent down. The rubble had formed a semicircular tunnel. On the far side there was a regular tile floor and an intact wall. "I think this is a part that hasn't collapsed," he said. "Come on."

They both carefully picked their way through the debris until they reached the end. It was indeed an intact hallway, with walls painted a neutral gray and a floor that would've fit in perfectly at a hospital or a lab back home.

"I've never seen a floor like this. Is it wood?" Tapov said as she tiptoed around like it might be lava.

"No. Floors like this have been around forever back home." It wasn't human, though. The colors and the texture weren't quite right. A thick layer of dust covered it, showing again that they were the only people to visit in a long, long time.

At the end of the hall were two regularish doors, complete with lever latches. The nearest one opened with only a little effort. When he looked inside, he realized what this place was.

"It's a lab," he said. And not any kind of lab. "Electrical, if this gear is what I think it is." There was brass and glass all over the place, but no tubes or hoses. It wasn't for chemistry or medicine. Thick wires hung from the ceiling connecting motors and gauges together. The ceiling held another surprise. "Light bulbs. I'll be a son of a bitch." They were big, glass bulbs, the kind you found in steampunk realms or maybe old movies about Edison.

The room itself was a classic long rectangle with counters around the walls and through the center. There, right in the middle, was another sign of what was happening down here. "They were fucking with quantum lattices." It was another giant box identical to the one they'd tried to trick Tapov's dad into handing over. Tapov made one of her annoyed princess huffing noises. Without looking up, he said, "It's the guts of a node, what makes it tick."

The devices around it were far more delicate, and included recognizable bits of electronics, transistors, capacitors, that kind of shit. A notebook of graph paper sat open with the hand drawing of an unmistakable circuit on it. Spencer touched it, but it didn't crumble. The paper was of a much higher quality, better than anything he'd ever messed with back home. It reminded him of the parchment Mike simulated in his medieval realms for things like magic books and spell scrolls. Sturdy stuff.

Spencer turned a few pages to find more circuit drawings, with notes in the same flat script they'd found on the paper scattered outside. One of them folded out into what was obviously a drawing of the device that was on the table in front of him. It allowed him to decipher the symbols they used on the page for the components he recognized that made up the device. There were other foldouts that described other smaller devices arranged around the big lattice box.

"What is it?" Tapov asked.

He considered it for a minute, trying to mentally fit all the parts together. It added up to a thing he'd never thought of before. "It might be an analog electronic lattice virus." Knowing she wouldn't understand what that was he immediately added, "Think of it as a node bomb. It doesn't explode, though. It, well…I don't know what the end result would be, but this is the delivery mechanism." He carefully closed the book and put it in his backpack. "This could come in handy."

Tapov looked around, eyes wide. "I don't recognize any of this, but you do." She locked eyes with him. "You said humans never visited our planet."

It was a weird conclusion, but this was a weird place. "We haven't. Humans haven't gone anywhere, like, ever. I'm it, sister, me and my Interpreter buddies. We're the first ones to meet people like you, period." It was another reminder. *He* was the extraterrestrial here, the bug-eyed monster, the invader from another world.

Whatever. Spencer gathered up a sampling of the smaller parts and components and dropped them into his backpack. When he turned around, he found Tapov giving him the stink eye. The princess didn't seem to like thieves. "What?" He motioned at the counters around him. "It's not like anyone's using it."

The other room's function was also obvious. Nothing screamed *executive* like a big office covered in dark wood paneling. It was all there: the side tables, the big wooden desk. Bookshelves lined the walls, and it was easy to tell which ones were made of the same paper as his notebook since they were the only ones still there. The carpet was thick and crunched into powder as they walked on it. For some reason it didn't blow up into big dust clouds. That had to mean quality. Fucking executives, they always got the nice stuff. It even had framed sheets of paper on the walls with fancy lettering. Had to be diplomas.

There was also a picture on the wall, a real black-and-white photograph, the first they'd seen. It was a group photo.

A group of Telirians.

The picture was blown up so you could make out everyone's faces. There were a dozen of them, maybe more, standing in two ranks on the front steps of a building, what might be the building they were in right now. They were stiff and expressionless, like they were in old photos from the nineteenth century. The clothing was different from what Tapov wore, and it was obviously manufactured and not handmade.

Tapov stared at it, mouth hanging open. She swallowed with an audible gulp. "But I don't…we never…this can't be." She turned to Spencer, obviously on the verge of losing her shit. "We were scattered tribes of savages when the nodes found us," she said slowly. "Spears and stone tools."

Now he recognized what the propped-up rectangles were on the desk. Spencer walked past her to get to them. "I don't think so," he said, and began turning the small picture frames toward her one by one.

A marriage photo.

A proud couple in front of an iron-framed house.

The same couple holding a baby in front of an elaborate buggy, with a lizard harnessed to it.

The same man, much older, seated, holding a different baby in his lap while a young couple stood behind him. A photo of the old man's wife, much younger than he was, stood on a lamp table beside him. Now that he'd moved around, Spencer saw that photo mounted on the wall next to the door.

Each time he turned one around Tapov got smaller, made a little whimper.

The room blurred and tears rolled down his face. He'd only ever been on her side of the fence when life decided to implode. It'd happened when his parents broke up. It'd happened again when he lost Fee. He'd never seen it from the outside until now.

It was the worst fucking thing.

She slowly sat down on the ancient, ruined carpet. Telirian weeping was a horrible, sad coughing sound, and they didn't seem to shed tears. Not that it mattered. Spencer sat down next to her and threw an arm over her shoulder. She leaned against him and shuddered with her sobs.

Eventually she stopped. "Do you think it's all lies? What they've taught us?"

He sighed. "Your version of history is one hundred percent bullshit. That seems obvious to me. But they're teaching you more than history. The rest of it is probably okay, as far as it goes anyway."

"These people...*my* people...they were trying to stop the nodes, weren't they?"

"I think they came a lot closer to pulling it off than you realize. That's the only thing I can think of to explain why you know absolutely nothing about them."

"But *why*? The nodes...they told us we would go extinct without them. They helped us survive."

"Yeah. We got a saying back home about that." His grandad had taught it to him. "*We have to destroy the village to save it*. The world is a fucked up place. I guess the galaxy is, too."

"I don't have any idea how to digest this, what to do about it. We don't know how to survive without the nodes. Nobody does."

He was glad she couldn't see his smirk. Mostly because she was right. Earth might know how to survive without it, but the rest of this galaxy would be well and truly fucked if there was no AC network.

She breathed deep. "Did they do this to your people, too?"

Well that was a complicated question. If he told the truth, she'd think there was a chance for them to go it alone. But there wasn't. They didn't know how to survive on their own anymore, and Earth was in no goddamned position to help. Humans fucked shit like this up all the time, meaning to do good for a people in need but screwing up because their ideas didn't match the facts on the ground. And that was with each other. The truth was that he trusted the nodes a hell of a lot more than humans in a situation like this.

"Spencer?"

"How could I know?" Deflection was the better part of valor. Now to sink it into a side pocket of truth. "I've never seen anything like this either."

"It would be one thing if they told us about this, said there was a war, and that we'd sent ourselves back to the stone age. But that's not what they say at all."

"They're hiding behind a simpler lie. It's easier to maintain. You don't go looking for your ancestor's treasure if you think it's a bunch of stone tools."

"We lost. The fight against them. We lost."

Yeah, Spencer figured that part would probably suck most of all. "You didn't have a chance. The nodes haven't shown you the whole deck yet, the technologies you'll live with. I haven't seen any of their weapons, but they must have them. Compared to what I'm seeing around here, what the nodes would've used would seem like magic. In a way, you should be proud."

"Proud? Of losing?"

"That they got this far. That machine in the lab? I didn't think it could exist. They wiped the memory of your ancestors out because they're scared of you. All those wrecked nodes out there? Your ancestors did that. They got so close."

She pulled away from him. "What do I do about this?"

"Hell, I don't know. I wish I did."

"Father will know." She sighed and then laughed a little.

"What?" Spencer asked.

"I thought nothing could make me go back to him until I'd proven myself. *Nothing.* And then you come along, an actual alien, and show me everything taught to my people for centuries is a complete lie. I have to go back now. This is too big for me to deal with by myself.

"We have a saying, at least I'd like to think it's ours: never defy the gods, they'll take it as a challenge. Boy, did they ever." She pushed herself off the floor. "Come on. We need to get out of here."

The river flowed against one wall of the cave, coming up out of the blind passage they'd entered from, and then a few hundred yards later, entering another one. Spencer knew they were in trouble because he heard that exit long before they could see it. Then the riverbank started to rise above the water level. The exit was at the bottom of a fair-sized gully, transforming their lazy-as-the-Mississippi slow mover into a pretty fucking terrifying set of rapids that ended in a hole.

A *dark* hole.

"Well there goes that idea," he said.

"You don't think it'll widen out and calm down on the other side?"

"The other side of what? We don't know what's on the other side, or that there is one."

"Can't you send your drone, like you did last time?"

It was a nice idea, but there was a problem. "It's built for lakes or slow rivers. Even if there's another big room directly on the other side, and I'm just about certain there's not, I could never get it back through those rapids. I do have an idea, though."

He walked back upstream until there was enough of an eddy pool to have gathered some driftwood. He configured the smartRope to wrap up a stick about a foot long and the width of his thumb. "We'll watch how fast the rope unreels. If it does slow down somewhere up ahead, we'll know it. That still won't make it safe, though."

"Why not?"

"It could be a flooded cave six miles long. I'll have to risk the drone to find out."

"But you will."

He shrugged. "*If* it slows down."

They walked back, and he threw the stick in. After a few swirls, it vanished down the hole. The speed did change.

It got faster.

When it hit the end of the spool, he commanded the rope to let go of the stick and reeled it in. "Nope. That's not a way out we can use."

It took a few hours of exploring to determine that there weren't any ground level exits, either. That only left one direction and created a new problem.

They'd done pretty well with rations and water so far. Nobody was gonna stuff themselves, but by being smart, sharing, and accepting the occasional stomach gurgle, he figured they still had several days until nutrition was a problem.

The issue they had now was power.

"I didn't count on needing the climbing harness at all, let alone doing anything useful with it," he said as he put it on.

"How much do you have left?"

He checked. "Fifteen percent." Not good. "You'll have to stay down here while I explore."

"Do you think there's a way out up there?"

"Pretty much has to be, otherwise the air wouldn't be breathable." Maybe. But fresh air had to mean *something* in a cave otherwise sealed off by a flowing river. "When I do, I'll lower the rope and pull you out." He'd at least find them a better place to spend the night. The petrified grass made him sneeze if he breathed too much of its dust, and the ruin gave him the creeps.

The next few hours were a grueling routine of finding a path that went up, hitting a dead end, clambering around the obstacles, and then towing Tapov across. At least she was no slouch at climbing. He had scratches on his back that would've been problematic if it weren't for some nanoHeal cream he'd brought along. Those claws were serious business.

He stretched out the remaining fifteen percent for a lot longer than if he'd gone straight up and then tried to haul her along with him. It was still exhausting and more than a little dangerous. Some of the rocks were sharp, and it wasn't like he was dressed for the occasion. By the time they got two-thirds of the way to the top, they were both covered in cuts and bruises.

But they kept hitting dead ends, and the power level of his suit only went in one direction.

He did have hope, though. Unlike the rest of the time they'd been down here, all the paths went up. Sometimes they didn't go up much. Other times they went up way too much.

"You said," she growled at him from a cliff face as he held the rope wrapped around what had to be a stalagmite or stalactite or some other shit, hoping it didn't let go before she got to the top, "that I only needed"—a clawed paw hit the ground as the rock cracked underneath the rope—"to wait for you"—the other paw hit, and she heaved herself up—"to find the way out."

"I'm not the Hulk, and you're sure as shit not Tinkerbell," he replied, not caring that she'd have no idea what he was talking about. "If I tried to lift you all in one go, you'd probably be hanging from the ceiling until I got help. This way you'll be out right behind me."

After a couple of minutes of heaving gasps with her hands on her knees, Tapov replied, "Assuming I don't drop dead after all this climbing."

"Well, there is that."

"What's a Hulk?"

The next climbing segment went by quicker while he explained *The Incredible Hulk* to someone who had never seen a comic book.

She wasn't as impressed with Tinkerbell. "We have legends like that. At least I think they're ours. Who knows?"

"Those probably will be yours. Tinkerbell was around way before we knew about the nodes."

"Do you think it's a coincidence we have similar stories?"

He considered it as he leveraged his way across the underside of a cliff. Spencer had grown to hate this type of climbing because it was too much like falling on purpose, especially when he had to climb blindly up and over an edge. The power level now read two percent. They were running out of time. "More like people who experience the same kinds of fucked up shit life throws at them will tend to come up with the same sorts of stories to explain why." He turned to see what their next route might be.

The fuck?

The cliff led to a passage, which was long. He saw how far away the opposite side was because it was lit up.

With sunlight.

He wrapped the rope around a big boulder and then held his end tight. The next two minutes were some of the longest of his life as

Tapov did a Tarzan impression swinging on the rope until she was directly below him, then climbed up. He knew she was struggling now because of how long it took. The suit wasn't the only thing running out of energy.

It didn't matter, though. There was sunlight.

"Come on!" she shouted.

The hole was small but proved no match against a motivated ape and bear, neither of whom had been outside in a week. Tapov was the first out, shaking dirt and rocks down on Spencer's head as she went. He was about to shout at her but then saw her hand, now not strange at all, reaching down for him.

She pulled him out with a heave. After blinking a few times in the light, he looked around. They stood on a tall hill on the other side of the broad plane they started out on. He could barely make out the trees that stood on the edge of the pit they camped in before setting out on this fiasco.

Now well above ground level, it was obvious what the mysterious craters represented.

"It's a city," he said. The craters were the remains of buildings, all undermined by some weapon or technique of the nodes. The place had been gigantic, probably the size of a city like Pine Bluff or maybe Little Rock. North of twenty thousand people at least.

Tapov sat down heavily. She barked out a sob and was silent. He sat down next to her, not a clue as to what happened next.

"They took this from us. The nodes. Why?"

"I wish I knew."

In the far distance to his right, where the city vanished into the horizon, four black dots, spaced apart evenly, appeared in the sky. As they flew, he barely made out the specks that fell from their bellies.

"Oh fuck me."

When they hit the ground, great spouts of dirt and fire shot into the air. Spencer started silently counting.

"What are those things?" Tapov asked as she stood.

He motioned for her to be quiet, still counting. *Four Mississippi, five Mississippi…*

"Spencer, seriously. What's going on?"

He got past fifteen seconds and still hadn't heard the explosions. They had a chance. "Those are bombers, and they're headed this way." He grabbed her hand. "Come on!"

Chapter 35

Helen

It looked exactly like what it was: an artifact that had been orbiting a remote star completely undisturbed for more than 250 million years. There weren't many things that would bring a well-educated Chinese person, proud and knowledgeable about their history and heritage, up short. An object that was constructed a quarter billion years before humanity itself had evolved did the trick nicely.

And yet, on another level, it was quite mundane. A simple square box, rounded on the edges and corners, wider and longer than it was tall. It was about the same size as a Chinese big box retail outlet. The vaunted seal that excited Maff was across the opening of a standard docking bay. Despite the time and the discontinuity of the Refounding, from the outside at least, it was indistinguishable from any other.

Maff had brought them into realspace several hours' transit time away to do an initial scan of the system to see if anything nasty lurked nearby. It gave Helen a chance to enjoy a long stint of weightlessness. No space sickness for her. The pallun had magnetic grips on their legs and stayed firmly on the deck.

Once the scan came up empty, she jumped them closer and made a map of the object itself.

Whatever it was made of was incredibly strong. There were signs of asteroid strikes all over the structure in a bewildering range of sizes, but none had significantly damaged it. Almost all of them were smudges. One was downright enormous, a pulverizing collision that covered a quarter of the underside but was, at best, a meter deep. It only revealed more of whatever the walls were made of. It had not breached the inner hull, nor had it imparted any spin. Helen couldn't make out any cracks. They built these things tough.

Before they boarded it, they had to settle on a plan.

"I'd say it's a matter of when, not if they arrive," Helen said as they discussed what to do with the ship.

"The ship will stay in realspace then," Maff replied. "We'll park it in that hangar and then seal the door. They'll have to come in the same way we do."

Sornik pointed at his men. "Bithern, Tollar, you're volunteered for guard duty. And no fucking around, right? That's our only way home. Poolin, Fulan? You're with us."

None of them seemed happy about it, but Helen had only ever seen them happy when they won at cards. Regardless, she was glad the giant Fulan would be coming with them. Pallun used manipulators to interact with the world, but they were proportional to the size of the individual in the suit. Fulan's were almost as big around as one of Helen's legs. If nothing else, he'd be good at getting doors open.

Up close, the plain box's edges were well out of sight, with its patchy blotch marks and pits making it seem much more moonlike. The massive hangar doors hadn't been spared any impacts but seemed likely to open.

Palatine had an external manipulator arm mostly used as a loading crane. It was easily reconfigured by adding a cutting tool. Maff used it to neatly slice the single metal band that mechanically locked the doors shut.

Alarms sounded on her control console as lights flashed on the doors in front of them. For an instant, she was back in her father's office, staring in horror as he prepared for a nuclear launch, fingering the syringe of drugs in the pocket of her uniform. She shook off the feeling. "What's going on?"

Maff threw a few switches and consulted screens only she could see. "The doors are powering up."

Americans often talked about how this, that, or the other thing was *mind blowing*. For the first time, she genuinely understood what they meant. "But this is more than two hundred and fifty million years old."

Maff and Sornik stared at her.

They must not have understood her. Maff's grasp of English was strong enough for this. She switched to that and said to her, "Nothing stays operational for that length of time. There's no way. It should all be…I don't know…rusted together."

"Ah," Maff said. "Now I am understanding why you are having the confusion." She switched back to Pallundian. "Human machines aren't like ours. If you don't use them, over time they'll stop working."

Sornik gave her a confused look. "What?"

Maff shrugged. "If you leave an Earth machine alone, it will vanish completely, all by itself. It can take some time, but it always happens."

"Oh, come on." He looked at Helen. "You said your people were advanced."

It might be easy for her to get overawed by bemian technology. Bemians themselves, not so much. "We are. Sometimes we wear shoes."

A new pattern of beeps sounded from Maff's console. "That it works doesn't impress me. That it can talk to our systems does. I've got docking instructions and a clearance now." She grasped the ship's manual controls. "Tell your men to prepare for landing. Helen, if you could monitor the scanners, I'll take us in."

Helen called out speed and proximity readings as Maff gently nudged *Palatine* toward the hangar. Alerts sounded from the console, and her stomach lurched unpleasantly as down suddenly became a direction.

Maff swore and threw some switches. "Well that's a surprise."

"Artificial gravity?" Helen asked. Gravity existed, somehow, in the transit dimension, but they'd all been floating while in space.

"I guess. It's the first time I've heard of it, but apparently *Palatine* was ready for it. It's a part of the landing sequence I've never seen until now. We would've crashed otherwise."

"It would seem that some important technology was lost in the Refounding, after all."

*

The outside of the cache was impressively tough but still showed its age. The interior? It gleamed. When the atmosphere changed from pure nitrogen to a breathable mix, part of an automated welcoming procedure of some sort, they exited the ship. It smelled like a new car. "There's no dust," Helen said.

"Why would there be dust?" Sornik asked. "We're the first people to set foot in this thing in millions of years. It's not a planet, it doesn't have weather."

He said it like there was nothing special at all about a structure this old that was this new. When they'd started out back on Earth, Helen hadn't taken Maff's idea of technology trade all that seriously. Earth's technology wasn't as advanced as bemian, but to Helen it was a difference in degree, not kind. Briefly being in charge of China had given her an eye for trade opportunities, and while there were plenty of those, aside from portal tech, Helen didn't see any game changers.

She was now inside one.

The hangar was the kind of antiseptic white common in high tech factories or military garages. It was tall but not all that wide or deep. "Perfect for ships like *Palatine*, but not the big cruisers. Maybe they didn't have big ships back then," Maff speculated.

Helen flinched a little when her bemian phone chimed with a connection request. Judging by how the pallun jerked back, they'd all gotten the same request. Helen traded shrugs with Maff and Sornik, then accepted it.

It was immediately apparent that while bemian communications tech had survived unchanged, Standard had not. The voice had a gentle, neutral tone, but it spoke gibberish to her. "Does anyone understand what it's saying?" she asked. They all shook their heads. "And the text?" It was bemian 3-D style writing, but she'd never seen any of the symbols.

"Not a fuckin' clue," Sornik said, shrugging with his manipulators.

They'd left their interpreter threads behind for obvious reasons.

"It may have lasted a quarter billion years," Helen said, ignoring the stunned shock saying the words sent through her, "but it wasn't meant to." Or maybe...she searched around. If the builders had any inkling that recovering from the disaster would take millions of years, there should be a sign of it.

"How you figure that?" Sornik asked.

"They didn't account for the way languages shift over time. If they had, there would be instructions located prominently that didn't rely on language. Humans did this by using pictures instead of words."

She searched and also used her threads to penetrate the local realmspace. Or, rather, she tried to. The base codes and protocols of the cache were compatible with modern bemian electronics, but it seemed that the interstitial areas of their realmspaces weren't. She'd have to bring this up to Mike next time he contacted her. His explanation would probably be too technical for her to follow in detail, but she'd get the gist.

She did a double take when she saw the door that led to the rest of the complex. Helen stood stock still, waiting for what she saw to vanish. Her eyes began to stream because she couldn't blink.

"Helen?" Maff asked from behind her. "What's wrong?"

She didn't dare turn away. "I need you to come over here." When the clacking of Maff's legs stopped, she pointed at the door. "What do you see?"

Maff switched to English. "This...this is not possible."

"No, it's not."

Attached to the door was a square of paper. It was the first time she'd seen paper since leaving. It had words written on it.

English words.

They said THIS WAY.

Chapter 36
Tonya

With Maff's coordinates, she could fulfill Tenor's wish to preserve pre-Refounding bemian culture, but it wouldn't be done in a day. Or a week. At a minimum they would be here for several months at least. They'd need to set up a base and account for logistics.

First, the base. After confirming that the controls in the threaded room worked within the bounds of her theory, she created a copy of this room in another pocket of the dimension it was in. She didn't have the patience to jump through the hoops Cyril would inevitably put in front of her if he found them before they were done.

The rest of the basic requirements, things like food, water, and a place to rest, wouldn't be a problem. She still didn't understand how to enter a room like this on her own from realspace, but once inside, it wasn't difficult to create and maintain a bridge between it and realspace. The room stood outside time in one respect, but in others it moved along with the rest of the flow. It wasn't a time machine so much as a time observatory. They could view the past and the future, such as it was and within the limits of the room itself, but traveling to realspace would place them in the same *now* as when they left. This room was flowing with the timelines of and around the catastrophe that led to the Refounding and would move forward only as they did.

The room went a long way toward explaining Cyril. If she lived as long as he did, she'd probably be able to ride this thing all the way to the present.

"We need to come up with a name for what happened, what caused the collapse," Tonya said to Tenor as they examined some promising locations.

He chuckled ruefully. "It doesn't have a name. The disaster itself has been wiped from history." He considered it for a moment. "The Rending? What would you pick?"

It was a little strange to be a wolfling from a civilization that didn't know any of this existed trying to come up with a name for it. But he did ask. "The Blackout?"

He looked at the end of the room that held the threads that terminated in the disaster, the terrible darkness beyond, with only the hint of light at the end. "The Undoing."

She rolled it around in her head. "I like it. Now," she said as she turned back to the threads, "how to help something survive it."

The time span from this point in history to their present was a giant challenge. She had no idea how to help anything survive for so long.

This confused Tenor. "What do you mean *for so long*?"

She stared at him, trying to comprehend a civilization that shrugged its shoulders at machines that lasted for time periods that humans measured in geologic eras. They spent the next five minutes talking in circles until she got over a hang-up that, to Tenor, was as profound to him as his inability to imagine time travel was to her. To a bemian, machines millions of years old were commonplace.

She held up her hand. "Okay. Machines don't break down out here, ever, no matter how old they are. I believe you. I do. I need to find out how it's done."

"Do humans always have to know how a thing works before they can use it?"

"No, but it helps."

*

They settled on creating the mother of all time capsules, a self-maintaining space station placed in a remote corner of the galaxy that would quietly watch the millennia pass as it preserved its precious cargo. How to build it turned out not to be a problem. A species called pa'ranti were already building them all over the galaxy, caches of artifacts meant to survive the onslaught of Andromeda. Their presence at the meeting may not have spurred a galaxy-spanning war, but it had begun nonetheless. Tonya and Tenor knew how it would end, but history prevented them from doing anything to stop it.

Theirs would be small on the scale of the other caches, which sometimes spanned whole planets. It would be about the size of eight big box retail stores like they used to have back home, two sets of four stacked on top of each other. It wouldn't be pretty, but it would be tough.

She let Tenor manage creating the list of artifacts to preserve while she spent time on the problem of why they were so durable. At timespans that long, the main obstacle to preservation was basic entropy. Machines were made of materials that were manufactured. Those materials were not in a stable state. Steel rusted. Food rotted.

Even if a material had no known method of rapid decay, like plastics, time always found a way to get rid of them. Coal was so prevalent back home because when trees evolved the ability to create wood—technically they evolved a complex organic polymer, effectively a kind of plastic itself—nothing on Earth could consume them. For millions of years, until organisms evolved ways of digesting it, trees fell over and sat there until fossilization turned them all into rocks.

So it didn't matter what a machine was made of. If it sat around long enough, it would not only stop functioning, it would be completely destroyed. Bemians had, somehow, found a way around this.

Tenor was right to question why she needed to know this. It wasn't necessary to understand how bemian tech lasted so incredibly long to use it. But she had to figure it out. Entropy was a fundamental law throughout the universe. Things broke down, always. Bemians didn't get to break that law without some sort of explanation.

Tenor finished compiling his wish list before she managed to compose the first postulate of a theory that might explain how they did it.

"I have a question," he said. "How are we going to pay for all this?"

Tonya smiled. "We won't need to."

Since history was so unsubtle about protecting itself, Tonya knew exactly what to do. She'd pick an item on his list, and then try acquiring it in the flashiest, most public way possible. Within hours, sometimes minutes, an alternative path to the goal would reveal itself. Back doors would be left unlocked. Auctions mysteriously rescheduled themselves so nobody else was there. The hoary chestnut of *don't let my wife sell my collection for what I told her I paid for it* played out several times at estate sales.

She didn't do it with the super exotic or rare items he picked out. Rather, she used this method to buy items low and sell them high, working their way up to the point they could purchase rarities directly without attracting suspicion. In a way, it was a version of time travelers using an old racing sheet to place bets on historic horse races. But they didn't have to worry about gangsters showing up asking inconvenient questions about their incredible luck.

As the collecting progressed this strategy wasn't the only way they acquired artifacts. Toward the end, examples of spectacular bemian art found their way to the collection in deeply weird ways. History itself seemed to want certain things preserved. Three of the eight main rooms had centerpieces that arrived in their own special ways.

An abandoned D-ship, lost for millennia, its species' home planet long ago recycled by the La'fan, nearly ran them over on a collection run. Its hold was taken up by *The Hunt,* a memorial commemorating the defeat of a mythical monster, carved from a single perfect ruby that weighed half a ton.

The next, known as *The Temple to the Silent One,* was discovered when the floor collapsed in a warehouse they'd bought as temporary storage. The hole created revealed an incredibly well-preserved temple complex clad in a material that, somehow, was a natural display screen that acted as a kind of active camouflage. The effect must've been to hide the entire enormous building in plain sight. Somehow it had gotten stuck and now displayed a day in the life of the people who worshipped there on its walls and columns. It had vanished sixty million years ago and was, improbably, missed when the La'fan recycled the planet.

Xenarka's *Blue Infinity* had arrived at their loading platform unannounced, the secret gift of the race that had created it, having just finished its thirty-third bi-millennial public exhibition. The note asked them kindly to look after it until the nameless crisis the pa'ranti warned about had passed. They would then ask for its return so it could be put on display once more.

For some reason Tonya was deeply moved by the idea that they would never get to display it again, that if the creators survived the crisis at all they would've forgotten its existence, and then themselves passed into oblivion. She was humbled that the Lord had entrusted her and Tenor with its preservation, along with the thousands of other artifacts they'd brought along. He did indeed move in mysterious ways.

*

Tonya found the answer to her entropy problem while they were reviewing their plans for the cache. Always happy to help someone who believed them, the pa'ranti set Tonya up with a construction crew and a space dock big enough to build what they needed.

She'd been reviewing blueprints for the machine spaces when something caught her eye. "What's this?" she asked the pa'ranti engineer helping her, an ewok-sized and shaped creature with scales instead of fur.

He looked at the spot on the blueprint. "That's the power source."

"No," she said patiently, and then pointed at a different area. "*That's* the power source." A fusion reactor spun into their shared 3-D space. It was one one-hundredth of the size it would be back on Earth, but she still recognized it. "What does this other thing do?"

He shrugged. "Okay, it's *part* of the power supply. They always come in pairs, output and exhaust. All power supplies have them, small or large."

If they all had them, then there would be smaller versions she could examine up close. An hour later found her tearing apart a cordless drill discarded in a corner of the space dock's machine shop. The recognizable battery had an unrecognizable object attached to it. It was a small black square barely a half a centimeter wide, textured with a rough surface that felt like Velcro.

She thought it *was* Velcro, but that had been a mistake. It was a much smaller version of the exhaust the pa'ranti pointed out. She could see incredibly delicate tendrils extending from this square, touching all parts of the device.

It had broken because the gearset had stripped long ago. The tendrils to that particular spot had fractured, perhaps because it'd been dropped or overheated.

She'd had many eureka moments in her life. Being deeply involved with a brand-new branch of physics meant they sometimes came at her fast and furious. All of them represented a high point, a payoff that said the work she'd done, the blood, sweat, and tears spent getting there, had been worth it. Until now, almost all of them had been abstract, theories coming together on a blackboard. This discovery was different.

It was how a galaxy worked.

"It's called an entropy pump," she said to Tenor as they made their final preparations. "Well, that's what I call it anyway."

"That's nice. What's an entropy pump?"

"Somehow it can drain disorder from a system and get rid of it. At its most fundamental, that's what wear and tear is: an increase in disorder. If a device can somehow get rid of that increase in disorder, it will never break."

"But things do break, they always have. These ancients have loads of broken things waiting on AC nodes to repair them. There were junkyards everywhere."

"That's due to accidents or misuse. Sometimes it's a bad design."

He shook his head. "Okay, so there's a little square inside it all that stops it from breaking. How does it work?"

People with no knowledge of a problem always jumped on the biggest weakness of her solution. It was uncanny. "I don't know. It shouldn't. The entropy has to go somewhere, but I can't figure out the mechanism or the destination. It…vanishes."

"Like we're about to do, right?"

"Exactly."

It'd taken a little more than six months to complete their collection and have it paid for, assembled, and then packed into their purpose-built cache. She let history tell her the safest way to get it to its final destination, which turned out to be renting their own automated D-ship tug and having it pulled out there anonymously.

She surprised him by taking them both back to the threaded room when they were done.

"I thought we put hibernation creches in the cache for us? That's not how we're going home?" he asked as she adjusted the controls for their final transit. Now they would use the room as a proper time machine, transmitting themselves forward. There would be no return.

"Oh no. I'm not gonna become the galaxy's oldest human by sleeping 250 million years."

"Then why'd we go to all that trouble? They were expensive."

"These controls aren't precise enough to make a jump directly to the present. There's a plus or minus two-year margin of error. I don't want to accidentally end up two years in the future, so I'm setting our destination for four years in the past. We'll make sure it's all still in working order, and then sleep *that* amount of time off."

"And if anything has gone wrong?"

"Your family will be around. *You'll* be around. Heck Maff will be around. We'll figure out how to contact someone and arrange a pickup. I think it'll work fine, though."

"Why?"

She suppressed a giggle. It was heady stuff knowing why time paradoxes were impossible. And she had the math to prove it. "Because none of those things happened."

There was a darker possibility, there always was. Four years was still plenty of time for things to go wrong. But Tonya could only work with what she could change. The Lord would have to take care of the rest. And He would. She felt that certainty like a warm embrace. She'd been working with one of His proxies, after all. History had taken care of her so far. Jesus would be happy to pick up the slack once she got back to where she belonged.

Tonya took a long look around the room.

"Do you think you'll miss them?" Tenor asked as he looked around as well.

They'd consciously kept their distance from the residents of this era on the brink of the Undoing, not only because they'd been dead for hundreds of millions of years from their frame of reference, but also because it made history's interventions a lot less intrusive.

"Maybe a little. It'll be nice not to constantly feel guilty around them." She'd never quite gotten used to knowing what was in front of the entire galaxy, and that she could do nothing about it.

"Yeah," he said. It looked like he might say more but then he shook his head. He'd been the inspiration for the whole thing, and the driving force behind deciding what would and would not be coming along. She could understand that he was overcome now that it was finished.

Tonya set her hands on the controls, which were a collection of bulbs and leaflike constructs. Not a TARDIS, by any stretch. She pulled the visor down on the space suit she was wearing in the unlikely event something had gone wrong with the cache. Regardless of Tenor's attitude, it *had* been out there for hundreds of millions of years. "Ready?"

He did the same thing and then nodded.

Tonya activated the sequence. There was no disorientation, no surreal splitting, no sensation at all. It was completely the opposite of the snapping disorientation of their previous trips through time.

One second they were in the threaded room, and a split second later, they blinked as the lights in the cache's main hangar snapped on.

Less than another second later, the main AI interfaced with their phones. *Welcome, Tonya and Tenor,* it said in the now archaic version of Standard it had been programmed to use.

"Time stamp?" This would tell her how long they'd have to sleep. The reply said it would be a little less than two and a half years until they hit the present. She'd take it. "Status summary?" she asked.

All collections intact. Hull integrity: 92 percent. Inner structural integrity: 98 percent. System integrity: 99 percent. Power system: 100 percent.

They must've taken a big hit at some point along the line, but it had been built to take big hits. At least they wouldn't have to stay in the suits. Once the atmosphere changed from preservation-friendly pure nitrogen to a gas mix they could breathe, she opened her visor. The air was cool and clean, smelling like a new hospital. Tonya thought she'd gotten used to the longevity of bemian tech, especially now that she understood the basics of how it worked. But to stand inside a time capsule that'd been out here for so long…

Tenor lifted his own visor and harumphed. "Lots of little anomalies in the logs."

She threw him a half smile. "The tech works; it's not perfect."

Alert: sensor monitoring in sectors nine and eleven is now offline.

"And more to come, it seems," he said.

Now that they were so much closer to the present, history's hand was nearly imperceptible. About the only thing she felt was a heavy need to stay in the cache. This was good news. The outside world was almost certainly one they'd recognize. With a little more time, they'd be able to leave with an incredible story to tell.

But they weren't there yet. "Come on, time to get to work."

Chapter 37
Mike

When he told Malafan where Spencer and his daughter's last known location was, the lord swore under his breath and shouted for his sergeant.

"Yes, milord?" Sergeant Eskol asked, a little winded. The soldiers had been drilling on a field about a hundred yards away.

"She went to the Interdict."

A broad grin split Eskol's face. "She did? Slurks do breed to the same color, milord."

Mike looked at Kim, who shrugged, then they both looked at Malafan.

"Let me guess," he said as he sighed. "In the galaxy, teenagers don't break rules and push boundaries. Will we have that peace?"

Kim barked out a laugh. "I can't speak for the entire galaxy, but on our planet, they do both every chance they get."

He sat down and motioned for them all to do the same. "The Interdict is strictly off limits, but a few teens in each generation take it upon themselves to find out why. They think they'll never get lost and never get caught, but they always do. The punishment can be severe."

"Unless you're the heir apparent, of course," Eskol said with a chuckle.

"Oh, they punished me, all right. It just wasn't in public."

"Cor," Eskol said in a half whisper. "Is that why you disappeared for a month after we got back?"

"It is indeed. And now she's out there."

"What is it?" Kim asked.

"Honestly, we don't know," Malafan replied. "A collection of sink holes that connect to a massive cave complex. Places like it are scattered all over the planet, but not common enough to need more than one name. We have our Interdict, there's another one in Kalfan's land..."

"Have you ever managed to see that one, milord?" Eskol asked. "Mounds as tall as castles *and* the pits and the caves."

"No, I haven't had the pleasure. At any rate, no Telirian has ever been allowed to explore them openly, and anyone who tries to do it on their own faces consequences."

"But you've both been down there?" Mike asked.

Eskol shrugged. "Like milord says, we was a couple of dumb teenagers, got lost, and then got captured."

"What's it like?"

"Wet and dirty to start, dusty and dirty after we found the river."

"River?"

Malafan nodded. "The Beshanta runs through the cave system. It comes out near Umalaza, a city several days' walk from here."

"Is that how you got caught? On the river?"

"Nah," Eskol said. "The river's a dead end. The lord's father here, he got suspicious when his boy and his friend went missing."

"And if it'd only involved Father, things would've turned out differently. I'd left a note, but he saw right through that." He smiled a rueful grin. "Does your society have a tradition about fathers being cursed to have children exactly like them?"

Kim nodded. "It does indeed."

"It's nice to know we have things in common. Father would've handled it discreetly, but Mother found the note. That's when the pintara crashed through the gate."

"You got that right, you do," Eskol said. "After his ma found out, she went straight to the nodes. The Servants of the Network went into a right tizzy, like they always do when someone goes against the wishes of the network. They dispatched fliers and then crawlers."

Malafan chuckled, eyes closed on a memory Mike wished he could see. "How long were we down there, anyway?"

"Let's see," Eskol said as he stared at the sky, scratching his chin. Mike was immediately reminded of Kim's uncle Kostas. Storytellers as a galactic staple. The parallels never stopped. "It had to be at least three days, but no more than five. We were a right mess at the end, drinking from the river, starving. We'd run out of rations."

"What else do you know about the caves?" Kim asked. "There must be other stories."

There were, but they weren't detailed. The one consistent element was the river. Everyone always found the river, and that was how the nodes found everyone. It disappeared into the ground far to the north, entering the cave system and trending southeast until it welled up from the ground on a high plateau.

"That's where we start," Kim said. "Nobody in that situation travels up the river."

"There's no way into the caves there," Malafan said. He stopped at Mike's smile. "Ah. I'm thinking you have a device that will help us find a way in?"

"We do, but there's more to the story. The nodes are going to sterilize the area. Exactly what that means I don't know, but it can't be good."

"They're in caves, though," Kim replied. "Wouldn't that keep them safe?"

"I don't think so," Mike said, and wished he could share the video the drone shot with the Telirians. A description would have to do. "From the air, the site is enormous. Sterilizing it will mean collapsing what's left."

Kim stood. "Then we better get started."

Malafan shook his head. "It will take far too long to get there."

"Oh, no, milord," Eskol replied. "That's where you're wrong. Let me show you what these aliens use for ground transport."

*

It was the biggest risk they'd taken since coming to Teliria. They needed as many people as possible to help with the search, but the mounts Malafan's men used would never be able to match the speed of the truck.

So they unpacked most of their camp to free up space, leaving it behind in a neat cube-shaped bundle hidden under piles of straw in the householder's barn. Now the truck bed was filled with six uncomfortable-looking men-at-arms hanging on for dear life as they rushed down a surprisingly good paved road.

"The nodes built them," Malafan said from the back seat.

Sergeant Eskol sat opposite him, with one of the lower recruits wedged between them. Per her usual preference, Kim drove while Mike made sure they didn't lose anyone sluicing through the turns.

"Why does it change to dirt outside your city?" Mike asked.

"We don't know. They built it to a certain point and then stopped. The whole planet has roads like this. They start well away from established towns and end well away from different established towns. It was generations ago. My grandfather told stories watching them get built when he was a boy."

Regardless, it let them make good time through the middle of the journey. They left more than one stunned caravan in their wake as they sped past.

That stopped when Malafan had them turn down a dirt road that ran through a forest of tall trees. The soldiers in the back quickly figured out how to brace each other to keep from getting thrown out.

The young soldier sitting between Malafan and Eskol, Mike didn't catch his name and so called him Ethan, pointed forward. "There, see that bend? Turn left onto the trail."

After about a hundred yards, the ground bent upward, quickly lifting them out of the forest. Kim slowed and then stopped before [illegible]ad made a hairpin turn and continued upward. A gigantic [illegible]ll thundered downward far in front of them. It was a couple [illegible]vay, but they could still hear its roar. Majestic didn't come close to describing it. Mike had been in Niagara Falls realms before. These put them to shame.

"That," Ethan said as he pointed, "is Tenara Falls. They're made by the Beshanta river, the one you think Princess Sarewith is following. We get to the top of this road, and we'll be able to follow the river to where it comes out of the ground."

They quickly climbed at least a thousand feet, giving Mike a commanding view of the forested plain below. A creature that wasn't quite a vulture and wasn't quite a pterodactyl soared on a thermal, searching for lunch. It was odd, but peaceful, then quickly obscured as Kim turned through the next switchback and put his window next to the cliff.

The road was for Telirian vehicles. It was narrow and steep. But now that they were up above the tree line, he could see two pairs of faint ruts worn into the road. They were much narrower than the truck's wheelbase.

Curious.

With a final dizzying turn, they reached the top of the bluff. On their left, maybe a mile away, the Beshanta river roiled its way over the falls. The road continued straight in front of them, turning toward the riverbank. On the other side of the bluff was a giant valley dotted with sinkholes. Thousands of sinkholes, stretching beyond the horizon.

They were pulling to a stop when four aircraft thundered over their heads, much larger than the drones which had chased them a few days ago. They seemed to take no notice of the truck or its occupants.

Kim stopped and everyone piled out. Mike got out some smartBinocs and found the drones in the sky.

"There's too many for them to be scouts," Kim said beside him.

"Look," the other soldier said as he pointed to the east. "There's more." That one scanned the skies with his own version of binoculars, made of brass. Two other soldiers were doing the same thing, in different directions with the other four scanning the low ground, looking for bad guys.

Not too shabby.

Mike checked the fliers out. "Identical. Same type, same number." Their smokey engines—probably low-bypass turbofans or maybe turbojets—made following their trail easy. "There's more on the way."

"How long?" Kim asked.

He could barely make the more distant ones out. "They don't seem to be heading the same direction."

"There!" The soldier following the nearest squadron shouted, pointing at the bombers.

Exactly together, each dropped a bomb. These were perfectly circular instead of aerodynamically oblong, but the purpose was obvious. Five seconds later, another set fell, and then another five seconds after that. By the time the sound of the first explosions reached them, at least five sets of bombs had been dropped.

"Lord Malafan!" The soldier scanning the southeast shouted as he pointed. "There!"

Beyond the river the bluff continued to rise to a peak that must've had a commanding view of the entire area. After a minute of scanning, he found what the soldier had spotted.

Scrambling down the slope, arms pinwheeling to keep balance at speed, were Spencer and someone who had to be Malafan's daughter.

"How deep is that river?" Mike asked.

"Let's find out," Kim said before Mike heard the rotors of the drone whir up to full speed. "Back in the truck!" She leaned on the horn, but they were probably still well out of range.

Eskol shouted Telirian too fast for him to follow into the truck. A moment later, Mike's ears nearly split from the most intense shriek he'd ever heard. The area around them was bathed in red light for a brief moment, but it faded quickly. Mike turned and saw that one of the soldiers had used what was obviously a kind of flare gun.

Startled, he turned to Kim. She switched to English. "The nodes must've built them. The language Telirians use doesn't have a word for gunpowder."

The soldier holding the gun had a big grin on his face while the rest of them stared up in awe. "It might be the first time they've used one," he replied.

"All right," Sergeant Eskol shouted in Telirian. "Now put it away before you set the place on fire." He turned to Mike. "Did it work?"

He checked. Spencer and Tapov had changed course and were now running straight for them. "It did."

"Good," Eskol said. "The nodes gave those flares to us. I don't know what the hell those things are," he said as he motioned vaguely in the direction of the bombers, "but in about half an hour, this place will be crawling with every kind of drone the nodes can send."

Chapter 38
Maff

Sornik and his crew didn't think that what Helen had found was writing at all. "It's a bunch of squiggles," he said while peering at it closely, then looked at Helen. "Like what we found in those old books. If you call it art, I'll believe you. I know people who'd buy it on the spot. But writing? Writing has depth."

It'd taken her months learning how to interpret human writing, so Maff understood his pain. "Whether or not you believe it is beside the point. That is human writing, but the only human to ever have set foot in here is standing in front of us. She didn't do it."

Sornik stood up. "Then who did?"

They all looked at Helen, who stared at the writing. She began picking at it. Or rather, what the writing was on. After a few moments, she peeled the writing completely off the door.

"It's written on a leaf?" Fulan asked.

Maff chuckled. "Paper. It's called paper. The humans use it to write on." She held up a manipulator to stop their protests. "I know, that part doesn't make any sense either. They have display screens like we're used to, but they also have this unnatural writing surface. Let the suit take the hit, you keep walking." *Roll with it* would've been better, but she didn't know how to translate that into Pallundian.

"More properly," Helen replied as she examined it, "this is a sticker." She folded a corner, then sniffed it. "And it wasn't manufactured on Earth. The folding resistance is wrong, and the adhesive uses a formulation uncommon for this application." She looked at them, disappointment at their dumb silence clear on her face. "Someone taught bemians how to make paper stickers and stashed some in this cache. But it hasn't been on the door for long. The adhesive is much too fresh. In fact," she said as she pressed the sticker into a notebook she'd pulled out of her pocket, "I think it's been here less than a decade. Probably a lot less." She sketched a few notes with a pen that'd been inside the notebook's binding.

"That's impossible," Sorkin said.

"You are correct," Helen said, completely unperturbed by the paradoxes they'd discovered. Maff didn't think she ever got upset if there was a mystery to solve. "I need more data."

Helen pressed the button to open the door. It pulled upward with a whoosh, revealing a long white sterile hallway.

"It must run the length of the cache," Maff said.

"Yes," Helen replied. She took a dozen steps, then turned around and looked at them. "Interesting." She spun on her heel and continued forward.

"Come on," Sornik said as they walked. "You gotta throw us an eddy here."

Helen peered at another sticker, identical to the first, near the end of the hall. They could now see that it didn't dead end but went left and continued out of their sight. Again after a few dozen steps, she turned and looked at them, nodded, then turned and continued down the hallway.

"Why does she keep doing that?" Fulan asked no one in particular.

Still facing away from them, Helen shook her head. Maff wondered if the rest of them felt like they were on a field trip with a prickly guide who didn't like children.

"I shouldn't be disappointed you wouldn't notice this." Helen stopped and turned around. "Last chance to guess."

Maff looked around. The hallway was white, the walls weren't decorated so much as they were covering up the machinery and cables of the cache. The lighting was bright, indirect, and industrial, banishing any chance of a shadow. The floor seemed to be made of the same material as the outer shell, a tough kind of concrete, only black.

It all seemed normal.

After the awkward murmurs around her faded to silence, Helen stretched out her arms.

"And that's supposed to tell us what?" Sornik asked.

She rolled her eyes, turned, and took five steps to stand against one wall of the hallway. "Life forms build structures to fit their body type." She took ten steps to cross to the other wall. "Almost all of the galaxy's life is taller than it is wide." She returned to the center. "You don't notice anything special about this hall because you're used to it." One of her eyebrows shot up, a human expression that meant she was going to solve her riddle.

"This structure was created for pallun."

Maff looked again at the hall, its shape, its dimensions, the color of the lighting. Helen was right. It was perfect.

"Coincidence," Sornik replied. "We hadn't evolved when this thing was built."

Helen tipped her head sideways. "Maybe. Maybe not."

"Look," Sornik said, "you may be here for...whatever you're here for, but I'm here to find things to sell." He marched past them and around the corner. "Finally!" He pressed a button next to the first door they'd seen so far. It opened with a clean whoosh. On the other side Maff saw bright lights and dark, distant walls.

"Fuck me," Sornik said, and then walked slowly inside.

It was their first proper cache room. Until this moment, the galaxy only knew them as vast, empty chambers, always with a roof torn off or a hole blown into the side. Every single one of them had been picked clean during a time so chaotic it didn't have a proper name.

This one wasn't empty.

In front of them stood a giant statue of a race Maff didn't recognize, sculpted from a material that was the color of deep blue water, made of the clearest crystal she had ever seen. It reminded her of a nursery rhyme she was taught by a petarkan child she met at a playground, about a kind blue prince and his crystal magic.

The creature was at peace, contemplating its own sculpture, duplicated perfectly in one webbed hand. It, too, held another smaller copy, just as beautiful, repeated again and again, twisting as it shrank, until it was too small to see. When viewed from the opposite side, it was obvious that the miniatures made up the largest statue. In an instant, she understood how the infinite could be encompassed within the finite, a concept she would've thought impossible until she saw this magnificent sculpture.

Six aisles radiated from the area of the statue going off into the distance. Unlike the hallways, the space was too vast to be lit continuously. It used regularly spaced fixtures, creating splashes of light. It emphasized the vastness of the place without making it feel like it was a cave.

"You two," Sornik said as he pointed to his men. "Pick an aisle and run an inventory scan from end to end." Their phones would make a video record that a node…that a node would *normally* be asked to scan and create a list of objects found. Toraz would process the data they returned, but she had a feeling nodes wouldn't be involved, at least not directly.

"As for you ladies," he said after his men had departed, "you're outside my chain of command. But I'd appreciate it if you volunteered for inventory duty."

Maff turned to Helen, who said, "We need find out how English words are on this ancient ship." Her tone was neutral, as was her body language, but Maff saw the tension underneath. She understood it. Sornik was ignoring a profound mystery to inventory a warehouse.

"And I need to make a status report in three hours. Last time I checked, your mystery doesn't have a deadline."

He had a point. "We'll help out," Maff said. Helen shrugged, but that was good enough for now. "And then we start following the markers after you're finished."

Helen smiled. "You'll at least be able to tell me what these things are."

She did her best, but it was tough. Maff recognized the basic types...sculptures, paintings, mosaics, realms, and constructs. But the variations were unique.

Helen wasn't as impressed. "They're not. They're all still similar enough to existing bemian tropes to be recognizable."

"No way. I've never seen anything like these things. It's all so beautiful."

Helen then proceeded to reel off a dozen details that not only showed how each piece of art was related to another, but how they were also related to more modern types. Her powers of observation were both annoying and intimidating in equal measure. Maff might never see art the same way again.

Helen elaborated on the way back. "It's inevitable. The nodes may be uplifting you from savagery, but they're also fitting you into specific molds. I'll concede that the treasures here are unique, but unique within strictly proscribed boundaries. It's becoming clear to me that the AC network restricts creativity in the name of social stability. What's puzzling to me is why it lasted so long, and then failed so spectacularly it created a discontinuity that completely cut the entire galaxy off from its own past."

Discontinuity was an interesting way to refer to the period before the Refounding. "What's puzzling to me is how I never questioned any of it until I met you humans."

"That's to be expected. Hundreds of generations of intelligent life forms have been trained from cradle to grave not to ask awkward questions, not to be curious, not to wonder." She sighed. "Sadly, I'm all too familiar with societies like these. I was briefly in charge of one."

"Hey," Sornik said as they returned from their survey. "Have either of you seen Poolin? He's not answering his comms."

"No, we haven't," Maff replied.

"Did he go back to the ship?" Helen asked.

"Nah, I checked, and they haven't seen him. Hey, Fulan,"

he said as the big pallun joined them from his aisle. "You seen Poolin around?"

Helen leaned toward Maff. "He went down that aisle, right?" she pointed to the one on the far left.

"Yes," Maff replied. "That's the one."

She nodded grimly. "Walk with me."

They did. When Sornik noticed Helen moving off, he and Fulan fell into step behind them. "What have you seen?" he asked.

Helen shook her head and kept walking. She looked quickly from side to side, stopping occasionally but never for long. Sornik and Fulan would occasionally shout Poolin's name, but the vast room only replied with echoes. What before had been a warehouse full of treasure now took on a more sinister feel. Maff was reminded of her encounter in the senescent center on the La'fan planet and shuddered inside her suit.

They reached the end of the aisle, which stopped short of the opposite wall, making a connecting aisle. Unlike the rest of the space, it held no shelves of its own. Helen walked about a quarter of the way and stopped, facing the wall.

"He's gone," she said flatly.

"Gone where?" Sornik asked.

She reached out and touched the wall with her thumb. It pulled inward and then up, revealing a featureless hallway no different from the one they used to get here.

"He went with whatever this came from," Helen said, then reached down. She'd spotted a blob of dust or dirt. Maff ran half a dozen reasons through her mind to explain why this single spot wasn't as clean as the rest of the cache. All of them were nonsense.

Helen held it out so they could see. It was a clump of dark green hair, long but bristly.

"He wasn't alone. Something else is on this ship.

"Something alive."

Chapter 39
Tonya

She rubbed the first of their guide stickers hard against the wall of the hangar bay.

Tenor examined it closely. "You're right. Now that it's in place, there's not a bemian alive who'd think that was writing." He'd taken to the word bemian almost as quickly as Maff had. Hang out with aliens, learn alien slang. "You've shown me how it works, and I still don't believe it."

"One down," she held up the sheaf of stickers, "twenty to go."

"And I'll give you a tour."

"Of this place?" It was simple enough in miniature reviewing the plans, but there were eight full cache rooms split on two levels. "It'd take all year."

He shrugged. "The highlights, then."

"And the fixes."

"Ugh, yes. The fixes."

Bemian tech was miraculously tough, but it wasn't foolproof. There were too many opportunities for Murphy's Law over the timespan they'd needed to cross. The normal way to maintain the cache would've been to install a node on board as a caretaker. But it would've reached out to all its buddies right away, allowing it to be mapped, tracked, and plundered long before Maff could get near it.

So they had to accept that *some* amount of wear and tear would inevitably occur and planned accordingly. That meant redundancy wherever and whenever they could afford it. And it worked, for the most part. The hull had held up beautifully. At one point a hundred million years ago, it shrugged off the impact of a planetoid they'd missed during their system survey. The environmental systems were also fine, allowing them to stow their space suits without worrying about stumbling across a compartment filled with poisoned air, or no air at all.

It was the ancillary systems, dust control, diagnostic repair drones, and video monitoring, that were hit hardest by the eons. And it was all their fault. The alert timestamps were from just after their arrival time.

This was an unfortunate prediction of her theory. They'd spent so much time in the deep past that a kind of tockion differential had built up between them and the present, which created a damaging energy discharge when it equalized on their arrival. It was a shame they hadn't caught any footage. There was a good chance that they entered with a Terminator-like lightning ball around them.

So as she pasted stickers to the hallways, Tenor swept up, revived dead repair drones, and marked broken cameras for those revived drones to replace.

They also enjoyed the exhibits. If Maff and her crew followed the stickers from the hangar, Xenarka's *Blue Infinity* would be the first thing they encountered. The sculpture was quite simply the most stunning example of ancient bemian art either of them had ever seen. It was so famous echoes of its existence survived in children's rhymes to the present day.

She sighed. "I want to spend the time we have left exploring all this."

Tenor's wing rested lightly on her shoulder. "Me too, and I'm the one who found most of it. But we didn't bring enough supplies, and it's not like we can leave the house to get more."

True, and if she was honest, Tonya was looking forward to a semi-enforced big sleep. The previous six months had been an exhausting scavenger hunt interweaved with yet another exploration of new physics. History's hand didn't guide her so much as it slapped her around if they stepped out of line. Like Yoda, she'd earned a rest.

The main sleep room was located in the center of the structure, what would become a kind of visitor's center. When its door opened, Tonya immediately knew there was a problem. What should've been clinically clean and odorless had a hint of nail polish remover in the air. Acetone, strong enough she smelled it in the vestibule of the room. The environmental controls must've failed, and wasn't that a great thing to find out about a place you were planning to stay...

It wasn't the environmental controls. A device had been attached to one of the sleep couches. With its hatch opened, she saw a torn hose leaking fluid onto the cushion inside. It shouldn't look like that. It should be closed up, no modifications, she'd inspected it right before they left.

"Tonya!" Tenor shouted as he shoved her so hard she stumbled and fell to her knees. There was a roar, a slicing whoosh, and a terrible scream as blood and feathers exploded everywhere. A big white wing landed on the floor with a wet slap.

Get up, she thought, *get up NOW!*

Tonya let training and reflexes take over. She rolled away from the sound and jumped to her feet. Tenor was on the floor, dragging himself away with one wing while the stub of the other spurted blood. Above him a dark, monstrous shape uncurled from the ceiling, flashing knives mounted on wrist straps. It was smaller than she remembered, but the coloring, shape, and most of all, the triangle of three glowing eyes were easy to recognize.

It was a tricorn, like the ones she'd seen walk out of the portal at the power plant.

All this took a microsecond to recognize, as did potential vulnerabilities. It was built roughly the same way as a human, so she had to hope it had roughly the same attack points. Joints designed to move one way would break if forced to move in another, necks were soft, pain disabled no matter what the size.

She didn't waste any time and immediately went for a knee after it'd hit the floor. It didn't feel like solid steel, but it was a hell of a lot stouter than a human's. She put a hand down and spun inverted with another kick to the exact same place.

The monster grabbed her ankle and flung her across the room as it fell. There was no time to feel the pain; she had to stay inside this thing's reaction time. She was lighter and faster, got up first, and tumbled forward in a roundoff that led into a back handspring, feet aimed straight at its head.

She connected solidly, feeling the energy of her move transfer straight into its skull. Pain tore through her side, and she was again hurled across the floor. The nurse in her knew what had happened and knew it was bad. The blades were short, but they were sharp and had hit her on the lower left side. She would need serious medical attention, or she'd be dead inside of an hour.

One thing at a time. She was in trouble, but she'd laid that son of a bitch out in the process.

"Tonya!"

Tenor's good wing beckoned at her from a short, dark hallway. The pain in her side overrode all her training. She could not fight, and the monster was getting up.

"Come *here*!" he shouted.

She recognized where he was, a tunnel the repair drones used to travel throughout the caches. Screaming against the pain in her side, she dove forward. His prehensile feather fingers grabbed her by the wrists and hauled her inside. A metal door slid over the passage's opening, muffling a frustrated roar. It also muffled the subsequent hit well enough that she spared a thank you to the now long-gone bemian engineers. They built things to last.

The pain in her side was replace by a horrible itching, so intense she cried out and pulled up her shirt. It must've used poison or injected nanomachines that were going to eat her alive…

Right in front of her eyes, the three long, deep cuts in her side stitched together. She got the absurd urge to compliment an impossible, invisible surgeon. The work was so fine she doubted there would be a scar. "What the shit?"

"Sa'dst," Tenor said. "Remember?"

They were the nanomachines that kept bemians healthy across absurdly long lives and had been distributed throughout the cache when it rebalanced the atmosphere. She'd understood their function as an abstract concept. After this live demonstration, she now had a much greater appreciation for them.

He waved a pink wing stub at her. "It'll take some doing to get this back, but at least I won't die. What *is* that thing?"

This time the blow against the door had a sharp ring to it, and the door slipped sideways a little. Not a simple brute. It had smarts enough to know how a crowbar worked. "Nothing good." She'd worried about being the oldest human being in the universe, but someone else had beaten her to the punch. "It used one our hibernation couches."

"But how did it get inside in the first place?"

"Those things work for Andromeda. It can influence humans across millions of light years and made me think it was a god when we met it. I don't know the exact mechanism but with that kind of power on tap it probably wasn't hard. It's not like we made keeping it secret a priority."

Her wound still itched like crazy, but she was free from the worry of a perforated bowel. Tonya could deal with it.

The door moved a little more, this time with a metallic screech.

"It doesn't matter. Come on, we have to get out of here."

Finding a weapon was out of the question. It wasn't from a lack of examples; they had plenty of blades in the collection. The problem was twofold: they were packed away, and the creature would have the same sa'dst coursing through him that had saved their lives.

She tried to open a maintenance hatch to a regular hallway. A hairy pair of clawed feet stood in front of it, immediately replaced by a huge arm with knives mounted on the wrist. In the slow motion of her panicked backpedal, she noticed it had claws, too.

Wonderful.

The only thing that saved them was that the creature was too big for the tunnel. It could get its head and one arm in. If anything, that made it more terrifying, a roaring and howling half thing straight out of a nightmare. Tonya felt the image burrowing into her mind, and now the long sleep wasn't as appealing.

"How did it know?" Tenor asked once they'd put more tunnel between them and it.

She considered for a moment. "It's tracking us?"

"How? We didn't exactly come through the front door."

"Maybe it can smell us? I don't know, all the monsters I've ever fought were fake. Come on, we can't have much time."

She'd made an extra sleep room a number one priority during construction. It was located on the second level, ninety degrees away from the first room's position to ensure they both couldn't be taken out by a single event.

Every time they came close enough to a door, they heard the creature nearby.

Finally, they got to the last junction before the backup room. By then, she had a plan. She'd be the distraction, and he'd open the door. Then it would be a foot race for her to get to the room.

"That's not a good plan," Tenor said after she explained it.

"Most plans usually aren't." This part of the tunnel was long and had two doors: one on each end. They sat between the two until they heard the creature outside. "Okay, ready? On three… one… two… *three.*"

They split, Tenor heading toward the door next to the room, and Tonya heading toward the opposite end of the hall. Thinking would only slow her down, so she ran straight through it, then skidded around the corner of the hall outside. "Hey!"

The creature was already halfway toward Tenor's end. It stopped, absurdly reminding her of a head nurse she'd worked for back in the day. The old battle-ax stalked the ward's halls trying to figure out where Tonya was copping naps during down times. Except for, you know, the three eyes, vicious mouth full of teeth, and arms the size of tree trunks covered in swamp colored fur.

Actually, there *was* a bit of a resemblance there.

She flipped it the bird. "Come on! I ain't goin' nowhere. *Come on!*" Tonya crouched in a combat stance and waved it over.

That did it. The creature threw back its arms and bellowed at the ceiling. It stomped toward her, gaining speed as it went.

Long ago, she'd found warm shelter in a train garage in a Philly rail yard. She only had to walk across a trestle bridge to get there. One night the inevitable happened, and she'd been halfway across when a train pulled around the corner. Trestle bridges didn't have anything between the ties, and she didn't know how to swim. As terrifying as that run had been, with a machine that would crush her without feeling a bump, horn blasting only a few feet behind her, this was worse.

That time, she was running *away* from the monster.

The only reason she had a chance was down to a dumb joke they'd cooked up drinking a little too much of the local wine finalizing the plans. "The size of the halls doesn't change the cost. We'll make it pallun size!" he said in a shouted giggle.

She spluttered. "Nobody will get it!"

"Brilliant!" They toasted the decision and made the notes.

So instead of a hairy creature filling a corridor as it charged toward her, there was a hairy creature charging down a corridor with about two feet of free space on either side of its outstretched arms. It was supposed to be five, but it had long arms that she hadn't noticed until now.

Oh well.

She flexed and abstracted the monster in her mind. It wasn't a creature trying to kill her, it was a movement test, an obstacle of wooden cylinders and sticks like the ones Walter set up in the backyard and forced her to run through dozens of times a day. Toward the end, he'd mounted knives on them as sharp as the ones coming for her head. She grabbed the bubbling outrage tied to the memory, a teenager with no clue why an old Chinese man would torture her this way, and channeled it.

She had one chance.

When it got so close she saw the slitted center of its eyes, red and boiling with rage, she moved to the left, selling it by fully transferring her balance and weight. The creature reacted perfectly, slashing knives with a roar of triumph.

She collapsed, using the momentum to roll forward as the blades flew through the space her head had been in a moment before. Now, as it was then in that back yard, she felt a snick above her ear. A lock of her hair departed upward. The only difference was the color of the stripe, purple then, but green now. *The things you notice running for your life.*

The creature had fully committed to its own move, so she helped it along by hooking a foot against its ankle and yanking hard. There was no time to watch the result, but the shambling thud spoke for itself.

So did the scrabbling of claws and the renewed stomping, too close behind. Now the little girl and the grown woman were running from the monster in the right direction. She heard vicious swipes as the knives cut the air behind her. At the right-angle turn before their room, she jumped sideways and burned the momentum that would've sent her into a skidding crash to dash along the wall for three strides. Tenor stood in the doorway before her, hopping and waving frantically, looking absurdly off balance with only one wing.

The creature, more massive and a lot less motivated than she was, hit the wall with what sounded like bone-cracking force as she rushed headlong through the door. She crashed face-first into the wall on the other side so hard it bounced her to the ground. She heard Tenor slam the door's control. It whooshed shut and locked. This backup room was smaller and stronger than the main one. Prybars would be useless here, and the only drones they could use were the ones stored inside.

"Are you okay?" Tenor shouted.

"Yes," she said as she rolled up, bleeding from her nose. "We need to shut the cache down before that thing gets out of the corridor. Hurry!" Fighting the adrenaline shakes and the blood

Chapter 40
Him

Moments after Eskol explained that the flare would bring the nodes, she got more bad news from their drone: there was no spot on the river shallow enough to wade across. She kept going anyway, now aiming to meet Spencer and his friend in the shortest time possible. They arrived on the edge of the riverbank in a skidding, dusty slide. The rumble of the bombers was now audible over the idling engine.

On the other side of the river, Spencer and Tapov were jumping and waving.

Mike called up a screen on the truck's virtual display and punched a few buttons. "Stay here." By the time she figured out it was for the winch, he'd already gotten it out and was yanking smartCable from it in big handfuls.

She rolled down the window. The bombers got a lot louder. They were close. "What are you doing?"

"Stay here! I'm bringing them over!"

Before she could shout at him to stop, he wrapped the winch cable around his waist, shucked off his shoes, and dove into the river. It was about thirty yards wide at this point. He was a powerful swimmer—they both were—but she didn't know how fast or cold the water might be. He didn't either, but her giant dope of a husband wouldn't let that slow him down.

On the opposite bank, Spencer got out some rope of his own and configured it into two basket shapes, handing one to Tapov as he put his own on.

"What are they doing?" Malafan asked.

"Getting ready for Mike," she replied. She used his progress to judge the speed of the current, which was pulling him downstream fast enough that Spencer and Tapov were having to walk quickly along the bank to keep up. "They'll attach to the cable, and I'll tow them all back to our side." She hoped. His plan was a good one.

She still would've appreciated at least a quick consult before he ran off.

He reached the other side, then got Spencer and Tapov attached to the line. She needed to find out who made the smartRope family of products. They wouldn't believe her endorsement, but she'd make it anyway. As Mike walked toward the bank with his crew literally in tow, she engaged the clutch and began to slowly reel it in.

"And we're expected to sit here?" Sergeant Eskol asked.

Once they were up to their shoulders, Kim sped the winch up. All three took that as a cue and began to float, sending them rapidly downstream. "Unless you have a boat or can fly, yes."

"What's happening to the water?" the middle soldier asked, as Kim noticed Mike and the other two had stopped floating and were now standing on the riverbed again.

They still had three-quarters of the distance to go. Kim stopped the winch to keep it from pulling them off their feet. "I don't know, the level is falling." The flow had been blocked somewhere. With all the bombs dropping debris must've stopped the outflow upstream.

One of the soldiers had been scanning the skies from the truck bed. He pointed to the right, upstream, and shouted, "incoming!"

Four node bombers roared overhead, traveling outbound from the ruined city. A moment later, there were ear-splitting explosions to her right. The massive noise faded out, replaced by a different kind of rumble, one coming up from her feet.

"Look out!" another soldier shouted from the truck bed.

A massive, wet boulder, easily the size of a house, rumbled down the edge of the riverbed nearest to them. It hit another boulder in the now-exposed riverbed, sending the gigantic rock bouncing several feet in the air.

It came down directly on the winch cable, neatly severing it.

Then there was a smell, an unmistakable combination of reeking mud and rushing water.

The river had been reduced to a bare trickle while Mike, Spencer, and Tapov picked their way across, gathering the cable as they went. As one, they looked up river, and even from this distance, she saw the pale panic fall over them. The smell was getting stronger, and now there was a rising roar. The rock must've been the plug holding the river back. No more.

She knew what to do.

She said, "Buckle your seatbelts. Tell the men in back to hang on." She checked that hers was safely fastened, too.

She only had the small realm that was a built-in part of her phone. It would be enough. Kim closed her eyes, sat back, and accessed it. Instantly, she was in a plain, basic office, like what you'd get in a trailer on a construction site.

There were lines of potential, and she couldn't remember how to breathe. Seams of power dimensions of nothingness, dark patterns potentials horizon to zenith…

Remember to breathe…

Like this, she could reenter the world from any point she chose.

Breathe…

Like the spot where the cable had split, not ten feet in front of her.

Breathe…

There was no time to contemplate the mystery, she pictured the spot in her mind and rammed her way through the realm and the transit dimension on the other side. The parted ends of the cable were at her feet. She grabbed the one that had Mike on the other end, her black crystal hands covered in coral lightning. She looked up in time to see he'd grabbed Spencer and Tapov, hugging them around the shoulders and turned away from the wall of water that collided with them.

A moment later, it collided with her as well.

She threw a hemisphere of power up around her to block the

current and sent more power down the cable to enclose the other end. There wasn't much she could do about the water trapped inside, but at least now they were protected from the current and the debris that was already buffeting against the shield.

She set her feet, threw the cable around her waist, and started hauling it in. There was no pain…she'd had more than one bomb go off in her face like this. A bunch of water wasn't a big deal. But it was a lot of mass. She was stronger than normal, but she wasn't Wonder Woman. Still, one hand over the other was better than nothing.

The river had only been completely stopped up for a minute or two, so the water level fell almost as fast as it'd risen. She thought *mesh* at her shields and was rewarded with the water trapped inside her hemisphere draining away with the rest of it. She didn't need to breathe transformed, but the folks at the other end of the cable did. A moment later, the water level had dropped to the point she saw them in the opposite sphere, soaked and coughing but otherwise okay.

Once the water was about ankle deep, she shut the shields off completely, leaving one sputtering teenager, one overawed Telirian…

And the love of her life. Only now did she let the absolute panic of what he'd done, what had nearly happened, what *would* have happened, enter her thoughts. The sobs drove her to her knees.

"Hey." An invisible force lifted her to her feet. "It's okay, I'm okay." The force pinned her arms and crushed her chest. It wasn't the first time this had happened, so she wrapped her arms around what to her was solid air. It was as close to a hug as she could ever get.

And for now, it was enough.

"Where the fuck did the truck go?" Spencer asked.

She stepped away from Mike and scanned around. It was nowhere to be seen. That was disconcerting. It might've gone over the falls. They had no idea what would happen if her realspace body was injured, fatally or otherwise, while she was transformed.

She looked at her arms, black obsidian with coral lightning playing underneath as always. "I think I'm okay?"

"What *are* you?" Tapov asked, eyes wide as saucers.

"That's Kim," Spencer said, distracted, still searching for the truck. "Kim, this is Tapov. Where the fuck could it have gone?"

A shout from downstream caught their attention, and they all broke into a run. Behind a low hill was a debris-choked group of trees near the riverbank. The truck's tailgate was an incongruous red rectangle sticking out from the center of it.

"Jesus Christ," Spencer said. "How high did the water *get*?"

Now that she knew her body wasn't at the bottom of a waterfall, it was time for a change. She motioned for Mike to stop, then pointed at the truck. "I'll be in there if you need me." Picturing the rift she'd created to enter the world caused it to appear next to her.

"Be careful."

She winked. "Always."

Kim walked through and exited the realm, opening her eyes to a dry—and empty—truck cab. She looked around and saw that the men had all gathered around a fallen tree nearby. The shouting must've been Sergeant Eskol organizing them. They were working together trying to lift the tree.

It'd fallen on one of them.

Mike, Spencer, and Tapov arrived at a run. Tapov screamed, but Eskol intercepted her, tackled her, and held her to his chest. Spencer joined them, saying soothing things she couldn't make out from where she sat. That, more than anything, let her know who it fell on, and what it meant. She locked eyes with Mike through the truck's window. He grimly shook his head.

As she got out of the truck, the soldiers managed to lift the tree off the body. They carefully set the trunk down so it would block Tapov's view. The tree had fallen across Malafan's shoulders, knocking him to the ground and crushing him. It was a cold comfort to know that there had been no suffering. One of the men covered the body with his cloak, the gesture made desperately sad by its gentle care.

Kim walked over to Mike. He smiled wanly at her approach.

"Thanks for saving our asses," he said quietly.

"My pleasure." She turned around. "Does this mean we're looking at Ontara's new ruler?"

"Preindustrial humans transferred power in a variety of ways."

Eskol stepped away from Tapov and barked out, "Oy! Company A of the royal guards will come to attention!" The men quickly formed up into two lines of three. Eskol then marched over until he was in front of them and spun around. "For-WARD!"

They then marched smartly up to Tapov, who seemed to be expecting it. She gently pushed Spencer away, visibly lifting herself out of the wreckage of her mourning. Kim had never seen that kind of bravery up close. Mike would scoff and say all she had to do was look in a mirror. He might not be wrong. In the moment, she felt a kind commonality here, a recognition of another woman accepting a tragedy she couldn't control far too soon because that's what had to happen.

Hopefully Tapov would do a better job of dealing with it than she had.

Kim leaned in toward Mike and said softly, "I think we're about to find out."

The soldiers got about three feet away and stopped marching. "I, Sergeant Eskol, as lead man of the lord's companies, regret to inform you of our lord's death." They dropped to one knee. "We therefore gladly acclaim you, Princess Sarewith, as Lady, new leader of Ontara. All hail Lady Sarewith!"

The soldiers answered with an impressive bellow, "All hail Lady Sarewith!"

In the pause that followed, she said firmly. "Tapov. My name will be Tapov."

When they did it a second time with the different name, Spencer, with a grin that stretched from ear to ear, joined in the kneel and shouted too.

When they did it again, so did she and Mike. As transfers of power went, it was bold, simple, and direct. She could only hope that it would stick.

When they stopped, the crump of exploding bombs could clearly be heard in the distance. The pathfinders had gone, and now the main force had set to work.

"Stand, please," Tapov, said, voice husky with emotions Kim could only guess at. "We have much work to be done." She turned. "Spencer—"

Whatever she was about to say was drowned out by the descent of dozens of node drones.

Chapter 41
Helen

She saw that Maff was at a complete loss when she delivered the news that they weren't alone on this craft, but Sornik wasn't.

"Bithern, Tollar, button the ship up and get down here. We got us a situation." He turned to her. "What is that from?"

She examined what she'd found. "Easier to tell what it's not from, which is human or pallun. So it's not one of us or someone like us."

"Not much to go on, lady."

"No," she replied, trying to fit the pieces of this puzzle together. "It's not." Helen closed her eyes, relaxed, then opened them again. Observation was the key to deduction, and deduction would solve the problem. "We're looking for a large creature, two to three times my size, bipedal and shaped in the way we are and you're not. It's got a heavy double coat of fur and will be a dark olive color in normal lighting." She crushed the hair in her fist, which crumbled to dust. It shouldn't have done that if it'd been recently shed, but this was an alien creature. Its hair didn't have to act like that of a mammal.

During her politburo days she learned to never voice her doubts. It undermined trust and allowed confusion when she needed certainty. So she kept this contradictory finding to herself. Sornik's two other men arrived, and they continued down the hall.

After they walked a few dozen meters, they found a T intersection. "Keep the cache wall on our right," she said and kept moving.

"What's that gonna prove?" Sornik asked.

"The cache room is on the other side of this wall. If we find another right turn, we'll be back where we started at the hangar." The caches were large, so it took some time to pace out the distance. In the end, though, she was right: it did bring them back to their starting point. "If nothing else this should make it easy to map."

"Well, we know he didn't go that way," Maff pointed to the corner that led back to the hangar. "Someone would've seen him."

"Do you think this hallway goes all the way around the perimeter?" Fulan asked.

"Yes," she replied. "In the obviously unlikely event of a hull breach, having the rooms away from the outer hull provides options."

"So let's walk the perimeter," Sornik said, then pulled out a pair of what had to be weapons, small soap-bar-shaped devices that matched what Mike described once. The rest of the men did the same. "And see what we can see."

Helen fell in behind the armed pallun and walked next to Maff. They passed the hallway where she found the hair sample. It was an interior hallway that probably ran the width of the ship and kept going. They discovered a door on the far side of the hallway, just before they turned the corner.

This opened on another cache room, themed in red where the previous one was blue. Taking pride of place this time was a giant tree sculpture with bright red palm leaves extending evenly from the trunk. Below the leaves were flying creatures, with riders poised to hurl spears at foes fleeing below them. If the riders were roughly human size, as most aliens in this galaxy seemed to be, then the tree the fliers circled was more than a thousand meters tall. Helen was proud of her analytical side, but she could only stand dumfounded before such beauty.

Poolin was nowhere to be found. Nor was there any creature hair. They did, however, find a second door in roughly the same position it as in the blue cache room. "They built it to be toured," Helen said.

"Toured?" Maff asked as she looked around.

"There's a flow to these aisles, going from most spectacular and large to quite modest and small. It lets the traffic flow in a single direction." If she didn't know any better, she'd think it was based on an Ikea store. Helen had spent her fair share of time in those getting her house set up in Virginia. The resemblance was uncanny.

She immediately noticed a change when they opened their exit. "Almonds," she said softly. The smell was faint but unmistakable. There were no trees here, which could only mean one thing. The way all the pallun around her flinched confirmed it. Cyanide gas was an important part of a pallun's internal mix. She was smelling almonds, but they were smelling a corpse. Poolin was close by, and the news wasn't good.

All four of the men went on high alert. Sornik motioned for Maff and Helen to stay back while he silently signaled the rest of them to move out into the hall. They disappeared from view.

"What do you think has happened?" Maff asked.

She was an adult, so Helen had no need to sugar coat it. "Poolin is dead, torn apart by the creature or creatures I found evidence of. It's big and fast." And quiet. Whatever had happened, they hadn't heard it.

A few moments later, there were shouted curses but no gunfire or other sounds of violence. "They've found him," Helen said. "Come on."

A few dozen meters down the hall was a small atrium containing two elevators on one side and a set of down stairs on the other. There was a second, lower, level, which she suspected because of the height of the ceilings. Now she knew how to reach it. At the opposite end of the atrium was an undecorated wall that had a large, heavy door set in it, partially open.

Suit parts and what looked like rags of tiger skin were scattered all over the floor.

The rest of them spoke Pallundian too fast for her to follow completely, but most of it seemed to revolve around swearing and revenge. Helen knelt down to the largest remaining piece of suit, a rough rectangle perhaps a meter long and maybe half that wide.

"Hey," Sornik said. "You shouldn't be here. The gas is dangerous to your types."

"Not anymore," she replied. "That's why we were able to smell it from that distance without it affecting me. He found the door in the blue room but didn't tell anyone. Is that typical?"

Asking questions gave the men focus, which settled them down. It reminded Helen again that while these were criminals, they were professional about it.

"Yeah," Fulan said. "He would've wanted to know what was on the other side first. Idiot."

"Indeed," Helen said as she lifted up one corner of the fragment with her pen. The underside still held a patch of Poolin's skin. Since pallun were basically intelligent balloons, it represented a major part of his body. "Location and gas dispersion means this happened less than an hour ago. Whatever he encountered, he met it here." But things weren't fitting together neatly. "There were no signs of a struggle anywhere else, no indication of a fight leading up to this point."

"I'd call this the sign of a fight," Tollar said as he pointed at a blast mark on the wall over the stairwell. "He went down with his wings spread."

True, as far as it went. But that wasn't the point. "And yet," she countered, "the only evidence we have of an alien presence is near the door to the blue room, which is quite far from here." She stood. "If he had encountered the alien where we found evidence of it, we should've at least heard *that*," she pointed at the blast mark, a large black soot ring surrounding a divot of the same size about three centimeters deep. "Yet there was nothing until we found all this."

"Hey, Sornik," Fulan said with his head poked through the open door on the opposite wall. "Check this out!"

The room on the other side was completely unlike any they'd seen so far, and while it answered many questions, it posed many more. It was much smaller than the cache rooms, not much more than a short hallway connecting to a square space that was four meters to a side. When the space was built, the walls would've been blank squares designed to make virtual screens easier to read, concealing storage cabinets behind them. A pair of hibernation couches still dominated the center.

Fulan huffed out a laugh. "Someone's got anger issues."

The wall cabinets had all their doors torn off. Claw marks scored deep channels across their frames. The supplies inside, all high-density food items, had been dumped out and then consumed, leaving wrappers and empty containers covering the floor like an alley behind a drug den. A door to a maintenance tunnel of some sort had been violently pried open. The hibernation couches were stripped out, with the cushions used to construct a low, broad bed.

Behind her, Sornik gave his men orders to scout the rest of the hallways and return when they finished. The last thing they needed was to get ambushed.

"Is this a camp site?" Maff asked.

"It is," Helen replied as she scanned the room. "And now I know how it got on board." She walked over to the couches. "Notice the drill holes, and these empty brackets. Mounts for an external life support system, big enough that it needed to rest on the floor. And it was installed in a hurry. Note the sloppy nature of the work."

Maff shook her head. "The seals were intact until we got here."

"Correct." As incredible as it was, the conclusion was inescapable. "These fittings were added before the cache was sealed. The creature was a stowaway, brought on board with the last of the supplies. The cache has been inhabited since its inception."

There should've been wonder and awe. Instead she got two barely perceptible shrugs. Whatever had used this couch was almost certainly the oldest living thing in the galaxy—by far—and they acted like she had said cabbage was on sale at the local market. It was truly an alien culture.

"I guess it won't have to sleep anytime soon," Sornik said.

"Indeed," she replied as she examined the detritus of wrappers and cups. "But that's still not the whole story. This mess wasn't made in the past few hours. There must be several weeks' worth of rations here."

"Maybe it woke up when I got here the first time," Maff said.

She picked up a discarded cup and examined the dregs left behind. There was more, but she couldn't put her finger on it. "That would explain it." But it was too easy. She was missing something about the garbage.

Her concentration was broken by screams and the sound of weapons fire. Sornik cursed and dashed to the door, weapons drawn. Maff and Helen were right behind him. When they got to the door, Helen saw brass legs being dragged down the stairs, a struggling metal crab failing to fight off a predator below. There was another scream accompanied by sounds of tearing metal. A cloud of gas billowed out of the stairwell.

Sornik pushed them inside. "Get back, that will definitely kill you."

Her analytical mind was roughly pushed aside as well, this time by the way those legs disappeared, dragged away by a creature she didn't understand. She needed space for her threads to expand into, a shower to clean off her realspace body, and most of all, to be anywhere else but here. The urge was powerful but absurd. There was no place to go.

Helen held on to that contradiction until her pulse settled and her threads uncoiled. Panic was never a good look on anyone, least of all the one who only had her wits to protect her. Although if what happened on that stairwell was any indication, pallun suits weren't much better. She distracted herself by reexamining the trash on the floor. It still bothered her, but she couldn't figure out why.

Sornik opened the door behind her. "Tollar and Fulan," he said in a hoarse whisper, "what do you see?"

The two remaining men stood on either side of the atrium next to the outer wall. They must've still been searching when Bithern had been taken. "Nothing," Tollar said. "Stairwell's empty."

They cautiously approached the stairwell, three pallun and one human. Helen concentrated on the observations to keep the gibbering monkey that had come with her human host at bay. There were no scratches. The creature had come up from the lower level, otherwise it would've been spotted by the others. She was trapped on a ship with an alien capable of tearing other aliens in powered armored suits apart. Her concentration slipped a little.

When they got to the bottom of the stairs, it was suspended entirely.

Bithern had indeed been attacked violently. There were pieces of pallun suit scattered in a trail leading out and away from the atrium, down the hall to her left.

In the far corner, underneath the stairs they'd used to reach this level, were the remains of a large bipedal creature. The fur covering its body was the same dark green as what she'd found outside the blue cache room. It lay curled on its side, dead long enough to have completely mummified in the preserving atmosphere of the cache.

Sornik and his remaining henchmen stopped. After a second, he said, "Well that's one less thing to worry about," and barreled around the corner chasing Bithern's trail before she could stop them.

"Wait!" she shouted, rushing to keep up. "We need to examine that!"

"Bithern first," Sornik called back, "your thing second."

It should've been obvious that Bithern was dead, but Helen understood the impulse. She'd respond the same way if it were one of her partners who'd been taken. Dark memories of how her friend Ji Cong died in a factory explosion briefly clouded her vision.

But not for long. Unlike Poolin, whatever had killed Bithern seemed to have spent an inordinate time disassembling his suit. The trail of amputated legs, disarticulated manipulators, suit plates, and sensors led them deep into this level's hallways. There were too many pieces.

"Stop!"

Her cop voice wasn't as good as Tonya's nurse voice, but it did the job.

"What?" Sornik shouted back.

"Bithern isn't that way. We're being led into a trap." She held up two leg segments. "What monster kills its prey and then takes it apart piece by piece as it runs? These aren't broken, they're disassembled."

A roar bellowed out from behind them. For a brief moment, the base reflexes of her host, what Spencer called her *inner ape,* completely took over. There was no question of fighting, there was only a need to run so absolute her feet were moving before the echoes of that roar had died. The pallun were all right behind her. The trail of parts continued forward. When Helen saw a hallway opening to her left, she took it. If the bottom floor was laid out the same way as the one above, this hallway would give them a shortcut to get back upstairs to more familiar ground.

Another roar sounded out, louder.

Whatever it was, it turned the corner behind them.

Helen skidded into another left turn and bounced off the far wall with her arms.

At the end of this hall was a closed door, heavy, thick, and scarred as if it had been worked on by power tools. In that door was a window, which held a sign.

It said in English:

We are here! 165782, connection Alpha

Still running straight for it, pallun clacking frantically behind her, Helen accessed her phone's virtual screen. There was a connection named Alpha displayed. She typed the code in and hit Send. The door ahead immediately flashed green lights and slid open. It was a lot more massive than the other doors she'd seen, at least fifteen centimeters thick.

"Into the room!" she shouted, and dove inside to the company of another, closer, roar. She bounced against the far wall of a hallway and was immediately enmeshed with pallun manipulators bracing against the wall. She barely heard the door slide shut over thuds and curses as the pallun stopped their run with each other's bodies. After more cursing, they got untangled, and Helen could see where they were.

It was a smaller version of the hibernation room above, much neater, with two couches in the center. The readouts on these, however, said they were active and occupied.

One thing at a time. Helen locked the door and changed the code. She heard nothing on the other side, a function of the door's construction no doubt. Regardless, Helen had already seen evidence that it was not going to be broken through easily.

Now secure against whatever it was out there, she returned to the chairs. The pallun were gathered around, looking at her expectantly.

"What?" she asked.

Sornik fidgeted. "We figured you'd, ah, you know, do that... observation thing you do. We didn't want to mess anything up."

Recognizing expertise was the trait of a good leader, and she already knew Sornik was exactly that. She never thought she'd hold high esteem for someone she wouldn't think twice about throwing in jail back home. But here she was.

She carefully assessed the outside of the couches, which were identical to the ones above minus the modifications they'd found earlier. She accessed their manifest and ID channels.

Being a trained interrogator, Helen knew how to hold still at a surprise, remain neutral without giving anything away. After a moment's reflection, though, she allowed a warm smile to bloom on her face. Her suspicions, unvoiced and mostly unarticulated until this moment, had been right.

"Well?" Maff asked.

Helen activated the wake-up sequences. "It turns out the builders of the cache came along for the ride."

"But who are they?" Maff asked.

Helen shrugged.

"Oh, come on," Sornik complained. "You're killing me here."

Helen tipped her head toward the couches. "Observe."

They hummed and whirred for a minute, then both couches expelled mist that was rapidly captured by vents above the chairs. There was a clack, some ratcheting, and then they opened up.

"Wait a minute," Maff said. "That's—"

Sornik shouted over her, "What the hell is Tonya doing in there?"

Chapter 42 Spencer

Of all the surreal reminders that he was on an alien planet, he would never have suspected being descended on by dozens of node-controlled drones would qualify. But it did. Drones were a hobby of his. He could spot the difference between an J382 and a J382bis—one had an external antennal that pointed left, the other right—from twenty feet away. Now the fucking things were floating all around him, and he couldn't identify a single one.

Tapov, who had transitioned from princess to lord...err, lady, probably...without so much as an *excuse me, but what the fuck*, didn't miss a beat. "My father has been fatally injured," she said. "We require assistance to bring the body home to prepare for burial."

A different drone found the truck. "What is the origin of this conveyance?"

Kim stepped up. She seemed a little shaky for a moment but then threw her shoulders back and went all badass. "I am Kimberly Trayne-Sellars, lead Interpreter for the La'fan. The conveyance is mine. Its origin is confidential." Then she said it again in a different language. At least that's what he thought, since the only thing he recognized was her name.

This caused all the drones that weren't working with Lord Malafan's body to swarm into a different configuration. It looked like the church ladies back home when a particularly juicy bit of gossip came out after service.

Mike spoke softly behind him, and Spencer nearly jumped out of his shoes. He'd been standing next to Kim not five seconds ago. Spencer could've sworn it. "We need to get that patch uploaded into their network. They're constructing a communications tower to connect to the galaxy."

"Well that should give us some time. Those things aren't built in a day."

"You don't understand." He motioned to the ruins behind him. "Those aren't regular bombs they're dropping."

No shit, Sherlock rang out in his head. The plain wasn't burning or collapsing, it was bubbling and frothing like that bad special-effects sequence in *Star Trek II*. Unlike that sequence, the one with the Genesis device, one side was wrecked, and the other was a flat, finished concrete slab. Equipment, structures, and other big shit started appearing on top of that, like some giant cartoonist was drawing it all in with an invisible pencil.

"How long do we have?" he asked.

Mike shrugged. "Couple of hours. Maybe."

Tapov had walked up while Mike was talking. "Can they be stopped?" she asked.

"I don't think so," Mike replied. "This will end with them connecting to the galactic AC network. They'll be at their most vulnerable then. Once the connection is complete, they'll get a block of updates that will make trying a big hack impossible. The thing is, we don't want them to stop."

She stiffened in a way that reminded him of Kim. Now he wondered if she'd insist on being addressed with a title. "What if *I* want them stopped?"

Mike, being Mike, totally missed the subtext. "Why would you want to?"

Spencer's mouth was going before his brain realized interrupting *Lady* Tapov might not be the best move. "You wouldn't fucking believe the shit we found down there."

Mike got an aha expression on his face. "There are actual surviving structures down there, ones not visible from the surface."

Tapov's imperious body language faltered. Spencer had been around her long enough now to recognize her being confused. "And they're evidence of a terrible crime. I don't know what we'll do about it, but it's evidence, and it needs to survive."

"One impossible thing at a time, please," Kim said behind him, making him jump like an idiot for the third time in a row. Either he was really tired or really freaked out. Considering the situation, Spencer decided it was time to embrace the healing power of *and*. "We need to get out of here before the committee makes a decision." Spencer checked, and the drones were still hovering in their little bug swarm. They must have been seriously freaked out.

Mike said, "I bet Ethan knows where a wrecked node is."

"Ethan?" Kim asked.

"The local we brought along. They're common enough; one has to be nearby."

"You think they'll let us drive off?" Spencer asked, nodding his head at the swarm.

Kim smiled. "Have you ever known me to ask permission?"

Mike chuckled. "The relationship between Interpreters and the AC network seems pretty complicated. They might not be able to stop us."

"I'm going with you," Tapov declared. The lady was back. "The men can handle..." she choked a bit but then got a grip. "The men will handle my father's body. I want to see what you're doing."

Oh boy. "So you can try it yourself?"

The pampered princess was there, but she didn't go past skin deep. The rest was steel, all the way down. He saw that now. Good. "If you'll teach me, yes."

Well, hell. If a bunch of naked apes could patch an entire galaxy, who was to say a single talking bear from the Middle Ages couldn't tame a globe-spanning network? "Get in the back, I need to get you hooked up."

Ethan, who turned out to be named Marnor, did know where one was, at the base of the falls, on the other end of the road they'd taken to get up here. They cleared the brush away from the truck while Tapov told the sergeant what to do. A brief sharp argument broke out and he shook his head. The days of telling her *no* were probably never all that many. They were officially zeroed out now.

The drones hadn't so much as bobbed in the air. The gossip must be incredibly juicy to them.

He opened the door for Tapov so she wouldn't get embarrassed trying to figure out how. She got in with a huff. "That went about as well as I thought it would."

"That bad?" he asked.

"Our families have played the same roles in each other's lives for many generations. I leaned pretty hard on that history. But that's not all. If he hadn't helped raise me and didn't know that I'd be responsible for helping raise his child, it might've been worse." She closed her eyes and rubbed her temple. "So yeah, bad. But not a disaster." When Kim got the truck in gear Tapov opened her eyes and checked the interior of the truck out. She opened her mouth to speak but then the whole world lurched sideways and down.

"Jesus fucking Christ on a crutch, Kim!" Spencer shouted. "Slow down!"

"You worry about your friend. I'll worry about the road."

It wasn't a road so much as it was a series of stone-paved goat trails going straight down. But complaining about it would only get him more growls from the driver's seat. So he reached underneath his seat and pulled open a drawer that held their emergency electronics. "Bemian phones interface with human nervous systems easily enough. Now we get to see if the reverse is true."

"I'll help," Mike said, then closed his eyes. He'd gone full flying spaghetti monster, giving him access to realm functions nobody else knew existed. They'd need all the help they could get.

He hung the pendant phone around her neck and activated its calibration and binding mode. It took some twiddling to get the synch right. In fact, if it wasn't for Mike working in the background, it probably wouldn't have happened. Earth phones weren't designed to work with different synch rates because *why should they,* so it was his backdoor hacks that got the job done.

Spencer started to teach her how to transition, but she stopped him. "That's a Servants of the Network meditation practice. We learn it in school when we're kids." She leaned back in the seat and closed her eyes.

He jumped and found her already equipped with a default avatar, a version of her realspace body dressed in a plain white jump suit. The realm itself was hosted by the truck's Bbox, so right now it was his current Subnautica sea base. Like most players, he'd built it near the lifepod that starts the game, about fifteen feet below the surface. The water was shallow and filled with tropical, but alien, fish and other life forms.

She stood, gaping at the big window he'd put in, then startled when a nearby gasopod's rumbling call sounded out, audible through the walls of the base. "Is this what your home world is like?"

He shrugged. "This is a game realm, but Earth has lots of places that are pretty close. The fish are different, though. But that's not important right now." He snapped his fingers, setting the realm back to its base default of a featureless white room. "This is."

Tapov nodded her head slowly. "So it wasn't all a bunch of chants and mumbo jumbo, after all." She chuckled. "I should've paid more attention during services."

"Services? None of this is new to you?"

"Oh, I wouldn't go that far. On one level, yes. This is completely new and freaking me out a little. But on another…the nodes have been teaching us about these things without us realizing they were doing it. We learn about this," she indicated the space around them, "as part of the Servant's teachings. Not everyone believes it. What happened to your planet when you learned the truth?"

The truck changed speed and started bumping. They must've gotten to the bottom of the road and were now heading toward the node. *Saved by the bell!* "No time for that, I have to give you the basics real quick if you want to help us."

But he didn't need to, she already knew them as nursery rhymes or prayers or some shit. They were all in her native language so he couldn't make them out exactly, but each time he showed her a basic feature she'd smile, spout some singsong gibberish, and then use it like she'd grown up with it. Which in a way, she had. He got a grudging respect for whatever the Servants were. Unlike the fundamentalist wackadoo Christians he grew up with back home, they'd taught her a useful skill.

The truck stopped not long after he'd given her a basic hacking toolkit. "In a way, it's like the biggest game of make-believe ever. Think of a plan, focus on the tool, and it will transform into something you can use."

"Make-believe?"

Right. He'd said that part in English because Standard didn't have the right words. He opened a comm screen to the outside world. "Hey, Kim, can you translate for me real quick?"

"Make it fast," she said as she got out of the truck. "We need you out here."

"Tell her that realms are mostly make-believe anyway, and the tools leverage that."

"I can't."

"Eh?"

"They don't have a word for that in their language, and it'd take too long to explain. Get out here."

The idea hit him like a hammer. *She didn't know what make-believe was. None of them did.* He thought of the imagination it must've took to use wire and transistors to make a device that went toe-to-toe with the nodes that were taking over their world. They'd lost that incredible creativity. No, that was wrong.

It'd been taken from them.

And taken so long ago they didn't remember it'd ever been a part of them. The need to make the nodes pay for that was almost physical, but then it was gone. The nodes had remodeled these people until they were totally dependent on them. One person could not change that in an instant.

"Spencer!"

He turned to Tapov. "Right. Never mind. We gotta go. Follow my lead and try to stay out of the way. Here's how to exit."

She shook her head, sang another little song, and vanished.

When he exited to realspace, he found they were in another woods-encircled clearing with a broken node in its center. Kim and Mike had already set up the field scanner. It must've taken him longer than he realized to exit the truck's realm.

Tapov examined it closely. "You set this up the last time, and the node exploded."

He forgot she saw that. "We, ah, made a mistake."

"Exactly what are you trying to accomplish anyway?"

He glanced at Mike and Kim, who shrugged at him. At least he had Kim to smooth over any language fuck ups. "It's a long story. Short version: the nodes haven't found our planet, and we're here to make sure they never do."

"But that's—"

"Impossible, yeah, I know. So who are you going to believe, what the nodes tell you or your lying eyes?"

The sound of jet engines rumbled in the distance. Kim looked up. "They must've come to a decision. The trees will hide us from the air, but they're bound to send ground-based drones to find us. You three need to get cracking."

"Us three?" Mike asked.

Kim marched toward the truck. "You three. Tapov needs to see how it's done. The glass girl has put me on ice hacking-wise, and Spencer's the only one who's seen a node's inner realm. You'll need to unlock the doors for him."

"And what will you be doing?" he asked.

She opened the storage locker on the passenger side of the bed and pulled out a quarter staff. He'd laughed at her when she packed it, but now it made a scary kind of sense. "They're drones, Mike. Robots." She twirled it in a way he'd only ever seen her do in the realms. It was like the stick was moving in six directions at the same time.

"You can't do that alone," he protested.

"She won't," a voice said from behind the trees. Sergeant Eskol stepped into the clearing a moment later, sweating and panting. He crouched, hands on his knees for a moment, then stood up. "I am too old to run that far that fast. At least it was downhill." Still facing away from the woods, he shouted, "All right, you lot! Form up!" The soldiers pounding up through the woods behind him stopped and formed two neat lines of three behind him.

He turned to Tapov and saluted. "My lady. Your father is being returned to Ontara, along with a message to send reinforcements here."

"Good. I'm placing the Interpreter," she nodded toward Kim, "in command of your squad for now. I have other duties to attend."

There wasn't time to camouflage anything, so they set up the camp chairs with the truck between them and where Kim was setting up.

"Time to go," Spencer said, then jumped.

This time he was ready and immediately activated the HUD extensions, giving him the metrics he needed to tell if a construct was small and up close or gigantic and far away. Again it was an enormous factory realm complete with cranes, cables, and a robotic assembly line. The defenders, red boxy constructs of various sizes, were also present, patrolling in ways that would make moving around the space difficult.

"Don't touch anything," he said to Tapov. "Mike? You out there?"

A rushing sound announced his arrival, not as an avatar but as a giant collection of remoting constructs that always reminded him of a sea anemone made of glossy white plastic. Tapov cursed and stumbled back and away from it, forcing Spencer to catch her when she stumbled on the cluttered floor and almost fell.

"Yep, I'm here, but exactly where *here* is..."

Tapov regained her balance and shrugged off Spencer's hand. She pointed at Mike's anemone. "Why doesn't he look like he does in the real world?"

"This is what I look like in *my* real world. I live between the realms," Mike replied. "I have a human body in realspace. I'm not sure—"

Spencer knew the sound of Mike winding up when he heard it. "Not now. We've got to get moving. Can you do anything about the defenses?"

One of the tentacles thwipped out and enveloped a small defense construct like it was catching a piece of candy thrown at its mouth, then yanked back into the main bunch. "Hmm," he said. "Definitely doesn't taste like chicken."

Sometimes Mike's impulsiveness made him fun to have around. Other times… "Jesus," Spencer said, "how did you know you wouldn't set off any alarms doing that?"

"Keeping it from setting off alarms is *why* I did it. I've upgraded Helen's original design to include what you could best think of as thread covers." A bunch of tentacles rose up from the main body and waved around. Now that they weren't going past his ear at Mach two, Spencer saw they had a bluish tinge the rest didn't. "The moment one of these envelopes a construct, it's inverted immediately, but since it's covered, it won't trigger a chain reaction. The anemone has a sting!"

"I only understood half of that," Tapov said to Spencer. "Care to explain?"

Spencer shrugged. "Some of those tentacles can eat things. Which is good, because all these red squares floating around? They're alarms and defenses." He turned back to Mike. "Don't you think it'll notice one of its guards going missing?"

"They're not that sophisticated. This is an internal space, the node's equivalent of the inner workings of a realspace body. Do you notice when one of your white blood cells dies?"

"Fair point." He sat down on the floor and motioned for Tapov to do the same. "Let 'er rip!"

The center of Mike's formation exploded upward and then out, grabbing red squares as it went. Spencer had never wondered what it'd be like to get eaten by a frog, but now that it was happening so close, it was hard not to try.

Tapov put her hands over her head and started to scream. He reached out to her and leaned in. "None of this is real."

"It seems real to me!"

"Remember the tools I gave you? Hold out your hand and think of something pretty."

She held out her hand, and to her credit, it only shook a little. A moment passed, then a miniature Telirian appeared in her palm. She was female, pretty, and dressed in their version of a ball gown. Tapov's gasp was audible above the whooshing noise of Mike's frog attack.

The resemblance was obvious. "Your mom?"

She nodded. "It was my premiere celebration. We had such a good time that night." With her other hand, Tapov gently touched the construct. "It's so real."

To Spencer's critical eye it wasn't, since she'd only created the external appearance. Some of Mike's constructs were accurate down to the subatomic level, complete with quantum effects. But as a first effort at construct creation, it was pretty goddamn impressive. Most people needed an existing construct for reference and quite a few hours of practice to get her result.

Mike finished dealing with the defenses as Spencer taught Tapov how to quickly save her construct into local storage.

"And that," Mike said after a thwip, "is," *thwip*, "that! Okay, Spence, you're up."

He hadn't managed to clean out absolutely all the defensive constructs. The realm was too big for that. In the far distance, there were still a lot around, with some already turning to fill the blank space Mike had made. It didn't matter, he had plenty of time.

"One network exploit, comin' up! Tapov, I need you for this one." He spotted the terminal connection in the same place as last time and started walking.

She boggled and stumbled into motion behind him. "You do?"

"I do. Some bullshit happened when I tried to interface with one of these last time, and it set off a shit ton of alarms. You see those doors and hatches scattered around? Every security bot in this place will come pouring through them if I try it." Plus there was that whole *can't remember to breathe* horseshit. Kim said it sounded like her power in action, which was twelve different kinds of fucked up.

They all thought that her power was connected with her inability to touch people. He liked being able to hug his mom. So yeah, Tapov got the ball for the touchdown.

Mike's probes shambled along beside them like a spaghettified tumbleweed built with slat blinds. "I'll hold off any reinforcements, but we need to hurry," he said. A screen drew itself into being beside them, showing Kim and the troops doing a bang-up job of turning bots into sparks and spares. "I don't know how long she'll last out there."

"Understood," he replied, then turned to Tapov. "I don't think you'll have a problem with this." He gave her a quick tutorial on what needed to be done. "Got it?"

She stared up at nothing, bobbing her head and mouthing what had to be the words to another of her Servants chants. "I think I do."

That wasn't good enough. "Not think, *do*."

She took a deep breath and pushed it out. "I do have it. But this only takes care of your planet."

"Well, yes. I told you that."

"What about mine?"

She would decide to throw a wrench into the works at this moment. "We don't have time for that now. We need to get the hack in. We'll figure out what to do next when we're done."

"But he," she pointed at Mike's rambling anemone, "said it'll be much harder later."

In the window, Spencer saw Kim's squad begin to fall back. "We don't have time for this, Tapov. You need to get started."

She stared at him, colder than he'd ever experienced. "This isn't just about you." He thought she was going to walk away and they'd be fucked, but instead she used her tools to initiate the hack.

"That's it," Mike said. "Just a few more seconds…aaand done. Wait, what?"

All the doors Spencer had pointed out to Tapov slammed open, but instead of attack constructs, a wave of squirreligators rushed out from them. "What the fuck?"

Tapov had her eyes closed, still connected to the port they'd used to launch the hack. "You have your goals, I have mine."

The squirreligators nearest them were literally chewing the scenery. When they'd consumed whatever they were gnawing on, all that was left was a white default surface. The rest rushed away in a scaly, toothy wave.

"My people need to be free of this scourge. You saw what we'd achieved. They said we were primitive savages, but they lied. We weren't the savages, they were."

"Spencer," Mike said, "if these constructs get out of this node, it'll put the entire planetary network at risk."

"So invert it."

"Then we lose our hack."

"Use your tentacles."

"There are too many of them. She's got a massive amount of talent for someone who's never built constructs."

"The nodes have been training them, disguising it as a religion. Tapov, you have to stop. Your people don't remember how to live without the nodes."

"We'll relearn. Those ruins aren't the only ones. They're all over the planet. You can help us, too."

"You don't want our help. We suck at helping on this scale. Look, I know what they did was wrong, fucking evil bullshit, but it was a long time ago." She shrugged faintly and nothing changed. "Tapov, when's the last time your people had a war?"

"What's war?"

"There, that's what the nodes have given you that we can't. Peace. Tapov, my people are peaceful now, but they only got there by slaughtering millions over hundreds of years. It's still not perfect. We blow each other up if we think we can get away with it. We've got bombs that are so powerful they can destroy our civilization. We've made *hundreds* of them."

"Why would any race build hundreds of bombs that could each destroy a civilization? That's insane."

"It is, and it gets worse. *We're the ones in charge of the bombs*. There's nobody to protect us from ourselves. But fuck that, we don't need those bombs to kill. People flew giant planes into giant buildings and thousands died. We fucked around with germs trying to make them more efficient at killing, and *we succeeded*. There are millions of people back home who'd be happy to murder the world because of what they read in books written thousands of years ago by goat herders and small-time con artists."

By now there were so many squirreligators it was hard to breathe through the stench of them. But they still rushed outward, a thundering tide rolling away into the distance. Tapov wasn't just good at this, she was fucking awesome.

She shook her head. The princess, the *Lady*, was unconvinced. "No civilization can survive such things."

"You're right, and we almost didn't. They taught us in school that two, maybe three times the only thing that stood between survival and armageddon was one person's decision. I can't say whether or not your civilization would've survived what we went through without the nodes because I don't understand how we managed it. What I can say is that you don't know how to survive without them anymore, and you good goddamn better well understand you don't want our help. We'd burn this place to the ground and then argue over the ashes."

She faltered. "I can't walk away from this opportunity."

"I understand that now." He checked the screen and saw things had gotten much worse outside. "Mike, they need you out there. Go." The waving white plastic tentacles vanished. On the screen, a new player entered the game as Mike fucking descended from heaven—or probably jumped off the roof of the truck—and started kicking ass. In the realm, Tapov's vicious little army had done a bang-up job of clearing them an easy path forward.

"Now," he said to her, "put those greasy little fuckers away." He stretched his arms out, put his hands together, and cracked his virtual knuckles in that awesome zippery way that never failed to satisfy. It was time, for the first time, for him to lead a hack run against a target that mattered. *Angel Rage, eat your heart out*. "We've got work to do."

Chapter 43
Tonya

Hibernation turned out to be more than sleep but less than anesthesia. There was a sense of time passing, and she did remember having dreams, but no details. When she became conscious enough to understand what was going on, a part of her grew nervous, maybe a little terrified. They'd left the monster out there. Her only guarantee of success was her faith in the Lord.

But, as it had been since she'd learned the real meaning of faith, that was enough. The familiar feeling of love, as indescribable as it was illogical, surrounded her. The Lord had protected them. She was home, after traveling in ways she was only now learning how to predict.

The whirrs and hums around her got louder and light slowly faded up. A ping from the chair itself hit her phone. When she answered it, a stream of bemian instructions flowed in telling her what to do, how to do it, and what to expect. The uncomfortable sensation of the waste disposal system disconnecting would've been worse if it hadn't warned her ahead of time. At the end, as instructed, she closed her eyes and held still as the sequence completed and the hatch opened.

She heard a voice she recognized from her time on Maff's race crew.

"What the hell is Tonya doing in there?"

Sornik.

Still following the directions, she opened her eyes slowly and let them find focus on their own. Helen, Maff, Sornik, and two other pallun she vaguely recognized peered down at her. Helen looked like she'd won a prize at the fair. Tonya had never seen her so happy. The rest seemed split between confused and afraid.

The couch itself lifted her up, which was good because her head was about a hundred pounds too heavy, along with the rest of her body. The instructions warned her to breathe and relax as it changed the drug cocktail it'd been feeding her through an IV in her arm. The effect was almost immediate, like a balloon getting inflated. The instructions said to stay still, but she did at least manage to roll her head toward Tenor's chair. Her breathing got a little easier when she saw he'd lolled his head her way as well. They exchanged weak smiles and winks. They'd done it.

She turned her head forward, already feeling stronger. "Monster." It was supposed to come out as a sentence asking if it was still out there, but that was the best she could do.

Helen nodded. "Yes, it almost trapped us. Good idea with the English message and the open channel."

Maff leaned in and handed her a bottle with a straw. "Here," she said. "This rolled out of the base of your chair." Over her head, another set of Maff's manipulators handed Tenor another bottle. "Have you guys been here since this was built?"

The fluid in the bottle was thick like a milkshake but body-temp warm. The flavor started out nasty and salty. The combination would normally throw her into heaves, but whatever was in it was exactly what her body needed. She didn't stop pulling on it until the straw growled against the bottom of the empty bottle.

It was like someone poured pure energy into her. She sat up and was only a little stiff, like she'd been in one position too long. She cleared her throat, then said, "No, only a few years." Tonya pointed at a locker behind Helen. "I'll give you the story if you give us our clothes."

Getting them on proved to be a good test of her strength and coordination. It started out a little harder than she was used to it being, from pulling them out of the storage bag to tying her shoes. But by the end of it, she'd call herself basically recovered. Pretty good for someone who'd spent the last two years taking the world's longest nap.

As she did, she told them the whole story, starting with Dean Shakson's idiotic sabotage. When she got to the encounter with Andromeda, Helen interrogated her thoroughly. Unfortunately Tonya could only provide vague impressions of his appearance, which disappointed her.

"I gave you observation training. Did you forget to practice?"

People who didn't know Helen would bristle at this attitude. Tenor ruffled up a bit at it. But Tonya knew her well. Instead of growling, she chuckled. "No, but your training didn't cover techniques to observe an alternate manifestation of a conscious galaxy capable of manipulating time. I was distracted."

True to form, Helen nodded to concede the point. "It was an important opportunity, but I understand."

Tonya went on. "As you guys now know, we weren't alone. I can't believe it managed to survive two years without using a sleep chair."

Helen shook her head. "It didn't survive. I knew there was something wrong with those food wrappers. They were too old. I think it probably lasted no more than a year after you shut the cache down. Its corpse is on the lower level of the elevator atrium."

"There could've been more than one," Tenor countered. "We were too busy running to check."

"Are there anymore sleep rooms like this on board?" Helen asked.

"No," Tonya replied. "This is the only backup."

"Then that was the only one," she replied. "There was only a single couch altered in that room." She sighed. "I have been such a fool."

Tonya motioned for Tenor to stay quiet. The rest of them must've been around Helen long enough to know not to reply to that.

Helen looked at them all, grim-faced. "They've found us. Or rather, me."

"The Interpreters?" Sornik scoffed. "Nobody got past my men. The ship is still secure."

Helen nodded. "I mean no disrespect to your men. The Interpreters have almost certainly been here for some time. Probably not long after Maff discovered the place. Tonya, can you access the station keeping system?"

She checked and got confirmation. "Yes."

"Run a test on the smallest correction thrusters. See if any of them report as failed."

She ran a diagnostic on all of them. "Exactly one, first logged faulty ten days ago."

"Two days after Maff found the cache." Helen closed her eyes and shook her head. "Such a rookie mistake. I'm better than this."

"What are you talking about?" Sornik asked.

"The Interpreters who attacked Maff must've installed a tracking device on the pinnace. When you pulled off the racecourse and stopped, they knew exactly where you were. They only needed to find a way in."

"But the seal was still intact," Fulan said.

"They didn't use that as the entry. They drilled through a maneuvering thruster to gain access to the machine spaces. They did it again to access the interior."

"The thrusters are too small," Maff replied. "You could only fit a small…oh…"

"Right. They used a small drone with a camera. Interpreters only need to see a place to reach it."

Sornik scoffed. "Why haven't they taken the whole place over?"

Helen turned to her. "Kim's smartLocks, right?"

"Yup." Tonya had put them there to keep the creature from somehow breaking into the network. The beast almost killed her but, in an ass-backward way that always seemed to happen to her, it had also saved their lives. "Three sets." She checked and got green lights from all three. "They're fully intact."

"So why haven't *we* taken over *them*?" Toraz asked. "Space them."

"The locks apply to everyone," Tonya replied. "I can't use the controls either. If I remove them…"

"The Interpreters are already in the network," Helen continued. "They'd get access long before we could. Besides, this place is too well engineered to be easily vented."

"More like impossible," Tenor replied as he gingerly tested the new wing that'd grown back during his sleep time. "We considered that with the monster, but we built the cache too well for it to work. We could do the atmosphere thing again, change it so it's unbreathable, wait them out."

"These aren't normal Interpreters," Helen said. "They don't need to breathe, and they're not cut off from support. There's no waiting them out. But they don't have infinite supplies. This was all smoke and mirrors, a sa'dst hack. I understand how that works. It uses an enormous amount each time, especially in a direct physical attack like the one that killed Bithern. They're out, for now. We have a window."

"For what?" Toraz asked.

Tonya had figured out part of the answer. "The cache has a sa'dst generator. A big one." It put out Mike's hacked version of sa'dst, so no worries about getting turned inside out, but that would take too long to explain to Toraz and his men. There was a missing piece. She turned to Helen. "You can't reprogram them on the fly?"

She shook her head. "It starts at the generator. If we unlock the network, I can't push my threads through it. It's too crowded. But if I gain direct access, then we'll have our own source." She grinned in that fierce way she had when someone challenged her. "They won't stand a chance against me."

Sornik rounded his body for a moment and then returned to his normal shape, the Pallundian equivalent of a deep breath. "Well we better get moving then."

"Wait," Tenor said. "What about the maintenance passages?"

Good point. "How much time do you think we have?" she asked Helen.

"I'd say less than ten minutes."

Tenor grimaced. "It took three times that long to get down here using the maintenance passages, and we were closer." He shrugged and then scratched his new wing frantically. "Don't mind me, we need to get going."

Sornik formed his men up in a flying wedge with him in the center. Tonya, Maff, Helen, and Tenor were put behind them. The men pulled out sets of what had to be weapons. He turned to Maff. "If this all falls into the storm, grab those three and haul ass to the hangar. Don't look back. Understand?"

"Perfectly."

"All right then. On three. One…two…*three*!"

The door swooshed open, and they rushed out. The door faced the wrong direction to get to the atrium quickly, but again, their silly decision for extra-wide halls paid dividends. The pallun pivoted to the right gracefully. They zigzagged down the side hall and then turned left. The atrium was no more than a hundred feet ahead, but the pallun skidded to a stop. Even through a forest of waving manipulators, Tonya saw why.

In the hallway ahead, three black glass humanoids with different colors of lighting coruscating across their skin stood in the way.

"How much, Sornik?" the big one in the center asked. It was vaguely reptilian, but she had a hard time seeing details in that transformed state. "How much for the two humans?"

"What the fuck is your problem, buddy? You axed two of my guys and now you think you can *buy* your way out of that?"

"It's not only money, Sornik." It was surreal hearing Pallundian spoken by a creature built that solidly, like a wrestler back home having the voice of a child. "A favor from Valsa Barton can open many doors. She's quite interested in them, you know." His companions, both humanoid but more catlike, nodded and slinked forward.

"Ya know what? You can stick that favor right up Valsa's ass. I've had enough of this shit. Light 'em up, boys."

The wild howls of their weapons tore at her ears. All three Interpreters were knocked off their feet but then were covered with hemispheres of energy the same color as their lightning. The faint beams the Pallundian weapons created bounced off, scoring nearby walls.

"Maff!" Sornik shouted. "Go!" He and his men charged the Interpreters. Inside their glowing shields, the Interpreters hopped to their feet but recoiled from the sight of three giant armored manta rays bearing down on them. Tonya didn't catch the rest of it because Maff wrapped a manipulator around her waist and lifted.

Everything spun crazily. "What are you doing?" Tonya shouted as she was roughly pulled against Maff's suit. Tenor and Helen thumped down beside her a second later.

"No time," she said and leaped into the air with a sideways spin. Legs and manipulators gripped the fixtures and framework of the ceiling as she ran upside down over the battle. Below them, the pallun impacted the interpreter shields hard enough to knock them around but not break them. Bolts of power sizzled off metal suits, and Tonya saw legs and manipulators tumble away.

When they were clear, Maff rotated back to the floor and ran up the stairs. "Pallun are not fighters, not like that. Suits are too vulnerable. When I saw that the pistols did not work, I knew they could only buy us time." They got to the top and she shouted, "Which way?"

"Right!" Tonya shouted back. "Then another right." She didn't realize how fast a motivated pallun could go. It was like riding a stampeding elephant on stilts. "Ignore the hall, keep going, then another right."

They skidded to a stop in front of the hangar entrance. They were almost as far away from the fight as anyone could get, so things here were eerily quiet.

"Put me down, Maff. But not them."

"Okay," she said slowly. "Why?"

"The sa'dst generator is high up on the far wall of the hangar. Tenor knows the access codes, and you can get them both up there to reach it."

As she set Tonya down, Maff asked, "What about you?"

"She's the rear guard," Helen said, then sat up. "Will it be enough?"

Tonya cracked her neck and stared down the long hall. She'd beaten one monster, and it had knives. These were normal size humanoids without her training.

That were made of indestructible glass and could shoot bolts of power around. Piece of cake.

"It'll have to be." She locked eyes with Helen. "Don't screw around."

She scoffed. "I'm not Spencer. Come on, Maff, let's go!"

They hadn't designed this part of the cache to be a tactical choke point, but that's what it ended up being. The door behind her was the only way into the hangar, at the end of a hallway that ran the length of the cache. They couldn't get behind her or come at her from different angles. The width of the hall was problematic. If one of them decided to ignore her and run straight for the door, Tonya would find it difficult to stop them. She'd have to rely on their arrogance and lack of tactical skills to make up the difference. She tore the sleeves off her shirt and wrapped them around her fists. She had punched Kim in that form once, and it was like hitting a block of marble. Padding would help.

Tonya had walked about ten feet away from the door when the Interpreters rounded the corner. Two instead of three, the reptilian leader and one of the cat people. She took a page from Mike's playbook and named them Alan and Betty, since introductions would likely be lacking.

"Ah, good," Alan said in Standard without breaking stride. "This makes our job much simpler." The tone was one she recognized from long experience, a cardiac surgeon who'd pat her on the ass as she walked by. He only lacked a lab coat and expensive shoes.

She relaxed her stance, letting her body's energy ground her and stabilize her. Professional fighters would take a step back to reevaluate when they saw her do this because it was an advertisement of skills. Again, these two didn't break stride. They either didn't know the signs or didn't care.

Good.

"Do yourself a favor," she said in English. "Go home."

They looked at each other, not knowing what to make of someone who spoke a language they didn't know and couldn't immediately learn through their threads.

"What did you say?" Betty asked in Standard.

The longer she kept them standing there, the more time Helen had to get her groove on. Exactly why they hadn't blasted her on sight with their energy bolts was a mystery she didn't need to solve right now.

"You're not wanted here," she said. "This place wasn't built for you. Go get your other friend and get out."

Alan laughed. "You know, I don't think we will," he said.

In English.

Ah, well. Tonya *had* trained her thread in it during her time at the university. It was an entire galaxy wired up into a single network, after all.

"Why don't you come with us? We were sent here because some important people want to take a closer look at you and your companion. This will go much easier if you choose to come peacefully."

"A closer look? I'm not a lab specimen, and I'm not interested in meeting any important people. You need to leave. Now."

They shared a glance, then resumed walking forward. "That's not how it's going to work, I'm afraid." They broke into a trot, and then a run.

Tonya set her stance, noting where they were looking, how their bodies were balanced, the ways their strides broke up as they readied whatever strikes they knew. It telegraphed their moves as clearly as if they'd called them like pool shots. The important part was that they both focused on her. No need to worry about someone running past for now.

Alan pulled slightly ahead at the last moment, fist cocked back to knock her sideways into the kick Betty was already shifting her weight to throw. Tonya pulled away in the opposite direction, sweeping a leg under both of them, hitting at the precise moment when their running strides left both feet in the air. It was like she'd kicked concrete columns, but the pain meant the blows she'd landed were solid. Out of contact with any surface, there was no way to control the change of momentum. They would've slammed into the walls in a normal sized hall. Here they flew in arcs, hitting the floor hard and skidding to the base of the wall.

Tonya tumbled forward to reposition herself between them and the hangar door while they staggered to their feet. "Ready to leave yet?"

They looked at each other unsteadily. *Yeah, that's right,* she thought. *Score one for the humans.* They started to run toward her again but, at the sound of a loud whooshing noise in the distance, stopped and smiled.

"We won't be leaving," Betty said, cat eyes glittering at Tonya like she'd caught the mouse. "And you *will* be coming with us."

Around the corner at the end of the hall, the third Interpreter stepped out. "Did anyone need some assistance?"

Behind him, a swirling shaft of black dust, obviously under his command, rushed in to fill the space. Tonya turned and ran but tendrils grabbed her ankles and she fell face-first to the floor. They continued wrapping her up until she was all but mummified, holding her at least a foot off the floor. Their lightning-coruscated faces turned up to her, grinning, as they walked through the hangar door. "Now, time to pick up your friend."

Helen's voice rang out behind her. "That will not be necessary."

The sa'dst holding her collapsed in a pile, dropping her to the floor. But the Interpreters didn't seem to notice. They stood there gaping in obvious horror at something behind her. Tonya turned to look.

The entire opposite half of the hangar had been completely remodeled. It was no longer a hangar at all, replaced by a gigantic stairway fronting a solid gold wall. At the top of the stairs stood a large humanoid dragon, Helen's features on its face. A horn sounded out in an unending, dissonant tone. It would've blown Jericho's walls down from here. If she hadn't already been on the floor, the spectacle would've put her there. The Interpreters were struck still where they stood.

Helen walked forward with confident grace, and as she did, the gold wall rippled and pulled. It wasn't a wall. It was a gigantic cape attached to Helen's shoulders. It slowly pulled down behind her, forming an enormous train and revealing a ruby-colored temple behind it. Tonya had spent months collecting billions of years' worth of artifacts for this cache, items of such beauty she sometimes had trouble looking at them without weeping. With those examples in her mind, she'd still never seen anything that matched the power and authority that Helen projected as she walked down those stairs.

When she reached the bottom, the horn finally fell silent. Into the crystalline quiet Helen spoke swiftly and confidently in Mandarin. Tonya's Chinese was strong enough for her to catch phrases like *old order is swept away* and *we will not be conquered.* She fell silent for a moment, cocked her scaly head, and then said a single word.

"Go."

The room erupted into a maelstrom of colored dust, reds, golds, and blacks that temporarily blinded her. It centered on the three Interpreters. Tonya heard screams over the roaring tornado as the dust concentrated completely on them. After a moment, it all spun away and evaporated.

The Interpreters were nowhere to be seen.

Tonya turned around to find a perfectly normal Helen beaming at her. "I told you I was better than they were."

The opposite side of the hangar was also back to normal, with *Palatine* sitting calmly near the wall. Maff herself clung to that same wall, Tenor still strapped to her back, next to a now wrecked sa'dst dispenser.

She climbed down and joined them. "That was the most amazing thing I've ever seen."

Helen bowed slightly. "Thank you." She got distracted, staring with eyes unfocused. The silence stretched until Tonya was about to ask if she was okay.

Helen nodded. "Right." Her gaze came back to them. "Maff? Take Tonya to the atrium and see what happened to Sornik and his men." She faced Tonya. "I know your nursing skills don't include pallun, but there might be some first aid you can do. Return as quickly as you can."

"What's going on?" Tenor asked.

"It's Mike. They need us. They're in trouble."

Chapter 44

Kim

She'd been a realm combat champion for about as long as that was a thing. *Realms are real* was a mantra they'd all chanted back in the day, because for the first time, being good at a video game made you good in the real world. It worked for her, too, but she had no way to show it. Not if the touch of a finger would send her into convulsions.

That wasn't a problem today.

The rifles they'd brought were too slow for this work, and the woods around them were too thick for archery to be effective. Kim, knowing that her life functioned as a self-propelled demonstration of Murphy's Law, had therefore planned for a situation where neither of those weapons would be appropriate.

She brought a stick.

And not just any stick. She'd custom ordered this one while she was still in hiding. No woman with any sense lived alone without *some* way to defend herself. It was a pistol at first. Then one morning she'd woken up on the couch with sunlight in her eyes, an empty whiskey bottle in one hand, her pistol in the other, and absolutely no memory of how any of it had happened. The pistol went into her bugout bag, and a special quarterstaff took up residence under her bed. The shaft was made of woven carbon nanotube rods capped with tungsten alloy ends. The result was a living thing in her hands that had no business existing outside a realm.

She named it Donny Donowitz and made Mike watch *Inglourious Basterds* to learn why. She'd given him a sized-up copy of the staff as a honeymoon gift. They spent their mornings at the resort doing katas with them as the sun rose.

The light weight was key. Realms taught her the coordination and muscle memory to do complex moves with her body, and she biked constantly to keep her aerobic fitness high. But realms did nothing to build muscle mass. The staff let her leverage physics and advanced materials to make up the difference.

Plus, she already had muscle in the form of six well-trained guardsmen and their sergeant. She'd been put in command. The first rule of officers was that they didn't know the rules. That's what sergeants were for.

She didn't have much time. "Sergeant Eskol?"

He reacted the same way sergeants did back home when she'd sometimes taken charge of a team of pros: a mixture of *who threw that grenade in here* and *what have I stepped in*? "Ma'am?"

"I have only one order: we need to stop anything from getting to those three people. I've got this." She twirled Donny so it shrieked a few bars of one of his bawdy songs, and then ended it by shattering a nearby stone the size of her head. The sparks that flew were a nice touch. "And that's what I can do with it. Where do you want me?"

He stared at the shards of the stone and nodded. "You hold the end of the line." He turned to his men. "Right! You lot! Picket formation and mind the lady! She needs a little extra space!"

Picket formation turned out to be a relaxed line facing the trail they'd come in on. Kim took the left side. "Any worries about them flanking us?" she asked.

He shook his head. "I'll be surprised if the first few waves don't expect us to stand aside voluntarily. The nodes are all about power, not tactics."

That was charming. "How long until they escalate?"

"This is the first time I've heard of anyone standing against them. I have no idea."

The first drone was a simple wheeled rectangular box, almost the same shade of yellow that heavy construction equipment used back home, and about as tall as she was. "You are trespassing and must leave." It moved forward.

Kim couldn't help it. She stepped in front of it, planted her staff, and slowly said, "None shall pass."

This seemed to confuse more than impress. It tried a few times to go around her, but she wouldn't let it. She thwacked it with the staff hard enough to leave a dent.

"You have triggered a disciplinary reaction," it said, the robotic voice making its Telirian words sound blocky and comical. "You are advised to leave this area before the reaction arrives." Then it left.

"Well that went better than I thought it would," Eskol said.

Kim couldn't disagree. "Any idea when—"

A dozen ground drones rolled down the trail at speed, and it was on. These were low-slung boxes, designed to knock bipeds down and, if the gear on their backs was any indication, restrain them with nets. Kim smashed the two in her sector so thoroughly the wheels literally fell off.

They came in waves, all different sizes and shapes. Some were as small as a lunchbox. One was as big as the truck and didn't come to a complete stop until Kim smashed an access hatch open, and one of Eskol's men rammed a sword into it. Fortunately carbon fiber was nonconductive, because she had to knock him away with it once it was obvious he'd hit a live electrical connection.

As the drones poured into the clearing, Kim got in the zone, a flow state where there was no staff and there was no Kim. They'd become a single entity that smashed and spun a tornado of destruction, leaving a trail of drone parts scattered in her wake. Then her mind got crossed up. In a first for her, she mistook realspace for a realm and tried one of her spider moves to the top of the staff. This required more core strength than she really had, and she slammed into the ground.

For a moment, all she saw was yellow hulls and wheels coming for her. One of the men shouted, "Kim's down," and they all fought toward her until she could get to her feet. It was great not to be restrained or captured, but the result was an unbalanced line that allowed the robots to push them back closer to the truck. She wanted the sergeant to reposition the men, but the machines didn't allow the time or space to do it. When three bots pivoted and turned the corner of their line, she tried to block them all. She lost her balance, hitting the ground again. The nearest drone lifted up a thing that was half trap, half net, and dropped it on her.

Almost.

It was stopped with a sparking clang by a different staff, one bigger and heavier than hers. Mike stood over her, laughing as he pushed it back.

He looked down at her with a smirk. "What kept you?"

He twirled the first drone into the other two and then rammed his staff through all three. Mike had arrived not a moment too soon. His staff had triple the mass of hers, and with the extra power they pushed back the tide, cramming the ground drones up the trail until they were almost at the spot where it all started.

Mike managed to fight his way to her side. "We can't do this forever."

She flicked one of the smaller drones into a larger one, causing both to tangle with each other and fly to pieces. "No kidding."

"I'm calling in the cavalry."

"The what?"

There was a splintering crash to her left, and a tree fell straight into the clearing. A new path had been cut through the woods. Combat drones were lined up behind a large, squat drone obviously designed for forestry. Their small line faltered in confusion. She didn't have enough bodies to cover that gap.

Kim began to shout orders anyway but was interrupted by a massive blast behind her that immediately caused the front of the forestry drone to shatter, scattering the pieces all around it. The entire battlefield fell silent, the drones as stunned as anyone else.

A familiar voice split the silence.

"Eat hot lead, you ass sucking, tree chomping, shit for brains motherfuckers!" It was followed by another explosion, which she now recognized as one of their rifles. This time it cut a swath through the robots trying to find a way around their destroyed tree cutter. A quick glimpse behind her showed him standing on the roof of the truck, handing the now empty weapon to Tapov, who handed him the third and last of the loaded guns. Tapov turned and started frantically reloading before he'd brought the gun to his shoulder.

That final shot seemed to announce the resumption of the fight, now punctuated with slugs ripping through the air every thirty seconds or so. The style of firearm may have been antiquated but the loading system wasn't, and Tapov got faster as she practiced.

It still wasn't enough. They were fighting an entire planet's worth of drones. It didn't matter how inept the drones were, how clumsy, how ineffective. All they had to be was lucky one time. Kim kept wracking her brain trying to come up with the unexpected move, one nobody would see coming, the middle choice that was hidden between two untenable ones. Nothing came to her. Her world turned into a sea of yellow metal smashed into sparking pieces by a staff that grew heavier by the second. All she needed, all she *desperately* needed, was a chance to catch her breath. But they would not stop.

The trees above them exploded in a shower of branches and splinters. Kim found herself flat on the ground before it had properly formed as a thought in her head. A heavy thrumming dominated all other sounds. There was a loud crack as a skein of lightning splashed over and around her. When it touched the drones, they stopped dead.

Kim rolled over and stared up at a swath of glossy blue metal edged with gold and red stripes. It'd basically blown open a hole for itself through the canopy above, creating a perfect cookie cutter shape of its outline. It took that long for her mind to put together what she saw into a coherent image that made sense.

Palatine.

And it kept making a hole, shattering trunks and ramming branches aside as it descended. Kim sat up and looked around, trying to find Mike. He was a few yards away helping one of the soldiers to his feet. All around her, Eskol's men were slowly standing up, brushing sawdust and branch ends off as they did. Kim saw Eskol himself lying facedown next to her, a heavy branch next to his head.

The wave of nauseated adrenaline that hit her forced her hand out toward him. She yanked it back quickly as the boiling sear of her touch madness shot up her arm. Instead of grimacing, she smiled. Touch madness had a use after all. Anyone else would have to check for a pulse.

A second later, he groaned and rolled over. "Even from beyond the grave that man gets me into the most ridiculous situations." He spotted the ship. "What in the seven pits of Skerrol is *that*?"

"It's our ticket out of here." She levered herself up with her staff and then offered one end to him. "Come on."

Spencer had already fishtailed the truck around, Tapov holding on for dear life in the passenger seat. The cargo door opened as he reached it. The rest of them limped and hobbled toward it as fast as they could.

Mike was bruised and bleeding from a small cut above his left eye. Battered, dirt smeared, and covered in sawdust, he still made her insides jiggle. Judging by the way his eyes flashed when he looked at her, he was thinking the same thing. Kim tried to brush her hair out, but her fingers immediately got tangled up in the twigs and splinters that covered it. A glance down showed that she'd not faired any better than he had, with torn, mud-spattered pants and a shirt that was more dirt than cloth and stank so badly of flop sweat her eyes watered.

Mike's expression didn't change, and neither did the smile on her face. *Love conquers all.*

Eskol stood on one side of the hatch while she stood on the other. After the last of the party ran inside, they hoofed it up the ramp themselves.

Helen stood on the second-level deck on the opposite side of the hold. When Kim nodded, she shouted, "Go, Maff! Go!"

The familiar stomach lurch told her they were now in the transit dimension, safely out of reach of the local network's forces. She gingerly picked her way past jumping and hugging Telirians to Mike. "The cavalry?"

He tapped his head. "We haven't talked that much, but I've always been able to contact Helen if I needed to. And I did. We weren't going to last much longer."

She heard the unmistakable whistling of pallun voices coming from the other side of the truck. Walking around it, she found the source. Three pretty badly beat up pallun were hanging from the bottom of the second-level walkway by large straps, surrounded by trays full of suit parts. "Move the vehicle, kid, we can't see!" said the one in the middle.

"What the fuck happened to you guys?" Spencer asked as he backed it up a little to unblock the view.

Kim quickly translated. All three huffed and the middle one said, "What the fuck happened?" He pointed up to where Helen still stood. "She's what the fuck happened. You humans, I swear to Turlanfador, buy trouble by the shipping container."

*

Their ad hoc leadership committee met in the mess hall, the pallun named Sornik via a simple remote camera since he was still repairing his suit, while the Telirian soldiers were learning card games from Sornik's men still in the hold.

After all they'd been through, Eskol and Tapov were still obviously in awe of the tech around them. "How about this," Tapov asked. "Will we get this?"

"Yes," Kim replied. "This is real bemian tech. We don't have anything like it back on Earth."

"Yet," Helen said owlishly. She'd been tense ever since they came on board. Kim hoped to pry that out of her during the meeting.

But first she had a more important question. "Did you complete the hack?" she asked Spencer.

"Fuckin' A, we sure did." He grinned at Tapov, who returned the expression but with sharper teeth. "And more."

That could mean anything, especially with Spencer. "Explain *and more*."

"Oh, don't get your tits in a twist. We were subtle."

"I wanted much more," Tapov explained. "But he talked me around to a different point of view."

Instead of destroying the planetary network, which Kim agreed would've been a complete disaster, they'd gone with a gentle touch. The nodes on Teliria had been programmed to give the Telirians themselves an incentive, and then two seemingly modest alterations to the node's directives. The incentive would encourage the Telirians themselves to recover their native language in both spoken and written form.

"There's literature out in the forbidden zones, but we have no idea how to read it," Tapov explained. "Spencer said Earth could probably help, but it would take a long time."

"And only after we let the rest of the planet know about all this," he said. "That's a decision beyond our pay grade, I think."

"Indeed," Helen said, and this time the whole room noticed how tense she was acting.

"Anything you want to tell us?" Kim asked her.

She shook her head. "I'm not done researching it yet." She closed her eyes and took a deep breath. When she opened them, she was visibly more relaxed, much closer to normal. "My apologies. I concentrated too many threads in the wrong place. Please, continue."

"The other two are things my father wanted," Tapov said. "The ability for us to have more than one child in a family, and for us to formally join the galaxy at an earlier date. I don't think the first will change much. We've been having one child per family for as long as anyone can remember, but he disagreed. Where we did agree, though, was that Teliria is more than ready to join the galaxy. The nodes were going to wait another five thousand years!" She made a disgusted sound and then gestured at the ship around her. "This is all new, but it's not shocking. They were frightened of us. Apparently we have been one of the more difficult planets to..." This time she got so angry she gripped her hands tight. "To *tame*. They couldn't agree on a timeline and so chose the longest one they were allowed."

"Buncha fucking cowards," Spencer said. "The place was pacified centuries ago. They have held back this entire goddamn planet because they didn't want to look bad in front of their node buddies. It's fucking weird, but it's true. We skimmed the notes of their last vote to join Teliria with the galaxy. They didn't come out and say it, but it was crystal clear that they'd been shaking in their nodey little boots about this place ever since they found it. I don't think they would ever let Teliria join."

"So we took another vote for them," Tapov continued. "Spencer and I turned ourselves into honorary node chiefs and held another election. The result was unanimous." She faced Eskol. The excitement of Tapov announcing this was obvious to Kim. She was almost vibrating. "Our grandchildren will be the first to greet the rest of the galaxy." She turned back to Kim, really all the humans since they were sitting together. "I hope Earth will be there to greet them, too."

"That's where I come in," Sornik said. "No problem. Forget about it. They'll be there. You can bank on that."

Chapter 45
Helen

It was difficult pretending to be normal, that she hadn't learned the true value of Tonya's cache before they'd left it. And the whole truth still wasn't within her grasp. That would take months at least, and only if all aspects of what she had planned came together. It was difficult to be normal in a situation like that.

But she managed.

Against all expectations, Mike and Spencer's patches had worked. The transmission facility finished itself bare minutes after they'd rescued everyone, and after it connected, the hack went out into the galaxy. Each time it installed successfully—to Helen it was more accurate to call it an infection, but Mike squirmed at the term—Mike received a brief note. The core worlds were already largely patched. At the rate he was receiving the notices, there was a good chance the entire galaxy, and Earth, would be safe from each other in a few years.

If only they had that kind of time.

She got to watch Mike and Kim act as true Interpreters up close negotiating Tapov's ascent to power, and what she'd unilaterally done to the planet's future, with the rest of the rulers of Teliria. It was strangely straightforward. The nodes had held them at a medieval level of government but had prevented power from accumulating to any single lord. Tapov's domain was roughly the same size as the majority of other territories. Remarkably, regardless of size—and a minority of holdings did vary by a large percentage—all had roughly equal access to enough natural resources to be maintained directly or through trade. It was all suspiciously neat and tidy. The La'fan had to be behind those distribution patterns. Earth's resources were never so evenly spread, and that strongly contributed to humanity's long history of violence.

The planet's governing structures made Mike and Kim's efforts to bring the rest of Teliria around to the idea that what Tapov had done was a good thing much easier. The nodes themselves treated it all with a blind eye. That might've been due to what Tapov and Spencer had done, or it might have been that the nodes were somehow glad these choices were made for them. The assumption that the nodes were nonsentient unduplicates now seemed to be an oversimplification. Helen would need to examine this more closely. It could be critical for the days to come.

They departed after participating in the grand celebration that commemorated Tapov assuming her title. True to Mike's word, the Telirians treated the sight of aliens as novelties to investigate instead of monsters to be feared. The goodbyes were more than cordial, especially between Spencer and Tapov. Helen knew their bond went deeper.

She asked Sornik how such things worked in the galaxy. He laughed it off.

"Most bemians are built on roughly the same pattern. They can't have kids, but they can have fun. You go into a realm and then..." He bonked some manipulators together. "Happens all the time."

They dropped Tenor off at the cache. Again, Mike and Kim were indispensable, working out an agreement between him and Toraz that kept Tenor in charge of his museum and let Toraz be the sole distributor of the items he'd intended to sell all along to keep the place going.

It was clear he and Tonya also had developed a deeper bond. Being older, things were more complex and subtle, especially for Tonya. Now that she'd spent an extensive amount of time observing her at close quarters, Helen knew Tonya's legendary easygoing ways were a camouflage over waters that ran deep, with raging currents and dangerous shoals. Tonya kept people a specific distance away from her soul because she had no idea what would happen if her control ever slipped.

Then it was time to drop off Sornik's crew, forcing Helen to directly confront a relationship that had gotten closer than she'd ever intended. It wasn't love of course. He wasn't Chinese or human. But it was a deep and abiding respect, perhaps affection, for someone who a part of her still insisted should be placed behind bars at the earliest opportunity. She'd probably wear the ruby necklace he gave her for the rest of her life.

Helen's entire existence hinged on her bedrock belief that law and order were what separated people from savages, yet two of her most intimate friendships, with Sornik and Jainlee, her departed alter ego and snake mother, were criminals of the first order. She still hadn't gotten over Jainlee's leaving, and now she had to put up with another emptiness that shouldn't exist, let alone be this painful.

"Yeah, well," he said as they stood together at the base of the ship's loading ramp. "You be careful out there. I don't want to hear about you getting in any trouble. Apparently your friends have made it impossible for me to take care of it if it happens."

She chuckled. Most people would say rescue or help. Sornik would take care of it, and this wouldn't involve hand holding. Unless the hand held a crowbar. "I'll be fine." His hug was strange. He used manipulators to hold her against his suit, and he was the wrong shape for a good fit. But Helen still found it comforting, profoundly so.

"You'll still be able to reach me." She'd anchored almost as many threads here as Mike had.

"I know. But I also know you. Stay honest, is all I'm sayin'."

She turned and walked up the ramp, grateful that the rest of the crew had kept to the front of the ship. She hoped they'd stay there. It took some blinking to clear her blurry eyes before she could tell.

It wasn't love. Not in the way she'd expected it anyway.

Fully fueled and resupplied, they set off for home. The trip would give her the time she needed to confirm without any doubt what she'd discovered in the cache's realmspace and how to overcome it.

This need to be completely certain turned her into a hermit. After reassuring Mike that it wasn't an emotional problem, that she was doing careful research and it required long periods of solitude, he ran interference for her and brought her the meals she needed to keep her realspace body going.

They were a week out when she finalized her conclusions and called everyone together.

Once they settled into various seats around the mess hall, she broke the news. "It started at the cache, with the Interpreters. I didn't kill them. I sent them away with a message."

"That's why you spoke Chinese to them?" Tonya asked.

"Yes. I couldn't risk a misstep in a second language no matter how fluent I am in it. I'd already taught the thread I used on Silaria how to speak it, so they'd learn how one way or the other, and Chinese is the better language."

Spencer snorted, but Kim shushed him. Helen gave him the eye, but all he did was grin and give her a *continue* motion.

"I told them that their master's plan had failed before, and it would fail again. He may think the old order is swept away, but that does not mean his will take its place. I told them that I was living proof of the first genuinely new race in more than thirteen billion years, that I was not alone, and that we would not be bullied or conquered. I stood before them as a single human, but I did not stand alone."

"I was there," Tonya said. "I barely understood the words, but they were moving. If you used them to send a message, I imagine it has been received. But what does it mean?"

"Andromeda didn't evolve, it was created. Created by a species known only as the elders, the first intelligent life in the galaxy, probably the whole universe. They thought they were making a guardian, an eternal being that would watch over the galaxy and protect it. That's not what happened. Almost from the start, Andromeda has worked to destroy the home of the people who created it. Each time it's come closer to success. Tonya, your Undoing isn't the first discontinuity in the history of this galaxy, it's only the last and greatest."

Spencer flopped back in his chair. "Please don't say until now."

She nodded grimly at him. "Until now."

"Ah, *shit*."

"That's why our next moves are so important. The other disasters follow a similar sequence, right up to the point that Cyril appears to make a final play to stop Andromeda. But now there's a difference."

Mike said, "Wolflings."

Her brother was always good at jumping to the right conclusion. "Exactly. *We* are the wildcard. Our technology isn't up to their standards, but we understand how it works. We can only draw on the resources of a single system, but they haven't had an innovation, of any kind, in *billions* of years. The Telirians were at roughly a level equal to the West's late industrial revolution when the nodes found them, and they nearly won the fight. Spencer, what would've happened if Tapov's constructs had managed to make it off the planet?"

He barked out a laugh. "Hell if I know, but it would've fucked their shit up pretty good. She's a damn fine construct creator."

"It wouldn't have been enough to go all the way," Mike said. "But he's right, it would've done serious damage."

"So it's still possible to defeat Andromeda, if we're clever and we're careful." She hadn't counted on it being so hard to say. She'd thought her time with the politburo had taught her how to lie effortlessly. Helen had been wrong about that. But it was what they needed to hear, for now.

The next part would be worse.

They spent the final week wargaming various scenarios, mostly strategy and logistics. Americans were extraordinary logisticians, and her family was no exception. It was almost enough to give her hope.

Almost.

Helen stood in front of the door after they landed. "Kim, I must apologize for what I have done, to you most of all."

She went from smiling and hopeful to serious in an instant. "Why?"

"It is the only way I can see forward. We *must* do this to have any chance of success." The truth was a different kind of hard. "I promise that you will never have to interact with him, personally or virtually. This was my decision, and it will be my responsibility."

Now Kim turned absolutely white. "Helen, what did you do?"

Mike's face went flat, and his lips vanished into a single line. He'd figured it out yet again, but instead of flared anger he got an expression of resignation. He nodded faintly to her and said, "Come on, Kim. Helen needs to take care of something outside before we leave the ship."

Helen exited through a side door as Kim's questions to Mike became louder and more frantic.

Their lab was dark and silent, but not empty. Standing in front of her was their last hope, and Kim's worst enemy.

"Helen Zhang, walking out of thin air. You do know how to make an entrance."

Matthew Watchtell.

He was evil and dangerous, and he was Kim's rapist. If he'd tried half of what he'd been convicted of in China, she would've been happy to be the one to stick the needle into his arm. She was quite proficient at that, after all.

But where China was too poor, too fragile to risk psychopaths running loose, America was rich and strong enough for them roam free. This was, as had become common recently, an irony for her. She would have to dance with a devil, again. Play dice with a demon, again. She would, again, compromise the bedrock of her beliefs. It was the only way to survive.

Because Helen had lied to her family. There was no hope. The sequence had already played out. Andromeda had learned well from its last defeat and kept its steps secret this time. But once Helen knew what to look for, the conclusion was obvious.

Andromeda had already won.

"Yes, I suppose I do. Come, Matthew. We have much to speak about."

THE END

Gemini Gambit will return with book 6

The Sins Of The Elders

www.ingramcontent.com/pod-product-compliance
Lightning Source LLC
Chambersburg PA
CBHW030420310726
48979CB00009B/1538/J

* 9 7 8 1 7 3 6 0 1 4 1 4 1 *